When Fates
Collide

Isabelle Richards

To: [signature]

Isabelle
Richards

COPYRIGHT

DEDICATION

I started reading this genre as a way to escape my crazy life. It is wonderful to jump into someone else's story and leave yours behind for a bit.
This book is dedicated to those doing the grind every day:
Come with me and escape....

ONE

I never expected to find myself in the back of a police car. It's certainly a life experience I wish I could have skipped. The A/C is out, and the windows in the back seat don't open. The oppressive body odor reeking from the front seat tells me these guys have probably been sweltering in this car all day. From the other smells, I'm fairly certain more than one person has thrown up back here, possibly today. Although I may be suffering in the back seat, between me and the two guys up front, I'm the lucky one. At least this isn't my office every day.

We're stuck in DC's infamous rush hour traffic, and all I see is brake lights for miles. Looks like I'm going to be here awhile. I'm careful to avoid resting my head on the head rest that's covered in God only knows what. Closing my eyes, I take a deep breath, and wonder how the hell I got here. What has my husband done now?

If I'd lived a simpler life, I'd be sitting back here thinking, "How is this possible? We couldn't be in trouble with the police." But nothing about my life has been simple. I've been expecting this day since we got married five years ago. Actually, if I'm being honest, I've been expecting it since I first met him. If he's finally gotten caught doing something, at least it will be over, and I'll be free.

I'm guessing this is serious. The police officers have refused to tell me what this is about. They wouldn't even let me grab my cell phone or my purse before taking me away. "Mrs. Preston, there's a problem involving your husband. You need to come with us," one of them had said. That's it, that's all I've got to go on.

After what feels like an eternity, we arrive at the police station. It's a bee hive of activity. Lots of press vans, men with cameras, and women wearing way too much make up for this kind of heat.

Sergeant Stinky opens my door, and he and his partner each grab an arm to force me forward. I'm not in cuffs, but it sure feels like I'm under arrest.

They bring me into a room filled with the sweet, sweet bliss of air conditioning. For the first time in two hours, I can breathe. I'm ushered very quickly through a lobby and down a maze of hallways until I get into "the room." It's straight out of an episode of *Law and Order*: pea green walls, fluorescent lighting, a big metal table, one way mirror, and no windows. I've now gone from hot, annoyed, and mildly concerned to straight up pissed off. *Ashton, what the hell have you gotten me into?*

An imposing man walks in, and my anger is replaced with fear. This guy means business. He is about six foot four, two hundred seventy five pounds, and has overworked detective written all over his face. "Ma'am, I'm Special Agent T. Greene. My partner, Special Agent Sullivan, will join us in just a moment. While we wait, can I get you anything?"

I desperately try to recall all those hours of *Law and Order* I've watched. *What am I supposed to say? What am I not supposed to say?* The best I can muster is, "Umm... Do I need a lawyer?"

Greene shakes his head and looks down at the table. "So, no one has told you?"

"Told me what?" Knowing Ashton, it could be anything from a Ponzi scheme or prostitution ring to a chop shop... And I'm probably at the center of it somehow. That bastard. I brace myself for what I'm guessing will be words that will change my life forever.

"Ma'am, I'm so sorry to tell you this, but your husband, Ashton Preston, is dead."

I should say something here. I should demand answers. I should cry. Weep even. But do I do that? Nope. I get a case of the giggles.

The absurdity of it is just too much to bear. My uncontrollable laughing fit turns into a laugh so hard that no sound comes out, and I can barely keep myself in my seat. If I'm not careful, I fear I'll actually be rolling on the floor laughing. I'm just lucky I don't wet myself.

Greene just looks at me as though I'm crazy, and I feel a little crazy. I try to gather my composure. Then someone else walks in, and I lose it again.

He stares me with a disdain that reminds me of the time when I was six and got caught in the church office munching on communion wafers as though they were regular crackers.

"We don't see that reaction too often, do we, T? Mrs. Preston, I'm Special Agent in Charge, Danny Sullivan. People respond to tragic news in different ways, but laughing hysterically is a new one for me. Why don't you tell me why you're laughing? I didn't realize death was so amusing."

Well, that comment sucks all the oxygen out of the room, and my belly laughing stops suddenly.

I struggle to formulate my thoughts, but when I do, they pour out of me like a waterfall of anger. "For the last three hours, I've been trying to figure out what the hell's going on. I've been dragged from my home and stuffed in a puke-covered car with Stinky and Stinkier, thinking Ashton has dragged me into some mess. As it turns out, the bastard is dead? But not just dead. He's dead and I'm in a pile of shit, right? Why else would you drag me down here, if there wasn't a heap of trouble? So please, tell me, what did he do? What has he left for me to fix?"

I hadn't intended to rant like that, but my emotions are spilling over. My cheeks are hot, and I'm breathing heavily as if I've just run a marathon. I must look like a raving lunatic. I'm sweaty and gross from sitting in the car with the Stinkies. When the police arrived, I had just stepped out of the pool. I'm still in my bathing suit and cover up dress and sporting pool hair. I can only imagine how frizzy and fried it must look from the combination of chlorine and humidity.

Greene sits in the chair next to me, then takes my hand. "Mrs. Preston, you do have my deepest apologies that the two police officers who escorted you here didn't inform you of your husband's death. I'm sure that all of this is very confusing."

"Your husband's death is part of a larger ongoing investigation run by a multi-agency task force, and there's very little I can tell you at this time. Let's go through this step-by-step, and I'll tell you as much as I can," Agent Sullivan explains.

My head is spinning. I can't believe this is happening. I keep waiting for Ash to jump out and say this is one of his elaborate pranks. Everything was a joke to that man.

Greene's hand over mine and the look of pity on his face make it hard to believe this is a prank. Greene doesn't strike me as a jokester. He looks weathered and hard—cop-like. But he has soft and caring grey eyes. He strikes me as the type that could bench-press a million pounds while defusing a bomb without even breaking a sweat, but who also likes to garden and read poetry in his free time.

"Your husband was in a car accident," Greene begins.

With all the trouble Ashton has gotten himself into over the years, he's been taken down by a car accident. I would've guessed it had to be something far more sinister or grandiose, like getting knifed leaving a strip club or being pushed down an elevator shaft. A car accident just seems too banal for Ash. He lived big and on the edge. I would have expected his death to follow suit.

"He was in a head-on collision leaving a farm in Poolesville at around eleven o'clock this morning. Both cars were driving at high speed, and both drivers were killed instantly." He pauses as the reality of his words soaks in.

The room suddenly feels cold. I wrap my arms around myself.

"Are you ready to continue?" he asks. I nod, and he pats my hand. "The farm at..." He looks down at a file on the table. "2849 White's Ferry Road has been under surveillance by federal authorities. Over the last four months, your husband has been spotted there on numerous occasions. Are you familiar with this location?"

"Agent Greene, my husband and I lived very separate lives. You probably know more about him than I do."

Sullivan speaks up sounding highly irritated, "Mrs. Preston—"

I hold up my hand. "Please, don't call me that. I've never liked it. Just call me Lily."

"Okay, Lily. Look, we brought you here because this case is about to get complicated and there's likely to be a lot of press. Your husband was in business with some dangerous people. We're concerned for your safety. We think it's best if you stay in FBI custody until we have a better handle on the situation."

"Hold up for one second. You're FBI? I was picked up by the local police. I thought you guys didn't play well in the sandbox."

Sullivan laughs. "You watch too many cop shows. For this case, we're working together on a task force with multiple agencies. The local police have the most space, so they get the home field advantage. There are at least fifty or sixty people working on this case from maybe half a dozen agencies. It's a big deal."

I'm dizzy and can't seem to catch my breath. A cold sweat breaks out on my skin, and I feel as though I'm going to throw up. I push back from the table and stand. Heading for the door, I try to run out of the room, but it's locked. Damn interrogation rooms.

Sullivan tries to stop me, but I give him a nauseated look telling him I may hurl all over his shoe if he doesn't let me out. He uses his magnetic badge to open the door.

I run blindly. I don't know where I'm going, but I need out. Someone calls to me, but I can't make out what they are saying. It's all just fuzzy noise. Nothing is clear or making sense, and all of my senses are dull. All I can see is the door to the outside, and I'm using every last bit of energy I have to get to it. I reach out for the door handle when I feel my feet leave the floor.

I'm suddenly being scooped up by... someone as I hear a voice with the most comforting English accent say, "Not so fast, luv. You're not going to want to go out there."

The man sweeps me away to an office. He's tall and solid, and his arms swallow me as he carries me. Once the door is closed, he slowly puts me down but doesn't let go. "Sorry to snatch you up that way, but they'd eat you alive out there," the stranger says in his hypnotizing voice.

I finally get a look at him. He's the most stunning human being I've ever seen—far more handsome than any model I've ever drooled over. He's tall, I'd guess about six foot three at least, and every inch seems to be perfection, from his dark blond hair to the crystal clear blue eyes that stare right into my soul.

I try to stop staring at his chiseled features, but I'm mesmerized by his eyes and his full lips. His arms are still wrapped around me, and for a moment I feel safe, secure. It's completely inappropriate for me to stay entangled with him. I know I should step away, but he's holding me so comfortingly that I don't want to break free.

While I'm lost in the oceans of his eyes, the door flies open, and I'm hit by a tidal wave of flashing lights. The lights are blinding, and for a moment, all I can see is stars. After blinking a few times, my eyes adjust, and I see a short man that looks and smells as though he's been living in a dumpster. He's barking questions at us, but I'm still so overloaded that I don't process anything he's saying. He might as well be speaking Greek. Before I can figure out what's going on, several officers burst through the door. Sullivan tackles the little man to the floor and slaps cuffs on him. Sullivan may be rough around the edges, but he can be my bodyguard any day.

Dazed and confused, I step back and shake my head. "Can someone tell me what is going on? Who the hell is that, and why is he taking my picture?"

"Mrs. Preston, there's still quite a bit we need to discuss. Can we please return to the interview room?" Sullivan asks firmly. "Agent Greene will escort you while I sort out this yahoo." He grabs the creepy photographer and storms out.

"You should talk to her in here where she won't feel like she's a criminal," the English stranger pipes up, heading after him. Before I can muster the words to thank him, he's out the door, leaving me with Greene.

I can't seem to wrap my head around what's going on. I feel as though I'm watching a movie after missing the first thirty minutes. I have no idea what's going on or who the characters are.

"Agent Greene, my head is spinning. I haven't even processed what you told me in there. I don't know why that guy tried to take my picture. And who is the Brit? Jesus, I feel like I've walked into an episode of *The Twilight Zone*!"

Before Greene can answer, Sullivan bursts back through the door. "T, there's been a development. We need to hit the road. Preston, you need to stay put. Don't go anywhere."

Just like that, they're both gone, and I'm left in the dust.

I sit on an uncomfortable plastic chair, stunned. Replaying the afternoon in my mind, I can't believe this is happening.

"What the fuck?!"

Hot tears stream down my face. I'd sworn I'd never let Ash and his crap make me cry. But here I am, in a police station, a blubbering mess!

The English stranger rushes back into the room. "Are you okay?"

"Oh, I'm just great. Why do you ask?" I snap back at him.

"Well, people don't tend to scream profanities at the top of their lungs when they're okay. Typically, it's only if they're very good or very bad. With the tears, I'm guessing things aren't very good right now."

Apparently, that "what the fuck," hadn't been in my head. "You are perceptive," I retort.

He crosses the room and hands me a handkerchief.

I raise an eyebrow at him and say, "Really? A handkerchief? I didn't think people really had these anymore. Is that an English thing?"

He snorts when he laughs at me. "Well, it's a 'being a gentleman' thing. So yes, I suppose it's an English thing, then."

I dab at my eyes with the handkerchief, and we sit in silence for a minute or two. I have no idea what to say to him.

He jumps up. "Okay, luv, we need to get out of here. Follow me."

"They said I have to stay," I respond.

"I know." He winks. "We aren't going far."

I look at him completely puzzled. "Who *are* you?"

"That, my dear, is a question that requires scotch. Which is exactly why we're getting the hell out of here. Don't worry, Sullivan and Greene will know where to find you."

"I thought you said we couldn't go outside," I say, confused.

"I've got a bloke that can get us out of here." He pulls out his phone and texts someone. "We'd better get moving straight away, before we miss our window."

For some reason, I follow him. With an ass like that, I'd probably follow him anywhere.

TWO

We go down a few flights of stairs to a parking garage. The Brit whistles using his fingers, and an unmarked police car rolls up.

"Your own personal cop taxi?" I ask with skepticism.

He chuckles. "Not quite. Just a friend trying to get you some breathing room. The press will be distracted with Sullivan and Greene leaving. If we move quickly, we can sneak out without anyone noticing." He opens the back door and motions for me to climb in. "Thanks, Sam," he says to the driver. "We both need to get out of there for a bit."

The driver turns around with an extended hand. "I'm Sam."

"Lily," I say after shaking his hand.

Sam smiles. "I know. All of us on the task force know all about you."

"Fabulous. Some husbands give their wives jewelry. Mine gave me a task force," I mutter to myself. "So, where're we going, Sam?" I ask. Since I'm leaving the safety of the police

11

station with two men who are complete strangers, it seems like a smart question to ask.

"Where I'm taking you, no criminal or member of the press would be stupid enough to go," Sam says with a smirk.

About two minutes later, I'm standing in front of a dingy dive bar. I look up at the sign. "Jack's? Really? This is the safe place that stops bad guys in their tracks? Is there some sort of force field I'm not seeing? Or is this place so sleazy that even the bad guys are too classy to come here?"

The Brit nudges me out of the car. "Thanks, Sam. Tell Sully and Greene where we are. Let's go, Lily. You need a drink."

I have to hand it to the Brit, he sure knows how to pick 'em. Jack's is a cop bar, owned by a third-generation retired cop who, oddly, is not named Jack. Despite the dive bar look on the outside, it's pretty clever on the inside. It has a big, solid wood bar that appears to have come straight off the set of *Cheers*, police memorabilia everywhere, and a whole wall dedicated to 9/11 heroes. There is even a mock cell. It's now close to six-thirty pm and the place is packed with those cops who are just getting off shift, some who are retired and come here to feel connected again, and women looking for a good man with good benefits.

Whatever trouble Ashton has gotten me into isn't coming in here to get me. As the Brit leads me to a table in the back, he nods to several of the off-duty officers. He must be a cop, but a British cop? Nah, his shoes are way too nice for him to be a cop.

He's by far the best dressed guy in this place, wearing charcoal grey slacks that look like they were custom tailored and a blue V-neck that makes his eyes stand out and highlights his toned physique. Even so, it isn't as much about what he's wearing but how he carries himself. He walks with bold confidence yet also seems completely approachable.

As we sit down, a large mountain of a man brings us a bottle of scotch, two glasses, and two shot glasses already full of God only knows what. I know nothing about scotch, but based on the label, I'm guessing it's top-shelf. I must be in for some serious shit if we need a whole bottle.

I open my mouth to rattle off a litany of questions when the Brit hands me a shot.

"Drink first, questions later."

It burns going down. Normally, I only do frou-frou shots with cute names like *Sicilian Whore* or *Sex With a Bartender*. I make a face that obliterates any chance I'd had of playing this cool. I'm fairly confident I look like a kid who's just stolen her first sip of alcohol.

The Brit laughs hysterically. "I thought all you Americans drank bourbon."

I cross my arms. "Listen, you. I drank your damn shot. You didn't say I had to do it gracefully. You said if I went with you, you'd give me answers. *Start talking*." I try to appear as intimidating as possible. Regardless of how attractive he may be, my patience is wearing thin. I've had too much thrown at me today to waste time playing games.

The smile fades from his face as he pours us each a finger's worth of scotch and takes a deep breath. In a very somber tone, he says "My name's Gavin Edwards. My wife was the other driver in the accident that killed your husband."

I hadn't seen that coming.

I stare at him in stunned silence. I still haven't really accepted that anything has happened to Ashton. If I think about what he's just said, I have to think about Ash, and maybe I'm just not ready to do that.

He takes a long sip of his scotch. "You now see why we needed the drinks," he says with a shy smile. "This is a lot to take in. Part of me is still dodging reality a bit."

I nod. "Sullivan said this is part of a bigger problem. Are we really in danger? How real is this?"

He shrugs. "I don't know as much about that part of the investigation. It seems that your husband was in cahoots with some major players in the drug scene. Since the accident was right in front of their hideout, it could draw unwanted attention. What the police don't know is how these gangsters will respond to all this attention. Especially with all the press this is going to draw."

"I imagine it will be a hot story for a few moments, but something else'll come up, and they'll migrate to that issue quickly enough."

He rolls his near empty glass between his hands. "My wife was Brooke Livingston."

Oh crap. Hollywood's "It girl." If it's true, there will be *True Hollywood Stories* about this accident for years to come and a media infestation that could rival a zombie apocalypse. Gavin will have it worse than I will. I can just fade into the woodwork, but the press will be all over him.

"So that guy, he was paparazzi?" I ask.

"Yes, it seems like there's been a leak. They know something's up with Brooke, but they don't know what. I think the latest rumor is that she's under arrest at the station for a DUI. We're working hard to dispel it, but a rumor is all you need in tabloid journalism."

I slam down the rest of my scotch. "The drinks," I say, pointing to the empty glasses. "This was a good idea." I pause and take a deep breath. "This is going to be a shit storm of drama, isn't it?"

He refills our glasses. "Yes, Lily. It is."

We sit in silence and drink slowly, both lost in our own sea of thoughts and emotions. After a few minutes, I look at him, but he doesn't seem to notice. He stares down into his scotch glass as though he's looking for answers. He's so amazingly handsome he doesn't seem real. As though he must be made of plastic or something. While his perfection is blinding, it doesn't quite hide the pain, and torment clouds his soulful eyes.

I touch his hand, and look into his eyes. "I'm so sorry that your wife has died. I'm sick with grief by the thought that Ashton has taken her from you."

"It was a head-on collision. They were both at fault. Both of them were driving way too fast down that little farm road, high as kites. They made their choices, and now we're paying the price."

Part of me wants to cover my ears and not hear anymore. I've avoided thinking about the details all afternoon. Ashton was a mess, a complete train wreck of disastrous life choices. The only way I ever managed to get up in the morning and keep living my life was by turning a blind eye to all his dirty secrets. As the truth comes out, my protective bubble is going to be popped, and I'm going to have to face all the darkness I've been ignoring. Five long years of denial are going to come back to roost.

"So, what was Brooke Livingston doing in Poolesville, MD? Don't you guys live in London?" I ask, attempting to change the subject.

Gavin gives a small laugh. "She wasn't always Brooke Livingston. She was born Bonnie Zabriskie in Maryland. It's a very well-kept secret. Her whole family still lives in Monrovia. They're Mormon, very devout. She was home schooled and kept isolated from anyone that wasn't in the church. When she was fifteen, she ran away to New York to become a model. Bonnie disappeared, and Brooke was born."

"Oh," I say taking a sip. "So she was home visiting family?"

"Sort of. Brooke had a lot of demons, and I was worried for her safety. I was traveling a lot for work, and I didn't feel she would be safe alone. To be honest, I knew if she was left unsupervised, she would probably overdose. I booked her into rehab, but she would sign herself right out. About four months ago, her addiction was out of control and I was desperate to save her. I tracked down her family, and they were eager to help. As I said, they're religious and felt that through the church they could reach her. I didn't really buy into it, but I hoped a change of environment and some parental love may help. I gave her a choice. She could either go to rehab again, come to see her parents, or I would divorce her. She chose to go home."

I look down at the table, not really knowing what to say. She had such a squeaky clean image that it's surprising to hear she was a junkie. But, then again, I only knew of her through the media, so what do I really know?

"I had no idea about her troubled past when I met her," he continues. "We met when she was in London filming *Covent Gardens*. I'm sure you've seen it."

I feel a blush creep across my cheeks. "I don't usually admit to it, but yeah. I watched religiously."

He laughs and flashes me a smile that stops my heart. Damn, this guy is hot. When the butterflies start in my stomach, I feel shame slap me. *He's talking about his dead wife! What is wrong with me? I'm going to hell.*

He takes a sip of his drink, then nods. "I hear that a lot. The show got great numbers, so clearly more people watched than will admit to it."

I chuckle. "Like reality TV. Everyone swears they don't watch, but someone must be. Networks are making a boatload of cash, and they keep churning out one abysmal show after another."

He smiles. "Precisely," he says. "Since *Covent Gardens* was a show for teenagers, maintaining a certain image was part of her contract. She worked tirelessly to appear put together and innocent: the perfect picture of the girl next door, the girl I fell in love with. When the show ended, she no longer had a reason to stay wholesome, and that's when things went downhill quickly."

I sip my scotch as I listen to him talk about her. His tone is somber and reverent, and I see loss and despair in his eyes. He's attractive, so it's easy to miss, but when I look closely, I see the emotional exhaustion written across his face.

"The first thing everyone saw when they looked at Brooke was her beauty. She's undeniably stunning, but beauty only goes so far. Her unrefined acting skills passed on a teenage drama, but she didn't have enough talent to carry her over

17

into movies or theater. When she couldn't find work, she became bored and restless. She made friends in London, lots of other Americans and washed up actors living off past success. Before I knew it, she got sucked into the fast life. Day by day, I lost her a little more until she was gone. I didn't know it at the time, but she'd blown through most of her money. That's when she turned dark. The lying, the cheating, the stealing... I didn't even know who she was anymore when I sent her here."

He takes a drink of his scotch and chuckles. "Wow, I've just dumped my sad, woe is me, story in your lap."

I smile. "It's fine, really. All of this is so overwhelming, it's kind of nice to hear about someone else's problems. It helps me avoid thinking about my own."

"Since I started helping the task force, I've been traveling back and forth to London. For months and months, I haven't been able to say a word to a soul about what's going on. Not about Brooke's drug problem, or how she's gotten herself mixed up with these thugs. I've had to pretend that she's 'working on a new project.' It's a relief to finally be able to talk to someone about it. The blokes in the task force are great, but, I swear they're always double checking everything I say to see if I'm really mixed up in this drug mess. Can never really let my guard down, you know?"

"That must have been hard," I say with a sympathetic smile.

"I swear I'm usually more tight lipped about my private life. With the paparazzi hiding around every corner, and all." He looks down and smiles. "There's something about you. I feel comfortable around you, I suppose."

I laugh. "It must be the deer in headlights look."

Before he can reply, the moving mountain of a bartender comes over. "Gavin, seems word has gotten out that you're here. A few gnats from the press tried popping in. We set them straight, but I wouldn't be surprised if there are more. You may want to move into the back room." Travis clears our empty shot glasses and says "FYI, *TMZ* is reporting Brooke Livingston's husband was seen canoodling—their word not mine—with a smokin' hot blonde."

Smokin' hot blonde? Really? I'm feeling anything but right now. I'm not bad-looking or anything, but 'smokin' isn't a word I would use. I'm about five foot eight, and my legs are my best feature. I've always been a swimmer, so I'm long and lean. Plus, I think the press calls any girl with long blonde hair hot. I'm no Brooke Livingston, that's for sure. Thank goodness my cover up is black and can pass for a sundress. Otherwise, I'd feel more ridiculous than I already do. After all day in a swimsuit, I'm ready for a shower and change of clothes.

Travis brings me back from my mental digression when he says, "Be careful you two. This could get out of control very fast. I know they're doing their best to keep this all under wraps, but you have got to stay out of the line of fire."

Gavin lets out a long sigh as he stands. He pats Travis on the back. "Thanks, Travis, we'll move on back. I hope this doesn't cause any trouble for you." He looks at me as he grabs the bottle of scotch and our glasses. "Come on, Lily. Seems like we're disturbing the peace."

He leads me to a table in the back of the bar. As we walk through the bar, several people stop him to say hello. When we arrive at the table, he places the glasses and scotch on the table, then pulls out my chair for me. Looks like chivalry is alive and well in England. After he sits, he pours us each a new drink.

I look at him bewildered. "How is it that everyone knows you? You're even on a first name basis with the cop bar bartender. Don't you live in England?"

"Well, that's Travis. He's a good chap. He owns the pub. For the past few weeks, I've been here working with the FBI. It was Sully's idea that we come here. Jack's is considered a private club, with dues and the whole bit. Their own bobby hang out."

I raise my eyebrow. "Bobby?"

He rolls his eyes. "Police officer."

I nod, vaguely remembering learning that in elementary school.

"As you probably know, the press is always interested in Brooke and me, so walking in and out of the police station everyday would have brought unwanted attention to the case. I bought a membership so I could meet with Sully and Greene on the sly," Gavin continues. "The regulars have been really great to me. I owe them a tremendous amount for their support and their secrecy. Any one of them could have sold this story to the tabloids for more money than they make in a year. But they've protected me and Brooke every step of the way. These are good people."

"Well, that explains why it feels like you are 'one of the boys' here. That was really decent of Travis to give us the heads up. I don't think I can deal with another photo attack." I shudder at the thought, which gets me thinking. "Is your life always like this? Having to hide out from paparazzi?"

"Sometimes. When I was younger, I was in the spotlight often. I was a bit wild, and my family has some very distant connections to the royal family. When I would get in trouble, the press would try to use me as a black mark against the royal family. It was really quite a stretch. You're probably closer to getting the crown than I am. But it sold newspapers. Back then, I thrived on it. Anything to piss off dear ol' Dad."

I let out a quiet laugh and nod, even though I can't relate. I didn't have the luxury of going through a rebellious stage.

I hear a chime, and Gavin pulls his phone out of his pocket. He taps away at it for a moment, then looks up at me. "What was I saying? Oh, yes..." He takes a sip before continuing. "Eventually, I grew up a bit, spent some time in the military, and disappeared from the public eye. Later, around the time Brooke came into my life, I became a story again. The paparazzi have followed us pretty closely since then. It's one of the reasons I sent her here. I wanted her to have time to detox and clean up without the press all over her."

That seems like a horribly flawed plan to me. I'm not sure what the press is like in England, but celebrity privacy is not something that is respected on this side of the pond. The poor woman was probably accosted on a daily basis. If he'd just kept her in England, she'd probably have still been alive. Wanting to keep these thoughts to myself, I nod and take another sip.

"It worked until she left her parents' house. She stayed committed to getting clean for about a week, until she got into a fight with her parents and then took off. I suspect they pushed the religious angle too hard and Brooke just couldn't take it. When her mother called to tell me about the fight, I flew here and went straight to the police. About a month later, the FBI contacted me. Brooke started staying at the farmhouse they've been surveilling, and they wanted my help to either get her out or get information from her."

He's certainly been through hell and back. Ashton was always a train wreck, but he was functional. He'd gotten up and gone to work every day. He was always late, but he went. I'd never considered sending him to rehab. Perhaps I should have. As that thought simmers in my brain, I motion to Gavin to refill my drink.

As he pours me another, he continues, "I tried for months to get her to talk to me, but she wouldn't take my calls. When I finally connected with her, I begged her to come home, but she just wanted more money. The FBI wanted me to meet her and see if I could glean any information about the men she was living with." He looks down and shakes his head. "I'll never forget that day. I met her at a park. When I pulled up, I barely recognized her. She was a shell of who she used to be. Her porcelain skin was blotchy and covered in sores. She used to have such thick, long black hair. When I saw her, she'd chopped it all off, and it was clear the rest was falling out. Everything about her used to sparkle, especially her green eyes. But when I saw her, her eyes were flat and vacant. She looked hollowed out, as though she was dead inside. She used to be so curvy, but she'd become emaciated, like she hadn't eaten in weeks. It's probably what saved her from being noticed. No one that saw her would have thought that she was Brooke Livingston."

Clearly upset by the memory, his eyes look glassy, and his face is flushed. He takes a sip of his drink and clears his throat. "My wife no longer existed, and all that remained was the addiction. Brooke was now this … person that I could no longer stomach to be around. She was irrational and erratic.

All she could think about was getting her next score, and she'd stop at nothing to get it. She'd flirt one second and then scream and scratch when I wouldn't give her money. Sully told me she'd been prostituting herself to pay for her habit. I decided to work with the authorities and do what I could to help them take down the dealers she was with. If she were arrested in the process, it would be awful, but at least she would be out."

I can't find the right words to say as tears well up in my eyes. I'm blown away by the depth of the love he felt for his wife. His bravery and courage. I ache for his loss and feel a pang of guilt for not feeling the same way about Ash. I should feel something. Anything. Pain, hurt, anguish. But I feel nothing. I'm numb, and that depresses me. Is this reaction shock or have I really become this cold? Has Ash broken me so fully that I'm incapable of emotion?

Gavin rolls his glass between his palms. "I'm sorry to have laid all that on you," he says sheepishly.

Before I have a chance to say anything else, his phone rings, the *Hawaii 5-0* theme song issuing from it. Looks like Gavin has a sense of humor. "That was Sullivan," he says after checking the phone. "There have been some developments, but the agents won't be back until morning at the earliest. He said it's not safe for you to go back to your house. An agent is going to come by in a few minutes to take you to a hotel."

I hear what he says, but it doesn't really register. I've drunk my weight in scotch and haven't eaten since this morning. My brain is hazed in a fog. All I want is to go home, shower, and climb into bed. But I can't do that. I don't know when I will be able to go home. And I don't even know why! It has been comforting talking here with Gavin, but it has allowed me to completely ignore the reality of the situation.

Meredith, the agent assigned to babysit me, arrives. She stands about five foot eleven and is built like a linebacker. No one is messing with this chick. When I stand up, the scotch suddenly hits me, and the ground moves beneath me.

Meredith catches me as I stumble, saving me from falling flat on my face. "Whoa there, lightweight! Let's get you to the car." She waves at Gavin. "Come on, Hot Stuff. You can hitch a ride."

"Why's he coming with us?" I say in what is intended to be a whisper but probably comes out loud enough for the whole bar to hear.

"I think we'd best get her some take away on the way to the hotel, Mer," Gavin says as he scoops me up and carries me to the car. "Something good and greasy!"

We drive by an all-night Mexican place—an insta-sobering trick I learned in college. As long as I don't think about what's really in this burrito or other pesky things like health codes, I'm golden. By the time we get to the Marriott, I'm feeling somewhat human again. We enter the hotel through the back entrance. I'm told I've been checked in under an assumed name: Kelly Kapowski. Classic.

I'm in the room right next to Gavin's. When we arrive at our doors, I look at him and have no idea what to say. This is such a bizarre situation. I don't think Emily Post has etiquette rules on this. Do I say, "I'm sorry my shithead husband killed your wife?" "Thanks for getting me trashed so I don't have to think about how my life is in danger?" "You're so beautiful it helps me forget that my whole world has turned upside down?"

I settle for, "Thank you for getting me out of the station and for sitting with me tonight. Have a good night." I unlock my door, but turn back around to face him. "Wait, will I see you again? What happens now?"

He pauses with his hand on this door handle. "I'll see you tomorrow. They'll bring us back over to the station tomorrow morning, and they'll tell us as much as they can about what happened today. Stop by when you're up in the morning. We can have breakfast." He comes over to me and looks me in the eye so intensely that it sucks all the oxygen out of me. "Don't worry, Lily. We'll get through this. Try to get some rest. You'll need it to get through tomorrow."

He gives me a hug that's as soothing as climbing into bed with sheets fresh from the dryer. So warm you just want to crawl in and never leave. This man has something about him that emits a sense of security. He lets me go and walks back to his room.

"He's something else, huh?" Meredith says, snapping me out of my trance. "Come on, Lightweight. You need a shower. You smell like a distillery!"

Meredith clears the room and then lets me in. No monsters under the bed or boogeymen in the closet. The room is a one-bedroom suite with a small living area. Meredith says she'll stand guard by the door all night. The bedroom itself has a proper door, so at least I can have a little privacy. There's no way I would get a moment's sleep with Meredith staring at me.

Eager for a shower, I head straight for the bathroom and turn the water on as hot as it will go. The scalding stream leaves me feeling raw. But at least I'm feeling something. I keep waiting for the day to catch up with me, but my mind is blank. I try to focus on the individual parts of the day, but it's as though my mind is determined to shut it all out. I guess this mental shutdown is why people drink scotch. You really can forget it all.

When I get out of the shower, I realize I don't have any pajamas, and I remember that I left a load of laundry in the washer. *Damn! Ashton gets so mad when it has that mildewy smell. Even when I use vinegar, it never gets it all the way out, and he...*

Then it hits me: Ashton isn't going to be upset about the laundry. He isn't going to get upset with me about anything. Ever. Ashton is gone. Huge tears begin to fall. Tears of loss and tears of mourning. Some are tears of relief. I cry myself to sleep.

THREE

The Mexican food did the trick. I'm hangover-free. When I wake up, it takes me a minute to realize where I am. The unfamiliar sheets and my nakedness throw me for a loop, until the previous day's events come back to me in pieces. After I find a bathrobe in the closet, I peek out the bedroom door to find Meredith doing yoga.

"Doing okay, Lightweight?" she asks, balancing in crescent pose.

"Yeah, I think the e-coli from that burrito ate all the alcohol," I retort.

She laughs. "I like you, Lightweight. You didn't puke in my car, and you have a sense of humor."

I smile at her.

"I spoke to Greene a few minutes ago," she continues. "The guys are back at the station and will see you later in the morning."

"Don't they need to sleep?" I ask. "They've been at this all night!"

27

She shakes her head. "That's life on the job, Lightweight. That's life on the job."

I feel a sudden deep appreciation for these men and women who are charged with keeping me safe. Lives have been lost, others are in danger, and Ash is at the center of this mystery. My selfish prick of a husband. Guilt consumes me, and I vow to be as helpful as I can so that this investigation can all be put to rest.

Reluctantly, I dress in my disgusting clothes from yesterday. I wish I had at least washed my bathing suit out in the sink, but the idea didn't occur to me until now. Once I'm dressed, we leave the room and walk to the car.

"Are we getting Gavin?" I ask.

"Hot Stuff's already down there. They called him in very early this morning." She unlocks the car doors with the remote. "Now, let's stop off at Target. You've got to grab some new clothes. You still stink!"

I open the door and slide into the passenger seat. "I don't have my wallet or anything," I reply.

She hops in and closes her door. "I'll spot you," she says with a smile.

"Thank you. I'll pay you back right away."

She laughs. "Please. It's more for me than you. I'm stuck with you all day in close quarters. A deodorized version of you would make this day much easier."

After a quick shopping trip and an even quicker change in the store's restroom, we return to the station. As we walk through the lobby, I notice the TV is set on some morning show. *Hot news from the Hollywood scene. Gavin Edwards, Brook Livingston's husband, was seen entering a DC hotel late last night with a very attractive blonde. This picture*

28

comes from a hotel guest that captured the two as they exited a cab and snuck in the back entrance of the hotel. Brooke's PR rep says she's in New Zealand working on a project, but rumors are flying that the Covent Gardens *star has been arrested for a DUI in Washington, DC. So we want to know: What is up with Brooke, and who is this woman on her husband's arm?*

There I am, walking into the Marriott. The picture isn't half bad considering the shape I was in at the time. As flattering as it is that they're reporting me in a positive light, the stroke to my ego does nothing to squash my fears. I'm petrified that the word is out and what that will mean. The FBI has been so cryptic about this investigation. I don't really have a grasp on what's going on, who the bad guys are, or what they could possibly want with me.

Meredith shakes her head at the TV. "Damn vultures," she says. "Now we've got to change hotels. Dammit!" She yells loudly enough to draw the attention of everyone in the lobby. "Let's go. The boys are waiting," she says with great irritation as she guides me to my interrogation room.

"Seriously guys, I thought we've moved passed the scary room with no windows?" I ask as I enter, trying to bring a bit of humor to the two very cranky-looking men.

Sullivan points to the same uncomfortable plastic chair that I sat in yesterday. "Sit down. We've a lot to talk about. The press has gotten wind of you, and it's only a matter of time before this blows up and takes the whole case down with it. The higher-ups are pulling as many strings as they can to keep this quiet, but that only works with mainstream press. The trash papers couldn't give a shit whose life they put in danger."

"Let's just focus on the new information, and we can worry about the press later," Greene says. I'm thankful he seems to be keeping his head. Greene has such a calming effect. Otherwise, Sully's intensity would probably send me right over the edge. "Meredith, can you get Lily something to drink?" he asks.

She nods and leaves the room.

"Before we start," I say. "I want to let you know that I know Ashton was trouble. Always in trouble, always making trouble, always looking for trouble. I don't know a lot of details, but I'll do everything I can to help you."

Sullivan nods. "We appreciate that. There are holes that need to be filled in, and hopefully you can help. We may ask you some questions that seem obvious, but just go with it. Tell us what you know. You'd be surprised the details people know but don't realize are important." He takes the cap off a pen and pulls a legal pad closer to him. "Let's start by talking about yesterday."

I hold my breath and flinch. I'm not ready for this, but it's happening, like it or not.

Before we dive in, Meredith comes back with a bottle of water. "Stay hydrated," she says. "I'll be down the hall if you need me." She gives me a reassuring smile and disappears once again. I wonder if it's obvious how nervous I am.

Greene moves closer, his voice softer than before. "As we told you, Mr. Preston was in a head-on collision. It's our understanding that Mr. Preston was speeding to get to a meeting with Mr. Jason Robertson, the owner of the farm, and an Anthony Maniglia at the farmhouse. Do you know either of these people?"

I tap my chin as I try to remember. "I remember hearing about a Jason, but I don't recall specifics. I tried to keep as much distance from Ashton's extracurricular activities as possible."

Sully jots down a few notes on the pad.

"That's okay," Greene says soothingly. "Mr. Robertson was a drug dealer and bookie. Mr. Maniglia was a financial backer of Mr. Robertson's, and he had ties to organized crime. We've obtained confirmation that your husband was in debt to these two men."

"He owed them some major dough," Sully chimes in.

"I wish I could say I'm surprised, but nothing surprises me when it comes to Ash," I reply. I'm curious how much he owed and what he did with the money, but I refrain from asking. Being curious and actually wanting to know are two very different things.

Greene continues. "Your husband was trying to blackmail his way out of the mess he was in. He claimed he had evidence that would be damaging to both men and that he would hand over this evidence to Maniglia in exchange for their clearing his debt. He was supposed to be bringing it with him to the meeting." Greene looks at me in the eyes, "You with me so far?"

I take a sip of my water and then nod.

"As I mentioned yesterday, there are many branches of law enforcement involved in this case—state and federal. We have evidence coming in from informants, undercover agents, and wiretaps. When we got confirmation of Ashton's blackmail attempt, everyone thought it would be our big break. We were lined up to take them all down, until your husband got into the accident. It put a wrench in everything."

I swallow hard as I try to process this information. Greene's story sounds more like a plot from a movie than something I could actually be involved in. "So you were planning on arresting Ash yesterday?" I ask.

Sully taps his pen on the table as he responds. "We were going to listen to their exchange over the wire, and once we had what we were looking for, we were going to arrest them all. Not only those at the farm, but others in the organization as well. The busts were supposed to be simultaneous, but all of that came to a screeching halt after the accident."

"Oh," I reply, digesting his statement. My mind returns to yesterday morning. Ash had complained I hadn't made enough bacon for breakfast and that I must have shrunk his shirts in the wash. I'd snapped back that if he ate less bacon, maybe his shirts would fit. He tried to keep fighting, but it just wasn't worth it to me, so I'd ignored him while he ranted and raved about all the ways I let him down. We'd spoken more in that conversation than we had all week. What would I have done if he'd called saying he was arrested? I probably would have laughed and told him to rot in jail.

Would I have said or done something different if I'd known it was the last time I was going to speak to him? Probably not. Our relationship was so broken that there really was nothing left for us to say to each other. A tearful good-bye would have been bullshit, and we both would have known it.

Greene coughs, and it brings me back to the present. "The accident threw a wrench in everyone's plans. The agents knew they needed to play everything very carefully so as not to blow their cover. We sent in special units to the accident to clear the scene and avoid arousing suspicion. Luckily, while

Mr. Robertson and Mr. Maniglia were essentially trapped in the farmhouse, they consumed large quantities of drugs and became very chatty. We got enough on record to sink them both for life."

Sullivan jumps in. "We knew they'd be worried about what evidence your husband had, and we suspected they would come after you. We stationed local PD in your home last night. As it turns out, we were right. At two eighteen a.m., two men entered your home. There was a shootout between them and the police, and both men were taken down."

My blood goes cold. "Is everyone okay?" I ask, the words barely squeaking out.

"Yes, everyone involved came back safely," Greene says in a soothing voice. "After we had proof that they sent someone to harm you, officers raided the farmhouse to arrest both Robertson and Maniglia. Both of them were high out of their minds and came out guns blazing. Both were killed."

Ashton may have been a magnet for trouble and had always wound up in over his head. But this... this is different. People have lost their lives. It's all too much. "Now that these guys are gone, do you think I'm in the clear? Is someone else going to come after me?"

"Lily, look," Sullivan says, almost sounding human, "The straight answer is we don't know. We think Maniglia was operating off-book, meaning this operation wasn't authorized by the higher-ups in his group. The rest of the organization isn't going to be happy that he had this little side project and that it comes with so much heat. I don't think they'll give you a second thought. But, that's just a guess at this point. This could be a sanctioned operation, and if that's the case, there are going to be some very angry and desperate mobsters looking to make this go away."

So basically, they know jack. I take another sip of my water. It doesn't soothe my fears, but it helps with my dry throat. One problem down, a million to go.

Sully taps that damn pen again. If he keeps doing it, I'm liable to stab him with it. "The bigger issue is—what else was your husband into? We have only just begun to sift through the evidence, and it's pretty clear he was involved with other unsavory parties and in trouble up to his eyeballs."

I nervously chew on a fingernail as I try to think about anything I might know that could help. "I wish I knew something, but I don't."

"We started going through his business offices and your home. Your home is now a crime scene, and you won't be able to stay there for a while. Now that the hotel is compromised, we need to find safe housing for you. You'll stay in FBI custody until we clear this all up. That could take hours, days, even weeks. We have no idea."

"Oh no! The business," I exclaim. "He has employees. Not many at this point, but they are good people that rely on their jobs. I have to do something." Ashton had been running Preston Construction since his father's death. When his father ran the company, PC was a big player in the Washington commercial construction market. They built office buildings, apartments—that sort of thing. He'd made his fortune on government contracts. At one point, he'd had hundreds of employees and contractors, but since Ash took over, all but a handful have left. He ran the business into the ground.

Greene pats my hand and says, "All assets from Preston Construction will be frozen pending further investigation. We have already spoken to the employees. I know it's hard, but that's how it has to be. We've found evidence of drug dealing and bookmaking in his office. We're guessing he was using the business as a front, but until the accountants dig through the records, we won't know for sure."

It was one thing when it was Ash screwing up, blowing through money. He was only destroying his life and keeping me from living mine. I could live with that. But this is different. People are dead. Lives have been destroyed. I know I didn't do it, but I feel responsible. Thinking about those poor people losing their jobs makes me sick.

"What do I tell people?" I ask. "Is this still a secret? What am I going to tell his mother?" The room spins as I start to panic.

Greene scoots closer to pat my back, but it's Sullivan that snaps me out of it. "We have to worry about your safety first. Then we have to consider the case being built against these guys. I think we can all agree we want to get these guys and stop them from hurting anyone else. As far as you go, we don't want anyone that may be watching you to think anything is up. You're going off the grid. You can't tell anyone about this, not yet. Post on Facebook that you are going on a trip, taking some 'you time' or whatever the hell girls like to do. Don't talk to anyone, no details to anyone.

"Just let us and the other agencies do our jobs. The more we learn, the more we can protect others from getting hurt." He has the bedside manner of a grizzly bear, but he is direct and honest. It's what I need right now.

"Of course, I understand. I don't really do social media, but I'll go under the radar. Please, do everything you can. No one else deserves to get hurt. This needs to end."

There is a knock on the door, and Sullivan grabs the legal pad before stepping out. Greene keeps talking, doing all he can to keep me calm, but my mind wanders while I take it all in.

I peel the label off my water bottle while I try to piece it all together. "How does Brooke Livingston fit into all of this?" I ask as the door opens once more.

Sullivan walks back in and tosses his pad on the table. "She was the key to it all really," he answers. "She started banging Robertson in exchange for drugs. The girl was seriously strung out. She used to be a looker, but man, how the pretty crumble when they're on heroin. Gavin tracked her down and tried to get her out with no luck. That's when he came to us. If he couldn't get her out, he was determined to help take down the whole thing. He got her to meet him a few times. She wanted cash. He gave her a little, but each time he planted a bug on her, her stuff, her car. Those wires opened the door for us in this case. We never would have gotten the investigation off the ground without it."

"At the time of the accident, she was driving to your house," Greene says. "Through the wiretap, we heard Jason tell her to go and see if she could find anything, in case Ashton didn't bring the goods. She was loaded up on a pretty nasty cocktail of drugs and booze when they crashed. Even if they hadn't crashed, with what she had in her, I doubt she would have made it out of Poolesville in one piece."

Greene and Sully exchange looks and shrugs. It's obvious they work together well. They have an excellent "good cop/bad cop" routine, and they seem to be able to communicate through telepathy.

Greene taps the table again. "That's all we can tell you at this time. Now, we need you to go downstairs and identify a few items from the wreck. When the cars crashed, they were both going so fast that the cars exploded on impact. Neither set of remains could be salvaged."

I swallow hard again. These words rattle around in my brain. Remains. Exploded. Salvaged. He speaks about it so clinically that it's easy to forget that we're not talking about events from a case file but rather something that happened to real people. To Ash. I let my mind drift, briefly considering what his last moments were like, and bile rises in my throat. I have to slam that door shut in my mind. I can't go there.

"This case has gotten a lot of attention. It's a career-maker. Every agency that can get a piece of it will try to. You'll be approached by everyone from IRS to ATF. Just answer them honestly. Don't let anyone bully you. We'll do our best to keep you posted," Greene explains.

Sully pulls the legal pad across the table toward him. "Before you go, is there anything you can tell us? Something we should look into? Anything or anyone that has made you nervous or uncomfortable?"

I rack my brain, desperately wanting to give them something to go off. "You know about Preston Construction, right? Well, Ashton would sometimes make jokes that they were somehow connected to the mob. I never really paid very much attention. Ashton always liked to brag like that. But maybe there's more to it?"

Sully scribbles on the pad with his left hand and motions for me to continue with his right. I can't believe he can actually read the chicken scratch he's writing. "Tell me more. What would he say?"

"His father was stabbed five years ago," I begin. Sully nods and motions for me to keep going. "Ash told me it was a former employee that attacked him, but nothing came of it. There was never an arrest. I don't even remember the police even being involved. I always found that strange. The man almost died, and nothing happened. It may not be what you're looking for, but it never sat well with me. After Franklin's stroke, Ashton took over the business and has been running it into the ground. I don't even know how the lights stay on. They only have a few remaining contracts. I've often wondered if there was something shady going on."

Sullivan nods as he writes. "Good, Lily. This is very good. These are the types of things we need to know. You never know what one uneasy feeling from the wife can lead to. I think this is good for now. I'll call you later with an update."

Afterward, Greene leads me downstairs to the evidence department to sit in yet another room without windows and wait. It's cold and reeks of bleach-based cleaner. The stench adds to my growing headache, and the florescent lights buzz above me, rubbing my nerves raw. It's as though they intentionally make this place the most uncomfortable and irritating setting on Earth.

After about ten minutes, Greene comes back with a file box with "Preston" written across the top in black Sharpie. He opens it and takes out several plastic bags. As he opens each bag, I'm hit with a smell that makes me gag. Something rotten mixed with fire. I miss the cleaning solution smell. I look at Ashton's burnt things spread across the table. The watch I got him a few years ago, the hat he asked me to find for him before he left, one of the cuff links he inherited from his grandfather. I touch them, expecting to feel something, some connection to him. I don't feel anything. They just feel cold.

"Can you identify these items?" Greene asks me.

I open my mouth to respond, but my voice is missing. My throat feels like sandpaper, and the words will not come out. I nod. He hands me paperwork to sign and lets me know Ash's effects may or may not be returned to me, depending on what is still needed for evidence.

As he repacks the effects, my chest tightens. He puts the lid on the box and then seals it with evidence tape. I feel as though he's just sealed up what's left of my life. As he leaves the room with the box, I want to stop him and take it back. Everything is happening so fast, and I still don't really understand what's going on. It feels as if I'm trapped on an out of control hot air balloon. I don't know how to get down or where I'll land. I just want off!

I'm suddenly desperate to go home. I need to feel connected to something that will ground me. When I tell Greene, he says I can't go back just yet, that I've already been through enough and I don't need to see that scene now. I can only imagine what that means and decide to take his word for it. I trust him. He asks me to wait in the lounge and assures me that someone will be with me soon to discuss where I can go from here.

I sit on another ass-numbing plastic chair and take stock of my life. My house is a crime scene, I'm completely alone, and I can't call a single friend. I'm so mad at Ashton I want to scream, but I'd have to yell pretty damn loud for him to hear me now. My head drops into my hands, and I rub my temples, hoping to fight off my growing migraine. After a few minutes, I feel someone sit next to me. I fan my fingers and look up to see Gavin's hypnotic eyes. I get lost in them for what feels like eternity.

Gavin takes my hands away from my face and gently wipes the tears away. Then he wraps his long, muscular arms around my shoulders, and I allow myself to lean into him. This man, whom I've known for about twelve hours, whose wife was killed by my husband, is the only person in the world I have left.

FOUR

"Hot Stuff, Lightweight, let's move!" Meredith's voice booms, breaking up the comforting moment. She claps her hands. "Chop, chop! I've got to get you two out of here. We've found press trying to sneak in, and with your growing popularity, it's only a matter of time before you're found again." She stands in front of me and lowers her voice. "We're going to a safe house. *Ándele!*"

She hands me an FBI jacket, a Washington Nationals baseball hat, and some aviator sunglasses. "Try to look a little less like Goldilocks, would ya? You're supposed to be under the radar," Meredith barks at me.

"I'll do my best, but your costume department is a bit lacking. I look like someone that got dressed in an airport gift shop," I snap back as I slip the windbreaker over my head. It's over ninety-five degrees out today with a hundred percent humidity, and this unbreathable vinyl is going to be miserable. But beggars can't be choosers, I suppose.

Giving me the evil eye, she says, "You're lucky I like you, Lightweight. I don't take crap from people. Especially people I'm hiding out at my house!"

"Oh, Meredith, you don't have to give up your home," Gavin chimes in. "I can't stand the thought of us invading your space. There must be another solution."

She waves him off. "It's fine, really, and easier than finding another hotel. Staff-wise, we're stretched thin. We don't have extra bodies to babysit you. There's top-notch security in my building. My roommate, who's also an agent, and I are both working this case, so we won't be home much. So for the time being, this is fast, simple, and safe. The deal is that neither of you leaves. You keep your asses inside where no one can see you. Got it?"

We both look at her and promise to stay put. She leads us out of the building to her car. We end up fighting traffic the whole drive downtown. Meredith lives in Penn Quarter in an amazing building, and her condo has a killer view. It's as though the Capitol Building is in her backyard. But for me, the best part is the rooftop pool. I can't begin to guess how FBI agents afford this place, and it certainly isn't my place to ask.

I walk around the living room, taking the place in. It's a beautiful condo. Modern kitchen, hardwood floors throughout the unit. She has the place decorated with contemporary furniture—clean lines and bold hues. Amazingly, there's no clutter. No pile of mail on the counter or stray coffee cup on the end table. Everything is so pristine that I would have guessed it were the model unit used for sales pitches. I know I'll have to be very careful to keep everything as tidy as I've found it.

"All right, you two, here's the deal: You don't leave. Don't answer the phone. Don't open the door unless I tell you to. And no, Lightweight, you may not use the pool. There's nothing but liquor in the house, so I'll have a patrol car bring by food for lunch and dinner. I'll call you to let you know when it's coming. Do not open to the door to anyone without asking to see a badge first."

She opens a cabinet in the kitchen stocked with liquor bottles. "My brother is a liquor distributor, so it's an open bar. Drink yourself silly if you want. As long as you *stay put*." She points around the room. "TV is there. Computer is there. Lightweight, make sure you set up your social media escape. Go to the beach, to Mexico, to the moon. I don't care, as long as people think you're out of town. Don't allude to your husband. Make it sound like he could be joining you, but don't specifically mention him. Got it? Hot Stuff, do what you need to do on your end." She looks at her watch. "Crap, I've got to get out of here. Call me or Sullivan or Greene if you need anything. Until then, plant your asses on my couch." She slams the door behind her as she leaves.

"That chick blows my mind. I wouldn't want to get on her bad side" I say, only half kidding. I plop down on the sofa, then smirk at Gavin. "And 'Hot Stuff', really?"

He throws a sofa pillow at me and sits down on the love seat across from the sofa. "We'd better get our homework done before she gets mad. What did they tell you to do?"

"I need to make it seem like I've gone on vacation. But what they don't realize is that I'm already pretty much off the grid. For the last five years, I've done nothing but take care of Ashton's dad. I've lost track of all my friends, minus the occasional hello from my friend, Emily. I don't even have a

Facebook account. They don't have to worry, I'm already MIA."

He furrows his eyebrows in a way that's very endearing. "That must be very lonely," he says softly. There's no judgment or pity in his tone, just compassion.

I shrug. "It was what it was. I had to grow up quickly, and compromises had to be made. I couldn't be a social butterfly and take care of Franklin."

"Was he ill?" he asks.

I place the accent pillow on my lap and lean back into the sofa as I describe Franklin's attack. "He wasn't found until the morning. The doctors were astounded he was still alive. He was in a coma for weeks and suffered a few strokes. When he finally came out of it, he required round-the-clock care."

"How devastating," Gavin says.

I nod. "He had an insurance policy that covered the facility, so we thought he was set. A few months later, he missed an insurance payment, and they terminated coverage. Ashton didn't want to pay for the facility himself, so Frankie came home with us, and I took care of him."

"That's quite a burden. How old were you?"

"Twenty-two. I was right out of college. At the time, we never expected it would go on as long as it did. He lived longer than anyone ever imagined. Frankie was quite the fighter. He grew up in New York, came from nothing. He worked in construction and worked his way up in the company, but he eventually scraped enough money together to go out on his own. Ended up making millions. Frankie became Franklin from Potomac. I was the only one that got away with calling him Frankie. Preston is actually his middle name, but he had it changed. I don't know what it was originally. I'm guessing something ethnic-sounding that ends in a vowel. Something that wouldn't go over well with the WASPs. He was determined to be rich. And he was. A lot of good it did him. He spent the last five years of his life watching his son blow through everything he had accumulated while he was stuck inside with me taking care of him. "

Gavin gives me another shy smile and quietly says, "I obviously didn't know the man, but something tells me if he spent every day of the last five years with you, it couldn't have been that bad. I can think of far worse ways to go."

I blush and shift in my seat, uncomfortable with his flattery. "I hope I made his last years comfortable. He was a womanizer and probably a crook. He certainly wasn't winning an award for Father of the Year, but I really cared for him. My parents passed away when I was young. For the nine years Ashton and I were together, Franklin was the only parent I had."

Gavin stands, turning toward the kitchen. "Thirsty? I'm going to get some water."

"Yes, please," I respond.

He opens and closes the cabinets until he finds the glasses. He fills them from the water dispenser on the fridge and carries them back to the living room. He hands me the glass. "I'm sorry to hear about your parents."

I take a sip of my water before placing the cup on the coffee table. "Thanks. I was really young when it happened. Old enough that I remember them but young enough that I don't really remember what it's like to have a family." The room suddenly feels warm. I'm typically reserved when it comes to talking about myself. I don't like people to know my story, especially when it comes to my parents. I'm not sure what's come over me. I pick up my water glass again, hoping to cool my hands down, but then I realize it's tepid. *Must be a British thing.* Every time Ash had gone to London, he'd bitched that they never use ice.

"Were you able to stay with extended family after they passed?" he asks.

I put the glass back down. "I raised myself, really. I was shuffled around between foster homes for a while. Then, I became a ward of the church of sorts. They sent me to a church-run prep school. Then I went to college. Like I said, Franklin was the only family I really had."

He raises an eyebrow. "Your father-in-law was family but not your husband?" he asks. Gavin shrinks back in his seat as his hand goes to his mouth. "Please, pardon me. That's very personal. You don't need to answer that. My question was quite inappropriate."

I shrug. "We're locked together in an FBI agent's apartment because my husband killed your wife and the mob may be after us both. We can't contact friends or family for support. You're all I've got right now. I think we're past the point of 'inappropriate questions,'" I say in a horrifically bad British accent. "All's fair, okay!"

"I told you it was an accident. Brooke was just as much at fault as Ashton."

"To answer your question," I say, cutting him off before he can go on further. I'm not ready to have that conversation with him, and it's far easier to talk about the past than reflect on the present. "Ashton and I met in college. Our relationship was good for college. I just wasn't smart enough to figure out that while playboys make exciting boyfriends, they don't make good husbands. Once real life began, he wasn't around much. Drugs to buy, girls to screw. He had access to his trust fund, the business money, his dad's money. And he spent it all.

"Money burned a hole in that boy's pocket. He would go out every night, 'til all hours. I'd see the receipts for the restaurants and bar tabs, thousands of dollars a night. That doesn't include what he put up his nose. Let's just say he kept the drug dealer's kids in new shoes.

"He would go on extravagant vacations, say they were for business. 'Lil, I'm wooing a client. I have to take him to Monaco,' or some crap like that. He thought I actually bought what he was selling. The truth is that I just didn't care anymore. Whatever we had between us was long gone by that point. I stayed for Frankie. He died about three months ago. I had just started making plans to get out and break free from Ash." I release a big sigh. "I guess he beat me to it."

My last statement just hangs in the air like a cloud of smoke. We're quiet until Gavin breaks the silence. "Well, you may not need to do your homework, but you can help me do mine. I'll warn you, in light of current circumstances, it's rather twisted and morbid."

"What do you have to do?" I ask with trepidation.

He crosses the room to get Meredith's laptop. "The FBI wants to maintain the façade that Brooke is still alive, well, and not addicted to drugs. So I have to use social media to keep her alive. I think it's a bit unnecessary. Her PR company has been doing it for well over a year now, ever since her addiction overtook her life. They were hoping that, after she hit rock bottom and rehabbed, she would be

47

marketable again. They were constantly worried about keeping her relevant. It was all about how many followers she had and all that nonsense. Now that she's gone, the FBI wants me to help them keep it up just a little bit longer so as to not draw attention to the investigation. I can't imagine it'll do much good, but I want to help avoid waves." He sets the laptop on the coffee table and boots it up.

"Man, that is really disturbing," I reply. "Where do we start? I heard on the news her PR people are saying she is in New Zealand. Do we just post things about what she's doing in New Zealand?"

"Yes, that's exactly it. It seems foolish, as the press already thinks she's being held for a DUI in Maryland, but this is how the game is played. I come up with a bunch of posts and tweets and whatnot that will be released throughout the day. I also respond to other's postings as she would have."

"Oh, this is twisted." I get up and walk to the kitchen, ready to look through cabinets. "If I'm going to help write the posts of a dead woman, I need tequila. Oh, look! They have lots. Good. We're going to need it." I return with the bottle and two glasses. I pound two shots before looking at Gavin. "Would you like some?"

He shrugs. "Tequila isn't my first choice, but why not."

I pour a shot and slide it across the coffee table. He catches it before it falls on the floor. I guess I need to reel in my fancy bartending antics before I make a mess.

Turning my attention back to the laptop, I Google spas in New Zealand and can't help thinking about why we're doing this. It just doesn't add up. "Can you explain exactly why we are doing all this anyway? I just don't get it. Is it to keep the press off our tail?"

"Yes, in part. Right now, we don't know what the potential 'bad guys' know. They may not even know that those blokes from the farm are dead. Since the FBI handled all things regarding the accident and subsequent standoff, there's no public record of it. No 911 call or police report. If these men think they're about to be exposed, or that you know more than you should, they'll come after you."

I pour another shot of tequila and shoot it. "So, as long as they think Ash's alive, they'll worry about him before looking to me. But if they think he's dead, they'll be knocking on the door with a pair of cement shoes and an invitation to sleep with the fishes."

He looks confused. "I'm not sure I understood that last part, but essentially yes." He pours himself a shot. "The other issue is the press. If the press finds out this involves Brooke, they'll go snooping around, and they may uncover her connection to this mess. The FBI wants as much time as they can to let this play out. With all the wires they have, they're just waiting for these blokes to hang themselves. If that happens, you and I should be in the clear." Gavin slams back his shot. "It does seem silly, I know. I have thought that they don't really need me to do this and they just want to give me something to do to keep me busy."

"Okay, I get it. I'll help," I say and get back to work. We research New Zealand and come up with activities and places she could have gone and post about them.

I tap my fingers on the coffee table. "Aren't people that are actually at these places going to realize that she wasn't there?" I ask.

"You would think, but stars do this all the time. If anyone says anything, you reply by saying something like, 'That's how good an actress I really am. You had no idea it was me'. Or, 'I'm incognito!' Believe it or not, it works."

I'm cautious about broaching the subject of my own tabloid appearance, but considering the project we're working on, it seems prudent. "Should we post a response to the TMZ story about you and me?" I ask.

He shakes his head. "This isn't the first time I've been accused of cheating on Brooke. When it happened in the past, she wouldn't respond. So I think it best if we just ignore the subject altogether."

My curiosity is piqued. "You don't just throw a statement like that out there and not extrapolate, sir." I hand him another shot. "Let's go. Give up the goods."

He rolls his eyes and does the shot. "I have a sordid past that has been frequently used against me."

I shake my head and motion for him to keep going. "Not good enough."

"As I told you, I was a bit of a rebel when I was younger. I guess I was acting out against my overbearing parents and was eager to get in as much trouble as I could. After an epic row with Mum and Dad, I left home when I was fifteen. Determined to make it on my own, I refused to accept help from family or friends. I had no money, went hungry. Often. Eventually, I met this bird at a party, and the next thing I know, I'm modeling."

I look at him critically. "Model, huh? I can see it." That's the understatement of the year. I'd probably have bought spoiled milk if his face were on the bottle. If he were in a commercial telling me to, I'd probably drink it.

He shrugs. "It paid the bills, kept a roof over my head." A devilish grin spreads across his face. "And it kept my bed occupied. I became quite involved in the life. Dating other models and starlets, living it up quite publicly. It was fun at the time, but I did a lot of things I regret. The press loved me because I always had a headline for them. *Royal Family Shamed Again.* If you're really interested, my debaucherous youth is immortalized on the front pages of *The Sun.*"

"That boggles my mind," I say. "I had my fair share of growing pains when I was younger, but I never had a camera in my face, and no one can Google me to read about it. I can't imagine how hard that must have been."

He taps his fingers on his thigh. "It certainly was daunting. But, at the time, I was acting out and encouraging all the attention, so I got what I asked for. And modeling helped me pay for school. Even though my past follows me around like a bad sidekick, in the end, it was well worth it."

I laugh. "I met lots of girls in school that left college so they could take a stab at modeling. I don't think I've ever heard of it happening the other way around."

He shrugs. "Oxford was always my dream. Modeling was just a means to an end."

"Oxford? Well aren't you a smarty-pants." I try to mask how impressed I am, but by the way he avoids my gaze and shifts in his seat, I'm probably failing. Good-looking and smart. It's a dangerous combination. "What was your major?"

"Medical Studies," he answers. "I had always wanted to be a surgeon."

Gavin is so prim and proper that I can't really see him as a surgeon. Maybe playing one on *Grey's Anatomy*... But being elbow deep in blood and guts? I just can't see it. He's too pretty. "Should I call you Dr. Edwards?"

He shakes his head. "No, I never finished my medical degree. Almost, but that doesn't quite count."

I pour another shot for each of us and slide one to him. "How come?"

"That's a complicated answer."

I look around the room. "In case you haven't noticed, we've got nothing but time."

He takes his shot and then pours another for each of us. "My parents did something that hurt me, and childishly, I needed to hurt them back. Going into the military was the one thing I could do to hurt them the most, so I registered for the Army."

There's clearly more to the story, but his tone indicates he's not interested in delving further into the subject, so I don't push. I take my shot and say, "We got sidetracked a bit. This all started when you said that the press would accuse you of being unfaithful. How did that come into play?"

He looks at me with raised eyebrows, which I shoot right back at him. I'm tipsy, trapped, and curious.

He gives in and finishes the story. "Just after I completed my second tour, I was called back to London. The family business needed new leadership, and I stepped up to take over. The press tried to turn me back into the kid I once was, but I didn't give them very much. I went to work and went home. Dreadfully boring. Until I started dating Brooke.

"The press was all over it. *Can America's Sweetheart Tame the British Bad Boy?*" He drops his head back and laughs. "You'd think they could have come up with something more clever! If they only knew it would be the other way around. Things were tame for a few years, until Brooke started to get bored with life in London. She was out all night, every night. I tried to save her from the attention. Her PR rep would tip off a photographer that I would be at this hotel or that bar with a woman, and that would be the headline. In exchange, they left her alone. Her career would have been ruined if there were covers of her doing drugs in the bathroom at a club or going home with some bartender or other scumbag she'd taken up with. I tried to save her from herself. I guess I failed big time."

"You said it yourself, Oxford. They made their choices, and now we have to live with them." I hand him another shot, and we drink in silence.

FIVE

As the sun sets, Gavin and I sit out on Meredith's balcony and watch the lights come on across DC while we sip on margaritas. In the thick, humid air of the evening, the tempting smells of restaurants waft up to us. Not one identifiable cuisine per se, just the delicious aroma of good food, reminding me how hungry I am. Meredith didn't lie. She doesn't even have basic staples everyone has in her kitchen. Not even a box of stale saltines or a can of chicken noodle soup. Her cupboards have booze and nothing more.

Meredith stops in around eight with some sandwiches. My tequila-based lunch and afternoon snack have me wobbly on my feet, and I fall on my ass on the way to the door to let her in. Unable to get up myself, Gavin gets the door for her. She drops the take out bags on the center island while shaking her head at me.

"Listen here," I yell with alcohol-infused confidence. "Making up fake vacations for a dead lady is hard to do sober!" I wince. "That didn't sound very good, did it? I'm sorry, Gavin. That was rather insensitive."

All three of us crack up laughing. It's a messed up situation, but at least we keep our humor.

"Alright, you two lushes. I have to get back. Take care of yourselves and keep your heads down," she says as she leaves.

As soon as she's gone, we dive into the take out. Meatball subs from Carmine's. One bite and I'm in heaven. Conversation is light while we scarf our food down—it consists mostly of moaning and my frequent requests for another napkin. Barely stopping to chew, I make an absolute pig of myself, but I'm hungry and drunk enough not to care. Not following suit, Gavin gets a knife and fork to eat his sandwich with.

"What are you doing?" I ask with my mouth full.

"Eating," he replies. "What does it look like?"

I wipe my mouth with a napkin and swallow. "You can't eat a sandwich with a knife and fork. It's un-American."

Gavin smirks. "I'm comfortable with that... You missed a spot," he says, handing me another napkin.

"Where?" I ask.

He circles his face with his hand. "Everywhere."

I take a big bite of my sandwich, letting the sauce dribble down my chin, and say, "Screw you!"

After we finish eating and clean up, Gavin and I return to the balcony. We instantly slip back into comfortable conversation. Talking to him is easy. Despite how refined he appears, he's kind and empathetic. He may come from a life of privilege, but he doesn't act superior. I've spent a considerable amount of time with rich people, and no matter how kind they seem, more often than not, they end up looking down their noses at poor girls like me. He, however, asks questions and seems genuinely interested in what I have to say. I can't remember the last time I had a conversation with a man and felt like he spoke to me and not at me.

We stay up all night talking about everything and nothing. We share the same dark sense of humor and laugh at things other people might find completely inappropriate. Just like me, he openly expresses his opinions on everything, even the most mundane observations, and the trait keeps us in active conversation. He looks like a pretty boy that has probably never worked a day in his life, but I learn that couldn't be further from the truth. There's much more to him than his looks. He is a deep, complex man with many layers. At times, our discussions become quite serious and intense. Not what I would have expected.

Once I'm yawning more than speaking, I leave him, needing to take a shower and get ready for bed. Meredith has let me borrow some of her things to sleep in, and it's nice to be in something clean, but I long for my own clothes. Hopefully I'll have them soon. Her shorts are enormous on me, but I have to make it work.

Meredith didn't really go into sleeping arrangements before she left, and it's unclear if she and her roommate are comfortable with us sleeping in their rooms. So, I look for linens to make up the couches just to play it safe. I'm stopped in my tracks by what I find when I return to the living room.

"I really don't feel comfortable taking over their rooms," Gavin says. "They've been kind enough to let us stay here. I feel it's an intrusion. So, I made a fort. What do you think?"

The makeshift fort would be any kid's dream come true it's so spectacular. "They teach fort building at Oxford, do they?"

He chuckles. "No, this I learned from years as an only child and years in the military."

The sofa cushions became the floor, and the sofa frames have been reorganized to create "walls" The three floor lamps are in a row in the center of the room, with sheets draped over them, creating a tent. He's also positioned the dining room chairs to hold up the blankets, extending the fort further out. It takes up the whole living room and is far better than anything I could have come up with. It's pretty impressive.

He gallantly bows. "Does the fort meet your approval, milady?" he asks.

Not wanting to give away just how impressed I am, I give him a bored look and say "Yeah, I guess it's all right."

He smirks and throws a pillow at me. "All right, my arse! It's an architectural masterpiece."

After we get settled into Fort Gavin, I say, "I take it back. The fort's pretty awesome."

He shifts on the cushions to face me. "As I said earlier, I was a medic. When we'd get to a new location, we'd need to set up quickly and get right to work. I had a lot of experience in tent construction."

I pull my blankets up around me. "What was it like when you were out there?" I ask but immediately regret it. "If it's too personal, you don't have to... My father was in the Marines, and I remember the subject of war was completely off limits."

"No, not at all," he replies. "I just haven't really been asked that. I'm told people find me unapproachable or intimidating. Plus, we Brits are a bit more formal than Americans. I'm not often asked direct questions about my service. But, I'm happy to answer. It's nice when someone just says what's on their mind. I rather like that."

I smirk. "As you can probably tell, I'm not one to hold back." As soon as the words leave my mouth, I realize they're a lie. I never used to be one to hold back, until I married Ash. I've spent the last five years turning a blind eye and biting my tongue. So much so that I'm not sure I really know who I am anymore.

"Ok, so my time in the military," he continues. "Well, it was... life-changing. I saw real bravery. Genuine courage. I was just some spoiled rich kid trying to prove a point, and these men were there to fight for peace and freedom. It gave me a whole new way to look at the world.

"I saw things that will forever be burned in my memory. Both pure heroics and epic tragedy. Being a medic, I saw the personal impact of war. I felt it every time I worked on a patient. One night, I was partying till dawn with supermodels, and a few weeks later, I was holding men's hands as they died. It was quite a shift.

"One day, in Afghanistan, we had a number of injured men in the field. I was out doing triage when we were hit. I was the only one to walk away, but I was hit by a bit of shrapnel."

He turns around and slowly lifts his shirt. Several deep scars run down the length of his back. I want to reach out to touch them, but don't. I've had my fair share of shit happen in my life, but nothing like that. I don't know the appropriate thing to say or do.

"I can't imagine how hard that must have been," I say, but it doesn't feel like enough.

"After I was discharged from the Army, I visited the families of each and every person that died while on my watch. I felt like I needed to do something for them, bring them some peace or closure. It allowed me to honor them one last time," he explains, turning back to face me.

I sit up so I can look at him more easily. "That must have been hard, to relive that over and over again."

"I couldn't save their sons or husbands or daughters or wives. It was the least I could do. That, I think, is the hardest part. No matter what you do, you can't save them all. And I have to live with that."

He pauses for a moment and then says, "These families. They are why I do what I do. My family's company, well it's been built under six generations of warmongers. Going back for centuries, my family's made weapons for the military. In the last thirty years, they'd started making weapons that could take out whole towns in one fell swoop. I couldn't stomach it. All the wealth they'd accumulated was blood money, and it made me sick. It's why I estranged myself from my family when I was fifteen. I couldn't bear that they continued to make weapons. I'd hoped that when I joined the Army, they would be more concerned for my safety, but instead they released a new automatic weapon. It was naive on my part, but their message was received loud and clear.

"When my father died and I was asked to take over the company. My plan was to stop making weapons entirely, but I soon learned it wasn't that simple. Weaponry is now a very small part of what we do. For the most part, we now make products that save lives. I shifted the focus of the company to communication and surveillance technology that can help soldiers better assess the field. If I was going to stay in this business, the focus was going to be preventing loss of life, not creating it."

I contemplate what he's just shared in awe. "How old were you? That seems like so much to have placed on your shoulders."

"I was twenty-four," he answers. "In the last four years, I've completely refocused the company. It hasn't always been well received by my board, but I keep making them richer, so that keeps them quiet. I know they're always looking for the chance to boot me out, so I have to stay on my toes and keep the money rolling in."

"That's a lot of pressure." I try to picture what all the responsibility would feel like until he smacks me upside the head with a pillow. "What the hell was that for?" I yell.

"Things have gotten a little too intense in here." He gives me a lopsided smile.

"Oh, you think starting a pillow fight is a good idea? 'Cause you don't know who you're messing with. Trust me. You don't want any of this."

"Please. You've got nothing," he says arrogantly and then throws another pillow at me.

"Oh it's on, Oxford." I shout. "It's on like Donkey Kong!"

We have a massive pillow fight that tears apart his well-designed fort. After almost an hour of strategic attacks, I manage to collect all the pillows and declare myself the victor. He disagrees, but she who has all the ammunition wins the war.

I quickly learn we're both highly competitive, and neither of us backs down from a challenge. Pushing each other's buttons keeps us from going stir-crazy while we're trapped in the condo for days. When I find Monopoly in a closet, I think it should be a fun way to pass some time. But after the fifth game, we find that we both become too cutthroat and the games get far too heated for comfort. Plus, we can't agree on the rules. He refuses to play with the Free Parking money pot, but I've never met a person that doesn't play with Free Parking! He insists that he plays by the *actual* rules where you auction off property, but who really plays that way? So, in the end, we agree not to play anymore.

Afterward, there are embittered debates about random things, like the last episode of *Lost*, the allure of *Downton Abbey*, and—most hostile of all—US vs UK. Everything from food to sports to which side of the road to drive on, we battle it out without resolution.

Our debates are broken up when either Meredith or Greene stops by with food. I've eaten far more pizza in the last four days than I care to, but at least there are plenty of leftovers for midnight snacks and early breakfasts. I wish they'd just go grocery shopping and let us cook, but I think they like to check in on us a few times a day. They haven't given us any further insights or information, which is making me crazy. But Gavin takes it in stride much better than I do.

Before long, Meredith is kind enough to bring Gavin one of his bags, so he has changes of clothes. But I'm stuck doing laundry every day to keep the few items of clothing I have to my name clean, as Meredith's clothes are just too big for me. Her clothes might not fit, but I have helped myself to her bathroom. Once a day, I climb into her deep Jacuzzi tub, armed with a glass of wine, some deep conditioner treatment, and face mask. I may be stuck in this condo, but it won't be with split ends or clogged pores. It feels wrong to pamper myself at a time like this, but I have to do something to pass the time.

The rest of our hours are passed by playing games. We play cards, which Gavin kills me at. But my level of patheticness amuses us both. At Scrabble, we're fairly evenly matched, but we frequently butt heads over British spellings versus American spellings. This again instigates the US vs. UK argument, which tends to go on so long as one of us is still hot under the collar. We're both too painfully stubborn to back down.

As the days wear on, we become too antsy for board games, so we search the apartment for alternative forms of entertainment. We find a Nerf basketball set and play HORSE. He wins. Later, we find a putter and set up mini golf courses around the furniture. He wins again. No matter what I come up with, it's followed by a comment of "I was captain of such-and-such" or "I won all regionals in blah, blah, blah." Perfection may appear appealing at first, but it can become pretty damn annoying when locked up with it for days on end.

At one point, I think I'll have the advantage when we play Pub Trivia, seeing as it's the "All Things American" edition.

"Oh, I've got you this time, Oxford," I boast. "You're going down."

He winks. "We'll see about that."

"You can't seriously think you can beat me, can you? I am the American here."

"I'm a bold man. I know I can beat you."

"Shall we wager?" I ask.

He waggles his eyebrows. "If you're brave enough." The daring gleam in his eye bores into me, sparking a surprising warmth inside me. His challenging tone sounds almost flirtatious, but it can't possibly be. He's been nothing but a gentleman, impeccably respectful to me and the fact that we are both in mourning. But, there's something in the way that he's looking at me that makes me wonder. Maybe I'm just seeing what I want to see. It's been so long since I've actually enjoyed spending time with someone that I could be misreading it.

"Oh, I'm brave enough," I brag. "Loser has to sing the winner's national anthem. With a smile."

"Done. It's on! You're going to regret this," he says with a smirk that, while it makes him even more attractive, just makes me want to beat him!

Question after question, he answers perfectly. I'm amazed but still confident. He has to slip up somewhere.

Then, it's my turn. The question: *Name the thirteen original Colonies.*

"Ah, the thirteen colonies that dumped your country's ass!" I list off the states from Maine to the Carolinas.

"No. Sorry, luv," he replies. "I think you're referring to that little temper tantrum you rebels threw, but you're wrong." We argue back and forth and back and forth, but in the long run he's right—Maine joined the country much later.

I throw a bit of a temper tantrum. "Okay. You win. You and your photographic memory and your nauseatingly perfect chiseled chin can suck it!" Then, I pout for a while. But I'm a woman of my word, and I grudgingly sing "God Save the Queen," which he enjoys far too much.

I do win at beer pong, which is apparently not as big in the UK. Finally, I've found something he's not good at. Spending four years at a party school has finally paid off.

With the exception of our intermittent little spat, we spend the days in comfortable conversation. At times, he talks about Brooke, and I can see the sadness in his eyes and hear the grief in his voice. She doesn't come up often, usually as a part of a memory he's sharing, but when she does come up, I can feel how much he's struggling. I think both of us are avoiding reality, which is easy to do while we're in hiding. I know I am. If I think about the real reason we're trapped in this apartment, I know my calm, cool, collected persona will come unglued.

This vacation to the state of denial has made it easy to forget we're two people with lives that have just been devastated by loss. Instead, we can pretend we're just two people spending time together. Because this arrangement is temporary, I'm comfortable exposing parts of myself to him that I wouldn't typically. We've quickly developed a strong bond, but I'm sure it will dissolve once the investigation finishes. He'll go back to his life, and I'll go back to mine.

Spending all this time together in confined quarters, chemistry is inevitable, but under the circumstances, it's both awkward and inescapable at the same time. Sometimes, when we're sitting and talking, Gavin looks at me as if I'm the only thing left on Earth. I have his complete attention. At other times, he looks ravenous, as though he simply wants to grab me and fuck me against the wall. It's tempting. After all the loss, fear, and confusion, I crave the connection. It's not about sex exactly, although a little action wouldn't hurt, but I covet the intimacy. To feel something real, alive. Something that wouldn't make me feel completely alone in the world. We couldn't… could we? I know I'm going to hell for even thinking it.

He's a bit of a workout nut. He'd have to be with a body like his. Every day, he has me doing his crazy exercises with him. Planks and burpees. It's awful. It's a good thing he has a sense of humor because I'm completely uncoordinated. We end each "session" in stitches, laughing at what an ass I've made of myself. Man, does he have stamina though. Thinking of it makes my mind wander to all sorts of places... I can only imagine what he could do with that stamina during other cardio activities.

The cherry on top of it all is that Gavin can dance. One day during our seclusion, I get out of the shower and hear JT's "Rock Your Body" blasting. I peek my head out of the bathroom to see Gavin busting a move like I cannot believe. I've never seen a man, in real life, dance like that. I watch him 'til the song ends and then burst out in applause.

He turns around and goes beet red, looking at me like a kid caught with his hand in the cookie jar. "Well, this is humiliating!" he says in his adorable English accent.

"Why? You're amazing! If I could dance that well, I'd dance all the time. I wouldn't walk anywhere. I'd just dance from place to place."

"Can't you dance?" he asks. "Everyone can dance."

I shake my head. "No. I don't dance. I can shake my butt a little. Enough to go to a club and survive. But it's a far cry from dancing."

He steps toward me. "Come here."

I step back. "What?"

He steps toward me again. "Come. Here."

"Why?"

He rolls his eyes. "Stop asking questions and just do it. Seriously. You can be so difficult."

"Are you going to make me dance?" I ask in a slightly whiney tone.

He holds his hand out. "I'm going to teach you to dance. Big difference. I'll teach you, and you will love it. Give it a bash?"

I point to his feet. "The only things that'll get bashed are your toes."

He grabs my hand and drags me across the room. I refuse to walk, so my socked feet slide across the hardwood floor. He puts Big Bad Voodoo Daddy on the stereo. I raise my eyebrows at him.

"All Americans should know how to swing dance. You invented it, for crying out loud. It's very easy and lots of fun. Just trust me and relax," he says, pulling me close to him.

"Trust you, huh? That's asking a lot. What if I break something? We can't even go to the hospital."

"Quit being such a baby," he scolds. Before I can protest again, he spins me. I twirl until I'm dizzy. When I finally stop to catch my breath, he says, "See? Wasn't that fun? Good. Now let's get started."

He teaches me the basics, and it only takes me about three hours to do it with some sort of rhythm without stepping on his feet.

When we stop for a water break and I have a chance to catch my breath, I ask, "So, aren't you going to tell me how you learned to dance? Is this an English gentleman thing as well? Like carrying handkerchiefs?"

"Ballroom dancing, yes. That's something we all had to learn. But the rest, that's from my Mum. She was a dancer. Could have probably been a professional, but she got married and did the proper thing for an English lady to do. She always loved to dance. We had a dance studio of sorts in our house, and we would dance all the time. Plus, I inherently have good rhythm. The rest just comes naturally."

Oh, I'd bet he has really good rhythm.

We dance till dawn, and I have the time of my life.

****

On the morning of our fifth day in captivity, Meredith brings us breakfast. Bagels with lox and whitefish salad from Bagel City. They have the best bagels in the area, but their locations are too far out of my way from my house to go regularly. There's no easy way to get across DC, and even bagels this good aren't worth that much traffic. I dive in with gusto and growl when Gavin tries to take some of the whitefish.

"Down girl," Meredith says. "I brought plenty." She slices a bagel for herself and smears on some cream cheese. "Time to talk shop for a few. We know from a source in the organized crime division that Maniglia's crew knows about Ash's death and that he and Maniglia were being investigated. I don't know more than that. But this is crunch time. If they are going to try to do something, now would be the time. So make sure you stay put."

It's the first news we've heard in days. I'd thought I would be relieved to hear something, but I'm not. Even though we've learned something, we still really know nothing. We don't know what the gang's reaction will be. They may not care, or they may want to kill me. I've seen every mobster movie out there, and I've always been under the impression that wives and families were kept out of these

67

sorts of messes. But that's the movies. Who knows what happens in real life?

Meredith takes a bite of her bagel and wipes the crumbs from her chin. "Gavin, the press has stayed tame. Whatever you're doing to keep them off the scent is working."

"If only Brooke were really feeding sheep in New Zealand like we've posted she is," I say with sorrow.

"Brooke made her choices," Gavin replies.

Meredith leaves, and we're both quiet for the rest of the afternoon. Gavin works, and I read a book I find in Meredith's room.

At five, Gavin appears at my side and hands me a shot of tequila. "I think this day needs a pick me up, don't you?" he says with a smile.

By seven, another bottle of tequila is gone, and we are playing I Never. Neither one of us really remembers if you drink when you've done something or if you've never done it, and it's really hard to play with two people, but we still end up laughing hysterically while we share stories.

At eight thirty, Gavin leaves to take a shower. I give in to my urge to Google him, and I find pictures from his modeling days. It turns out he was a Calvin Klein underwear model—back when they were hot and didn't look like waifish heroin addicts. Good God Almighty! There are no words to describe the perfection that is this man. Every inch of him looks as though it was carved out of granite. His glorious pecs, the eight pack—eight pack!—just begging to be licked. And the deep cut of his abdominal V... *I bet Calvin sold a whole lot of boxer briefs that year!* While I'm drooling, the doorbell rings. I figure it must be Meredith coming back with dinner. As I'm opening the door, I think,

Why would she ring the doorbell? Then everything goes black.

SIX

I come to in the back of a van. My hands and feet are bound, and my mouth is covered with what smells like duct tape. My eyes aren't covered, which scares me to no end. I've seen enough movies to know that if your abductor lets you see them, you don't live to tell about it.

Fucking Ashton. It's bad enough he had to throw his life away, but did he need to take mine down with him? When I met him all those years ago, I'd known he was trouble, but I'd thought he was just enough trouble to keep my life interesting. I should have known enough to turn around and walk in the other direction.

I can hear the tick of my watch as it counts down what I guess are the last minutes of my life. My heart pounds, and I struggle to get what air I can through my nose. I need to calm down. Why spend my last few minutes in a panic attack? That reaction may be the tequila talking, but I go with it.

I have no idea how long we've been driving when the van stops. Apparently, there has been someone behind me the whole time because he whispers into my ear, "He's going to want to talk to you, so I'm taking the tape off. Don't scream, or it'll go back on." He rips the tape off my mouth and then puts an atrociously smelly bag over my head. My skin burns from the removal of the tape, far worse than from any waxing. The upside is that I still haven't seen anyone's face.

The man picks me up and carries me over his shoulder, caveman-style. He chuckles. "No one would hear you anyway." He walks for a while. I listen, trying to pick up any clue that may tell me where I am, but all I can hear is the crunching under his feet.

I'm set down hard on what I guess is a tree stump. *Damn that hurts!* A bruised tailbone seems minor at this point, but it still sucks. He taps me on the head, and then I hear the crunching of his footsteps as he walks away.

I'm left alone for what feels like forever. I call out, but no one answers. Maybe he was right, no one can hear me.

The air is hot and thick with humidity. The heavy air makes the smell inside this bag even worse. Mosquitoes feast on my bare arms and legs. He must have taken me out of the city because Rock Creek Park is never this buggy. I have no idea how long I was passed out. We could have been driving for hours.

I play out worst case scenarios in my mind. Not a good game to play when you are trying to stay calm. The bug bites become so uncomfortable that all of my energy is focused on willing them to stop itching when I hear the crunching of several sets of footfalls.

"If you're trying to torture me with mosquitoes, it's working," I joke to let them know I'm supposedly calm. "Well, it's a toss-up between the bugs and the smell of the bag. I'm not sure which is worse. But well done on your part."

I hear a chorus of deep belly laughs. Sounds like three or four different voices, all male. One of them has that raspy, phlegmy laugh of a lifetime smoker. I'm cataloging all this information as though it will be helpful in some way, assuming I don't die here. I have no idea how I'll survive, but it gives me something else to think about.

"You're funny, Mrs. Preston," Phlegmy says with a thick New York accent. "Too bad your husband was such a *fessacchione*."

"We apologize if you are uncomfortable." This man is younger, with a smooth, polished voice. "This shouldn't take too long at all. We'll make it quick and painless."

Oh shit. They're going to kill me. I decide that going to hell might be worth it if I can torment Ashton for all of eternity for getting me into this.

"We have gotten word from our friends in law enforcement that you have concerns, Mrs. Preston," says another man, who sounds exactly like Joe Pesci. "The longer these concerns continue, the longer we'll have undesired attention. We don't like unwanted attention."

I gulp, preparing myself for them to put an end to my concerns.

I hear someone coming closer very slowly. With each crunch of leaves under his foot, I jump. These woods are remarkably silent. All I can hear are footsteps and heavy breathing. I imagine this person is psyching himself up to do something stressful, like slamming an axe into my forehead.

A cold hand touches my arm, and I flinch. I can feel hot breath on my neck. I'm slowly turned around on the tree stump. They must not want to see my face when I die. The bag is slowly lifted off of my head.

I close my eyes, and suck in the fresh air as though I'm taking my last breath. After a few moments, I dare to open my eyes. There's a slight, elderly man standing in front of me. He's unassuming in his posture and dress, but I have a strong feeling this is the man running the show.

"Hello, Mrs. Preston. I'm sorry for all of the theatrics. My business partners felt more comfortable taking precautions. They'll be angry with me for revealing myself to you. But I'm eighty-four years old. I can do as I please. As long as you don't turn around, you'll be safe. And I trust you, Mrs. Preston. I don't say that to many people."

Too afraid to speak, I nod.

He smiles. "Your husband has left you in a compromised position. He owed my great nephew quite a bit of money. He made some very bad decisions and involved some very dangerous men. It was all … careless." He closes his eyes and shakes his head in disappointment. "Not the way I do business."

"Ashton was a child that never grew up. He never appreciated the consequences of his actions," I say in hopes of showing him I understand who my husband was and distancing myself from him. "When he saw something he wanted, he took it, without thinking about who he was hurting."

He pats my arm and says, "Yes, I know. My name is Lorenzo Grimaldi, and I'm Franklin's godfather. Do you know much about Franklin's upbringing? Did he talk about where he came from?"

"Very little," I respond with a mix of fear and great curiosity.

"His father, Antillo Messina, was my best friend. His whole life. Antillo wanted a straight, American life for his son and did everything he could to raise Franklin to be a hardworking, honest man. And he was, for the most part. It was his father's wish that Franklin wouldn't be part of my way of life. I respected that wish.

"That isn't to say I didn't help out from time to time, but what he didn't know didn't hurt him. Franklin worked hard for everything he had. I couldn't have been more proud if he'd been my own blood. If only his son had followed in his footsteps.

"As I said, Ashton left you in a compromised position. In a typical situation, I would hold you accountable for his obligations. Even when someone has an unexpected departure, the debt must still be paid. I'm well aware of your financial position and that you have no means to pay down your husband's debt.

"But I'm also aware of how you cared for Franklin in the last years of his life. That son of his would have put him in a state-run home and let him rot until he died if it weren't for you," he says with disgust, as though it offends him to even have to speak of Ashton. "You cared for him as though he were your own father. He lived out his last days with dignity."

"Franklin was like a father to me," I say. He nods as though he understands.

"Because of your kindness, I have cleared your debt. Additionally, you'll be under my protection against other... associates that your husband may have wronged. He was involved with some dishonorable men. I'll do all I can to ensure you won't be harmed. Start a new life, Lily. You'll never see me again, but trust me, I'll be seeing you."

And just like that, there's a rag over my nose, and everything goes black.

SEVEN

I'm awoken by a gentle slap to the face. "Wake up, Mrs. Preston, and listen carefully. You will tell the FBI you cleared your debt. If you tell them you saw anyone or give them any other details, our deal is over. Trust me, you need that protection, so keep your trap shut."

I hear the man talking to me, but I'm still in a haze.

"Tell me you understand, Mrs. Preston," he says growing impatient.

"I understand," I whisper. The next thing I know, I'm pushed and hit the ground hard. A car door slams, and then tires squeal. As the world comes back into focus, I see a van speeding away. My hands and feet are free. I try to stand, but I'm too wobbly. I guess I've been drugged. Looking around, I try to get my bearings, but I'm so disoriented that everything is still a bit blurry. I'm in an alley of some sort, but have no idea where.

I open my mouth to call for help, but my voice is shot. Barely a whisper comes out. I don't know how long I lie in the alley before someone comes out of the building. I recognize the someone as Travis. *I'm outside Jack's!* They brought me to the one place I'd definitely be found. They sure are crafty, I'll give them that.

Travis recognizes me right away and runs over. "Lily, everyone has been looking for you! Let's get you inside and call Sully. Are you hurt?"

I shake my head no as he scoops me up and carries me in. He puts me down on a sofa in the office, and I immediately lose consciousness again.

The next time I wake up, I'm surrounded by people in a hospital room. I recoil from the overload. Someone yells, "She's awake," and Meredith and Sully come running in.

"Everyone out. *Now*," Meredith orders. "Girl, when I tell you to stay put, you stay put. What the fuck happened to you?"

Sully hands me a bottle of water. "Here, you probably need this first. Looks like you may have been drugged. We're waiting on your tox screen to come back to know for sure."

After slowly drinking the water, I'm ready to tell the story. "I heard the doorbell ring. We were expecting Meredith to come with dinner, so I went to open the door. It occurred to me too late that you could just unlock the door when you came."

I give them all the details up until the part where I met Lorenzo. "They said I was bringing them unwanted attention. That my debt was clear. I think you were right, Sully," I say. "I can't remember exactly what they said, but I think that what Maniglia was doing was off their radar. They just want it all to go away. Why take the heat for something they didn't profit from?"

He puts his pad away and pats me on the leg. "Ok, sit tight while I go run this by the organized crime guys," Sully says as he walks out.

Meredith looks as though she wants to kill me. I may be more afraid of her than I was the mobsters. She yells at me for about fifteen minutes, and I hang my head in shame for messing up. It seems to have been completely forgotten that I've just survived the scariest thing that has ever happened to me.

Greene comes in and says, "Enough, Mer. The girl has been scared shitless. Give her a break. You okay, kid?"

Before I have a chance to respond, Sully bounds back into the room. "You must have gotten a pardon from on high, Lily. Organized crime said that about an hour ago they were messengered a package with tapes, flash drives, and files on Maniglia. They're still sorting through it, but there's enough there for us to take down everyone in his ring. There's info on prostitution, coke, meth, bookmaking, bribery, extortion—the whole enchilada. Heads are going to roll! We have nothing on any of the higher-ups, but the organized crime guys say this was a gift. We get to take down this crew, and in exchange, we leave them alone. The crew that operated off-book gets cut out like cancer. It's a deal with the devil, but sometimes you take what you can get."

"So does that mean I'm out of witness protection?" I ask. "I'm not in danger anymore, right?"

"Don't know that yet, kid. This particular case will be closed. But we don't know what is still out there. For now, you can come out of hiding, but we are going to keep in touch," Greene says. "You can't go back to Meredith's house as it's now a crime scene. Someone will take you over to another hotel. We'll watch your room tonight."

"Greene, look at me," I say. I try to stress my words with my gaze when I say, "I know I'm safe."

He raises an eyebrow. "You leave anything out of your statement?" he asks. "Is there something you aren't telling me?"

I shrug. "Greene, I've told you all there is to tell. Just trust me when I say I know I'm safe."

"When you're ready to talk about what you're not telling me, you know where to find me. In the meantime, you've had a rough day, let's get you discharged. I'll get someone to drive you over there now. You'll still have to come by the station later to give a statement and sign some papers. But for tonight…" He looks down at his watch. "Make that today."

Twenty minutes later, I'm blinded as I walk out of the hospital into the afternoon sun. A Town Car pulls up to the curb, and Sam, my escort from that first night with Gavin, jumps out and opens my door for me. It's hard to believe that was only a week ago. I feel as though I've lived a lifetime since then.

Sam takes me to a room in the Hyatt this time. After clearing my new room, he hands me a bag. "From Meredith," he says before he leaves. I take a peek. Brand new pajamas and a change of clothes for tomorrow. I turn her house into a crime scene, and she still gets me a change of clothes. I owe her big time.

I take another scalding hot shower, trying to burn any remnant of the last two days off of me. The crazy adventure is finally over, and I'm relieved. I can breathe a little easier and finally go home soon. I've wanted nothing but to go home since the moment I found out Ashton was dead, but now that it's going to happen, I realize I'm not sure what I'm going home to. Maybe just a gigantic empty house filled with bad memories…

EIGHT

After getting out of the shower and changing into fresh pajamas, I hear a knock at the door. When I open the door, Gavin scoops me into a bear hug that cuts off my oxygen supply.

"I was so worried about you," he whispers in my ear. "I'm so relieved you're safe."

"I'm sorry you were worried," I squeak out. I pat him on the shoulder. "Can't. Breathe."

He releases me with a laugh. "My apologies. I'm just so happy to see you." He shakes his head. "You have no idea the horrible things I've been imagining." He looks me up and down, as though he's examining me for injuries.

"It was scary, but I'm here now. I even have all my fingers and toes."

He looks at my hands, focusing on my fingers. I can almost hear him counting in his head to make sure they're all there. He lets out a sigh and touches his forehead to mine. "You're here," he says.

This sweet, tender moment touches me. Moments ago, I'd been feeling completely alone, as though I could disappear off the face of the earth and no one would notice my absence. And here comes this man, making me feel like I'm not entirely on my own. My emotional floodgates open. Everything I've been holding in since I was taken—about Ashton, all the fear and anger—just comes pouring out of me in heavy sobs.

Gavin is kind and gentle, holding me, letting me get it all out. I'm appreciative that he doesn't just tell me to be strong or say it's going to be alright. I know all of those things, but at this moment, I need to feel it all. All the things I've been stuffing down inside me, ignoring and avoiding, I need to face. I let the wave of emotion hit me so that I have a chance of getting through this. My brain is a hot mess of grief, relief, fear, confusion, and sheer exhaustion.

I'm not sure how long I cry, but from the look of his shirt when I pull away, it must have been a long time. He's soaked through. I look up at him, feeling completely swollen from crying, and say, "You may need a new shirt."

We both laugh. I'm temporarily distracted from my emotional disaster area by the thought of Gavin without a shirt. My mind blissfully wanders back to the boxer brief ads I'd found earlier, and, for a moment, I forget everything. He snaps me back to reality when he kisses the top of my head and turns to leave, saying he'll be right back.

Before long, he returns to my room in pajamas. While I lament not getting to see him shirtless, Gavin in pajamas has become one of my favorite things to look at over the past week. I never tire of looking at him. His tight t- shirt shows off a well-defined torso. His pants rest low on his hips, allowing a glimpse at all his abdominal glory.

When I come back to my senses, I see he's brought two containers of Ben and Jerry's with him.

"I'm a closet ice cream junkie. I bought these downstairs earlier." He holds up the containers. "Chunky Monkey or Chubby Hubby?"

His English accent makes me giggle. I feign not hearing him to get him to say the names two more times before he catches on.

He rolls his eyes and says, "If you're going to make fun of my accent, I get to choose first." He goes with Chunky Monkey and throws the other container to me. He takes two wrapped plastic spoons out of his pocket.

The ice cream is heavenly. Peanut butter and fudge with salty pretzels. Pure euphoria! I point my spoon at him. "How can you be a closet ice cream eater and look like you do?"

"I work my arse off so I can eat ice cream. Well, you know that at this point. Plus, I'm a fairly healthy eater minus the Chunky Monkey."

I'm sent into giggles again. I love the way he says that.

We sit on the bed and eat and talk. He doesn't ask me anything about what happened but instead tells me funny stories about all of the agents he's met during the time he's been here. Like when Sully got so drunk they locked him in the fake cell at Jack's. Or the day Greene had to bring his daughter to work with him because his wife was sick and she kept him running around in circles. He has me in stitches, which is so nice after the day I've had. I don't know what it is about him, but he sets me completely at ease.

Too much at ease apparently. I look down and realize I've emptied the container in my hands. "Damn it, Oxford. Why is it that I seem to end up doing everything to excess when I'm with you? I've eaten this whole pint, and I feel like I'm going to explode. You're too distracting with your funny stories and your cute accent. I stop paying attention to what I'm doing and keep shoveling it in. Tomorrow, I will not eat or drink until I feel like I'm going to be sick!" I throw a pillow at him and then roll over and moan.

He puts his remaining ice cream down, apparently having enough restraint not to eat the whole thing. "You have collywobbles? Come here. I'll rub your belly! Come on, snuggle up!" He motions for me to come closer.

"Do I have what? Is that contagious?" I tease.

"You love my Englishness, and you know it. Now come over here and let me rub your tummy."

I curl up next to him, and he gently rubs my stomach.

I have to admit, it does help settle my stomach. Very soon, his rubbing does more than that. I feel a warming down south, and my toes start to curl. Ashton and I hadn't slept in the same room in years. Once he'd started sleeping around, I saw no reason keeping up the pretense. The thought of sleeping next to him made my skin crawl. I can't remember the last time someone has touched me with such a gentle caress. As over Ashton as I may have been, this still feels strange. He only died a week ago, and here I am, in bed with the hottest man to ever walk the planet, overrun with thoughts of the myriad of ways I can molest him.

In all the time we've spent together the last few days, we've never gotten too close. I've made a conscious effort to keep a healthy distance between us. A throwback to my

Catholic school days, a least a yardstick's length between us at all times. Not that getting closer hadn't crossed my mind. Often.

This is the closest we've ever been. Soon, the air in the room changes. It becomes charged with electricity. I think he feels it too because his touch changes from soothing to seductive. The sensation overtakes me, and every nerve ending in my body is standing on end. My breathing becomes heavy, and I bite my lip to stifle a moan.

I suddenly feel him shift next to me. "I'd better put the ice cream away before it melts," he says as he jumps up. "I'll be right back."

I try to calm myself down while he's gone. I drop my head into my hands. *What am I doing? The man's wife just died, for crying out loud! Ash just died!*

I'm sure I've misread things. He was just being a nice guy trying to calm a hysterical friend. Not even friend. I'm just this crazy woman that he's been stuck with all week. There's nothing going on here other than my libido. She's been asleep for so long that she must not remember how to tell the difference between a nice guy and a come on. Since I married to Ash, nice guys haven't been part of my frame of reference.

Gavin returns but stays in the doorway. He avoids meeting my eyes while he picks at his cuticles. "Maybe I should go back to my room and let you get some sleep. You've had such a long day."

A feeling of dread overshadows my shame. "I don't want to be alone," I whisper. Now, I'm the one avoiding his eyes. "With everything that happened tonight, I just don't want to be alone right now. I know everything's all clear now, but I can't shake this feeling. I'm… I'm scared."

He looks at me with sympathetic eyes as he steps into the room and closes the door. "Oh, of course. I'm happy to stay. I don't want to leave you alone, but I also don't want to make you uncomfortable. It was one thing when we were in our fort. It was fun and games, completely innocent." He stares at the bed. "This is different. It's a hotel. You're a recently-widowed woman. I would hate to be … inappropriate."

I laugh. "Didn't I tell you we're long past inappropriate?"

We both chuckle, and then there's an awkward silence. He plays with the carpet seam with his toe, looking uneasy.

"Yes, I'm a recently-widowed woman, but I'm not going through the typical mourning process. My relationship was over years ago. I was more like the hired help than Ash's wife. I took care of the laundry, made sure the gutters got cleaned, and stuff like that. We slept in different rooms and barely saw each other. He started cheating on me almost as soon as we came back from our honeymoon. Maybe before. The only reason I stayed was to take care of my father-in-law."

I'm not sure why I've just said all that. Gavin wasn't asking for permission to make a move. He was just being respectful. My confession has taken an already awkward situation and put it through puberty—now it's the tallest girl in class, with no boobs and horrible acne. Making things worse seems to be a special skill of mine.

Gavin shakes his head and furrows his brow. He looks as though he wants to say something but chooses not to. He just keeps shaking his head, a scowl on his face. He looks disgusted, and I feel ashamed.

"I know it sounds horrible. I feel wretched just hearing myself say it. My only hope is that this is one of the stages of

86

grief or I'm in shock or something." I look down and pull at a loose thread on the bedspread. "With everything that he's done to put me in the position I'm in, I'm so angry. It's horrific that he lost his life. I would never have wanted that. But I'm not sad that he's not a part of my life anymore. I know I'm a horrible person for admitting this, but for the first time in a long time, I feel a sense of freedom."

"That anger will go away in time," he says softly.

"Maybe it will. Maybe it won't. It'll take a lot for me to make peace with what he's done. The fact of the matter is I wasn't in love with him. Hadn't been for a long time. After what I went through today, I don't know if can ever forgive him."

He crosses the room and sits next to me. "Do you want to talk about it?"

I tell him the whole story, every detail—minus my bravado. I become so animated that I pace the room, talking excessively with my hands. He listens, not saying anything.

After I get the whole story out, I'm spent and a little breathless. I sit next to him on the edge of the bed. He doesn't say anything for quite a while.

When he finally speaks, his voice sounds strained, as though he's trying to hold back his emotions. "If only I hadn't been in the shower, I—"

"Gavin, this isn't your fault. Who knows what they would have done to you if you had been there? Clearly, they don't like witnesses. Things worked out for the best. I'm back and safe. Hopefully, this is all behind us now."

"When I walked out into the empty living room with the door wide open, my heart seized. I called out to you, searched every nook and cranny of that flat, and there wasn't a trace of you. While I waited for the FBI to arrive, I searched every floor, knocked on every door hoping someone saw you. I must have looked like a madman. I probably scared all of the tenants. When Meredith arrived, I went with her to look at the security footage. The guys were dressed in police uniforms and had badges, walked right passed the guard and carried you out the back. Your body was limp, and I was petrified you were ... that I would never see you again. I just couldn't bear the thought. I've already lost one person I care about from this calamity. I can't bear to lose another."

I pat his hand. "It must have been traumatic. I'm so sorry you had to go through that. I probably would have been a hysterical mess if the roles had been reversed."

He pauses for a moment, tracing the art deco pattern on the bedspread with his finger. "I know we've only known each other for a short amount of time, and we met under such unorthodox circumstances, but in the last few days, I've come to fancy you. I wish neither of us was caught up in this mess, but I'm thankful I'm going through it with you."

He looks down and away as if to hide his emotions. I reach my hand up to gently touch his face and turn it toward me. "Me too. You're all I've got these days, Oxford." I lose track of my thoughts as I get lost in those eyes again.

We stare at each other for what feels like forever, the chemistry between us building with each passing second. I'm not sure who leans in first, but the next thing I know, we're kissing. The kind of kiss that makes you feel like you're floating. Sweet, sensual, and pure magic. I'm still mesmerized by the connection when he pulls away.

"I'm so sorry. That was a mistake." He brings his hands to his lips as he stands up and walks toward the door. He hangs his head as he rakes his fingers through his hair. His back is to me when he says, "I should go." He runs out the door before I can say another word.

The kiss was deliciously intense. So intense it bolted him right out the door. *What have I done?* Gavin has been the only stable thing in my life, and I've just fucked it up. Why? Because he has a whisper-light touch that makes me tingle all over? Because those full lips and hypnotizing eyes pull me in like a magnet?

I know he's mourning Brooke, and I'm… well, I'm not sure how to describe what I'm feeling about Ash. My emotions are so jumbled and confused. In a very short time, Gavin and I have gone from strangers to close friends. Today was an emotionally charged day, and we've both leaned on each other. Probably more than we should have. I hope this is nothing more than a momentary lapse in judgment. One that felt damn good.

This kiss could destroy our friendship, and I need him in my life more than I need to be kissed. Kissing would be a bonus, but this isn't the time to be greedy. I decide to head to bed and hope Gavin will have forgiven me by morning. I've been running on fumes for days and I desperately need to recharge, but I can't shut down. My body and brain are exhausted, begging me for sleep, but it never comes. I keep replaying the kiss over and over in my mind, wishing I hadn't done it, and at the same time, wishing I could do it again.

After tossing and turning for too long, I jump out of bed. I need to talk to him. Throwing caution to the wind, I run from my room. I make it to the hallway before I realize I have no idea which room he's in. I return to my room, call the front desk, and ask for Gavin's room. No Gavin Edwards.

"Oh, right," I say. "What name is my room registered under?"

The front desk guy is clearly irritated that I have interrupted whatever he's doing. "Uh, you don't know your own name?"

"Look, dude, just tell me the name." I throw an equal amount of irritation back at him.

"Eve Moneypenny?" He sounds very confused. "Is that, uh, your real name?"

"How do you not know who Moneypenny is? Do you live under a rock? Please tell me what room James Bond is in."

"Uh, there isn't a James B—Oh, wait, there is. Ms. Moneypenny, I can't release his room number. I can put your call through though. Have a good night."

The line rings and rings until I'm redirected back to the dipshit at the front desk. Frustrated, I call Meredith, knowing she's probably still up and working. She barks his room number at me, and then yells at me about something I don't stick around to hear. I imagine I've hung up and made it down the hall long before she realizes I've dropped the call.

The elevator is taking forever to arrive. But my emotions have taken over, and I can't waste another second to find him, so I take the stairs. When I hit the tenth floor, I run down to ten twenty-three and knock gently on the door. "Gavin. Are you awake? Please let me in!"

Nothing.

"Gavin, can we please talk about this? I don't want anything to be weird between us."

I bang on the door for another ten minutes before I give up and plod slowly back to my room. Deflated, I wait for the elevator, giving myself time to I wallow in my disappointment. First I kiss him, then I harass him. It's not shocking that he won't answer the door.

When the carriage doors open on my floor, I drag my feet as I walk sluggishly down the hallway toward my room. When I get there, I see that I left in such a hurry that the door is still open. Today has not been my day with doors.

I walk in, desperate to climb into bed and pout, when I'm suddenly scooped up by Gavin. He pulls me into a clutching embrace. "Bloody hell, woman! What is your aversion to closing doors? I thought you'd been snatched again!"

The comfort of his hug is inviting, and I'm tempted to never let him go. He has that sexy masculine smell, sweat with a hint of soap. He's dressed in running shorts, shoes, and a tank top that shows off his amazingly toned arms. I'm guessing he went for a hard run because his clothes are slightly damp.

"You're going to give me a heart attack if you keep doing this to me," he says before letting me go.

When he releases me, I flick the brim of the baseball cap that he's wearing backwards. "I thought guys stopped wearing their hats like that like ten years ago." I smirk before turning to pull the door closed behind me.

He laughs as he readjusts his hat. "Some looks are timeless." He hands me a bouquet of sad, wilted flowers. "Here. I got these for you."

"Thank you for the dying flowers?" I say with sarcastic curiosity. "I was just thinking this hotel room could use a little potpourri."

He smiles sheepishly. "I went on a run to try to clear my head, and a gentleman on the street corner was selling them. I wish I had gotten a better look at them though. They are rather pathetic, aren't they?"

I bring them to my nose, and they smell as though they've just crossed the line from fresh to rotting. "It was a sweet gesture, regardless. I can't even remember the last time someone bought me flowers."

"I'm sorry for what happened earlier, and I feel worse about the way I handled myself. I didn't express myself well, or at all, really." He takes the flowers from me and sets them down on an end table, then sits down. "Running out on you was cowardly."

I join him on the edge of the bed, keeping a respectable distance. "You have nothing to apologize for. An innocent moment got carried away. Can we just forget it?" I ask. "It would break my heart if something came between us. A crazy twist of fate has brought us together on this insane ride, but we're on it together. I can't navigate this without you. Let's just pretend it never happened."

He cups my face and tilts it so he can look straight into my eyes. He says to me with the softest, most tender voice, "I panicked because I can't imagine getting through this without you, and I don't want to mess that up. We're both going to have a tough go of it in the next few weeks. We need each other. I don't want that to get mucked up." He scoots closer to me. "Lily, I had to pull away because I didn't want to stop. But I had to stop. This is the wrong time to cross lines we can't uncross. We need to grieve and find closure in our lives before we start new chapters. Does that make sense?"

I wrap my arms around him. "Of course. I understand." As I pull away, our eyes meet again. I feel myself being drawn back in, but neither of us tries to fight the urge. Our lips meet, and it's enchanting. His lips softly envelope mine, the tip of his tongue tempting me by slowly tracing my lips, drawing me further and further into his kiss.

My heart races with each touch of his lips to mine. I want to run my hands all over his body, but I hold back. I know that's not what he wants right now. I use all my might to refrain and focus on enjoying the moment while it lasts, knowing that any second he'll come to his senses and pull away. But he doesn't. Instead, he wraps his arms around my waist, pulling me closer. I can feel his excitement growing. Running shorts don't leave much to the imagination.

As the passion grows between us, our bodies writhe against each other. We hold hands rather than exploring each other the way I know we both want to. The heat between us becomes intense. My body yearns for more contact, and I'm not sure how much longer I can control myself. He pulls away, but this time he doesn't run. He gives me a look that says he wants to devour me. He's breathing heavily, and his muscles are tense and rigid as though he is forcing himself to hold back.

"Why is this a bad idea again? I remember you giving a reason, but I can't for the life of me remember what it was. Hard to imagine something that feels like that not being a good thing," I say, challenging him.

I know he's fighting with himself, and I'm being cruel by egging him on. I know I shouldn't. I should respect his choice. The thing is I just don't want to. So, I keep pushing the envelope.

I lean in and whisper in his ear, "Was that really so bad?" My voice oozes with seduction. I have no idea where this sexuality and chutzpah are coming from. This side of me has been dormant for years. Gavin's unleashed something in me. Something primal. And I like it.

He shakes his head and takes in a slow, deep breath. "You little minx."

"If this is too much for you, you can always walk away," I say teasingly. Judging from what I feel through those running shorts, he might have trouble walking.

Gavin looks down at me with pleading eyes. I'm not sure if he is begging me to stop or begging me to keep pushing him. I lean forward and gently blow on his neck, getting as close to him without actually touching him as possible. A slight tremor ripples through his muscles, telling me it's taking everything he has to hold himself back.

A deep growl comes from somewhere deep within Gavin as he pushes my shoulders back and I fall back on the bed. At that moment, the room phone rings. A few seconds later, his cell phone follows suit. We look at each other, knowing we have to answer. It's two thirty in the morning, and our agency pals wouldn't call unless it was urgent.

We separate, trying to catch our breath and regain composure.

"Maybe you were right. Kissing's a bad idea," I say, trying to lighten the mood.

He gives me a Cheshire Cat grin. "Clearly a bad idea".

I pick up my phone. "Lily, wake your ass up!" Meredith screams before I have a chance to say hello.

"Hello to you, too," I say, not trying to hide my frustration.

"There's a car downstairs. Get in it now and get down here."

Before I can respond, she's gone. "Looks like we need to get dressed. Did they tell you what was going on?" I ask.

"Cortez, their PR person, called my mobile. They think someone has the story. I was going to issue a press release later today, but she thinks I need to act now."

Back to reality.

Gavin heads back to his room to shower quickly and get dressed. I just throw on the clothes that Meredith packed for me. I don't really care what I look like. I won't be issuing any press releases.

We meet around the backside of the hotel and climb into the backseat of the squad car. Ten minutes ago, we were engulfed in passion, and now we've done a one-eighty and are about to dive into a deep pool of grief, mourning, and guilt.

I can't get a read on him. His posture and body language don't give anything away. He's composed and controlled, nothing like that conflicted man that was in my hotel room just moments ago. I'm not sure what to make of it. I'm jealous of how assured he appears. In the blink of an eye, he's gone from sweat-drenched workout wear to looking like he could work a runway in his charcoal slacks and white oxford. I, on the other hand, have bitten all my nails down to the quick, my hair is a fly-away mess, and I'm wearing jeans that are far too big with a tank top that's a pinch too small. Emotionally, I'm as disheveled as I must look.

Gavin reaches out and grabs my hand. He gently runs his thumb along mine. It's such a simple gesture, but it soothes my anxiety. As we get closer to the station, he leans over and whispers in my ear, "This is going to be complicated. There's a lot going on for both of us. I'm here for you, every step of the way." When we arrive, he kisses my forehead before stepping out of the car.

NINE

When we walk into the building, it's a zoo. The entire taskforce has been called in. The agency acronym alphabet soup makes my head spin. Everyone is chiming in about how their case could be blown if this story has leaked. Lots of testosterone, too much caffeine, and not enough sleep are the perfect recipe for the erupting volcano of craziness before me. Wanting to avoid the eruption, I sneak out and find a quiet corner that I hope will keep me out of the chaos.

"Her parents can't find out from the news," I hear Gavin say. "Greene, we must go out there and tell them. It would be cruel for them to find out this way. They've suffered enough."

"Of course. Let's go," Greene responds.

Sully comes up to me while I'm eavesdropping. "The Bureau pays decent money for snoops, you know. I'd be happy to get you an application if you're looking to make a profession out of it."

My face must give away my embarrassment. "I'm hiding out from the insanity of the meeting in there. I didn't mean to intrude. I just needed out of that room."

"Yeah, they're going to Brooke's parent's house."

I think about the finality of what Gavin's about to do. After today, I'll have to make a similar phone call to Ashton's mom. It's about to get real.

He snaps in front of my face, bringing me out of my thoughts and fears into the present. "Hey, you with me? We need to chat now."

"How can I refuse an offer that enticing? Let me guess, we're going to my favorite room?" I ask sarcastically.

He gives a gentle tug on my elbow to get me moving. "It'll be better in there."

The more time I spend in this interrogation room, the less intimidating it appears. It isn't scary for me anymore as much as it is annoying and depressing. The paint is chipped, the legs of the table are speckled with rust, and based on the amount of dust and grime on the floor, I'm guessing it hasn't been cleaned since the linoleum was installed.

Not wanting to sit in that butt-numbing chair, I lean up against the two-way mirror. "So what's up now?" I ask.

He points to the offending chair. "Sit down."

I'd normally have given him some push back, but a sleeping backside is less of a hassle than a fight with Sully.

"Your house burned down last night. It's a clear arson case. The arson team is there investigating, but it's pretty obvious. The point of origin, accelerant used, and the fire pattern are similar to other cases we have seen related to organized crime. Maybe it's payback. Maybe they want to make sure whatever your husband had on them burned to the ground. Maybe it's a reminder that they can always get to you. At this point, we're not sure, but we're investigating."

For once, I don't have a smart-ass comment. My bravado is all tapped out, and I can't pretend that I've got it all under control anymore. I can only sit in my chair and look at the cracked linoleum tiles.

The circumstances are completely different, but I can't help feeling déjà vu. I was thirteen when my house burned to the ground, killing my parents. Here I am, thirteen years later, and my life has been turned upside down and inside out all over again.

Lucky number thirteen.

"Come on, Lily. Give me something, here. Some wisecrack so I know you're okay. Maybe throw an insult or two my way," Sully says, with a tone that makes me think he's actually worried about me.

"I've got nothing for you," I say quietly. "Thank you for telling me in here. I can't do this in front of the army out there."

"Do you want to know more details, or do you want to talk about this later?" he asks me.

I pick at a chipped nail. "Is there anything left?" I ask.

"The main house is gone, the pool house and the carriage house are both gone. The fire department got there when the garage caught fire. The shed with all the lawn equipment is fine. I'm pretty sure the cars are salvageable. But when we ran your financials, we found that several of the cars are in default. I'm not sure how all of that will play out. That's for the bean counters to figure out."

"It's hard to imagine it gone. That monstrosity was Frankie's pride and joy. He loved having parties, showing off the obnoxious opulence." I try to swallow past the lump in my throat. "I know the money's going to be a mess. Ash handled it all, so how can it be anything other than a mess? I was only given enough money to manage the household. Ash was in charge of everything else."

Sully pats me on the shoulder. "I'll keep you posted as I find out more, okay?"

"Thanks, Sully," I sigh. The hits just keep on coming. That house had never really felt like home to me. I'd always felt like a guest. It was Franklin's house, never mine.

If I'm being honest, I've felt like a guest just about everywhere since my parents died. I was shuffled from foster home to foster home. It wasn't until the church took custody of me and sent me to boarding school that I stayed in one place for more than a few months. Boarding school may have been a place to live, but it wasn't a home.

Because of that, I've never gotten too attached to anywhere I live, so I'm not devastated that the house is gone now. But at least it was a place to stay. Everything I own is now ashes, and I have nothing but the clothes on my back.

As I think about it, it
occurs to me that everyone related to me, even if just by marriage, has perished in some horrible way. What are the fucking chances? I must be cursed.

"Lily," Sully says, snapping me back into reality. "I want you to start thinking about anywhere Ash may have used as a hiding place. My theory is that someone was looking for something or trying to destroy something. If it wasn't at the house, they're going to start looking other places, and they'll start with you. Did he have another office or an apartment?

Maybe a safety deposit box? You said he was having affairs. Was he paying for a girlfriend's place?"

I pull my legs up to my chest. Thinking about Ash's collection of whores and other nefarious deeds is the last thing I want to do. As much as I want to shut everything out, I don't have that luxury. The boogeyman will come calling if I don't come up with some answers. "I can't think of anything. I often wondered where he was meeting his concubines. If I had to guess, he'd have had a place for himself, something with a rotating door perhaps. He got bored too easily and didn't care enough to want to keep any one girl housed. Maybe when the accountants go through the money, they'll find something."

Agent Cortez knocks on the door. The press conference is about to begin. The official statements make it seem like a simple car accident on a winding country road. Nothing underhanded at all. No mention of the fact that they were both on enough drugs to keep an entire frat house high for a month. Not a word about organized crime. The press goes crazy with questions. I've never seen such pandemonium.

Thinking that this'd be a good time to sneak away, I turn to leave. Unconsciously, I look around for my purse. But then I realize that I don't have a purse. It was at my house. I don't have a wallet or cell phone. I've lost the few pictures left from my childhood. The only thing I have to remember my parents by is the cross I wear. It's a tiny, gold cross on a thin necklace that my parents gave me for my first communion. I just so happened to wear it the night of the fire, and haven't taken it off since.

Not knowing where to go or what to do, I return to my interrogation room. The moment the door clicks closed, my knees buckle, and I collapse on the filthy floor and cry. How pathetic is it that this room is the most familiar thing in my life?

Sully finds me some time later. The waterworks are still flowing. He gives me a small smile. "I was waiting for that hard exterior to crack. You're a tough girl, but no one's that tough. You've had a lot thrown at you over the last week."

I wipe the tears from my face. "It's just so damn confusing. I hate Ashton. He's brought nothing to my life but pain and disappointment, but he's all I know. We've been together for so long, and now... he's dead. Gone forever. I can't even yell at him for all the shit he's put me through. I want to scream at him, slap him until my hand hurts, and then switch to the other hand. But I can't. Instead, I have to start my whole life over again. It sounds like the money is all gone. The house is gone. I know I can start fresh. I've done it before. Hell, I'm a pro now at reinventing myself. But, just because I know I can do it doesn't mean that it doesn't really suck."

He kneels in front of me. "I can tell you're a survivor. You're a strong girl. You're hurt, but you'll heal, and you'll rebuild. Lean on Gavin. You'll be good for each other right now." He looks down at his watch and says, "Come on. Let's get you out of here. There's nothing else you need to do right now. Let's get you back to the hotel. You need to get some sleep, okay?"

I nod. He holds his hand out and helps me up. As we're walking out, a young officer chases after us.

"Mrs. Preston! This is for you, from Meredith," he says as he hands me a duffle bag. That woman is a life saver. Clothes, underwear, a tooth brush. Enough to get me through a few days. Where would I be without her? Sully takes me back to the hotel and orders me not to leave until I've gotten some sleep. The police have agreed to pick up the tab on the room for a few more days, until I figure out what to do next.

I climb into bed and pass out.

****

I wake to the feeling of hot breath on my neck. It scares the hell out of me, and I jump out of bed, ready to kick someone's ass.

"What's wrong, Lil?" a very sleepy and now-panicked Gavin says.

"*Gavin!*" I yell in relief as I throw a pillow at him. "Dammit, Oxford, you scared me to death." As I really look him over, I see he's wearing boxers—and nothing else. The sight of him literally takes my breath away. I let out a little cough to hide my reaction. It's going to be very hard to concentrate with all of those muscles out in the open.

He holds his hands up. "Sorry, I didn't mean to frighten you. I got back a little while ago, and couldn't bear the thought of going back to my room alone. It's been such a crap day. I snatched your spare room key earlier when you were gone and I was about to go looking for you. I didn't think you would mind." He shakes his head and stands. "I shouldn't have been so presumptuous. I can go."

I drop back down onto the bed. "No, it's fine. You just caught me off-guard. Clearly, I'm still a little jumpy. Plus, it's been years since I shared a bed with someone." I pat the other side of the bed. "Take a load off. It's been a crap day for me as well."

We lay in bed, talking for hours. He gently strokes my hair as we share the horrors of the day. I may have lost everything that I own, but Gavin had to tell those poor people their child is dead, and he was bombarded by paparazzi. I know it's probably only going to get worse for him too.

We both cry a little and comfort each other. As we always seem to do, we get sidetracked telling stories that make us laugh. Having him here feels good. Safe. I may not have a home, but at least I have the comfort of his arms for the moment. The fact that I get to run my fingers along his magnificent abs while we vent doesn't hurt.

After a while, the conversation slows. We've discussed so much, and yet there's so much left to say. The tension built by the thoughts we're both trying to ignore fills the room. After a few minutes he squeezes me in his arms. "I'm so thankful you're here," he whispers in my ear.

I look up to face him, and his eyes are clouded with worry and guilt. "What's wrong? Besides the obvious, I mean."

He shakes his head.

"You can tell me."

"When I was talking to Brooke's mum, she said that the last time she saw her, she knew Brooke was gone. She may have still been alive, but the person that was there wasn't her daughter. When Brooke left their house, they resigned themselves to the fact that it was only a matter of time. It's gut-wrenching to watch a person walk to their grave and know you're powerless to stop it."

Brooke's self-destruction has caused him so much pain and anguish for so long. It's hard to hear him talk about the cross he's borne for her. I didn't know the woman, but from what I've learned about people living with addiction from my life with Ash, she was probably selfish and conniving and unworthy of the mound of guilt he's burying himself under. I have zero empathy for her. It may make me a bitch, but that's how I feel.

"Much like them, I feel like I've been mourning Brooke for years. Which is why my feelings now are so befuddling. My wife has just died, and yet I lie here with you. I spent the day looking forward to coming here and seeing you. Seeing your smile, hearing your laugh. God, it's the perfect elixir for all this heartache. What kind of selfish wanker have I become?" He sits up and moves toward the edge of the bed, holding his head in his hands.

I pull up behind him but keep my distance. "You don't have to feel guilty, and you aren't being selfish. What we've been through is almost insurmountable. A bigger challenge than most people face in the totality of their lives. And we've been through it together. It's only natural that we've leaned on each other, learned to appreciate each other. You've changed my life in this short period of time, and if you walk out the door and I never see you again, a part of me will always love you for what you've done for me. How you've been there for me." I rest my chin on his shoulder. "What's developed between us has nothing to do with Ash or Brooke except that they're the reason we're both here. We're just two people trying to make sense of a messy situation."

"I care for you more than I should, and that puts this dark cloud around the first honest connection I've had with another person in … in as far back as I can remember. You've become this bright light amidst the years of darkness I've been in. I don't want to feel bad about that."

"Then don't." I place a gentle kiss his on shoulder. My intention is to be comforting, as he's clearly upset. But as my lips touch his soft skin, my intentions become less pure. One kiss becomes two, and then three. With each kiss, I feel my lust grow. I slowly kiss my way from his shoulder to his neck. I run my fingertips slowly up and down his stomach and across his chest.

I feel his heart pounding as his breathing becomes faster and heavier. A quiet moan escapes him when I nibble on his ear. After about thirty seconds, he abruptly turns around and pulls my mouth to his with a passion I've never felt before. His kisses are intense and seductive. He teases me with his tongue, which ignites my excitement. With each kiss, I long for more, but I'm hesitant to push too far.

Gavin's hand moves from my hair down my neck. He slides it down the side of my rib cage, gently tracing my breast en route. My whole body shivers. He's still only touching over my clothes, but his hands on me send a jolt straight down to my core.

Our kissing becomes frantic, as though we can't possibly get enough of each other. His hands wander from the small of my back across my stomach. My skin feels as if it's on fire. Each time he touches me, it both soothes the ache and inflames me more.

Gavin's hands make paths across my stomach, as though he's debating if he should go further. When his fingertips brush the side of my breast again, I moan and arch my back, giving him the green light. His thumbs graze my nipples through my shirt, and my whole body starts to tingle. Never in my life have I been this turned on from a PG-13 make out session.

His hands slide down my body to my thighs. Starting behind my knees, Gavin's fingertips make long strokes up the backs of my thighs. He slowly moves his hands around to the front of my thighs, gently tracing up the length of each one, as if he is trying to make it to my apex but isn't quite ready. As Gavin gets closer to my center, my body craves his touch even more. It's pleasure masquerading as torture.

His fingers make it to the outside of my boy shorts. He runs a finger along the seam before allowing his fingers to just barely cross the barrier. My body is crying for him to touch me as his fingers slowly tease the very top of my leg but don't yet reach my center. Finally he moves to touch me there, his fingers brushing up against my entrance... and the fire alarm goes off.

"Bloody hell! *You must be fucking kidding me!*" he screams into a pillow. We look at each other and laugh. "Looks like we set the fire alarm off," he says, giving me a playful glance.

We both get dressed and exit the building, only to find out it was a false alarm. Some fraternity prank. At this point, we realize we're both starving and decide to get a late dinner. The temperature has finally cooled off thanks to today's late-afternoon thunderstorms. For the first time in weeks, the night air isn't oppressed by heat and humidity. The perfect night to stroll around the city. We walk to The Burger Joint down the street. I haven't eaten much in the past few days, so I pack away a cheeseburger, fries, onion rings, and a chocolate shake. I introduce him to the deliciousness that is dipping your fries in your milkshake. Odd but delectable.

"You aren't a shy eater, are you?" he asks as I polish off the rest of my shake.

I point a fry at him. "Shut it, Oxford. I now have some pent up sexual tension, and I'm hoping the chocolate will help relieve it."

"We do seem to be cursed, don't we?" He laughs. "Aren't fraternity brothers supposed to promote sex, not prevent it?"

"I think the word you are looking for is cock-blocking. And, in my experience, frat brothers are only interested in sex that directly concerns them. If they aren't involved, they might as well spoil it for everyone."

We both laugh and then go quiet for a moment. I drag an onion ring through the ketchup. "So, is that what we were about to do?" I ask, my voice dripping with curiosity.

I think I've caught him off-guard because Gavin blushes and then stammers. It's the most adorable thing I've ever seen. "Well, I don't know about that," he says, flustered.

"You're really cute when you're embarrassed," I say with a smile. This makes him blush even more. It's strange to see someone so stunningly handsome blush. It's like hearing a dog meow. It just doesn't go together.

He wipes his mouth with a napkin. "I don't know where things were going today. I wasn't really thinking at all. The moment carried me away. Being around you, I get simply primal. It would have been proper to keep our distance."

I wink. "Where's the fun in being proper?"

He pauses for a moment, looking pensive. He points at me. "You started it," he declares. "It was you! Not me! It was you and your shoulder kisses. You're the naughty one trying to steal my virtue."

"Yup," I admit. "You'd best remember that! I'm not sure I can show such restraint again!"

I can see the wheels turning in his mind, and he gets a mischievous grin on his face. "Can you tell me what that would look like exactly?"

I throw a fry at him. "Come on, oh virtuous one. Let's get going. Oh, and Gavin?"

"Yes?"

"Can you say naughty again?" That accent makes me wild.

He leans in and whispers "naughty" in my ear in a seductive tone and then kisses my neck. If it were possible to melt, I would be a puddle on the floor.

We walk back to the hotel slowly, just enjoying the night. Despite the late hour, there's still a number of people out and about. The conversation eventually steers to the topic of his favorite places in London. He keeps chatting on, but I don't hear a thing he says. All I can hear is the pop of my protective bubble bursting.

"Gavin," I interrupt him. "Do you know when you're going to go back? I mean, I'm guessing that's what's going to happen next, right? You have to go back to London?"

"I haven't been thinking about it, but I need to start. Brooke's family will be holding a private ceremony for her funeral, but we decided that I shouldn't attend. It would just bring in the media circus, and they don't deserve that. As of now they have anonymity, and I'd like to do everything I can to keep it that way."

Gavin gently lunges to the side, helping me avoid a massive puddle.

"Brooke's PR company wants me to hold a big flashy memorial, which is exactly what Brooke would have wanted. The thought of it disgusts me. Everyone will pretend that she was the innocent victim of some random car accident. One more giant lie that I'll have to sit through with a stiff upper lip."

He lets out a deep sigh and runs his fingers through his hair. "Plus, I need to get back to work. I've been here for weeks, and my company has been on autopilot. My staff has been picking up the slack for too long now."

"I bet they've missed you," is the best I can come up with to say. I really don't give a shit about his staff or if his business is suffering. I don't want him to go.

"What about you? What are you going to do?" Gavin asks in a tone that sounds as though he's afraid of the answer. Maybe he senses that I'm not really ready to think about it.

"I need to call Ashton's mom and tell her what's happened. I'm sure together we'll figure out what to do. When Franklin died, there was a big service, but Ashton's made a lot of enemies. A big thing may not be necessary. Personally, I'd rather just ignore the whole thing, but I'll do whatever Darlene wants. I need to find a place to live, and fast. The FBI is only paying for the room for a few more days. And then I have to figure out what to do with my life."

"You have a lot on your plate and not a bean to support yourself. Let me help you," he pleads.

I thread my arm through his elbow. "That's sweet. But, I need to do this on my own."

"Don't be stubborn. You don't have to do it all on your own," he insists.

"I got myself into this mess, and I'll get myself out." Between my tone and body language, I hope I'm making it clear this isn't an issue I'll be pushed on. Thankfully, he backs off.

We walk another block before he pulls me close to him. He kisses the top of my head and says, "I respect that you want to do this on your own. It's commendable. Just know I'm here if you need me."

It's quite a statement and a lovely sentiment, but I don't really believe him. He lives four thousand miles and a very large ocean away. I'm so grateful we've had each other through this. I'm not sure I'd still be vertical if he weren't here. But once he leaves, I'm sure that will be it. A phone call here and there, some texting, an occasional email.

As we enter the hotel, Gavin's phone rings. "It's my office."

I look at my watch. "It's almost midnight."

He smirks. "Not in London. I'd better take this," he says. "Why don't you head up to your room? I'll come up and see you after I finish."

I nod and start to walk away. I've made it about halfway to the elevator when he suddenly grabs me and spins me around before planting a deep kiss on me. As we break apart, he winks and walks away, picking back up on his call without missing a beat. That man sure knows how to make a girl feel special

TEN

"I'll come up and see you when I finish." It seems like such a simple statement, but it could mean *anything*. A friendly handshake goodnight. Or watching a movie. Playing cards? Or wild, crazy sex. The possibilities are endless.

While I try to decipher his complex code of guy speak, I hop in the shower to make sure I'm 'sexy ready'—just in case. I shower for so long I nearly turn into a prune, so I finally get out and dry off. Still no word from Gavin.

By two, I'm too revved up too sleep because I'm trapped in an internal debate about what to do. Do I wait up all night for him to come by? Call? Say 'Fuck 'im!' and just go to bed? What's the protocol here? It's been so long since I've had to deal with the games played between men and women that I'm completely at a loss. Disgusted by my indecision, I get dressed and head to his room.

He opens the door to his room looking haggard. Quite the turnaround from when I saw him a few hours ago. His room looks as though a bomb has gone off inside. Suitcases and clothes everywhere. "Lily dear, I'm so glad you're here. I was just going to ring you. I have to leave in just a few hours.

I wasn't intending for it to happen this fast, but chaos has erupted at home. Since word got out about Brooke, it's been pandemonium. My offices were essentially attacked by the press. No one can get anything done. Someone released Brooke's address, and there are people camped out there. Someone broke in and tried to steal her clothes to sell on eBay!"

I sit down on the edge of his bed. "That's disturbing. Who would do that?" A stupid question, I know. The world is full of morons that would pull those sorts of stunts, and even bigger morons that would spend a small fortune on the pillaged souvenirs.

"I'm just gobsmacked," he continues. "Where were all these adoring fans when she was trying to make a go of it after *Covent Gardens*? Certainly not buying tickets to her films or going to her plays. The PR person says that this is what happens when someone was in a cult classic like that. Even if she wasn't making movies anymore, she was still in the public eye. I'm still trying to wrap my head around it, but I don't have time to stop and think. I have to pack and go. My flight leaves at six. The car will be here in an hour and a half."

I'm just as gobsmacked as he is. I'm not ready for him to go. I know he has to, and I completely understand why, but I don't want him to. I don't want to spend my last bit of time with him pouting, so I say, "How can I help?"

He kisses my cheek. "Aren't you wonderful. Would you mind helping me pack? When I came, I only brought an overnight bag, never expecting to be here this long. As my trip extended, I just shopped online for whatever I needed."

He looks around the room. "As you can see, it got a little out of hand."

This makes me laugh. "Gavin, you are such a clothes whore!" A well-dressed one at that. He always looks as though he's just walked out of a Ralph Lauren ad, and now I understand why. The man has exceptional taste and an unhealthy shopping habit to match.

"Fourteen pairs of shoes? Really?" I laugh, but deep down, I'm jealous. The only shoes to my name are the flip flops on my feet.

"I was a model, remember? I was spoilt by all the best clothes, and I became accustomed to it. I'll admit I have a bit of a shopping problem. I hate to go to the shops. But get me on a website, and I point and click my way into trouble."

"I can see that." I shake my head. "I can't relate. I despise shopping."

I sort through the mountain of clothes and come across the shirt he was wearing when we first met. It's the same blue as his eyes, is so soft, and smells just like him. I hide it in a corner, hoping to snag it for myself. A little something to remember him by.

We tell stories and laugh as we pack and get him organized. Before we know it, it's three fifteen, and his car is meant to arrive at any moment. Both our faces fall when we catch sight of the clock. I look at him, trying to find the words. There's so much to say, so much we haven't talked about.

He takes me in his arms and kisses me as though it's for the last time. I'm absorbed into his embrace, and I melt into the kiss. When we break apart, I have tears streaming down my face.

"Oh, no. I can't stand to see you cry," he says as he wipes the tears. "Run upstairs and get dressed. Ride with me to the airport. I know there's so much left to say and talk about. We can't leave like this. Please?"

I couldn't possibly say no. Especially when he gives me that look. Those baby blues could get me to do just about anything. I grab my memento as stealthily as possible and run upstairs to change. My choices are slim: an FBI tee and shorts or an FBI tee and sweats. I'll fit right in with the tourists.

I open my door to find him there. The car is waiting. We hold hands as we make our way down. I'm gripping his so hard I'm amazed I haven't cut off his circulation. He practically has to drag me along as I walk as slow as molasses to the back door.

Before we get in the car, he captures my face in his hands and tilts it to look at me with those amazing eyes. "This isn't goodbye, Lily. I promise. I don't want to leave you, especially like this, but if I don't, my life is positively snookered. And—"

"Gavin," I stop him. "I understand. You have to go. Please don't feel bad." I move to get in the car, knowing that if I don't do it now, I'll lose my nerve. "Plus," I say after we settle into the seats. "They have these things called telephones and computers. I don't personally have one right now, something I must resolve soon."

"Oh, Lil, I totally forgot. How can I leave you here without anything? What will you do? How will I get in touch with you? You don't even have my bloody mobile number! Bollocks!"

"You're so cute when you speak British!" I lean over and give him a sweet kiss. "I think you could read me the phone book and it would get me hot and bothered."

He pats my knee. "While I love the distraction, this is a real problem. How will I talk to you? Seriously, Lil. I can't not talk to you."

He looks genuinely bent out of shape about this, which touches my heart. "Gavin, I'll get a phone. Once the insurance thing is all worked out, I'll get a new laptop. I promise I'll be reachable." I pause for a moment, giving him a half-hearted grin. "Plus, you're going to be so busy, you probably won't even have time to talk."

He looks at me like I've just backed over his dog with my car. A cross between heartbroken and angry. "That's bullshit, Lily. I—" He stops himself. He looks furious. His face is flushed, and he's biting his lip so hard I'm afraid it's going to bleed.

I reach over to try to connect with him, but his muscles tense at my touch. His eyes that usually look like a warm ocean are now cold as ice.

This mood shift shocks me. I'm not even sure what I've done. "I didn't mean to upset you. Please talk to me. We only have a few more minutes before we get to Dulles. I don't want it to end like this."

"That's just the thing, Lily. In my mind, this isn't the end. You speak about me leaving with a casual disdain that guts me. As though the moment I get on the plane, this," he points back and forth between us, "disappears. I'm not ready to abandon the bond we've created just because I'm leaving for now."

He runs his fingers through his hair. "I've never felt this way about anyone. Ever. Those five days in that apartment with you were like a slice of heaven after almost two years of hell. Leaving you now, it feels like I'm walking away from the promise of something amazing, and I hate it. But it must be done."

I sigh. "The idea of the debacle I called a marriage opening the door to a happily-ever-after is charming and enticing. But that's not how things work out for me. I don't ride off into the sunset and live the fairy tale. You're going to go home, mourn, and move on with your life. You're going to realize that this connection we have was just a bi-product of our shared experience, and our friendship will get tucked away in the back of your mind, lumped in with all the other memories regarding Brooke's death. I don't want it to be that way, but we have to be realistic here. Things like this?" I point back and forth between us. "They don't work once you go back to the real world."

I'm pushing him away. I know I am. As much as he wants to believe there's hope for us, I know that there isn't. I don't have room in my life for any more disappointment or things I can't count on. The last thing I want to do is hurt him, but I can't delude myself either.

"You're wrong," he says quietly. "I don't know how to convince you of that, but you're wrong."

Not wanting to look at him, I watch the landscape of the Dulles Toll Road pass by. The atmosphere in the car turns tense. Every pebble we drive over feels like hitting a speed bump at seventy-five miles per hour. I feel myself shrinking into the corner of the car, wishing I hadn't run my mouth. Why couldn't I have just played along until he left and then been grateful when those few-and-far-between emails showed up in my inbox?

The airport comes into sight, and I brainstorm how I'm going to try to end this amicably.

"Come with me," he says breaking the quiet.

"What?"

"Come with me, Lily. To London. You have nothing tying you here. Just get on the plane with me, and we will figure it out."

I'm taken aback. Nothing like a grand gesture to stop your heart. Part of me wants to go with it, to be swept up into the romance. But I can't. My life is a mess and I need to get my head on straight. Riding off into the sunset would just be avoiding the problem. I need to fix me first. I will not jump into another relationship simply because it promises to be a quick, easy escape from my past.

I reach across the car to hold his hand. "You have to go home and get your life together, and I have to do the same. It would be amazing to just run away with you. But everything would catch up to us."

He sighs deeply. "I know you're right." He pauses, a pouty look spreading across his face and making him look like a spoiled toddler. "I just don't like it!"

We arrive at the airport and I'm dreading saying goodbye. I lean into him to pull him into an embrace, but he pushes me away. "No. I'm not doing it this way. I have a few more minutes, and you're coming in with me!" He tells the driver to circle for thirty minutes and then return for me.

I follow him into the airport, even though I know I'm just prolonging the pain of the farewell.

Gavin checks in, ignoring the ticket agent's snickering at his ridiculous amount of luggage. The airport is practically empty, which gives it an air of privacy as we stroll the concourse trying to enjoy our last few moments together. We talk about nothing at all of consequence, just random stories that make us both laugh. He has a laugh that can brighten any room, and it's infectious.

I look at the clock on the wall. "You need to get going or you won't make it through customs. You remember how much you're bringing home, right?"

He perks up, as if he's seen something out of the corner of his eye. He kisses me and says, "Stay here!" Then he runs over to the security checkpoint and quickly disappears from view.

I stand there, feeling like an idiot, for close to fifteen minutes. There's still no sign of him, and I have no idea what he's doing. *Is he skipping out on saying goodbye?* I wouldn't have expected something so cowardly from him, and I'm not the one who just insisted that "this"—whatever "this" is—is more than just a case of two people bonding through tragedy. And yet, I'm the one standing here by myself.

After nearly twenty minutes, I decide he must be gone. There's no way he can come back and still make his flight. It's not like he has to worry about his carry-on luggage. He can just point and click his way to another new wardrobe. I turn to walk away when I'm plagued by an image of a TSA agent tackling me for leaving a suitcase here. That's how my luck would go. I meet Prince Charming, who bails on me at the airport, and I get arrested for abandoning "suspicious baggage" in the concourse.

"Lily! Don't Go!"

Turning back around, I see Gavin running the length of the concourse on the other side of security, loaded down with shopping bags. He heads for the door that leads back to this side of the lobby, panting heavily.

What the hell? He left me to go get airport souvenirs? I put my hands on my hips and stare at him as he comes to a halt in front of me. "I live here, I don't need Washington DC tchotchkes."

"Don't be cheeky," he says, out of breath. "When I flew in, I needed a new cord for my iPad, so I stopped in this shop I saw when I landed. It sells computers and mobiles, and I thought, 'Who the hell is daft enough to buy a computer or mobile at an airport?'" He points his thumbs at his chest. "Well, this bloke is bloody daft enough! I gave up my last few moments with you to know that I would be able to talk to you when I land. It was well worth it!" He hands me the bags that hold a brand new iPhone and Macbook.

"This must have cost a fortune! At an airport no less! I can only imagine the markup." I try to hand the bag back to him. "It's too much. I can't accept this."

"Luv, I just sprinted through a very large airport, in loafers by the way, so that I could have the peace of mind of knowing I would get to say goodnight to you tonight. Bloody hell, woman! Don't ruin my moment with your rubbish. Take the damn gift and kiss me!"

I relent and kiss him with such fervor that it borders on inappropriate.

"Now that was a sendoff," he says with a smile. "I have to go now. They wrote your new mobile number on the paperwork. I've already programed all of my info into the phone. As soon as you get it up and running, email me with all of yours, please. I'll be devastated if I land in London and there isn't a message from you." He picks me up and kisses me again. "I'll see you before you know it." Then he walks away. I watch him go back through security. My heart hurts a little, wanting nothing more than to believe him that this isn't goodbye.

After the car picks me up, we get stuck in traffic. I wish I had spent more time looking at Gavin on the drive over rather than looking at the roadside, because I've got nothing to do but look at it now. It gives me time to take in the last eight days. The drama and excitement is over, and now it's time to focus on the mundane and the boring. How to put food on the table. Getting a table to put food on. Procuring more than three pairs of underwear. The basics.

Before I can start the next chapter in my life, I have to conclude the previous one. While I'm sure it would be easier to just keep moving and try to forget, I have people other than myself to think about. Ashton's mother deserves more than that. Darlene is a good woman that, sadly, has not been a big part of our lives. She met Frankie when they were fourteen. They married right out of high school and, from what it sounded like, they were happy in the early years.

When Frankie started making some money, they'd decided to have Ash. As Franklin climbed the social ladder, Darlene Costanzano from the Bronx couldn't keep up with the Potomac ladies that lunch. So Franklin had divorced her and left her with nothing. From what I understand, she was so shocked and heartbroken that he was actually leaving her that she couldn't muster the strength to fight back, and the bastard took advantage of her weakness. He said he wanted custody of Ash and for her to stay away, and her response was, "Well Frankie is so smart. He knows best." Poor woman didn't know what had hit her.

She loved Ash, but he'd always looked at her as though she were trash. Darlene hadn't even come to our wedding because she didn't want to embarrass anyone. After her divorce, she moved back to New York. To this day, she lives with her sister in the same apartment they grew up in. She's never remarried, never even dated. Franklin shattered her.

I've always felt a connection with Darlene. We were both thrown into worlds very different from the ones we knew. When my parents died, I'd been thrown into an elitist prep school—very different from the small, rural town I grew up in. Darlene had been thrown into the high society of Washington's elite. The difference between us was that I adapted and she never could.

I tap my fingers on my thigh while I wait for her to answer the phone. When she does, I skip the pleasantries and get right to the point. "Darlene, it's Lily. I need to tell you something important."

"Oh hello, dear."

I inhale, hoping there's some courage mixed into the overly recycled hotel air. "Ash was in a car accident. He died, Darlene." There's complete silence on the other end. "Are you still there?"

"Yes, dear. I heard you. I'm not sure what to make of it... I think I'm in a bit of shock," she replies.

"I think I'm still in shock too. I keep waiting for him to say this was one of his pranks."

"He has always been such a jokester," Darlene laughs.

She agrees to come down tomorrow to help me figure out what to do. It'll be comforting to have someone parental around. At times like this, I really miss my mother.

After I get off the phone with her, I make a call to my only friend in the world, Emily. We went to the same high school, but she's two years older than I am, and we didn't know each other then. I finally met her during my first week at the University of Arizona, and from that day on, we were inseparable—kindred spirits. We both had secrets to keep and were looking for a distraction from them.

We lived together for four years, and I've missed her terribly. Despite being the one to encourage me to get together with Ashton in the first place, she had been vehemently against me marrying him. As a result, after Ash and I were married, Em and I had drifted apart. Even so, I know that even after all of this time, I can call her and she'll be there for me.

"Lily? Oh my God, how are you?"

"Em, I need you." I tell her the whole story.

"Cocksuckermotherfucker," she shouts. Her nickname for Ash has always made me laugh. "I cannot believe he's done this to you. Well, actually, I can totally believe he's done this to you. This is his flavor of bullshit."

I laugh. "He always said he was destined to be famous. Well, he'll be infamous at least."

"How are you dealing with all of this?" she asks. "I've always wanted you free of that asshole, but not like this. I just wanted him to live a long and pitiful life with a venereal disease that made his penis fall off."

God, I've missed her. "I think I'm in shock. I'm sad and relieved all at the same time. I feel awful about feeling relieved, which then makes me sad. It's a vicious cycle. I need to plan the funeral and find a way to put this all behind me."

She promises to get time off from work and fly into town tomorrow to help me sort through everything. For the first time since all of this has happened, I feel like I'm taking steps forward.

After I hang up with Em I send Gavin a text, as requested, so he has my number, and then I slide under the covers. Craving sleep, I close my eyes and try to clear my mind. Nine-thirty in the morning in a downtown Washington hotel is about as quiet as a pre-school after snack time. Clopping feet storming down the hallway so hard the floor shakes—it's like a heard of Sasquatch are staying on my floor. Tourists bickering about which Smithsonian to start at. Business people chatting about their widget presentations. And I'm fairly sure I hear a man kiss a woman good-bye just before dialing a cell phone to say good morning to his wife and kids. Men are scum. To drown out the hallway drama, I turn on the TV and promptly fall asleep to a rom-com.

I'm woken up by the blaring tune of "God Save the Queen." I jump out of bed and look around the room, trying to figure out what the hell is going on. Gavin woke me the same way at least once when we were staying at Meredith's, so I feel momentary surge of hope that he's back—until I see the light of my new phone shining from my nightstand. I look at the caller ID, and it says "Oxford". I'm laughing so hard I can't get the word "hello" out when I answer.

"There's the laugh I adore," Gavin says.

I prop up a pillow and lean back against the headrest. "You've managed to one-up me, Oxford. Oh, I'll have to rectify that. When did you manage to find the time to download this ringtone?"

"I move fast when I'm motivated. Knowing this was going to make you smile and think of me was very motivating."

"Well, mission accomplished. I'll always smile when I hear this song."

"Because you have finally accepted British superiority?" I can hear his pompous smirk through the phone.

"No, silly, because it means I get to talk to you. It will be the best part of my day. And this does not mean Brits are sneakier!"

"As long as we both can admit that I'm winning this war." I can hear how big his grin is through the smugness of his tone.

The air conditioning clicks on and the room goes from sweltering to polar almost immediately, so I pull the scratchy hotel blanket up around me. "Oh it's on, Oxford. It's on! I don't know how or when, but I will get you back. Mark my words, you're going down!"

"I look forward to it," he replies.

"So, anyway, you made it safe and sound. Is it good to be home?"

He sighs. "Not yet. From the moment I landed, it's been one fire to put out after another. I tried to manage as much as I could while I was away, but there's so much I've let slide while I've been away. It's going to take me a year to get things sorted." He sounds weary. The whole time he was here, I never heard him sound so spent. I suppose it's all catching up to him.

We make each other laugh with humorous observations from our day, like my spotting of a three-hundred-pound man in a speedo riding a scooter down Wisconsin Avenue and his recounting of the gentleman he sat next to on the plane that spent six of the eight hours with a glob of pudding on his chin. This man is going to give me deep laugh lines that will never go away. In the background, I hear his driver announce that they're approaching their destination, but the crowd may prevent them from getting much closer. They must be at Brooke's. I may be four thousand miles away, but a heat spreads across my cheeks, and the bed becomes suddenly uncomfortable. Or maybe I'm uncomfortable. I quickly jump off the line before I can feel more awkward than I already do. It may have been rude to hang up so quickly, but chatting with him as he pulls into his late wife's driveway doesn't feel proper either.

Feeling the need to wash away my guilt and confusion, I take a long bubble bath, which I follow up with a horribly romantic movie trilogy about two people who randomly meet in Paris, fall madly in love for one day, and then spend a decade trying to find love in other places, but still somehow keep coming back to each other.

I fall asleep wondering what will happen between Gavin and me. While a happily-ever-after for us seems as likely as a heatwave in Alaska in December, he's made a mark on my life. Every man I meet moving forward will pale in comparison. Perhaps that's my punishment for falling for a guy the day his wife died.

ELEVEN

Morning comes too quickly. I want nothing more than to pull the covers over my head for one more day, but there's a little boy in the hallway that wants his "zoobie" and it doesn't seem he'll stop screaming until he gets it. It's the perfect motivation to get my act together and find a place to live. I call my credit card companies to have them issue new ones. Since mine were only melted, not stolen, they inform me they can overnight the new cards. *Why didn't I do this sooner?*

The next three hours are spent talking to the insurance company and the mortgage company. It's not a great situation, but I won't be underwater in the end. A year or so back, Ashton had taken out a big mortgage on the previously paid-off house. I owe a lot, but not so much that the insurance settlement won't cover it. Sadly but fortunately, Franklin had a lot of expensive things in the house that were all insured. So whatever doesn't go to paying off the mortgage company, I'll get.

My policy coverage will thankfully provide a much-needed stipend for living expenses until my claim is resolved, which really saves my hide. I'm told a check will come next week, so I just have to make it until then. I introduce the family lawyer and accountant so they can get to work sorting out the estate and repaying all of Ash's debt. The lawyer seems to think that, between the settlement and what I'll get when I sell the land, I'll have a nice cushion. The last call is to a family friend that sells real estate. I'm determined to get the land up for sale as quickly as possible.

Greene and Sully stop by to take me to lunch, and they bring me the best gift—a new copy of my driver's license so I don't have to go to the DMV. These men are saints. They catch me up on all of the FBI gossip. When we leave the diner, they remind me I only have a few more days in the hotel before I'm on my own. Time to find some new digs.

Greene's wife, Ellie, calls to tell me about a place that may be right up my alley. A colleague of hers is getting married and needs someone to sublet the last four months on a condo in Georgetown. It's a bit far from a metro stop, but other than that, it's a perfect location. I've always adored Georgetown. Before I know it, I'm eagerly signing a lease with TG Inc., the owner of the condo.

Later, Darlene calls to let me know that she's in town but needs to rest after her train ride. We decide to meet for brunch tomorrow. Most times, I would have enjoyed this rare chance to see her, but I'm dreading the plans we need to make. At least the restaurant we've chosen has a Bloody Mary bar. I'm going it to need it.

Em calls around six, and just knowing that she's nearby helps me breathe a little easier. Emily Harrington gave herself the self-imposed nickname Queen Bitch long ago, and it suits her perfectly. She's the epitome of high maintenance. She knows exactly what she wants out of life and never apologizes for it. At first glance, she appears to be just another beautiful, rich airhead. In reality, she's anything but. Her chestnut hair, green eyes, and legs that go on for miles distract people from the fact she has an IQ of 170. She's constantly being underestimated, and she gets off on humiliating the people who do so. Coming from obscene wealth, she wouldn't have to work a day in her life if she chose not to, but she's too smart for that. Em would get far too bored just being a socialite, so she works for fun. I've never really understood what it is she does exactly. Something about analyzing the economy and stocks. It's all over my head.

Being the pampered princess she is, she refuses to stay in my mid-level hotel and checks us into a suite at the Mandarin Oriental. She's said she's staying for a week and she wants us to be comfortable. Better her dime than the federal government's.

Em takes one look at my FBI-inspired apparel and decides it's her personal mission to restock my wardrobe. If it were anyone else, I would never allow it. But Em's trust fund money was grown from ill-gotten gains, and she's always seen it as blood money. She likes to do good deeds with it, and playing dress up with me seems to be her good deed for the day.

After exhausting ourselves pounding the pavement between the high end stores in Georgetown, Em demands dinner. An unapologetic food snob, Em will only eat at five-star restaurants and wouldn't be caught dead eating somewhere that lacked linen table clothes, disproportionately small servings, or food that average people can't even pronounce. Cityzen is in the lobby of our hotel and meets all of her qualifications. I'd known it would when I saw that they only offer a tasting menu. For someone that hates to give up control, it's always perplexed me that she prefers meals with a menu dictated by someone else. It's a foodie thing, I guess. Me? I'd have been happier with a burger.

Over our cold lobster soup, she catches me up on all of her escapades and all of the gossip about everyone we went to school with. She's stayed in touch with all of our sorority sisters that I haven't spoken to since before my wedding. Five years have gone by, but it doesn't sound like I've missed much. People have jobs instead of classes, but for the most part, they're still partying their way through life. While it makes me long for simpler times, I'm not sure I could ever go back to that life.

It amazes me that Em still talks to everyone. U of A was never the right place for Em. With her intelligence and high society upbringing, she belonged in the Ivy League. During her senior year of high school, her parents died in a tragic and highly publicized murder-suicide. Had she gone to Harvard, as planned, she would have been bombarded by press and ridiculed by the blue blooded student body. Instead, she changed her last name and moved to Tucson to the playground for wealthy kids that want to attend as little class as possible. U of A gave her sanctuary. In the four years she attended the university, I was the only person that figured out her true identity.

After the sommelier delivers our second bottle of wine, she raises her glass. "To you, my darling Lily. Life has dealt you bad hand after bad hand, but if there's anyone that can rise from the ashes and set the world on fire, it's you. You'll get through this, and you'll be stronger for it."

We clink glasses, and I smile, but I'm not quite sure how to respond.

She swirls the wine in her glass. "The last time I saw you, you were just a shadow of yourself. Your body was here, but your spirit was MIA. Cocksucker, I mean Ashton, had sucked the life out of you. I couldn't bear to see you like that again. Hence my distance. I never stopped loving you, but I couldn't watch you be a doormat."

Em's never been one to pull any punches, but that's why I love her. "I had to stay. For Frankie. It was worth it, and I'd do it all over again. Even though it cost me my backbone and self-respect."

She tilts her glass toward me again. "Here's to your reincarnation. Hopefully that backbone of yours will rejuvenate in your new life." She sips and then warns. "I can see a flicker of life in your eyes, and I expect it to stay. If you go all *Body Snatchers* on me again, I will not hesitate to take you out. I watch *The Walking Dead*. I'm a zombie expert these days."

She's not wrong. I shudder thinking about how numb and empty I had become over the last few years. "I'll hold you to that," I reply. "I never want to live that way again. It's not living when you've lost your soul."

"That's what happens when you marry the devil, my dear," she says.

Before I can respond, a team of servers swap out our soup bowls and replace them with plates of black bass and eggplant. When they leave, I glare at her. "You can spare me your 'I told you so.'"

She holds her hands up in defense. "I don't need to say it, my dear. You've already been punished enough. Gloating would simply be poor manners."

I know that this won't be the last time we discuss this subject. But I'm happy it's laid to rest for the moment. Conversation throughout the rest of the night is light hearted, mostly focusing on Em's dating life. Em rejects the notion of monogamy. She loves men, loves sex, and isn't ashamed of the fact that she's got a guy in every port. Despite the fact that she makes it very clear to each would-be suitor that she'll never be the girl he takes home to mom, she gets at least four or five marriage proposals a year. Who can blame them? Em's stunningly beautiful, and she has a way about her that makes you feel like the best version of yourself. She pushes you, demands the best of you, and knows how to grab life by the balls. It's addicting. But like most addictions, the high only lasts so long. As soon as she feels a guy falling too fast, she cuts him off cold turkey.

Two more bottles of wine take us to last call. Somehow, we manage to stumble to our room afterward.

Too tired to take off my dress, I crawl into bed fully-dressed. The flashing light of my phone catches my eye. I've missed a million calls and texts from Gavin. I send him an apologetic text and hope he understands.

Two minutes later, God's saving the queen again. "Allo, Guvnah" I say in a horrible cockney accent.

"Oh, luv, I think that may be the worst impersonation I've ever heard. All of England is groaning right now."

I fingercomb my hair in the hopes that it won't be too much of a rat's nest in the morning. "That bad, huh? Sorry I missed your call. I went out with Em and left the phone in my room. We moved hotels. Now I'm staying at the swanky Mandarin," I say, slurring my words. I proceed to drunkenly ramble on about random details of our night.

"Oh," he chuckles. "You're positively hammered! Let me ask you a question, and then off to bed with you. Have you seen my blue shirt? I can't find it anywhere. Do you remember packing it?"

"No, Gavin. I know nothing about it," I try to lie but can't help laughing hysterically.

"Oh boy, you're totally legless. Get some sleep, dear. You have a long day tomorrow."

"Gavin?"

"Yes, luv."

"I miss you."

"Me, too. Good night, Lily."

Motivated to change, I slip into said blue shirt. I take a seductive photo and send it to Gavin. At least, I hope it's a seductive photo. Drunk selfies are rarely as good in the morning light as they were the night before.

Moments later, he responds.

G: Glad it's in safe hands. It's my favorite shirt. Even more so now. Looks much better on you anyway. I bet it would look better off you too.

I'm smart enough to throw my phone across the room without replying. With the wine flowing through my veins, sexting seems like a great idea. Thankfully, I have enough sober brain cells to know that if I open that can of worms, I'll die of humiliation in the morning.

TWELVE

Planning a funeral is one of the hardest things a person has to do in life. Planning a funeral for a lying, cheating husband while hung-over? So much harder. Em and I meet Darlene the next morning. Em lectures me about my wearing sunglasses inside, but not all of us are blessed with the amazing ability to drink all night and wake up bright-eyed and bushy-tailed the next morning.

After a strong Bloody Mary that's really just vodka with a splash of tomato juice, we make plans for Ash's memorial. Having only recently planned Franklin's funeral, I'm able to contact the same vendors we used then and ask them to replicate what they did before. Em, being the best friend in the world, has already contacted all of our old school friends that would want to be there. I log onto Ashton's Facebook account and make a post with the date and time of the service.

Initially, I'd wanted to skip having a service. I've been so mad at Ashton that I'd wanted to give him the same respect he gave me—absolutely nothing. He doesn't deserve to be memorialized. But after planning the service, I'm ultimately glad I did. Not for him, but for me. Now I can fully close this chapter of my life.

Because of the circumstances, we decide to have an Irish wake. Ashton was in no part Irish, but he would have appreciated any opportunity to have an open-bar party held in his honor.

As weird as it seems, Gavin has been the biggest help for me through the whole ordeal emotionally. I have so many conflicting feelings. He's listened as I tried to sort through them. Guilt, anger, relief, frustration. It should have been awkward talking to him about my roller coaster mental state, but it hasn't been. When I try to talk to Em, I get, "Well, you made your bed" or "I told you not to marry him." I can be honest with Gavin without judgment.

The day of the funeral is sweltering hot, one-hundred-degree heat with one hundred percent humidity. It feels like Ash's still getting the last word even from the great beyond. If he has to rot in hell, so do we. Like most interactions with Ash, we all leave feeling dirty and in desperate need of a shower.

The nice thing about being the widow at a funeral is that no one really expects anything out of me. I refuse to sit there and say what a wonderful man he was or how I am going to miss him. Thankfully, people get that. No one tries to rewrite history and make him into a saint. I can't count how many times I hear, "He was lucky to have you," and, "It may not have seemed like it, but in his own fucked up way, he loved you." There may be some truth to that, but I'm still so hurt that I can't see anything redeeming in our relationship. So many years of my life wasted that I can't get back. But it was my choice. I could have left, but I stayed to take care of

Franklin. I made my choices, lived with the consequences, and now it's time to move on.

The reception is somber and quick. In just a few short hours, it's over. The bill is paid, the servers clean up. Signing the receipt brings finality to it. This is the last time that bastard's going to stick me with a huge bar tab. As the limo pulls away, I look over my shoulder and realize he's really gone. I shed my final tears for him on the drive back to the hotel. Ashton is now just one of many tragic memories of my past.

The next day, I wake up and go straight to Social Security to change my name, effectively erasing the last thing connecting me to this life. Goodbye, Lily Preston. Welcome back, Lily Clark.

We spend the last day of Em's visit hanging out by the pool, drinking fruity drinks, and watching attractive men. She's already plotting my next fix-up. I want to tell her about Gavin, but I decide to hold back the details.

I take a sip of my margarita. "There's someone, but I don't want to talk about it yet. It probably isn't going to amount to anything but a good friendship."

Sitting up, she slaps her hands on her thighs. "OMG, were you cheating on Cocksucker? Good for you. See, your balls didn't totally disappear."

"I did not cheat on Ashton, although I wish I had. It's been five years since I've had sex. *Five Years*! Do you know how long five years is?"

She narrows her eyes and glares at me. "How is that possible? You and Ash used to fuck like bunnies."

"Once he started screwing every other bunny that shook her tail in his face, there was no way I was going anywhere near his penis. Which is a shame. The sex was the best part about us, until coke became part of his daily regimen. By that time, he barely had two brain cells to rub together, and he became… let's just say soft and uninspired. I've had root canals that were more pleasurable. It has been a long drought."

She looks at me as though I have three heads. "How did you do that? A b.o.b.?"

"Oh, a lady never tells. But I will say one thing: spin cycle. Old-school but effective."

"I suddenly regret never trying to do my own laundry," she replies. She pats me on the arm. "So, tell me about this mystery man?"

"Nothing to tell yet. He's been there for me while I've been dealing with everything. He's a wonderful guy, but it's complicated and probably won't go anywhere."

As I take a sip, she asks, "Did you bang him yet?"

I choke on my drink and start coughing. "No," I reply once I can breathe again.

"No one would judge you if you have."

"It's not that I haven't thought about it, but it hasn't been the right time. We haven't had enough alone time. He's not the type of guy you screw and walk away. He's a guy that, once he gets under your skin, he'll become so imbedded that he'll become a part of you. It'll be painful to cut him out of your life. I'm not sure I'm ready for that, so I'm proceeding with caution."

She applies more sunblock to her shoulders. "You know I don't speak commitment, so I didn't follow a word of that. You've been tied up in a bad relationship for too long. It's time for you to have a little fun. Casual fun. If Mr. Imbedded can't handle that, maybe it's not the right time."

I shake my head as I rub in a glob she missed in the middle of her back. "No, it's not the right time for either of us. And when I am ready, I don't want it to be wham, bam, thank you, ma'am. I've learned my lesson. A relationship can't be all about sex. Just a lot about sex," I say with a wink. I take the last sip of my drink, and Em motions to the waiter to bring another round. "If I'm being honest, I'm kind of scared. Which I know sounds completely afterschool special, but I am. It's been a really long time. I've only slept with two people in my life—Ash and Garrett."

A wide smile spreads across her face. "Ah, Garrett Stone," she says in a dreamy voice. "Now there was a high school hottie."

I nod. "He sure was. Hot, but a terrible lay. But, we were seventeen, what the hell did we know?

The waiter drops off our drinks, and Em takes a sip of hers. "I don't know what you're talking about. I had amazing sex when I was a teenager. But then again, I've always been better at spotting the boys with God-given talents than you are."

Ignoring her comment, I say, "So are the rules different when you're an adult? I'm guessing there isn't so much angst about when to sleep together."

She shrugs. "It depends. Me, if I want to screw, I do it. I've never been one to worry about if he'll respect me in the morning. I'm interested in his penis, I don't need his respect. I have enough respect for myself. But that's not you. You've never been able to see sex as a mutual pleasure transaction. So, you may want to take things slow. You married Ash, so clearly you don't have that need for mushy feelings to have sex, but if a guy didn't call you after, you'd probably be heartbroken. It'd be like he'd liquidated all of your self-worth and lost it in a Ponzi scheme. I know you. So, take it slow."

"Probably sound advice."

Emily chatters on about all her conquests. Working in such an intellectual field, the academic types she works with are not used to a girl with as much freedom of sexual expression as she has. She thrives on it. Emily is all about stirring the pot and adding shock value.

The conversation slowly turns to work, and she asks what I'm going to do next. My degree is in journalism, and right out of college, I'd had a great job at *The Washington Post*. The pay was crap, and I wrote about things like co-ed kickball and how to turn empty lotion bottles into cell phone charging stations, but it was a start. After Franklin was attacked, my career was put on hold, and I have no idea how to get back on track now that I'm this far removed from the workplace. "I don't know what I should do," I respond. "But I have to do something, and fast."

Em rolls her eyes at me. "Man, you really are oblivious aren't you? How many people came up to you telling you how impressed they were with the article you wrote for *The Post*?"

I had been rather proud of the article I wrote about Franklin and the changes he'd helped foster in real estate development in Washington over the last forty years. It had started out as an obituary but turned into something far more reflective. When the obit editor had called asking for my piece, I told her it wasn't fit for print. She insisted I send it to her anyway. The next thing I knew, it was in the Living section. I've always found it odd that the obits are in the living section...

Em snaps her fingers in front of my face. "Hey, you still with me?"

I nod and reach for a bottle of water. "Sorry, the heat's got me a little dazed. What were you saying?"

"You're an amazing writer. You have a voice that captivates people and draws them in. Start writing feature stories and sell them freelance," she suggests.

I feel the rusty gears in my brain starting to rotate.

She lowers her sunglasses and fixes her gaze on the group of guys in the cabana across the pool. "Eh," she says, returning her glasses to the bridge of her nose. "Cute from far, far from cute. Now, what was I saying? Oh yeah. Between all the people Franklin was connected to and all the people you know from college and high school, you should be overflowing with stories. I actually have a great idea for one that would make a good series, and I can get you a connection when you want to sell it."

I look at her skeptically. "Do you really think I can make a living at that? It seems like one of those things that everyone says they can do before they quickly learn that all that glitters isn't gold."

She rolls her eyes. "With that attitude, it sure won't be. I said you could do it and be successful. I never said it would be easy. You'll need to work your ass off, but in the end, it'll be worth it."

I tap my chin as I consider her idea. "I did get a lot of attention from that article. I bet I could talk to the guy from *The Post* and see if he can point me in the right direction.

Amazon may have bought *The Post*, but I'm guessing the news still works the same."

Together, we plot some article ideas, and I actually think I feel a spark of hope for the future. Writing is the only thing that has ever come naturally to me.

"Oh," Em says as she hands me another daiquiri. "You need to write a blog too."

"About what? What the hell would I write a blog about?"

"Who knows? Surviving a cheating husband. Starting a new career in a bad job market. Or, how about this? You can write about starting your life over. People in this economy are constantly reinventing themselves. So are you. The journey won't be easy, but it'll give you lots of material to blog about. You know how hard it is to start over, how isolating it can feel. Wouldn't reading about how someone else was getting through it make it all easier?"

I'm less than certain about the blog idea, but at least for the first time in a long time, I see a path for my life. A chance to make my own choices and be who I want to be, not an abridged version of myself created to fit in.

****

After we tire of the pool, we go back to our suite, and my real estate agent calls to tell me that someone has already inquired about the land. The fire marshal has declared that the house is no longer a crime scene. It is, however, still a danger, and I've received a notice that we need to raze what's left of the house. Apparently, someone must have been watching the situation closely because almost as soon as the house was released back to me, the bid was put in. Thirty thousand dollars higher than I would have listed it, in fact, all cash with a ten-day closing. My agent couriers the papers

over, and I'm shocked when I see the buyer's name: Lorenzo
Grimaldi.

I'm not sure what to think about it. It wouldn't be the first
time I'd wondered if Lorenzo were connected to the fire. I've
never been able to figure out how burning my house could
benefit him, but now that he wants to buy the land from me,
my curiosity is piqued. When I hear the words "all cash," I
wonder if he's using counterfeit bills or if this isn't an
elaborate scheme to recoup the money Ash had owed him.
The list of possibilities is as long as the line of creditors
looking for payment. Knowing I don't have much choice, I
sign the papers and hope the sale doesn't come back to bite
me in the ass.

THIRTEEN

Em gives me a lift back to my sublet on her way to the airport. It's a cute one-bedroom on N Street with parquet floors and a retro chic design. The kitchen cabinets are bright blue, and the furniture looks as though it was lifted from the set of *Happy Days*. There's even a jukebox in one corner. The playlist is full of nineties alt rock. The fifties décor mixed with angsty grunge is an odd mix, but I don't mind it.

With my meager possessions, moving in doesn't take long. I put my toothbrush in the toothbrush holder, set my few items of clothing in a drawer, and poof!—I'm moved in. A few hours later, FedEx delivers a package for me, which takes me by surprise since *I* don't even know my own address yet, let alone anyone else. It's a collection of random but sweet gifts: some wine goblets, framed photos of London, and the highest thread count sheets I've ever seen— a housewarming gift from Gavin. The sheets seem like a curious choice of gift as I would only give sheets to someone if I planned on breaking them in together. If I read between the lines, I wonder if he's extending a subtle invitation to get between the sheets.

Since moving in has taken less than five minutes, my afternoon is free. I call Owen, my contact at *The Post,* to invite him to buy me lunch. Owen was my boss when I first started at *The Post,* and he's always had a sweet spot for me in an older brother sort of way, so he readily agrees. One we meet up, we walk down L Street to a trendy salad bar restaurant. Fifteen dollars for weeds that someone calls a salad seems like a rip off to me, but I won't turn away a free meal. Even if it has dandelions in it.

Owen gives me some great advice about delving into the world of freelancing and even gives me my first lead. DC is in no short supply of corrupt jackasses with trails of collateral damage in their wake worth reporting on. He knows of a few families with children with special needs that have been screwed over by shady lawyers working for the public school system.

I've even started to give Em's blog idea a whirl. I create a pen name—Rose Evans, my mother's name. In case I end up making a huge ass of myself, I don't want it to undermine my professional writing. Em's right—there are lots of people starting their lives over, either after divorces, starting new careers, or any number of other situations. I call the blog *Taking a Mulligan.* My vision is *Sex in the City* meets the unemployment line.

Despite the fact that he's an ocean way, Gavin has been the supportive drive behind all of it. He's full of creative inspiration and unique perspective that's always giving me something to mull over. He may be swamped at work, but he still always makes time to talk to me. We Facetime often, which helps. Video chatting makes it feel as though he could be in the next room rather than on another continent. He, of course, looks as amazing as ever and keeps my imagination running wild. For me, on the other hand, the webcam and camera phone make me look terrible. It's worse than fluorescent lighting, a really bizarre combination of shadowy in some areas and washed out in others. He keeps calling, so I suppose he can't be that put off by my less-than-stellar appearance.

It's already been three weeks since he left. Every time we speak, the words, "When can I see you again," are just on the tip of my tongue, but I don't have the guts to ask. Once I ask that question, I go from a good pal he talks to daily to a needy girl with unreasonable expectations, and I lose my own good pal.

When Friday afternoon rolls around, I'm finishing up a batch of interviews for my article when Gavin starts texting me trivia questions. All of the answers have to do with Washington. He must be really bored, so I indulge him. On my way back home, I climb the stairs up from the Metro, texting Gavin about my interview, when he writes back,

G: You look amazing in that skirt today.

I can't recall if he saw what I was wearing when we video chatted earlier. Kind of random, but I'll always take a compliment from a hot man. I write back,

L: Thanks for noticing.

He then writes back,

G: I can't wait to take it off with my teeth!

Gavin, you naughty boy!

L: Promises, promises. I look forward to collecting on that! I'll have to remember to wear this when I see you next.

Suddenly, I feel a hot breath against my neck. "How 'bout we give it a go now?"

I spin around to find Gavin's azure blue eyes staring back at me. He sweeps me up and spins me around, kissing me passionately.

"I can't believe you're here!" I literally squeal with delight.

"I was going to plan a romantic holiday, but then it occurred to me, why waste all that time on travel? I don't need amazing geography. All I need is you."

"When did you get here? When did you plan it? How did you find me?"

Not truly caring about the hows and whys, I don't give him a chance to answer before I kiss him. As our kiss deepens, our bodies push against each other as if being drawn together magnetically. His hands have moved from my neck and hair to the backs of my thighs. "Let's go to your flat before we get arrested."

As we walk back to my apartment, anxiety hits me so hard I misstep and almost fall off the sidewalk. He's telling me about his flight over, but I don't hear a word. I'm lost in my own thoughts. *Do I need to shave? What underwear am I wearing? I hope my bra and panties match. Are we really going to have sex, or is he going to want to take it slow? It's been so long... What if I'm terrible? Birth control? Do people discuss that anymore?* I'm internally panicking while I try to look collected and confident.

Lost in my panic, I cross Potomac Street on auto-pilot without pausing to look for oncoming traffic. It's a wonder I'm not struck down. Because that would be just my luck—a hot British guy surprises me for a romantic weekend and I get plowed down by a co-ed rushing to get to class. But that doesn't happen. I cross the street, hot guy in tow. Maybe my luck is changing.

"Lily, have you heard a word I've said?"

I stammer as we walk up the stairs to my apartment, "Um, I–I—" I look over my shoulder and smile. "Sorry. I'm a little flustered. This's such a surprise."

My hands shake as I try to get my key in the door. My mind and body are fraught with anticipation. As I fiddle with my key, Gavin stands behind me and whispers, "Whatever could you be thinking about?"

He runs a finger down the back of my thigh as he kisses my neck. I lose track of what I'd been doing as I melt into him. "Did I put naughty thoughts in your mind?" he asks with a snicker.

"Are you having trouble concentrating? Maybe I can help with that." He slides his hands all the way up my skirt and traces the edge of my underwear.

I finally get the damn door open. As soon as I've closed the door behind us, he grabs me and throws me on to the sofa.

"Don't you want the tour?" I ask casually, knowing a tour is the last thing on either of our minds.

He kisses me like a madman, which turns me on faster than a light switch. "I think I can find my way. Don't you worry," he murmurs as he kisses my neck. He tries to unbutton the tiny buttons on my blouse, but they don't want to cooperate.

"Need some help?" I ask coyly.

He tears my shirt open, and buttons scatter across the floor. "I think I've got it," he growls. I'd loved that blouse, and my wardrobe is still severely compromised, but it's so worth it.

I tug at his shirt, but he tries to resist, probably thinking he's in control. I pull my body away a bit and say, "It's only fair. A shirt for a shirt." My playful game seems to excite him, and he quickly pulls his shirt off, exposing his spectacular body.

He kisses my collarbone, slowly moving across to my shoulder. He grabs my bra strap with his teeth, pulling it down to expose my breast. He gently strokes my nipple with his thumb, sending shock waves through me. His mouth slowly kisses downward until he finds my nipple, which he gently licks, then sucks. His hands move around my back to unhook my bra and free my other breast. While his tongue teases one nipple, his thumb mimics his attentions with the other. Every nerve ending in my body is on full alert, and my panties are drenched.

I rock my hips toward him, grinding myself against his erection. His eyes roll back as he moans. That slight contact seems to energize him further as he becomes even more aroused, licking and tugging more fervently.

I'm so turned on that I feel as though I'll explode if he doesn't touch me. I intertwine my legs with his and maneuver my hips so that I rub against him, leaving a trail of my wetness behind, which makes him groan.

I'm completely wrapped up in the moment and the intensity, but then suddenly my brain turns on. We haven't talked about this at all. That's what mature adults do, right? They have "the talk" before they have sex. I think I read that somewhere. A civil war breaks out within me. My body screams for more while my brain lectures about birth control.

"Gavin, we should slow down a second," I say breathlessly, not sounding very convincing. "Should we talk about this first?"

His hands move from my breasts down to my skirt, which he proceeds to tear off of me as though it were a piece of paper.

"Lily, I've been thinking about doing this for weeks. Don't spoil it with talking—unless you're screaming my name, that is. I flew four thousand miles so I could finally find out how good you taste. I fully intend on completing my mission. Now lie back and prepare to have your mind blown."

Well, when he puts it that way...

He kisses his way down my stomach to the top of my thong before his fingers pull it down and toss it across the room. I look down at his unbelievably toned shoulders and scarred yet beautiful back. This man is truly amazing. As he turns back to me, he kisses my knee before moving his way up my thigh to my center. I'm full of anticipation. If he doesn't touch me soon, I'm going to have to touch myself. I can't wait another second.

At that moment, his tongue finds my clit, and slowly starts massaging. He licks and sucks, and my body responds instantly to the sheer pleasure. His fingers continue to massage my nipples while his tongue laps up my wetness, driving me ever closer to ecstasy. Gavin has awoken sensations in me that I'd forgotten existed. While at one point in time, I'd had an active sex life, I've never had this before. I become greedy, screaming out, "Don't stop!" as I grind myself against his touch, utterly fucking his mouth. It doesn't take long before I'm screaming in delirious bliss. My orgasm is hard and powerful, leaving me feeling high.

We are both breathless for a moment before I turn my attention on him. I momentarily debate my mode of attack. Sex? Blow job? What's a girl to do? I go back and forth in my head for a split second. At this point, the condom question would totally kill the moment, so I opt to follow his lead. I want him. I want to give him as much pleasure as he has given me. My body yearns for him, but I decide to take it slowly. Devilishly slowly!

I turn into the crook of his neck and kiss him gently, seductively. I make my way up to his ear and whisper provocatively, "That was my favorite skirt. Totally ruined because someone couldn't be patient. I think you're going to have to practice some patience." I look him in the eye with an intensity that lets him know that he's in for something good.

My kisses start off soft and wet, licking and sucking my way down his chest. While my tongue plays with his nipple, I start to unbuckle his belt. I slowly pull his pants off but leave the boxers on. My mouth returns to his delectable abs while my hands run ever so gently up and down his thighs. My touch is so soft it's almost weightless but just heavy enough to make his body tense with anticipation.

As my kisses move further south, I run my tongue along the edge of his boxer briefs, occasionally pulling at the elastic with my teeth as though I'm about to pull them off. But I don't.

I abandon his stomach and move my attention to his thighs, running my tongue up his toned quads, almost making it to the Promised Land, but not quite. Each time I travel up his thigh, Gavin gasps and moans softly. I'm torturing him, but I know he's loving every second of it.

Feeling he has endured enough, I finally pull his boxer briefs off slowly, and I get my first look at him. He's enormous. Almost intimidating. But I'm a girl that likes a challenge. I run my fingertips up his impressive length. As I reach the tip, I trace my fingers around his engorged head. Gavin moans, and I know I've just hit a sweet spot.

My tongue follows the lead of my fingers, starting at the base of his shaft and gently licking my way to his tip. After circling his tip with my tongue several times, I take him deep into my mouth. I'm amazed I'm able to take him so deeply. A girl learns she has new skills every day!

My hand strokes his shaft as I plunge him into my mouth. With each suck, he moans in a way that drives me crazy. I feel him getting harder by the second. By the way he's white-knuckling the sofa cushion, I think he's getting close. "Oh God, Lily!" he screams as he releases into me.

We lie there. Breathless, exhausted, and content.

After our breathing returns to normal, I look up at him and say jokingly, "So, what do you think of the place?"

He laughs and pulls me toward him to kiss me. "Better than I ever could have imagined."

I run a finger down his well-defined chest. "If that's what's going to happen when I walk through the front door every day, I might not let you leave."

He reaches behind him for a blanket to pull over us. "Just imagine if you came with me to London. It would be even better."

I swallow hard. "That can get better?"

"Yes, luv. Everything's better in London."

I roll my eyes, trying to think of a comeback, when my phone rings.

"At least they were kind enough to wait until we finished before interrupting us this time," Gavin says with a wink.

I chuckle as I cross the room and dig my phone out of my purse. It's a number I don't recognize, so I send it to voicemail and return to Gavin and all his scrumptious muscles. I snuggle against him, taking him in. His strong jaw; eyebrows so perfect I have to wonder if he gets them waxed. For all the flack Brits get for having bad teeth, the stereotype clearly doesn't apply to Gavin. Pearly white and flawlessly straight. He makes me wish I'd worn my retainer more after my braces came off. And then there're his eyes. If heaven has a color, it's the color of his eyes.

I had thought that if I ever saw him again, the chemistry would be gone, that the sparks that I had felt before would be nothing more than static. Man, was I wrong... The heat between us is scorching, too intense to be denied. I know he's going to leave again and I'll be left in the smoldering ashes of my broken heart, but I can't stay away. Not now. Gavin may be the death of me, but what a great way to go.

A deep grumble roars from inside Gavin's stomach.

"I suppose I should feed you, huh?"

His hands go to his abdomen. "Well, that's embarrassing. I skipped breakfast because I was running late, and then I worked the whole flight and skipped the meal."

"I have nothing in the house, so let's go out."

"Where do you want to go, and how dressy should I get?" he asks. "You know I've packed for all occasions."

I roll my eyes. "You're such a girl," I tease. "I was dressy and pretty before, and now that outfit's in desperate need of a seamstress. Now we go super casual. Pizza and beer?"

"Oh, thank God. I'd have taken you anywhere and been happy to do it. But I'm really not up for a four-course meal." He leans over, kisses my neck, and whispers, "I'm already thinking of dessert!" He pauses for a moment and looks at me very confused. "Wait a minute... You hate beer."

"I can't believe you remember. I *do* hate beer. The place I have in mind has cider on tap, so I'm all set." I place a chaste kiss on his lips. "You're just too sweet for words, you know that? A man that actually listens. Amazing!"

We step outside into the pleasantly cool evening. A storm must be coming in because the sky is blanketed with menacing clouds. "Should we grab a brolly just in case?" he asks.

"A what?" I ask.

He looks at me as though I'm missing the obvious. "An umbrella."

I scrunch my face. "Don't have one of those yet. I'm sure we'll be fine. I don't melt."

He goes back into my apartment anyway and returns shortly with an umbrella. I take it and tuck it into my purse. "Well, aren't you a boy scout?"

"What kind of Londoner would I be if I didn't have an umbrella on hand at all times?" he replies.

I lock the door. "Is it really as drab and dreary as books make it seem? I've never been."

He puts his arm around me. "It can be, but I've always felt it adds to the character of the city." As we walk to the restaurant, he describes his favorite places and things about the city and lists the myriad reasons I'll love them. He knows me far better than I'd realized because his reasoning is spot on.

When we get to the restaurant, we decide to risk the rain and sit outside to enjoy the comfortable night. The patio has a great view of the Potomac, and it's too nice to pass up. We quickly place our order, not wanting to tempt the rain gods by dilly dallying. The server soon returns with our drinks. I take an eager sip, but it takes all my effort to swallow. I slide the glass across the table, grimacing. "I believe this pint of piss belongs to you." I grin watching him catch it as I hear the muffled ringing of my cell phone. Not recognizing the number when I pull it out, I send it to voicemail and turn off the ringer to avoid further interruptions.

"It's a good thing I didn't try your apple juice. I'd have spit it out. I don't know how you drink that syrupy sweet stuff. It's ghastly." He slides my cider to me and then takes a sip of his beer.

I smirk. "Spitters are quitters." He laughs, causing him to choke. Miraculously, he keeps all his beer down, but his face is as red as a tomato.

He points at me. "You're a naughty girl."

"Say naughty again."

He raises an eyebrow. "Only if you're good."

"I think I've demonstrated I'm not a quitter. That makes me very good."

He shifts in his seat. "We need to change the subject, or else I may have to throw you over my shoulder and drag you back to your flat before the pizza arrives."

I stick my tongue out. "Party pooper."

"Don't stick it out unless you're ready to use it."

I cock my head. "So much for keeping it clean, Oxford."

Our flirtatious banter is interrupted when a server bumps the table as he sets down a huge tray of food for the diners to the right of us. The server is grossly overweight, which isn't terribly surprising since he works in the best pizza place in town. What is surprising is that he doesn't feel the draft when his crack is exposed for the world to see. I'd have thought all the fresh air would be good for the acne that covers his ass, but to his and my dismay, it clearly hasn't been. As he bends over to place a plate of eggplant parmesan on the table, his butt is shoved right in my face.

"Well that was a mood killer." I say after he's left.

Gavin takes a sip of his beer. "He could market himself as living birth control. There's no way anyone could spend time looking at *that* without it killing their libido."

"I'd have sympathy for him, but he put those pants on this morning sans belt. My sympathy left with my appetite."

To lighten the mood, Gavin tells a story about going to school without a belt when he was twelve and his best friends spending the day "debagging" him. Apparently, they don't call it "pantsing" in England because pants are underwear. "We call them trousers," Gavin corrects in a snooty voice.

Our pizza arrives just as I flip him off. We order another round of drinks and dive into our meal. As we eat, the conversation is easy and filled with embarrassing stories of our youths. I tell him about the pizza-eating contest I won in the fifth grade, beating out the boy I had a crush on. I'd gloated a little too much and later ended up puking all over him. Derek Oarsman had called me Puke for the rest of the time I lived in Ashfield.

The crisp, cool cider goes down quickly, and before I know it, I've had four rounds. At eight percent alcohol, the buzz has hit me hard by the time the server clears our empty plates and returns with our box and the check. With the liquid courage flowing, it seems like the perfect time to have an awkward conversation. "Before we head back, I thought maybe we should talk about something," I say trying to mask how uncomfortable I am.

"You can talk to me about anything." He looks at me through narrowed eyes. "What's wrong? You look really nervous. Remember, we're past inappropriate. All's fair."

I drain the last of my cider. "Sorry, I'm being a tool. I don't know why this makes me so awkward. The last time I had this conversation, I was eighteen. It didn't faze me then, but it seems I'm totally tongue-tied now. I don't know if post-college adults even have this conversation."

He covers my hand with his. "Just tell me."

My hair is sticking uncomfortably to the back of my neck. I flip it over my shoulder and take a deep breath. "Well, I thought you should know that I know that I'm clean and I'm on the pill. I wasn't for a long time, but I recently thought it was a good idea to go back on it."

"Oh, this conversation," he laughs. "You're too funny. In my wilder days, I thought I was invincible. I didn't get tested as often as I should have. I was tested when I got married and remember thinking how happy I was that I didn't have to deal with that again. I had a newfound appreciation for monogamy—until Brooke came to me and told me she had caught hepatitis from one of the men she was sleeping with or sharing needles with. She didn't know which one."

I'm not sure if I'm embarrassed for bringing up a painful memory or if I'm freaking out that I may have just contracted an STD. A vice tightens around my lungs, slowly squeezing out the air. My heart starts to pound as I get lightheaded.

"Lily dear, you look dreadful. Are you feeling okay?"

"No, Gavin," I say through gritted teeth. "I'm not okay. You just dropped a bomb like that and actually expect me to be okay?"

"Jesus, I'm sorry. I'm perfectly clean. Brooke and I hadn't been together like that for months at that point."

Air floods into my lungs, and my heart stops thumping like a rabbit's. "Oh, thank God."

He stands, reaches for me, and then pulls me into a tight embrace. "I'm a cad. I should've explained myself better. During the twenty-four hours between when my blood was drawn and the results came in, I was petrified. It gave me a whole new respect for sex. I'm proud of you for bringing it up. Many women wouldn't have. If it makes you feel better, if you hadn't, I would have."

I can appreciate where he's coming from. Once I'd found out Ash was sleeping around, I was so disgusted I wouldn't have even screwed him with someone else's vag. No fucking way.

I take a step back and nod toward the door. "I'm ready to go. How 'bout you?" I ask, hoping to get out of this awkward conversation.

The streets of Georgetown are packed. Gavin takes my hand as he navigates the crowd. When we make it to a quiet side street, he asks, "Why did you go off the pill? Where you trying to have kids?"

The question catches me so off-guard that I trip, almost falling flat on my face. "Oh God, no!" I shout louder than intended. "Certain people should never procreate, and Ashton was one of them. I knew that a long time ago. I was in a similar situation to you. He was sleeping with anything with legs, and that was a firm boundary for me. After a while, I got lazy and just stopped taking my pills, and I never went back for refills."

"So how long has it been?"

My cheeks suddenly feel hot.

"Look at you," he says. "This conversation is making you blush. You're one of the most brazen women I've met. I've never seen you bat an eye at a personal question, and you're squirming right now."

"I'm just nervous," I reply. "It's been a long time. A *very* long time. And from the sound of it, you've slept with half of England."

"I did not," he says indignantly. "Well, I sort of did. But it isn't anything you need to worry about. If it makes you feel better, it's been a long time for me too. Why do you think I'm in such good shape? I've got to burn off all that energy somehow," he says with a wink.

I feel a faint buzzing from my pocket and am reminded that I'd turned my ringer off during dinner. I pull the phone from my pocket to see that, in addition to a slew of calls from numbers I don't know, Em has called five times in the past hour. I quickly dial her back.

"Em, what's up? Where's the fire?" I ask when I hear the line connect.

"Um, hello? Your life just exploded all over the internet. How are you taking this so well?"

Gavin mouths *What's wrong?,* and I shrug. "Slow down. What are you talking about?" I ask.

"Fuck. You haven't seen it, have you?"

"Now I'm worried. What are you talking about?"

"There are pictures of you and a certain British gentleman all over the tabloids. Apparently, you've been carrying on an affair for months, and they have pictures to prove it. There are pictures of you from today for crying out loud. While I'm on the subject, you wore those heels with that skirt? Have I taught you nothing?"

I look at Gavin. "Seems as though we're trending."

We turn the corner toward my apartment, and I see a gaggle of photographers waiting by the main entrance. Gavin grabs me by the shoulders and turns me back around the way we came. "Just keep walking. We'll go to a hotel tonight. Unless you want to spend the few days I'm here posing for the press," he adds with a wink.

FOURTEEN

We weave up and down the streets of Georgetown, hoping that we haven't been spotted or followed. Gavin's hand rests firmly on the small of my back as he walks onward with commanding purpose.

As we approach a large brick building, the door swings open. A man leans out of the doorway and says, "Good evening, Mr. Edwards. We weren't expecting you."

Gavin shakes the man's hand. "Marcus, hello. How is Julia?"

"Very well, sir. Thank you for asking," Marcus replies as we walk through the door.

As I walk through the door, I notice a small sign. The Four Seasons. I stop and do a double take of the building. From the outside it looks like every other building in Georgetown. I'd never have guessed it was a hotel. I tug on Gavin's arm. "Hold up Oxford. I can't afford this place."

He glares at me. "As if I would let you pay."

He puts his hand on my back to nudge me forward, but I stand firm.

"Gavin. No. One night in this place probably costs more than my rent for the month. Letting you pay for dinner was one thing. But you footing the bill while we deal with this mess is another. I'm not comfortable with this."

This sort of extravagance was how it had started with Ash. Expensive dinners, lavish weekend getaways, and sweet presents from Tiffany's that come with a hefty price tag. The next thing I knew, he was paying my sorority dues and had bought me a car. At the time, it was as though I'd found my Prince Charming. Well, my lottery ticket was more like it. Without Ash's help, I would have had to work forty hours a week to afford college and living expenses. So I'd let him spoil me. At the time, it had seemed harmless, but after we were married, I realized I was a kept woman, and he treated me as such. I'd allowed myself to be bought. Clearly, I didn't have enough self-respect to take care of myself. Why should he have had respect for me? Even so, I don't intend to allow that to happen again.

Marcus steps back inside and closes the door, giving us some privacy.

"I understand where you're coming from," Gavin replies. "But I did come into town for a business meeting and my company was fully expecting to pay for my lodging while I was in town, but I'd initially declined since I was going to stay with you. Don't think of this as me paying. Think of it as you shacking up with me while I stay here. Plus, the staff here is top notch, and they place high value on the privacy of their clientele. I was here for weeks, and no one caught wind of it. I can say with absolute certainty that if we go to another hotel, where I don't have a pre-existing relationship, someone will sell us out in a heartbeat."

I lean against the cool brick wall, brainstorming alterative solutions, but I come up empty. "Are you sure your company is okay with this?"

A smile spreads across his face. "Yes, I can assure you my company is perfectly comfortable with this arrangement. Now can we please go in? Or would you rather wait out here to be caught by the paps?"

Begrudgingly, I follow him into the swanky lobby. There are no other guests around, just a handful of impeccably-dressed staff members quietly flittering around, all eyes on us. My flip-flops echo on the pristine marble floors, drawing unwanted attention to me.

Before we get to the front desk, a woman in a deep purple pantsuit appears and hands Gavin a key card. "Here you go, Mr. Edwards. You're suite's waiting for you."

"Thank you, Carmella," he replies, slipping her a tip. As we make our way to the elevator, Gavin stops to chat with a few other hotel employees. He seems to know everyone's name, their kid's names, and their hobbies. He has this magical ability to connect with every person that crosses his path, and he does so with such authenticity that people are drawn in. Living in Washington as long as I have, I've certainly met enough charismatic people that possess a similar ability to work a room, but after talking to those sorts, I always feel the need to go through a HAZMAT decontamination cleaning. Gavin, on the other hand, genuinely cares about the people he meets and radiates nothing but sincerity and warmth.

The elevator opens on the second floor, and he instinctively steers me towards the right.

"Why am I always being shuttled off to clandestine rooms with you? With no luggage, by the way."

As he opens the door to our room he says, "I guess you'll just have to be naked then, won't you!"

I'm flabbergasted when I enter the room. This isn't a hotel room. It's the size of a house. There's a full size dining room. To the right and down a few steps is a gigantic living room with a TV nearly the size of the wall it's mounted on. But what captivates my attention is the enormous terrace that's at least as big as my whole apartment. I wander and find a bedroom with an amazing view of Georgetown and the Potomac. The bathroom is also to die for—a deep tub designed for two as well as a shower that's bigger than an SUV and has more shower heads than I can count. Whoever designed this bathroom had more than simply bathing in mind.

I've been in some very nice places, but this room blows them all out of the water. "It's the *Rain Man* suite of DC."

"It is rather remarkable. I always stay in this suite because it allows me to get business done here. I have a great relationship with many of the chaps I work with, and rather than sit in stuffy board rooms, we'll go golfing, come back here, sit on the terrace with a pint or two. Then we'll eat downstairs. The restaurant downstairs, Bourbon Steak, is one of my favorite places to eat. It's a great schedule, and I get lots accomplished. Not a bad way to spend a work day."

He's interrupted by a knock at the door. "Hold that thought," he says. He returns with Marcus, who's pushing a cart laden with four bottles of Perrier Jouet, a pair of champagne flutes, and four pints of Chunky Monkey.

"Clearly, they know you well here. It almost feels rehearsed. Is this your schtick when you bring women here?" I'd known Gavin was smooth, but to have the staff on-call to bring champagne to the room upon arrival seems more sleazy than smooth.

"Mr. Edwards is a valued member of the family here at the Georgetown Four Seasons. We always keep plenty of Chunky Monkey on hand. The champagne is for another suite, but I'd be happy to bring a bottle to you, if you would like." He places the ice cream in the mini fridge hidden in the bar. "Good night, Ms. Clark. Please don't hesitate to call if you need anything." With that, he's gone.

I go behind the bar to scope out what other hidden treasures may be hiding back there. "How'd he know my name?" I ask. When Gavin doesn't answer, I stand up. His back is to me while he looks out the window, arms crossed.

"'It almost feels rehearsed?' Are you bloody kidding me?"He sounds pissed, furious even. Not a tone I've heard from him before.

"Um," I stammer.

He turns around and glares at me. "You caught me," he snaps. "I planted paparazzi outside your home to lure you here to get into your pants. I guess the jig is up!" He spins back around to face the cityscape.

I instantly recoil, feeling like a bitch. Too ashamed to meet his furious gaze, I look down as I apologize. "I'm sorry. Of course you wouldn't."

"I'm not like your husband. Please don't make me pay for his sins," he spits before walking out onto the terrace.

I've really stepped in it, haven't I? He couldn't be more opposite to Ash if he tried. Clearly, I have trust issues, and I need to learn that not all men are lying, cheating scum. All of that is going to take time.

I touch his back, hoping he'll turn to me. When he doesn't, I squeeze my way between him and the railing so he has no choice but to look at me. The hurt is written all over his face, and it feels like a dagger to my heart.

"I'm sorry. In my life, when things seem too good to be true, they typically are. It's a knee-jerk reaction for me to always look for the catch. It's still hard for me to believe that you're here with me. Part of me keeps waiting for the bubble to burst. I just hope I'm not the one to pop it by being an idiot. Can you please forgive me?" I give him my best puppy-dog eyes, hoping he will come around. The last thing I want to do is hurt him. And, if we're stuck hiding out from the press together, it will be far more fun if he doesn't hate me.

He finally looks me in the eye. "I know you have issues. I'm chock full of them myself. I'm overreacting a bit, I know. I'm acting like a mopey cow. What we have is... uh..." he stammers.

He pulls away from the railing and paces a bit, which I've noticed he does when he's trying to work something out. It makes me horribly seasick when he does it during our video chats. I've learned to just give him room to process. He'll tell me when he's ready.

"I have so many thoughts and they are all jumbled. Some of this may come out poorly, so just bear with me. Women have always thrown themselves at me, and I've never had to work for it. I didn't have to try. I didn't even have to be particularly nice."

"Wow, Gavin. Just lay it out there, why dontcha?"

"Just listen, please. I'm not trying to be an arrogant cad. I'm trying to be honest. When I was younger, I had plenty of women but no one I ever really cared for. I was a selfish wanker, and women would put up with it. They didn't want me. They just wanted my money or whatever piece of Britain's bad boy they could get their hands on," he says with an eye roll.

"At a certain point, I looked at who I was, and I made myself sick. Going into the army helped me grow the hell up. It helped me realize how precious life is, how hard it is. I had a new respect for the people around me. I decided I'd never use someone that way again. With Brooke, you see… Um, well how can I explain," he stammers.

I get queasy at the sound of her name. I really don't want to hear about their relationship, but I know I have to. If I want to know him, I have to know all of him, and clearly this topic is upsetting him. Squashing my insecurity, I nod for him to go on.

"She was so alive when I met her, but then she got lost. I tried to help her find her way, but because she was living this double life, she was always at arm's length. She was in my life, but she never really shared my life. That was how she wanted it, and I went along with it because it was easy. I never had to try very hard for her because she didn't respect herself enough to expect that of me."

He stops pacing and comes toward me. Grabbing my hand and looking me in the eye, he says, "Then I met you, and it was like my eyes opened for the first time. You're not someone I have to try hard for out of necessity. I want to try hard for you. I want to give you everything. Do everything for you. I think about you nonstop, and your happiness is like oxygen to me. If you're hurting, I can't breathe. It shakes me to the core.

"I've never felt like this before. So when you trivialize it and make it sound like you're just another notch on my bedpost, it wounds me deeply. I'm not with you because I'm mourning and looking for comfort. I'm not with you because I'm looking for a shag. I could do that a lot closer to home if I wanted. I don't want that. I'm with you because I'm consumed by you... every moment of every day."

He kisses me softly and gently, and I feel like I could kiss him forever. Slow and soft begets deep and passionate with roaming tongues and hands. He scoops me up into his arms and carries me to the bedroom.

Our last experience had been fire and lust. This time, it's tender and seductive. His hands move tenderly over my body, as though his fingers are trying to memorize every inch of me. Each gentle touch heightens my senses, making me yearn for him.

He slowly peels my clothes off, and I do the same to him. While there's a burning need to remove all barriers between us, we take our time, wanting to savor every second. The anticipation is delicious, and rushing the moment would be a sin.

Our kisses become more impassioned as the heat between us grows. My hands can't get enough of him. Tracing the contours of his body is erotic. I get lost on the hard plateaus of his abs, the slopes of his biceps. Every part of him is so well-defined, like a sensual wonderland for me to explore.

Tracing along my jaw, his fingertips slowly make their way down my body. He finds my breasts and gently caresses them. Running his thumbs over my nipples, he makes me moan. Feeling the way my body reacts to him, he continues, making quick circles with his fingers. I cry out in delight and turn my hips towards him. We writhe against each other as we kiss, building the anticipation between us. His erection grows with each kiss as our bodies move together. I can feel its rigid enormity. One of Gavin's hands travels the slow trail from my breasts down my stomach. It's deliciously slow torture. Enjoying his soft caress but so desperately needing him to touch me elsewhere.

I can't wait another second. I need him. My body craves for him to be inside me. I look at Gavin as I push him to the bed and straddle him.

"Are you su—"

I kiss him before he can finish. I've never been so sure of anything in my life. I gasp as I guide the tip of his cock into me. It's been a very long time, and he's far more well-endowed than I'm used to, so I need to take him in slowly. I lower myself on his throbbing erection. Inch by inch, he stretches me.

As he slides further inside me, Gavin lets out a primal moan, which only builds my confidence. His hands run up and down my body, caressing all the right places. Each touch sends a tidal wave of euphoria over my body. I'm lost in the sensation, not able to think or speak. All I can do is feel, and what I feel is mind-blowing.

Once he fills me completely, I tilt my head back; he hits me in depths I didn't know possible. Each thrust brings an explosion of pleasure. Suddenly, his thumb starts to rub my clit. The feeling is so intense and I'm hungry for more. I rock my hips against his, craving more friction.

The pressure mounts, and I know I'm about to come. I scream his name as I climax. Not wanting it to end, I continue my ride, pounding him deeper and deeper inside me. The sensations start to build again, which drives me to go even faster and harder than before. The look in his eyes tells me he's ready to explode. I clench myself around him as we both go over the edge.

We collapse from exhaustion and pure ecstasy.

Gavin rolls so I lie beside him, facing him as he cradles my face in his hands. "There are no words to describe how spectacular that was," he says as he kisses me softly. The sex may have been powerful and intense, but the intimacy I feel in the afterglow is even more so. I feel truly, profoundly connected to this man. There's no question about it—I'm falling for him. I spend the rest of the night showing him.

FIFTEEN

The bright sun wakes me up, and I'm disoriented. Groggy, I lie there, trying to figure out what time it is. Hell, what day it is. Gavin and I have completely checked out of the real world, doing nothing but talk, laugh, and have crazy, passionate sex for what seems like forever. I can't remember the last time I wore clothes. We don't even have to think about food. Good ol' Marcus keeps sending up trays of nosh and, of course, more Chunky Monkey. It's been pure bliss. Gavin isn't in bed next to me, so I have a feeling our sexcapade may be over and the blinding sunlight is my wake up call.

I shrug into one of the plush robes in the closet and wander in search of Gavin. I spot him on the terrace in nothing but boxer briefs, and the sight makes me feel all warm and tingly in all the right places. However, my libido is instantly smacked down when I see his angelic face turned dark by a fury I have never seen from him before. He's on the phone giving someone a tongue-lashing—and not the good kind.

My instinct is to go to him, but I give him some space. If this were a conversation he wanted to have publicly, he would have stayed in bed. We had mutually decided to unplug while we were here, and it was the best decision at the time. No texts or emails or anyone interrupting. Just him and me. But, since he's on the phone, I guess we're plugged back in, so I might as well be too. I turn on my phone to find my voicemail inbox full and a million texts waiting for replies. There are tons of numbers I don't recognize, which I decide to ignore for now. Em has sent a bunch of furious texts. Rather than sort through them all, I just call her.

"Where the fuck have you been? I've been worried sick! Do you know what the hell has been going on?"

"Hello to you, too. Gavin and I have been camped out in a hotel. There was a ton of press at my apartment, so we came here and have been lying low. Can you please tell me what all the drama is about?"

"The press is saying that you broke up Brooke and Gavin. I can't sugarcoat it. They're calling you a home-wrecking whore. The story is spreading like wildfire. It just keeps getting bigger and more out of control."

"How is this possible? I didn't even meet Gavin until after she was dead!"

"But the rest of the world doesn't know that. And there are so many pictures of the two of you! Fucking camera phones. That FBI guy called me when he couldn't get a hold of you. Sounds like there's a zoo outside your house. They're going through your trash, harassing your neighbors. Doing anything for some dirt on you. I've even gotten a ton of calls.

"Do you remember Chelsea Nixon from school? She was on *The Today Show* with pictures of you. Bad ones."

My stomach churns. Chelsea and I knew each other in college, but we never got along. She'd never liked that her boyfriend and I were good friends. He broke up with her senior year, and she'd blamed me, even though I was already with Ash at the time. She would have access to some pretty good dirt on me. Em gives me all the horrid details. It sounds like Chelsea had a shoebox filled with mementos of all of my worst moments, just waiting to crucify me with them. Dancing half-naked on a bar in Mexico. Another of me dressed up for a Pimps and Hoes party wearing practically nothing. Me laying seductively on the roof of Ash's car, again half-naked. Did I not wear clothes in college? *Ever?* It was Arizona, after all, and the dress code there is different from anywhere else. Sparse clothing is typical. But still, seeing it all laid out is scandalous.

Until this moment, I'd never been relieved that my parents were dead. Bile rises in my throat, and I think I'm going to throw up. I hang up on Em and run to the bathroom. I'm able to avoid being sick, but I break out in a sweat and can't seem to catch my breath. The cool marble against my skin helps to calm me down. After pulling myself together, I splash cold water on my face and brush my teeth. As humiliating as it is, I've got to go out and face the music.

I may have been out of the game for a while, but I am a trained journalist. I know that the best thing to do is to just let this story burn itself out. Something else will catch the media's attention soon enough, and it will blow over. I just can't give them any more ammunition in the meantime. But it will take all my restraint not to fight back.

Gavin comes back a few minutes later, looking defeated. Apparently, I don't look so hot either because he says, "I take it you've heard." He sits down on the bed and wraps his arms around me. Usually this makes me forget everything in the world other than him, but not this time.

"This horrible girl from college seems to have found a collection of 'Lily's Most Mortifying Moments' and has shared them with all of America. Suddenly, I'm a money-grubbing whore that likes to break up happy couples in my spare time."

"Luv, I've got my PR people on it. They think it will fade soon. Right now, the press knows very little about you. It seems like some blogger felt there was a story here and started buying up photos of us -"

"Why the hell were people taking photos of us? We're nobodies!" I hear myself say the words, and I know they aren't true. He is almost/not really British royalty and he was married to a Hollywood starlet and thus that makes him somebody. Being with him now seems to have made me a skank. I shake my head and sigh "I know why. I just wish this weren't happening. I mean, haven't we been through enough?"

He kisses the top of my head and rubs my back. "I know, luv. This isn't fair. We'll figure everything out together. I've been on the phone all morning trying to see what we can do to squash it."

I look up into his gorgeous eyes, and my nervous stomach begins to settle. He gives me a soft kiss that makes me want to forget all of this drama and just kiss him, but the responsible part of me knows that kissing isn't the answer.

"Can you say squash again," I tease, trying to lighten the mood.

He rolls his eyes and kisses me.

"I interrupted you. Please tell me the rest of this horrid story. I've got to know what we're dealing with. Sadly, just kissing you all day will not solve all my problems."

He laughs and kisses me again.

The long and the short of it is that some blogger started selling the story that Gavin and I have been together since long before Brooke died. The angle then morphed into Brooke being so depressed over the affair that she committed suicide by driving into the other car—among other crazy theories. That's when the fruitcakes must have come out. Seems this was a slow news week, because the story got a ton of play. Even some D-list actors swear Brooke had started talking about how devastated she was by the affair before her death. It seems they claim to have seen me sneaking around London with Gavin for weeks. Which is amazing considering I've never been to London. Then Chelsea appeared on the scene and painted me as a gold-digging slut.

Everyone wants their fifteen minutes of fame, I guess... except me.

A million questions brew inside, and I fire them out all at once. "So what do we do? What do your PR people think? And are they your PR people or Brooke's PR people?"

"Mine. Don't worry. They aren't worried about how this will impact DVD sales of *Covent Gardens.* They think we should release a statement that your husband died in the accident with Brooke, that I've only done what I can to help you through this difficult time, as you're all alone with no family to speak of. They think we should play up all the tragedy in your life. At least then, they'll stop painting you in such a poor light."

My stomach churns. "Urg, I don't want to cry victim. That's not my style."

"That's exactly what I told them you would say," he says as he kisses my forehead. "Sully called and weighed in as well. He was not pleased with this development, as you can imagine."

Hearing this news makes me wince. My pride has taken quite a beating already. I don't want to think about the tangible dangers that may still be lurking out there.

The phone rings, snapping me out of all of the merry-go-round of horrible scenarios playing through my mind. It's Gavin's PR group calling with a new batch of ideas. He puts them on speaker so I can weigh in as well. Most of the angles have Gavin looking like the altruistic hero, which I'm not opposed to, but I'd have preferred it not be by making me look like some pathetic girl who can't stand on her own two feet.

I'm trying to build a career as a journalist, and that won't happen if I look like some floozy. Of course, based on the coverage from the last forty-eight hours, that may be my destiny regardless of what we do.

"What if we just ignore it?" I ask.

"Ms. Clark," says a snooty voice from the other end of the line, "it could go either way. They could forget you and move on. Or they'll sink their teeth in further."

The room feels like it's spiraling around me. I tap Gavin on the arm and point to the door with my thumb. "I'm going out on the terrace for some air," I say as I bolt out of the room. I plop down on a double chaise and absorb the warm sun, trying to block out all the crazy "what ifs" that are running through my head.

About two minutes later, Gavin lies down next to me and holds my hand. I can tell he's frustrated. He's still breathing heavily, he's fidgety, and his eyes have ferocity behind them.

I lean over to kiss him, in the hopes of soothing some of his anger. "My gut says to lay low and let this pass. If, in a week, it doesn't die down, we can put out a statement. Not one that makes me look like some hooker you're trying to save. Okay?"

He puts his arm around me. "In this whole sordid affair, you're the innocent, and they're raking you over the coals." He slaps his free hand against the arm of the chair. "Bollocks! It infuriates me!"

He bites his lip and looks like a light bulb has just gone off in his mind.

"I hope you know I couldn't care less about the press and what they say. I'm not at all bothered about this in regard to me."

I love the way he says "at all," with the long, drawn out "a." So simple and yet so sexy. *Oh, he's still talking.* Damn, that accent gets me every time.

"I'd be happy to walk out there right now and tell them to piss off. You and I are together and happy, and if they don't like it, fuck them. But, if I were to do that, it may be worse for you in the long run. Bloody hell, this is a cock up."

"Wait, what?" I ask.

"I said I'd tell them to piss off!"

"Not that part. The other part."

He gives me a Cheshire cat grin. At last, his agitation melts away. "Well, we are, aren't we?"

"Gavin Edwards, are you asking me to go steady?" I ask in my best girl-next-door voice. It makes him laugh.

"Well darling, I suppose I am."

I lean into him and say, "Do you really think I would have done all that we have been doing here these past few days if we weren't together? What kind of girl do you think I am? You can't believe everything you read in the papers, you know!"

He doesn't respond at first, and I fear he hasn't gotten my joke. Then he shakes his head and laughs. "See, this is why I adore you! Even with all of this, you're still smiling. You are extraordinary."

Relieved that he understands me so well, I kiss him deeply. One kiss turns into another, then another. Hands start wandering, and very soon, my robe falls to the floor, and his boxers go flying.

"Gavin, we're on the terrace," I whisper as he kisses my neck.

"I told you, they can piss off. If I want to do naughty things to you on the terrace, I bloody well will. Let 'em put pictures of that on *The Today Show*."

"Well, let's make sure to give them a good show."

He plunges into me, and I scream with pleasure. Whoever said size doesn't matter has clearly never experienced someone with an abundance of it. There are times for smooth and gentle, but this is not one of them. I want to forget about the press, my sullied reputation, and all my anger and frustration. There's no better way to do that than to be thoroughly drilled by this extremely hot man.

The sheer pleasure absorbs any other emotion. All I can feel is my building orgasm. Gavin hits my sweet spot, and I come hard, but I'm not done.

I look deep into his eyes and say, "Harder."

He smirks, as if to say, "Challenge accepted," and satisfies my request. I can tell from his body language that he's about to explode into me, but I'm not ready. "Not yet!" I order.

My bossiness seems to excite him further because he lets out a primal moan. He does as he's told and hammers into me. He ravishes me until he pushes me over the edge yet again. I come so hard I think I may lose consciousness for a moment. I'm in a haze of ecstasy, my whole body tingling, and my brain still hasn't quite checked back in yet. I can't remember a damn thing about anything other than the full body high I have.

As I start to come around, I remember I'm not alone here. Gavin is lying there next to me, also looking like he needs some recovery time. I feel slightly guilty that the whole experience was purely selfish. I made it all about me and what I'd needed. And man did I need it. Something tells me he didn't mind.

He catches my eye and smiles. "Feel better?"

I nod and smile. "Sometimes a girl just needs it hard, fast, and dirty."

He cracks up laughing. "Well, I'm here for you anytime you need to work through your feelings. Want to go again?"

"Oh, I'm good and knackered," I reply. "I can't move yet. My muscles are complete mush."

He scoops me up in his arms and carries me inside. "Look at you speaking British. I must be wearing off on you," he says as he kisses me.

He brings me to the massive bathroom, sets me down on the counter, and draws me a bath. "You, my luv, need a good long bath after a proper shagging like that."

"Care to join me?" I ask.

"I might take you up on a shower later, but I've got a few calls to make. Take your time and relax. You'll need your energy for later," he says with a wink.

Between the sex and the bath, I'm feeling fabulous. I find Gavin on his laptop, typing furiously. His blond hair is a total mess, but he pulls it off. So sexy! His brows are furrowed in thought.

I wrap the robe around me tightly. "If there's anything on there about me, I don't want to hear about it. I'm floating on my orgasmic high and have no interest in coming down. The bad news will be there tomorrow."

We agree not to talk about the bad press. We only have one more night, and we don't want to waste another second on anything negative. We order burgers from Bourbon Steak and attempt to watch a soccer game. I know enough about soccer not to make an ass of myself, but it isn't my sport of choice. He tries to teach me about the players and the nuance of the game. His enthusiasm is adorable. We bicker about whether it's called soccer or football. I couldn't care less, but it annoys him to no end. I love pushing his buttons.

At halftime, he jumps up and drops his phone into the docking station, a sneaky grin plastered on his face.

"Get up," he orders.

"No way. You're up to nothing but trouble, Gavin Edwards. I will have no part of it."

"Get. Up."

"Fine," I say with an eye roll and a foot stomp. "What torture are you subjecting me to now?"

Lively music streams from the speakers, and he says, "Time for you to learn how to jitterbug." I recognize the song blaring through the stereo as "Jump, Jive and Wail" by the

Brian Seltzer Orchestra. Gavin grabs my hand and twirls me around the room. I'm terrible at the dance, but it's a lot of fun. Not that I'll ever admit that to him. My dance lesson lasts for the length of halftime, but the second the game is back on, the music is off and we're back on the sofa.

After the game, we head to bed with Chunky Monkey. It's a good thing I'm not wearing pants because they wouldn't have fit after my gluttony.

"How come ice cream is your thing and yet I'm the one who always ends up with the stomachache?"

"Because, luv, I have a well-defined sense of moderation, and you are just *so* American. You want it, you want it now, and you want all of it, even if it hurts."

I pelt him with pillows. "You may have moderation, but I have ammunition!"

Our pillow fight becomes a rumble in the sheets, effectively burning off my ice cream indulgence. The post sex calm takes over us both, and I inch closer and closer to sleep. My mind takes stock of how perfect this arrangement feels. Being with him, sleeping in his arms. This time has been a slice of paradise, but in a few short hours, he has to leave. We haven't even talked about it.

"Gavin?"

"Hmmm," he responds, half asleep.

"Don't go."

"Come with me."

"I can't," I reply.

"You can."

"I can't. Don't go. Just stay one more day."

He takes a deep breath and rubs his eyes, surrendering to the fact that he's not going to sleep just now. "Lily, dear, I have a company with thousands of employees I have to think about. I have to go back. Explain to me why you can't come with me. Help me understand." He's questioning, not pushing, and I'm thankful for it.

"I'm not really sure I understand myself. I just know I can't."

"You know more than that. Just start talking. It will come out. It doesn't have to make sense at first. It will eventually. Trust me, just talk."

I take a deep breath and just say the thing that first comes to mind. "I settled for Ashton because it was the easy, supposedly safe choice."

He snorts.

"I know. Irony's a bitch. I knew I wasn't in love with him when I married him, but I thought I would still be able to live a good life. Boy, did it backfire. It was like when I married him, I made a deal with the devil and I gave up my soul in the negotiations. He sucked the me out of me. I have to take the time to put myself back together again. If I were to run away with you, it would be amazing, but it would fail. I need to be whole before I can be with you or anyone completely… If you swept me away from here and all my troubles, you would be my knight in shining armor, but I would make a lousy princess. Does any of this make any sense?"

"It makes perfect sense. I've reinvented myself a time or two. I know exactly what you're talking about. You need to be able to look in the mirror and feel good about who you're looking at. That takes time to sort out."

It's astounding how well he understands me. He's so grounded, while I'm an emotional disaster area. I feel like I should have yellow caution tape, cones, and flashing lights wrapped around me. Gavin deserves better than that. The realization hits me like a right hook.

"I feel like I'm asking too much to ask you to wait. You deserve to move on with your life. You shouldn't be held back because I'm damaged goods."

He wraps his arms around me and lets me cry. He doesn't tell me it'll be ok or any other bullshit that I'm not interested in hearing. He just lets me get it out. When my sobs stop, he looks at me and wipes the tears away.

He brushes the hair out of my eyes and tucks it behind my ear. "Silly girl. You're not damaged goods, you just need to heal. It's a journey you need to do on your own. But if you think I'm going to bolt because you need time to take care of you, you're mad. Take all the time that you need. I'll be here. Until then, I'll take what I can get."

I take a moment to soak in what he's just said. "You're overwhelmingly sweet and nauseatingly mature. How are you so damn grounded? I don't know how you can be so secure with how messed up everything has been. I'm in awe of you, and at the same time, you scare the shit out of me. You're so confident and stable, and I'm still struggling to find equilibrium. I'm flawed and selfish and broken. You set the bar so damn high. I can't live up to that. I'm going to let you down.

"Don't get me wrong," I continue. "You just said the most perfect thing. Exactly what a girl wants to hear. What I want to hear. But that's the thing. It's so damn perfect. To believe that it's real, that you really mean that? Scares me to no end."

"Luv, slow down. The last thing I want to do is put more pressure on you. I don't have expectations. I'm not setting the bar at all! You couldn't possibly let me down. And I'm far from perfect. Yes, I'm fairly grounded, but I didn't get this way overnight. I've had a lot of heartbreak, and I've caused a lot of heartbreak. All of those experiences shaped the way I deal with things. What gives me confidence and security is us. You and me. Like I said, this is different from any connection I've ever had with another person. I have no doubt in my mind that we'll make this work. This is too good to fail."

His words make me gasp for air. They're shocking, soothing, and suffocating all at the same time. He winces at my gasp. I'm sure I have a look of panic on my face.

"I don't feel like I'm helping," he says. "I leave tomorrow, and I'm not scheduled to be back in the US for almost two months. Take that time to think things through, take care of yourself. We can meet then and see how you feel."

My throat feels as dry as the desert at the thought of not seeing him for two months. "I don't want things to change. I don't want to lose you." Talk about love bipolar. I want him, but I'm pushing him away at the same time. I'm such a train wreck.

"Nothing's changing on my end, okay?" he says reassuringly. "Let's get some sleep. My car is going to be here in a few hours. We don't have to solve everything tonight." He kisses me and rolls over. This is the first night that we've slept together without being wrapped around each other. It feels like he's already left. I lie awake all night, watching him sleep and running through "what ifs" in my head.

When he wakes up, he acts as if nothing has changed, but something feels off. He's full of affection and playful banter, just as always. He goes about getting ready completely casually. But he feels reserved, a bit distant. I feel as though he's put guards up.

Soon, Marcus calls to let him know the car has arrived. I get dressed, expecting him to ask me to come with him.

He pulls me toward him and kisses me. "I have a present for you." He hands me a fancy Four Seasons envelope. Inside, I find a schedule for a full-day spa package.

"I've booked a whole day for you downstairs at the spa. What better way to start taking care of you than by having someone take care of you? I don't know what most of this means, but I've been assured that you'll love it."

"When did you plan this?" I demand, disappointed I won't be asked to join him on the ride to the airport. I hear the words as they come out of my mouth, and I cringe. "Sorry, that was so rude." I kiss his cheek. "Thank you. This is so thoughtful and beyond generous. You didn't have to go through all this trouble. I'm just shocked you had a spare second to organize this."

"I know you didn't sleep last night, and I—"

"How did you know?" If he knows I was up all night, then that must mean he was up all night too.

He gives me an eye roll. "Please, Lil. You may think you're fooling the world, but to me, you're an open book. You need to unwind and relax, and I'm hoping this will be the first step in getting you there. I called while I was getting ready. Remember, there's a phone in the shower," he says with a sly, sexy smile.

Oh, I remember the phone alright. I think it's permanently imprinted into my back from one of our many go 'rounds in the shower.

"Too bad you won't be around to enjoy the outcome of my day of buffing and polishing. I'll be all shiny, smooth, and exfoliated, with no one to appreciate it." I give him a pouty face.

"You can tell me all about it. In vivid detail," he says with a naughty grin. "Alright, luv, my car awaits. You have the room for tonight. I've asked a security company that I've used in the past to go by your place and make sure the maggots are keeping a safe distance before you head back.

"On that note, some other new story broke last night, and I'm thinking you may be yesterday's news now. Seems like some New York politician is a coke fiend and enjoys the company of young prostitutes. Very young male prostitutes. It should be a big enough scandal to make you a thing of the past."

I release a sigh of relief. "I couldn't be happier my fifteen minutes of fame may be over!"

He gives me a quick kiss and says, "Let's hope so! I've really got to dash. I'll call you when I land." One more peck and he's gone.

I instantly regret what I said last night. I'd swear I feel him pulling away, but maybe I just think he is. Either way, I'm going to go crazy overthinking it all. I guess it's a good thing I have a day full of pampering ahead to try to forget the mess I've just made.

SIXTEEN

The spa day is marvelous. I'm scrubbed, soaked, rubbed, waxed, polished, and painted. I feel relaxed, my skin is as smooth as glass, and I think even my laugh lines may have disappeared.

Trying to soak up the end of the summer sun, I lay out on the terrace to work on my blog. I've got to hand it to Em—the blog was a great idea. Every day, it seems I have a new follower or two, and the writing itself is highly cathartic. However, I am having a bit of trouble turning my press nightmare into general terms that anyone can relate to. I try to spin the experience into a post about how snippets of the past can haunt and shape the future. It comes out pretty well, if I do say so myself.

Despite my long break from journalism, I feel like I'm easily getting back into a groove with my writing. My last piece about the plights of families with children with special needs got far more attention than I expected. It was picked up by a few papers across the country. The initial success has given me the confidence to go for round two.

Em has a promising idea for a series of stories about people from all walks of life whose lives were changed by the recession—farmers, plant workers from Detroit, techies, housewives, doctors, veterans. Her idea is to show a piece of how real Americans have been impacted across the board. It's a big undertaking, but what an amazing piece it could be. The focus wouldn't be so much on the economy as it would be on how we, as a nation, have changed. Em's convinced that when it's done, *Time* will be all over it.

I call her, and together we brainstorm for hours. By the end of our call, I feel energized and ready to hit the ground running tomorrow. I look over at the clock and see it's almost ten. Gavin should have landed hours ago, but I haven't even received a text. I know I'm getting the space I asked for, but I'm not happy about it. There's a big difference between not wanting to pick up and move to London and not wanting to talk to him every day. I miss him already. But how can I complain without seeming like a contradictory nut job?

There's a knock at the door, snapping me out of my pity party. My hopes soar, thinking it's Gavin and that he must have decided to stay after all. I sprint to the door only to find the night concierge, Raul, on the other side. My hopes shatter.

"Ms. Clark, my most sincere apologies. This package was to be delivered to you hours ago. The wait staff was on its way up to bring your nightly Ben and Jerry's when I saw it was still at the desk. I am-"

"No worries, Raul. Thank you. Good night." Once the parcel is in my hands, I don't wait for an answer before slamming the door.

Knowing it must be from Gavin, I tear open the package. He's left me another shirt of his that I love, with a note to call him when I'm wearing it. I immediately put it on, taking in the heavenly smell that is Gavin.

It's far too late London time to call him. So I take a selfie and send it with an apology for not calling sooner. Texts clearly travel across the ocean far faster than planes because mere seconds later he calls. I answer by saying, "You should be sleeping. Do you know what time it is in London?"

"I was worried when I didn't hear from you and couldn't sleep. I've been up working, just going to push through the rest of the night." He sounds weary. I picture him hunched over his desk, his hair wild from a long night of raking his fingers through it every time he looks at the clock wondering when his self-absorbed girlfriend will call. Hmmm... girlfriend?

"Don't know what kind of fleabag establishment you've stuck me in, but they sat on this package all day. They just now brought it up to me when they escorted my dates for the evening to my room."

"Dates?" he asks, a tinge of fury in his tone.

"Yup," I reply. "I'm having a threesome with Ben and Jerry."

"The things I would love to do with you and ice cream," he says seductively. "If only you ever left any."

"Shut it, Oxford." I rub my stomach as a blush creeps across my face. "I'm very sensitive about my ice cream-eating. Now that you're gone, I foresee many lonely nights with just me, Ben, and Jerry."

I picture him biting his lip to refrain from making a comment about how I ought to come to London and make it a foursome. Not wanting to talk about travel plans, I cut him off before he has a chance to speak. "Thank you for my spa day. It was heavenly. What a perfect gift to top off a perfect weekend. I loved it, almost as much as I love my new shirt."

"Can't have you walking about starkers without me there, can I?"

"One of these days, I'll be with you without being smuggled off to a hotel without a stitch of clothing."

"That will take all the fun out of it," he teases. "I rather like you without a stitch of clothing." I try to come up with something sexy to say, but he continues before I have a chance. "Lily, dear, I'm going to get back to work. I've been neglectful of my business obligations, and I'm simply drowning in it. Can we speak tomorrow?"

"Sure, no problem. I—"

"Great. Cheers, luv. Sweet dreams." And he's gone.

I suddenly lose any appetite for ice cream. I climb onto what had been Gavin's side of the bed, hoping to curb the feeling of growing distance between us.

SEVENTEEN

The next morning, I enjoy one last swim in the enormous tub before I have to check out. I'm going to miss my glamorous Georgetown hideaway, and I drag my feet getting ready to go.

As I'm leaving, Marcus stops me. "Ms. Clark, Mr. Edwards left strict instructions that his suite is to be made available to you anytime the press starts hounding you. Consider our doors always open as a sanctuary. I do hope that you will join Mr. Edwards next time he is in town."

I shake his extended hand. "Thank you, Marcus. Take care."

Stepping outside, I stop for a moment to bask in the sunshine. It's a gorgeous day, too nice out for a taxi, so I decide to walk home. On my way, I get a call from Greene. He tells me that the feds and banks have seized all they are going to. Franklin's car is the only thing left I can claim. He says I can come pick it up at one of the FBI facilities' impound lots any time, so I hail a cab and head on over.

I run over to Greene when I see him, and he gives me a warm handshake. "How you holding up?" he asks.

"Chopping wood and hauling water. You know, trying to rebuild my life under the watchful eye of the American public," I say with a smile.

"Yeah, I saw the tabloids. Damn parasites. Looks like you took my advice, though. Gavin's a good guy. Considering your late husband, I had grave doubts about your taste in men."

I kiss him on the cheek. "Greene, if Ashton hadn't fucked up my life, I never would have met you."

He gives a gentle tug on my ponytail. "One day, you'll have to tell me how a pretty, smart girl like you ended up with such a dirtbag."

"It's simple, Greene. I was young and dumb." I suck on my lower lip, remembering. "We met in college, and he was just what I wanted at that time. Someone that was going to keep my life simple. I was running from my past, and he was a safe place to hide. I didn't ask questions of him, he didn't ask them of me, and I always had someone to go home with. It was far from love, but it was perfect for college. After school, Franklin helped me get an internship here in DC, and then one thing led to another. We'd been together for so long at that point that it just happened. I never even considered what I was getting into. It was familiar and safe. Or so I thought."

Greene gives me a one-armed hug. "Someone should have told you that you deserve better."

I lean into his embrace. "Someone did, and I didn't hear them. Youth is wasted on the young, right? So, where's the car?" I ask, giddy as a kid on Christmas morning with anticipation. Franklin had a 1952 Ferrari 340, one of only four in existence. It had been designed as a race car, and the rumble of its engine can be felt blocks away. Now that I know he was from Italy, I can see why he'd treasured it so. He loved that car and wouldn't let anyone but me drive it. He only made that concession because he'd refused to ride in my old Jeep after his stroke. Every Sunday, we would take it out and just drive all day with nowhere in particular to go. If there was one thing I could have saved for Franklin, it would have been this car.

"Lil, we've got to talk about this. It's more complicated than just signing a release form."

I hear her purring before she comes around the bend. The impound attendant looks as though he's died and gone to heaven. I look at Greene as I climb in. "Want to go for a ride?"

"I thought you'd never ask," he says with a big grin.

We head out on Route 50 towards Annapolis, blasting classic rock as loud as the stereo will go. Knowing we need to talk, once we get to Annapolis, I take him to Mike's for crabs.

After we're seated at a table overlooking the water, I say, "So, how do I get to keep the car? It must be worth a fortune. With all of Ash's debt, I'd have figured someone would have had their hooks in it."

Greene takes a sip of his water. "Well, as it turns out, Franklin left it to you, not Ashton."

"*What*? How did I not know that?" I pause to think about it for a moment. "Never mind. I know the answer to that." Ash was such a bastard that I'm sure he'd known but planned on keeping it for himself anyhow.

He laughs. "You don't have to be a detective to figure that much out. We had well established that you were not involved in any of his wrongdoings, so there was no reason for anyone to stake claim on it. Oddly enough, it was in the second detached garage, which we'd thought was just for lawn equipment. And the keys were in it. A lesser detective would have been suspicious about that. But you were in FBI custody, so you couldn't have done it."

Our half bushel of crabs is delivered. Greene and I grab our hammers and dig in. "That's really strange. I can't think of why the car would have been in that garage. But I really hadn't thought about it since Franklin died, so it could have been moved and I may not have noticed."

Green squeezes a little lemon on his crab. "Well, it's peculiar, and peculiar doesn't settle well with me. I had the guys in the auto shop check it thoroughly. Needed to make sure someone didn't leave it as a trap…tracking device or explosives."

That stops me mid-bite. "I thought I was in the clear now. I can tell you it isn't Grimaldi. So who should I be worried about?" I drop my crab claw on the table. "What aren't you telling me?"

"We don't think it's Grimaldi either. But I do think there's something you aren't telling me. Putting that aside for a moment, we've been keeping our ear to the ground for anything related to your husband. Some recent chatter we've picked up has led us to understand some things in your husband's records we didn't at first. He was in over his head with people that've long memories and big egos. Being screwed over isn't an insult they'd be quick to forget. These men demand their pound of flesh, and more often than not, they get it."

Losing my appetite, I put down my hammer and clean my hands with a wet wipe. "We were worried they'd come after you, but once the media attention to the case died down, we didn't hear anything more. It seemed like they'd moved on. That was until your face was plastered all over the funny papers. Suddenly, your name's popped up a few times in conversations that have made me uncomfortable. Nothing so serious as a direct threat, just dangerous people acknowledging that you're still alive and they're still out some serious cash."

Across the restaurant, I see a man get down on one knee to propose, the intended in her chair frozen in shock and delight. He has so much hope and happiness written across his face. The world is at his feet, just wanting to be seized. I envy his optimism. He hasn't seen how dark life can be. He still believes in happy endings.

Greene picks up another crab and hammers away at a claw. "Officially, the FBI isn't taking action at this time. But, I'd like to take a bit more precaution."

Wishing my water were something stronger, I take a long sip. "You're freaking me out. Is there or isn't there a threat? What kind of precautions are you talking about?"

"We don't know if there's anything to be worried about yet. This could just be my spidey sense on the blink. But I think now's the time to play it safe. I want you to put the car in storage. It draws too much attention, and you're too much of a target in it. And I want you to move again."

"Come on, Greene, again? I know it isn't permanent, but I just got settled. " I'm protesting, but deep down I know he's right.

"The damn press is all over you. They're camped out in front of your door, and your neighbors are complaining. I know your landlord isn't too thrilled about it either."

"How would you know that? Has he called?" I ask. He looks at me smugly, and suddenly it all makes sense. "So you're the TG in the TG Inc. on my rent check."

He nods, chuckling slightly. "What does the T stand for anyway?" I ask.

"Taegan. But I've been T to everyone as long as I can remember. Taegan's too tough to say, I guess."

I lean back in my chair and stretch. The knots that the masseuse removed yesterday have already come back with vengeance. "So, landlord, where should I move to now? Have any other condos for me to sublet?"

"Nope, this was a just a fluke that happened to work out. I got called over yesterday when someone broke in. We caught the guy. He didn't get anything, but that's because you don't have anything there. While I was there, I packed up the few things you do have."

I shove a piece of crab in my mouth. "Wow. I'll try not to let the door hit me on the way out. Where am I supposed to go tonight?"

Greene reaches across the table to wipe a piece of crab off my chin. "Meredith is on assignment, won't be back for a while. She said you can stay at her place as long as you need."

"Yes, I have such fond memories there," I say sarcastically. Actually, the truth is, I have spectacular memories there, minus the whole kidnapping thing.

"What about her roommate?" I ask. "I can't imagine she's going to be too eager to have me show up again."

"McCarthy? He's never home, and even if he is, you'll get along great with him. He's a riot. My favorite person to go on a stakeout with."

A boy roommate? This feels like trouble.

"Stop right there," Greene says, obviously sensing my hesitation. "Before you let your mind wander, Max's in a long term relationship. You'll have no worries there. Plus, he knows Gavin. They got pretty close while we were looking for Brooke. You couldn't be in safer hands. And like I said, he's never home anyway."

I motion for the check. "All right, Greene. I'll stay at Meredith's, I'll keep my head down, and I'll put the car in storage."

"Great, I have just the place, run by a retired FBI agent. I can run the car over there myself if you want," he says with a sheepish grin. "This way, we know you won't be followed or anything."

"Sure, sure," I say with a raised eyebrow. "This has nothing to do with you wanting a test drive, huh? Just remember, Greene—you break it, you buy it."

He taps his fingers on the table. "It'll make us even for the window I have to replace at the condo."

I grimace, thinking about the never-ending list of damages caused by this whole situation. "Okay, we're even. Now take me to my new temporary home."

As we leave the restaurant, I reach out to hand him the keys but quickly change my mind. "Why did you make me come and get the car if you were just going to have me put it in storage?"

"It was drawing a lot of attention being in evidence, more than I was comfortable with. I was asked about it by people who shouldn't have had so much curiosity about the case. I've started wondering if we have some guys on the take. Today, there's a mandatory sensitivity training. Everyone in the department is supposed to report, so it was a good day to sneak it out of impound and get it off the grid."

I lean against the car. "If it's mandatory, how'd you get out of it?"

He coughs into his hand. "Got the flu. Don't I look sick to you?"

I hold the back of my hand up to his perfectly cool forehead. "Yup, real sick."

"If someone starts sniffing around about the car, that'll tell me we have a mole somewhere."

"Sounds like something out of a crime novel. I sure hope your spidey sense is wrong."

"Me too, Lily. Me too."

I hand him the keys, and he drives like a bat out of hell all the way back to the city.

EIGHTEEN

Everything in Meredith's apartment reminds me of Gavin. It's going to be hard to get over him if I'm reminded of him everywhere I look. Trying to keep busy, I unpack. Greene only collected a small suitcase and two boxes worth of stuff, so ten minutes later, I'm settled into Meredith's room and left with nothing to do but think about Gavin. Disgusted by what a "mopey cow" I've become, I head up to the rooftop pool and swim until my body cries for mercy. It hurts, but in the best way.

I decide a long hot shower is in order after I hobble back to the apartment. Eventually, my arms and legs stop screaming, and I throw on some sweats and crash on Mer's bed to read some research material. After rereading the same paragraph ten times in a row without retention, I put it away and call Gavin. A very groggy Gavin answers, and I realize my error. "I called you crazy late again. I'm so sorry. I promise I'll get used to the time difference."

"Luv, you can ring me anytime. I've wanted to talk to you all day." I fill him in on the car situation.

"We know Grimaldi isn't a danger. If Greene is hearing stuff about you, I think we need to take it very seriously. He's not the type to overreact. Promise me you'll be careful."

I adjust the pillow behind me. "I wouldn't be surprised if he, Sully, and Mer set up my staying here as a way to keep an eye on me."

"However it came about, it's a good idea. Meredith called me this morning to tell me about it. She said the building has just upgraded its security. There should be no repeats of last time.

"That's a relief," I reply. "Greene said you know her roommate?"

I hear the sheets rustling on his end, and I picture him sprawled across his bed. It makes me wish I were there with him. "Max is a great bloke. You'll get along well with him, and I'll be able to rest easy knowing he'll keep you safe. You'll really like his girlfriend. She's a laugh a minute."

I gently pull my cross back and forth along the chain around my neck. "Greene says he isn't around much, so I'll likely be on my own a lot. Maybe you'll have to come back and keep me safe."

"You know there's nothing I'd like better. But, my luv, I have a company that needs me."

He pauses as though he has more to say. Most likely he's about to rant about how I should come and see him in London. Not in the mood, I speak before he has the chance. "Time for bed, Oxford. I'll talk to you later?"

"Good night, Lily. Sweet dreams, luv."

The next morning, I wake up and have no idea where I am. My brain starts to piece together yesterday, and after a moment, everything clicks. A new day, new home, another chance to start over. Begrudgingly, I get out of bed.

Today, I need to stop talking about changing my life and start actually doing something. I don't want to have one more conversation about how my life is in flux. If I'm going to declare that I'm in control of my life, I'd better take control already.

I throw on some running gear and pack my backpack with work supplies—my laptop, some files and pens—and run the four miles to Politics and Prose, an independent bookstore that was my favorite place to write and be inspired once upon a time. I haven't made it down this way in years, which could explain how I've forgotten about the enormous, painfully steep hill en route on Connecticut Avenue by the National Zoo. After the punishment I'd doled out on my body yesterday, my limbs are threatening to quit on me before I've made it halfway up. Panting for air, I slow down until a group of kids starts to snicker and point. They piss me off enough that I kick it into gear, keeping up a steady pace all the way to the bookstore.

Politics and Prose is a popular spot for writers. When I arrive, the place is packed, but I'm lucky enough to snag a seat when a woman leaves. As I settle in my seat, the familiarity returns, and I feel a surge of motivation. Today is about embracing opportunity when it presents itself—not just for talking about change but actually making it. The good thing about this blog, besides it being great writing exercise, is that it'll keep me honest. I'm determined to only write the truth, and a blog about someone doing diddly-squat definitely won't be successful.

Once my post for the day is written, I dig into my article. A ton of research is required to write the type of piece I want, and I've barely made a dent in my pile of reading when I notice the sun has set. The whole day has gone by in the blink of an eye. I hear my stomach howling for some attention, so I pack up and call it quits.

I debate running home verses taking the Metro. It's dark, but this is just about the safest part of DC. I decide to brave it. The run downhill is a piece of cake compared to the run there was. During my run, I have this nagging feeling that someone's behind me. I stop several times and look around, but I don't see anyone. It's probably all in my head, but I can't shake the feeling. I'd swear I hear another set of footfalls keeping pace with mine. Either there's someone following me or I'm losing my mind.

As soon as Meredith's building is in view, I sprint to the door. During the elevator ride up, my mind races, worrying that someone really was following me. By the time I lock the door behind me, I'm in a full-blown panic. I call Gavin and get his voicemail. I know I shouldn't, but I keep calling. After the fifth time, he answers.

"Lily, is everything okay?"

I pace the living room, flailing my arms as I shout into the phone. My words come out in one long jumble. "*No*! I think someone followed me home. I didn't see anyone, but I *felt* someone. I'm probably imagining the whole thing, which is even more upsetting. I don't want to turn into a crazy paranoid person."

"I'm so very sorry I didn't answer. I was in the shower."

"Oh, so you're naked. Now, I'm paranoid and horny. Thanks, Oxford, you're a lot of help," I joke, actually letting out a chuckle despite myself.

"I'm happy I can make you laugh. Sorry for getting you all worked up. I promise to rectify that as soon as I see you."

I sit down on the sofa and plop a throw pillow in my lap. "I miss you. I ran home, and all I wished was that you were here waiting for me."

"Wait. You went running? My little Lily that whined like a little girl when we did a little calisthenics? What's gotten into you?"

"You got into me. Now you aren't here to get into me, so I have to run off my sexual frustration."

He chuckles. "Who knew I would have such an impact on you!"

I roll my eyes even though he can't see. "Oh, can it, Oxford. You know exactly the impact you have."

"As much as I'm enjoying this discussion of my sexual prowess, I have to run. Figuratively, not literally. I've a conference call to China in a few minutes. These late night calls are just dreadful."

"Yeah, you and your naked, sexual prowess go call China. I'm off to shower by myself. Who knows what I'll get up to in there all by my lonesome?" I blow a raspberry for childish effect.

"You minx! You're truly evil, you know that?" I hear another phone ring in the background. "I really have to ring off now. Good night, luv. Cheers."

I check the lock on the door so many times that I worry I've suddenly developed OCD. Three glasses of wine later,

I'm finally calm enough to hop in the shower. But I take Meredith's softball bat with me, just in case.

As I'm toweling off after, I hear noises outside in the apartment. Panicking, I grab the bat. I stay in a batter's pose for what feels like an eternity, ready to hit a line drive through someone's skull if they try to come into the bathroom. Surprisingly, the mystery guest makes no move toward the bathroom, but I do hear him or her puttering around the living room and kitchen, whistling. What kind of sadistic, cold blooded axe murderer's out there whistling while preparing to send me to my doom? When the whistling turns to singing and the smell of onions wafts through the air, I realize that either my supposed killer is making me my last supper or perhaps I've misread the situation.

Just as I'm considering peeking out, there's a knock on the door. I scream, then immediately cover my mouth, realizing I've just given away my position.

A deep voice laughs. "You can come out, you know. I won't bite. Dinner'll be ready in ten. Gavin told me you're a hearty eater, so I made plenty."

I open the door a crack, bat firmly in hand, and a round face with enormous dimples pops into view.

"Hey there," the man says.

I jump and scream again, clutching the bat with both hands again. My brain starts to do the math and I finally figure it out. I step out from behind the door. "Max?"

"Yup. Who were you expecting?" he asks.

My heart starts to settle. "Sorry for the screaming. Last time I was here, I was kidnapped, so I'm still a bit jumpy."

He crosses his arms. "You mean you're not over that yet? Jeesh. Someone's a drama queen. No worries then. Come on out, get some grub, and we'll get acquainted."

Relief washes over me, and I start to calm my pounding heart. I lower the bat and try to catch my breath.

He points to the floor by my feet. "You dropped your towel there, Slugger. Not that I don't love a free show, but it might be better if we were properly introduced first."

I glance down, taking in my previously unnoticed nakedness. I gasp, turning beet red, and run for Mer's room where I slam the door behind me. I hear his deep belly laugh echoing, even from behind closed doors. I get dressed but stare helplessly at the door, not ready to return to the living room to face my humiliation.

"Oh, lighten up already," he yells from the kitchen. "If we're going to bunk together, shit's gonna happen. It's no big thing."

When I finally come out, with clothes on this time, he walks over with his hand out. "Max McCarthy, at your service." He points to the glass dining room table. "Now sit and eat. I made fajitas."

Max is one-hundred percent Irish, from his red, curly hair to his millions of freckles. He's about six foot two, with a strong, broad build. From the commanding way he speaks to his imposing posture, everything about him screams, "I'm a cop." He also has a thick Boston accent that reminds me of my childhood.

I sit down at the table and unfold my napkin, amazed that he's actually remembered to put out napkins. "I'm sorry I freaked out on you. Greene told me you're never home, so I was caught off-guard. Something creepy happened earlier, and I'm on edge. I was sure you were here to kill me."

He brings over a plate of grilled peppers, chicken, shrimp, and beef. "As a rule of thumb, killers don't usually sing. But I hear what you're saying. Sorry to have ruffled your feathers. Go ahead, dig in."

I take a tortilla and stuff it with rice, beans, and guacamole. "Yes, when I heard *'It's 5 O'clock Somewhere,'* I guessed I might be in the clear."

"Ohhh, a smart ass, eh?" he says in a *Three Stooges* voice. "We'll get along great."

After taking I bite, I say, "This is amazing!"

"Thanks," he replies. "I have seven brothers and sisters, and I was always on cooking duty."

I add a little sour cream to my fajita. "If you can cook so well, why was there no food in the house when I stayed here before?"

"Mer refuses to cook. Won't even make herself cereal. So, when I'm not in town, there's nothing around."

As it turns out, Max is a chatterbox. He spends the whole meal telling me his life story and not once allowing me to get a word in edgewise. He has a wicked sense of humor, and I laugh until my sides hurt. Greene was right. Max's as harmless as they come.

He's so busy talking that he's barely able to eat. After a particularly long spiel, he shoves the rest of his first wrap in his mouth and reaches out to assemble another. "So, tell me what gave you the heebie-jeebies today."

I put my wrap down on my plate. "It felt like someone was following me. Not that I saw anyone or anything. I just had a feeling like I was being watched. I'm probably just being paranoid."

"Slugger, with everything you've got going on, I'd trust your gut. I read your file, and there're some nasty names in there. Press and actual criminals both. You need to keep your eyes open and trust your instincts. I'm persona non grata with my girlfriend right now, so I'll be around a bit more than normal. I'm starting to think that may be a good thing."

"Can you help me get some pepper spray? I heard DC has a policy about it and it's hard to find."

He nods. "Mer should have a little one we can put on your keys."

"Thank you. Even if I never use it, I'll feel better having it."

He gives me a thumbs up. "Got to keep my roomie safe. What kind of agent would I be if you got axed while living here?"

I glare at him. "That makes me feel so much better."

He takes a big bite. "I live to serve," he says with his mouth full.

Stuffed, I push my plate away. "So, what did you do to get on the outs with your girlfriend?"

He wipes his mouth. "She saw some pictures of me undercover in… let's just say 'a compromising position.' I don't blame her for being pissed. There's no way I could be with someone that disappears for weeks at a time doing God only knows what. I'd lose it."

Thinking about me and Gavin, I say, "It must be hard for both of you to be apart for so long."

"She's a DC cop, so she understands why I do what I do, and for the most part, she's okay with the tough schedule.

But deep down, she's still a broad, with a broad's heart and a broad's emotions. Right now, the broad is winning out over the cop. She always gets over it, but she needs some time." He looks down at the table with sad eyes.

"That must be tough," I say as sympathetically as I can.

A light bulb seems goes off in his head, and he suddenly jumps up. "That reminds me, I'd better have Greene talk to her. She won't take calls from me right now, but if I don't let her know about you staying here, boy, my goose will be cooked!" He grabs his phone and starts texting.

I collect our plates and bring them to the kitchen. "I'm happy to talk to her, if you think meeting me would help," I offer while I'm rinsing off the dishes.

Max brings in the leftovers and puts them in Tupperware. "Once Greene tells her you're Gavin's girl, she'll settle right down. She already knows all about you."

"Oh, yeah?" I ask. Is there anyone Gavin doesn't know?

"Yeah. That boy's got it baaad. Me and Sabrina, my girlfriend, we were with him the night you went missing. Damn, he was a mess."

I let out a quiet laugh, but don't respond. What am I supposed to say? That night wasn't a picnic for me either.

"Sabrina's probably your biggest fan. She hated Brooke— hated that show she was on, hated what she did to Gavin. Brina comes from a family of junkies and has no respect for them. No tears were shed by her when Brooke died, I can assure you that."

Sabrina sounds like a tough customer. "I hope I get to meet her," I lie.

Once the dishes are done and the counters are wiped down, Max tosses the dish towel on the center island. "On that note, I'm going to hit the hay. Good night new, short-term roomie. See you *manãna*."

When I get into bed, I check my phone and see I have a text from Gavin:

Max just pinged me and said, 'Holy Hell. Lily is enfuego. Especially naked! Hot damn! On top of that she has a helluva baseball swing. P.S. Cricket is for pussies.' Care to explain?

I respond:

Nope, my naked stories are my business :) And cricket is for pussies. Glad to know I have an ally in my war against the UK.

G: I may be rethinking how happy I am that you're staying with Max. If I didn't know firsthand how madly in love he is with Sabrina, I would be more concerned. Now that I know that you'll be walking around naked with each other, my confidence is waning.

L: Don't get your panties in bunch, Oxford. It was a harmless mishap, and he was a perfect gentleman. He and S are on the outs, though.

G: I'm still not happy. Have to stop thinking about you naked and start thinking about my call. Talk to you tomorrow.

L : What? You can't focus on work thinking of me lying here naked?

G : NO!

L: What if I told you I was lying here naked and very wet?

G: Lily...

L: SO, so wet. I can't remember the last time I had an orgasm. Can you remember my last orgasm?

G: That's not fair

L: No? Why not? I'm the one that's all wet with no one here to help. Whatever is a girl to do?

G: Lily, if I break some sort of international diplomacy rules because I'm distracted, envisioning you lying there doing naughty things, I will be in deep shite. I have to be a grownup here. Want to call me in an hour? We can pick up where you've left off.

L: Relax, Oxford. Like I'm coordinated enough to masturbate and text. I'm just trying to get you all hot and bothered.

G: Mission accomplished.

L: Go back to your call. Don't cause an international incident. Goodnight, Oxford.

G: Goodnight, luv.

A minute later he sends me a picture—of him, completely naked and clearly aroused. So much so that my girly parts actually tremble at the sight. Game, set, match to the Brit. A text follows:

G: I play to win Lily. Don't you know that by now?

That limey brat! I turn the light out, go to bed, and have very steamy dreams.

NINETEEN

Over the next few weeks, I fall into a comfortable pattern of working all day, then dinner with Max most nights. Since I'm trying to work on giving my life balance, I've signed up for Bikram yoga and painting classes at Glen Echo.

In the mornings, I run to Politics and Prose, work all day, and run back home. It's been a great place to work, and the exercise has been great for me. There are many regulars who use the bookstore as their office, and we're all friendly to one another. It's like an office for we self-employed schlubs.

I start each morning working on my blog. I couldn't be more surprised at its success; more and more readers every day. I have no idea how they're finding me, but they keep multiplying. In addition, my readers have been making great comments that have spurred fascinating discussions. I'll admit that, originally, I didn't think the blog idea had any merit, but it seems to be taking off, and it's very satisfying.

Em's idea for the article series is also proving to be brilliant. The research has been captivating, and as I find people to interview and highlight in the piece, I feel both obligated and privileged to tell their stories. Every day, I'm waiting at the door to the store when they open and staying until the sun goes down.

When I run home, my pepper spray is always firmly in my hand. I never see anyone, but I feel eyes on me. Each day, I try to ignore it, telling myself that it's all in my head, but I can still feel someone lurking in the shadows, watching me.

Max's gone this week, and after an unsettling run home, an empty apartment only accentuates how alone I am. I know I should just take the Metro or hail a cab, but the stubborn streak in me refuses to let them win. If I let them scare me out of living my life, I've let them win. Whoever they are.

On Friday, the streets are abnormally crowded for a summer night in DC. A storm is expected this weekend, so maybe everyone has decided to stay in town instead of escaping to the beach. My invisible sidekick is there too. I can feel it. Each time I'm bumped, I nearly jump out of my skin. I feel the world swirling around me. I look around, and while I can't make out any faces, they all seem like they are watching me. My heart races. No matter how deep a breath I take, it feels as though the oxygen isn't getting into my lungs. Panting, I sprint as fast as I can home and bolt the door behind me, collapsing once I'm inside. Is there really someone there or am I just losing my mind? Panic sets in as I start to question my grip on reality. I'm not sure what's worse—that there may be someone after me or that I'm imagining that there is.

Jumping at every sound I hear, I grab the bat and position myself in the farthest corner of the bedroom. Desperate for human contact, I call Gavin, but I can't get words out, just hard sobs.

He's gentle and doesn't push for answers. He whispers soft, soothing words into the phone until I start to settle down. "Lily, please tell me what's happened."

I wipe the tears from my eyes. "I don't know. I felt like someone was after me again today, but it's probably all in my head. This whole experience is just killing me. I feel like I'm losing my mind. I'm seeing shadows and boogeymen."

"I'm so sorry, luv! Is Max there?"

I pull my knees up to my chest. "No, he isn't. I haven't seen him all week."

"I'm sorry you're alone at a time like this. I wish I could be there."

The sobs start again, and my words are garbled by my exaggerated breathing and sniffling. "I wish you were here too."

"You could... Never mind."

After carefully making sure the coast is clear, I slink to the coffee table, grab the box of tissues, and blow my nose. "Just say it Gavin," I say in a nasally voice.

"No. I won't. It's not productive."

"Just say it," I insist.

"If you came here, you'd be safe. I'd protect you," he proclaims.

"You can't guarantee that. Whoever is after me could follow me to you, and then we'd both be in danger."

"I don't think that would happen, and even if it did, I can keep you safe. You'd be safer here than you are there. Alone."

"Do you have a crystal ball?" I shout. "I sure as hell don't. I'm safest near the FBI. And even if you could keep me safe, this's my mess. I need to fix it. I don't need to bring it across the pond and drag you into it."

"That's where you're wrong. You don't have to handle this on your own. I'm not telling you to move here. I'm suggesting you take an extended holiday until we can figure it out together."

"I don't need you to figure it out for me. It's my problem to solve. I do not need you to save me."

"You're so bloody stubborn. Why won't you let me help you?"

"You don't want to help me. You want to take care of it. I don't need you to take care of it. I need you to be there for me while I take care of it. If you want to help me, back off. I told you I can't run away with you. I told you I'm not ready, that I need to work on me. Pushing me to hop on a plane to London is *not* helping me. It's suffocating me!"

"You're being melodramatic. I'm offering you safe haven."

"Some safe haven. Because of you, I've lost my privacy. I've been humiliated on national television. If I were to come to London, the press would come after me even harder. I can see the headlines now: *Whore Moves into Brooke's House.* Won't that be a nice clip to send with Christmas cards this year? If you are so desperate to save me, Gavin, why don't you save me from that?"

There's dead silence on the other end of the line for nearly a full minute before he speaks again. "This isn't productive. I've offered to help, but you don't have to accept it. It's your life. Good night."

Before I can say anything in response, my cell phone beeps, telling me the call has ended. Infuriated, I get into bed and stare at the ceiling. Now I'm paranoid and pissed off. A horrible combination.

The next day, I go my through usual routine. Run, work, run. After my fight with Gavin, I'm more determined than ever not to let my fear get the best of me. I will not be a victim. I will not be intimidated. I refuse to hide. Fortunately, I don't feel my shadow followers today, so I'm breathing a little easier. Perhaps even they can see they shouldn't screw with me today.

I ignore Gavin for the whole weekend. I'm still too angry to be "productive," so there's no point returning texts or calls. I don't know why he can't understand that I need support, not a savior. When I allow my mind to wander to darker places, I wonder if our relationship is really about us or about his need to make up for what happened with Brooke. Like he's trying to salvage something from the ruins of his past failures. In my less-estrogen-influenced moments, I tell myself that I'm making something out of nothing, but the thought's still there, in the back of my mind.

On Monday morning, I wake to a knock on the door. A florist delivery man stands there with a gigantic potted plant full of beautiful white flowers. *Who the hell is sending me a potted plant?* I thank the man for bringing it in and open the envelope. There's an information card stuck among the blooms that tells me the plant is a peace lily and how to take care of it. Behind it is another envelope.

I'm waving the white flag. I understand you need time, and I'll do my best to give it to you. I won't stop offering, because I always want you to know that I'm here for you. But I promise to do my best not to push.

Can we call a truce?

Gavin

Well, I give him bonus points for creativity. I've never heard of a Peace Lily, which is surprising because my mother was obsessed with lilies and grew every type she could get her hands on. The flowers are beautiful and I don't want to keep fighting with him, so I send a text:

Truce accepted. Thank you for the beautiful flowers. Let's try to talk tonight. I promise I'll play nice.

He calls me around three thirty. I'm in my writing zone, so it's a horrible time to break away, but I do it anyway. I throw my laptop in my bag and step outside the bookstore to take the call. The traffic from Connecticut Avenue is oppressively loud, so I walk around the back of the building.

"Hey there," I answer. "Thank you again for the flowers. They make the whole apartment smell beautiful."

"You're welcome. I figured out you weren't going to return any of my communication attempts, so I needed to try a different approach."

I kick a pebble across the parking lot. "I needed some space. I—"

"You don't need to explain," he interrupts. "Let's just let sleeping dogs lie, okay?" It's the best thing he could have said. I have no interest in rehashing this argument since I know we'll never agree.

"Sounds good to me."

"I think a part of it is that I miss you," he explains. "I'm going through a lot, and I wish I were with you. You're going through a lot too, and I want to be there for you as well. It's hard."

"I thought we were letting it go," I reply. He's not wrong. I miss him more than I ever expected to. He's the first person

I think about when I wake up and the first person I want to share good news with when I get it. When I'm scared, I crave his comfort and reassurance. I need him, and I don't want to. It makes me bitter that he's not here, angry that he had to leave, and I take it out on him.

"You're right. Sorry. Look, I have to hop on a plane to Berlin in about five minutes, so I must go. I wanted to at least call and make sure we're okay."

"We're okay. Don't worry."

"Oh, I'll always worry. It's who I am. That's part of my package."

"Thank goodness there are so many other wonderful parts to your package. I can overlook your hero complex. Just because you look like a superhero doesn't mean you have to be one."

"I look good in a cape. And really, there's no other situation in which a cape is appropriate."

This makes me smile for the first time in days. "You in spandex and a cape... Hmmm, happy thoughts."

"Good to hear that smile in your voice. I'll call you when I can. But probably not until late tomorrow. I'm swamped with work."

"Okay, Oxford. I'll talk to you soon. Safe travels."

I let out a deep breath full of tension and relief. I'm glad to not be fighting, but nothing has been resolved. The issues are still there. He can't leave London. It's simply not an option for him. I know I want to be with him, but I'm not ready to move across the ocean, and I'm not sure my heart can handle this long-distance relationship.

Fortunately, Max gets back into town on Monday night and is home the rest of the week, which takes my mind off things. From what he tells me, it sounds like Sabrina isn't budging on their breakup. His heartbreak is my gain. I'm relieved to come home to a person instead of an empty apartment. We get along well, and having such a good cook to have dinner with is very nice. Life is much less lonely with him.

****

Max wakes me up by blasting Jane's Addiction from the kitchen as loud as possible. I struggle to get out of bed and walk out to tell him off.

"Whoa, angry zombie bitch is *not* a good look on you."

"Good morning to you too, jackass," I bite back. "What's with the morning serenade?"

He flips the eggs he's cooking without a spatula. Just one smooth flick of the wrist sends the eggs flying into the air, and he catches them effortlessly with the pan. "We've got to talk."

"Really? I figured you woke me up just to torture me."

He ignores me as he futzes around, cooking his breakfast.

"Yo! Max, want to share?"

"Are you done being an angry zombie bitch? 'Cause I can wait."

"Fine," I say through gritted teeth. "Whatever do you wish to discuss, dear?"

He slides the eggs onto a plate and hands it to me. "That's better. So, the news is we have to move out."

"Max, you must be kidding me. I just got here!" I know I shouldn't shout at him, but I can't believe what he's telling me. Greene had led me to believe I'd have a few months here before I had to move.

217

He cracks two more eggs into the pan. "I don't make the rules, sweetheart. I just enforce them. Meredith has been transferred, and she's got to sell the place. It goes on the market today. I wonder if she has to disclose that someone was kidnapped here. Or is that just with murders?"

My stomach grumbles, but I can't eat. I push the plate away. "Max, I do not love you right now. Stop trying to be funny. I've got to figure out what I'm going to do."

"Well, I know what I'm going to do. Sabrina has agreed to let me move in!"

"Ah, so that explains the annoying happiness. When did all this happen?"

He puts three pieces of bacon on my plate, ignoring the fact that I've made no move to pick up a fork. "The law sleeps for no man, Lily."

Picking up the bacon, I move it to his plate. "What fortune cookie shit are you selling me? The sun isn't even up yet. English please."

"Mer and Sabrina figured this all out yesterday. I got a text twenty minutes ago."

"So you're out of the loop, huh?"

Max stomps his foot. "Shut up, I'm in the loop," he says like a whiny child. "Well, I'm moving in with someone in the loop." He does a ridiculous happy dance. "And the sex embargo has been lifted!"

What a dork. A dork with a place to go—while I'm back to square one. The money from the sale of the land has gone through, so I guess I should just buy a place of my own. The thought's a little intimidating. I'm not ready for that kind of commitment. However, it does make more financial sense than renting.

After only one day on the market, the condo sells. Max and I have to be out in three weeks. Max, of course, can't wait to move in with Sabrina. He's kind enough to offer to go condo shopping with me, and he tries to keep his gloating to a minimum. I know I want to be in the city, but other than that I'm open. Unfortunately, as my price range is quite a bit below my current living arrangements, each place I look at is a bit disappointing.

Gavin and I are like ships passing in the night. We constantly miss each other's calls. We can't seem to master the time zone issues. I haven't told him about the living situation changes because I know he'll say I should just move to London. I don't want to have that conversation again. I know I'm being distant, and it's probably clear I'm holding back. Each time we talk, it goes nowhere, and one of us gets off quickly out of sheer frustration. It's not good.

Work is my focus. I'm making headway on my writing projects and have gotten to the point that I have to travel to do my interviews. I go to Detroit to meet several former auto plant workers, along with a former auto executive who went from making two million dollars a year to tending bar just to keep the lights on. I travel to Iowa and meet several farmers and their families who tell me their own heartbreaking stories. My last trip is to Phoenix to meet former techies that lost it all when their companies abandoned their satellite offices in the desert.

These stories become bigger than just a snapshot of the economy's impact on real Americans. It's become about the way that people adapt to trauma and reinvent themselves. Each person I meet has had their life turned upside down and inside out, and yet they've all persevered. Quite remarkable.

I'm making great progress researching backstories for my piece when Gavin calls. We've barely spoken in days, but I just want to type my notes before I lose my train of thought. I foolishly pick up and basically ignore him as he goes on about some problem he's having. My half-listening skills are so pathetic that I can't even begin to guess what the problem may be.

Understandably, he gets frustrated, and I finally just shout at him that I have to go and hang up. I throw my phone in my bag and try to pick up where I'd left off, but I'm too upset to work. My mind blanks. I can't recall what I'd been thinking before the call, and now I'm pissed. Pissed at him for calling while I'm working. Pissed at me for losing my temper when I haven't talked to him in days. Pissed at him some more for living so goddamn far away. Out of frustration, I kick at my bag but miss completely and stub my toe.

Trying not to howl and draw even more attention to myself, I reach down to massage my foot. A pair of flip-flops worn by surprisingly well-kept man feet step into view.

"You okay?" Mr. Pedicure asks.

Just wanting him to go away, I ignore him and continue to rub my foot.

The man taps my shoulder and crouches down. He has my cell phone in hand. "You chucked this."

I take my phone and gently toss it on my table. "Thanks," I murmur.

He stands and leans against the bookshelf adjacent to my table. "I'm Charlie, Charlie Murphy," he says with an outstretched hand. "You look like you're having a tough day."

"Yeah, Charlie Murphy, you could say that. Hi, I'm Lily." I shake his hand. "Thanks for getting my phone."

Charlie's good-looking, with wavy chocolate-brown hair, olive skin, and golden brown eyes. He's around six feet tall and well built, clearly someone who works out. He's no Calvin Klein model, but he has the "boy next door" thing working really well for him.

"Why the tough day?" he asks.

I could never begin to tell a complete stranger the truth, so I give him the simplest non-answer. "Boyfriend drama."

His golden eyes find mine. "Well, I find that hard to believe. Any guy fortunate enough to have you should be thanking his lucky stars."

I sigh internally. We were having such a nice moment, and he had to ruin it by flirting. The last thing I need is another man trying to get into my life. If he only knew what I was really like, he'd run in the opposite direction. I'm like that one piece of candy in the chocolate box, the one that looks so yummy on the outside, but once you take a bite, you find out it tastes like rusted nails, and no matter what you do, the taste lingers in your mouth for days. With just that one bite, the whole box is ruined.

"If only it were that simple, Charlie," I reply. I look at my watch and see it's starting to get late. I quickly shove my things in my bag and say, "I've got to run. See you around."

I run home and find Max halfway through a bottle of scotch and a bunch of empty beer bottles scattered around the kitchen. How does that saying go? Liquor before beer, in the clear, beer before liquor never sicker? I think Max is probably in for it, by the look of things.

After twenty minutes of trying to make heads or tails of his drunken babbling, I think I have the story. It seems things with Sabrina took a turn for the worse. She'd tried to lay down some new rules for life together, and it did not end well.

"Pull up a bottle. Mer's brother dropped off a bunch of new samples today. This scotch only sucks at the beginning. By your sixth or seventh shot, it tastes less awful."

I pour him a glass of water and place it in front of him. "What a ringing endorsement. I'm a tequila girl. The scotch is all yours."

He pours the water into the pot of a nearby plant, refills the glass with scotch, and slides it across the table to me. "Listen here, Slugger. You can drink with me, but we drink like men. No sharing our feelings. No crying. No overanalyzing. Absolutely no head shrinking. We talk about men things, like guns and cars and boxing and stories where we were badasses. So, if you're going to sit at this table, check your vagina at the door."

I bring the glass up to my mouth, but the smell is so foul I can't bring myself to take a sip. "You know about boxing?" I ask.

"No, but that doesn't mean we can't talk about it. Who says you have to know about something to talk about it? Didn't I tell you we're talking like men here?" He's hilarious when he drinks. He already talks with his hands when he's sober. When he's drunk, it's more like his whole body moves when he speaks.

I pat him on the arm. "How 'bout them Redskins?"

Max shoots the rest of his drink, sighs, and says, "Sabrina loves the Redskins." He lays his head down on the table and starts to cry. So much for talking like men.

He pours his heart out for about an hour, mostly incoherently. At one point, he becomes convinced he needs to run to her and beg forgiveness. He stands up, takes three steps to the door, and then crumples to the floor in a heap, passed out. I try to get him to bed, but he's out cold. I pull the blankets from his room and make him a bed on the kitchen floor before curling up with my own pillow next to him, determined to keep an eye on him. The last thing I need is to wake up to a dead roommate.

All of his talk has made me feel horrible for the way I treated Gavin today. I try to call him, but his phone goes right to voicemail. I've never known him to turn his phone off before. Suddenly, I miss him so much it hurts. I dig out his blue shirt and put it on. It no longer smells like him. I feel as though I'm losing him.

TWENTY

When I finish my first cluster of stories, they've completely surpassed my expectations. Em helps me shop them around, and we find there's a lot of interest. I'm also getting calls from magazines requesting me to write specific pieces. I feel like I'm actually making a go of this freelance reporter thing.

One of the assignments is taking me to Boston next week. It's a medical piece, and I'm feeling a bit out of my depth, so I've buried myself in research.

Lately, Charlie's been at Politics and Prose every day too, working from open to sunset just like me. He's a sweet enough guy, and I have to give him credit for his effort. He always compliments me on how I look, which is a little surprising when I run there every day and generally look like a wreck. His crush is cute, but I'm careful not to encourage it. There's only one guy I want crushing on me.

One day, the bookstore has to close midafternoon—an electrical issue or something. Before I can start my trek home, Charlie asks if I want to grab a late lunch together. I know it may send him mixed signals to say yes, but I'm starving. We walk to The Grille From Impanema, a Brazilian restaurant in Adams Morgan. It's one of my favorites. Not only does the owner always make it a point to stop by and tell me stories about her childhood in Brazil or the crazy antics of her grandchildren, but they offer Brazilian-style tapas. I never pass up on the opportunity to try a little bit of everything on the menu. Judging from the way Charlie's eyes bug out when I order, he must not be used to a woman who orders more than a salad. All I can say is thank God for yoga pants!

After we place our orders, Charlie and I stare at each other, not knowing what to say. I'm nervous, and I don't know why. I never get anxious talking to people, but there's something about him that makes my mind go blank. He's not remotely intimidating, though. Quite the opposite. He has this 'aw shucks' look about him that makes him seem so sweet and innocent. If he only knew the darkness in my life, he'd probably run away as fast as his legs would take him.

"So, Charlie, you from around here?" I ask, trying to break the awkward silence.

He smiles shyly. "Nope. I just moved here from Chicago."

I unfold my napkin and lay it on my lap. "That's a big move. What brought you here?"

"I was working at *The Tribune,* but got booted out in the last round of 'downsizing.' I started doing some freelance work and found out that if you're doing freelance, DC is a pretty good place to be. So here I am."

"There's no shortage of stories here, that's for sure!"

"Have you always lived in DC?" he asks at the exact same time I say, "Are you from Chicago originally?" We both quietly laugh. I gesture for him to go first.

"I'm from McCallsburg, Iowa originally. Grew up on a farm. Pop always wanted me to take over, but I get queasy at the sight of blood. After the third time I passed out into a big pile of manure, I told him farming wasn't for me. It broke his heart when I left for Northwestern." He points to me. "Your turn. Are you from here?"

Crap. I don't want to talk about me. Right now, he's just sitting across the table, looking at me with bright eyes, as though I'm just a typical woman who lives a typical life. If I tell him the truth, even a modified version of the truth, that light in his eyes will disappear and be replaced by pity or fear.

I can't deny that I love the way I feel when he looks at me that way. For that brief moment, I feel normal, and I don't want to lose that feeling. Is it so wrong to want to have one small part of my life that's just about me and not my drama?

"Lily?" he says bringing me out of my thoughts. "Are you from around here?" he asks again.

I smile. "Yup." I point behind him. "Oh, look. Our food's here!"

The food is amazing, and as usual, I've ordered way too much. That doesn't stop me from putting it all away though.

I manage to shift the conversation away from our personal histories and steer us toward more professional subjects: stories we've written, stories we've botched up horribly, upcoming projects. Occasionally, he asks something personal, and I either dodge the question or feed him a white lie. The conversation flows easily, and we end up staying till long after the dinner rush has come and gone.

It's nice to be with someone who's not surrounded by drama. No paparazzi. No hit men. Charlie's just an average guy. His days seem to be filled with ordinary things like going to work, going home, and spending time with friends. Rinse, repeat. His biggest problems are an occasional flat tire, too many parking tickets, and annoying landlords. And, he's here. In the US. The same time zone and everything. The simplicity is enticing.

Charlie understands my work and is excited about my projects. To be fair, Gavin is too. In fact, he often has really good ideas, but Charlie understands the technique and strategy that goes into the work. It's nice to talk to another professional in the same industry. And if I'm being honest, I'm starved for attention. I guess that's really what it comes down to.

Our server gives us the evil eye from across the restaurant, a clear sign we've overstayed our welcome. I leave a huge tip and pick up my to-go bag. "Thanks for hanging out with me," I say to Charlie as we walk out the door. "This was fun."

"Can I give you a lift?"

I smile. "I'm good."

"You sure? Where do you live? You might be on my way. I get nervous thinking about you running home at this hour. There are some scary guys out there."

He smiles and gives me those eyes that make me want to believe the world is just full of rainbows and puppy kisses. He's such a sweet guy, and I should come with a Surgeon General's warning that being in my life will result in being sucked into a black hole vortex of death and destruction. I feel like a selfish bitch for even spending time with him. Max has warned me about letting anyone new in right now. Not only for my protection, but for theirs as well. I need to keep

Charlie at a safe distance so when the shit hits the fan, he won't be hurt by the fallout.

I smile. "I'll be fine. Thanks, though."

He shakes his head, looking disappointed. "My father would whip me if he knew I'd let a woman walk home alone. I can hear my grandparents rolling over in their graves! You're killing my reputation as a gentleman."

I pat my stomach. "I need to work off the enormous amount of food I put away."

He frowns but holds his hand up in defeat. "All right. Just be careful."

I wink. "See you, Charlie."

I walk away from Charlie feeling lighter. This afternoon has been a little vacation from my life, and it was delightful. But, sadly, I know it was all a lie. Charlie may be a fun distraction, but he can never know the real me.

My good mood has dissipated by the time I get home. The dark funk I've been in for weeks has returned. When I open the door, Max grabs his dinner plate and bolts to his room. I can't say I blame him. Lately, I've been cranky and short-tempered. I don't mean to jump down his throat all the time. If only he'd stop saying things that drive me crazy, we'd get along so much better.

It's not all on him—I know I'm to blame. I'm not sure what's wrong with me. It's as though I've lost patience for everything and everyone. I could really use an emotional makeover. Despite my downright nasty behavior at times, Max sticks by me. I'm lucky to have him, even if the sound of his voice is like nails on a chalkboard these days. Thankfully, I manage not to kill him long enough for him to finally take me condo shopping.

After looking at what feels like a million places, I think I've found one I'm happy with. Not as swanky as Meredith's building, but it does have twenty-four hour security. I make sure Sully and Greene give it a once over and award the security their seal of approval before I put in my bid. I want to be in a high traffic area, and the building is in DuPont Circle. Doesn't get much more high traffic than that.

It's a two-bedroom with a den, so I could set up a proper office and comfortably work from home. There's even room for Max. He swears he and Sabrina are going to work it out, but I'm not holding my breath. I still haven't met her, but she doesn't strike me as the type to back down. I've yet to hear anything about this woman that sounds as though she's worth the headache and heartache she causes. I'll never say it to Max, but I secretly hope she doesn't take him back. He deserves much better.

I suppose Gavin's friends could be saying the same thing about me. Most of the time, we only exchange voicemails. When we do speak, we spend more time bickering than talking. If he asked, I couldn't tell him one thing that's currently going on in his life. I'm not sure if it's because he hasn't shared or I haven't been listening.

He's still the first thing I think about in the morning, and throughout the day, a million little things come up that I want to share with him, but I don't. Why don't I? How simple would it be to send a text to let him know I'm thinking about him? When I look critically at all of our exchanges in the last few weeks, it's always been me who starts the fight. He tries, but I always push him away. I wish I understood why.

Scared I might push him right out of my life, I've decided to work harder to improve our relationship. Over the week leading up to my trip, I make a concerted effort to call at good times and to focus on him when we talk. Once I've let him back in, I'm smiling again. It's like a blanket of sunshine has wrapped itself around my life. I smile at people on the street, instead of cursing them under my breath. Even Max notices that Angry Zombie Bitch has taken a leave of absence. When Gavin and I are in sync, it's as though all is right with the world again. All of this long distance is still hell, but when it's good, it's *so* good. I have to hope it'll all be worth it one day.

******

A few days before my flight to Boston, Em calls to tell me she'll be in town for the night. She's scheduled to be a talking head on some news show about the economy earlier in the day, and then tomorrow she's guest-lecturing at GW. In between, she has a full evening planned for the two of us. I don't know where she finds all the energy, but I dutifully get gussied up to hit the town. I glance at the clock and realize she's due any moment, so I quickly finish getting ready.

Max lets out a wolf whistle when I walk into the living room. "Well, look at you, letting your inner hooker out! Can that skirt get any shorter?"

I put my hands on my hips and glare evil death rays at him.

"No, really, it's a question," he says with a smile. "Can you even call that a skirt? It's more like some fabric hoping to be a skirt but not quite getting it done. Just who are you trying to catch with that trap you're wearing?"

"Thanks, Dad. You always say the sweetest things." I put my lip gloss in my clutch. "My best friend's in town, and we're going out. I'm twenty-six, and I've been living like I'm forty. Actually, I think most forty-year-olds probably live a more exciting lifestyle than I do. I deserve a little fun, right?"

"Sure, Slugger. You deserve all the fun you can muster. Just don't conjure up the wrong kind of fun. You're spoken for, don't forget."

I stop at the mirror in the hallway and try to tame a fly-away lock of hair. "Catching a few male glances'll help my ego and won't cause any harm. So chill!"

He snorts. "Oh, you're gonna catch some glances, all right."

My phone dings, alerting me to a text. I dig my phone out of my clutch before crossing the room to kiss him on the cheek. "Em's downstairs. I'll see you later. Don't wait up."

He looks disappointed. "She isn't coming up? I was hoping to meet the mysterious Em. Are you coming back here after?"

I wipe my gloss off his cheek with my thumb. "Not tonight. You'll meet her another time, after we move into the new place."

"First of all, Sabrina and I'll work it out. As much as you want me to, I ain't movin' in with you. Second, bring your pepper spray and text me when you get to her hotel."

I give him my best teenage-girl eye roll and hair flip combo move. "Whatevs on both counts. Good night!"

Before I can fully open the door, Max bolts across the room and slams it closed again.

"Damn, who knew you could move that fast?"

"Lily, I'm serious. You need to change." He pulls his phone out of his pocket and snaps a quick picture. "Don't make me send this to Greene and Sully. One look at this picture, and they'll have the whole FBI out after you. Should make for a fun evening. You, Em, and thirty guys in cheap suits watching you like a hawk. Change."

I reach for the door knob again. "No."

He gently grabs my wrist, preventing me from turning the knob. "Don't push me, Slugger. I push back harder."

I stomp my foot as I let go of the door. "Fine, I'll text you from each place I go, and I'll call you when we get to her hotel. Okay? Call off SWAT."

Before he can answer, there's a knock at the door, and Max gently hip-checks me out of the way to open it. "Wow. Do you believe in love at first sight, or should I open the door again?"

Em stares down her nose at him as she walks past. "Does that line ever work?"

"I don't know. You tell me?" He takes Em's hand and kisses it. "You must be Emily," he says in a voice I'm sure he thinks makes him sound cool.

"Guilty as charged. You must be Boston Max."

"Never been called that before, but hey, I like nicknames given to me by pretty women. How—?"

"What in the hell are you wearing?" Em shrieks as she pushes Max out of the way. "I said get gussied up not hussied up." She drags me by my arm into my room. "Get in here. What's wrong with you? Are you trying to look like a hooker?"

"That bad? I'm not going for slut. Just trying to show a little leg," I say.

She slams the bedroom door. "You look like you're trying too hard. Where did you even get that skirt? Can you call that a skirt?"

"Slugger, I think I've found my soul mate," Max shouts from the living room.

"Yeah, you two are quite the pair!" I yell back.

When did I inherit so many parents? I've been parentless since I was thirteen, now I seem to have them coming out of the woodwork.

Twenty minutes later, Em's picked out an outfit she finds suitable, and I'm dressed in something that's not from the hooker chic collection. I've been running my ass off for weeks, so I'd wanted to show off my killer legs, but I suppose I don't need to look like a tramp to do it. Clubbing attire has never been my strong suit. It's hard to find that perfect middle ground between saintly, sexy, and slutty. I often end up either too conservative or too risqué.

When we finally leave the bedroom, Max gives me the universal signal to spin around. I oblige and give him my best catwalk, which I'm sure makes me look ridiculous. It sets the two of them into giggle fits.

"Get dressed, Boston. You're coming with us," Em says. This is so out of character for her that I wonder if I've heard her right. Men typically have to work very hard to get an Emily invitation.

Once Max has thrown on a new outfit, the three of us head out to SAX. I've never been before, but I've seen plenty of Ashton's receipts for the place. It's a burlesque club of sorts, very *Moulin Rouge*. As we walk in and look around, I say, "I get why Ash spent so much time here."

"What? Cocksucker came here?" Em asks. She takes her hand off the railing and looks at it as though she's been contaminated. "Suddenly, I want to leave. How often do you think they sanitize this place?"

"Perfect," Max says. "I can tell Sabrina this was all research on the Preston case. We're still trying to track down Ash's secret hiding place. I'm not just going to a club where the staff struts around in lingerie. I'm following a lead."

"Want me to check your purse there, Maxine? 'Cause I really don't do the whole sappy 'What'll my girlfriend think?' stuff. Man up, pick up your skirt, and come drink, or cart your ass back home," Em says as she walks authoritatively down to our reserved area.

Max watches her go and says, "I seriously think I'm in love, Slugger. That woman... Wow."

I link my arm through his as we follow Em. "Be careful, Max. Em's a man-eater. She'll chew you up and spit you out without thinking twice. She doesn't do boyfriends. She doesn't do commitment. And she really doesn't do love."

"She might be the perfect woman," he says in a dreamy voice.

We drink and laugh and then drink some more. Tonight has turned out to be just what I needed.

Em points at me and looks at me with one eye closed. "You seem like you are getting your groove back, but something just isn't right," Em says.

"Yeah, I know," I reply with a shrug. "I'm trying to get my life together. The work part is great. The blog is taking off like wildfire. It's all thanks to you, Em. Since you started pimping it, my blog has just exploded. I have like twenty thousand followers. Last week, the actress that's in that new rom-com started following, and she's been reposting and tweeting about it. Yesterday, a woman on *Good Morning America* started following. It's just taken on a life of its own!"

Em holds up her shot glass with one hand and flips me off with the other. "Here's to my brilliant idea. Fuck you for doubting me."

I flip her off in return. "I'm sorry for doubting you," I reply.

"So, that's work," she says. "What about you? What are you doing for you?'

"I'm trying to figure that out, but it just isn't going anywhere. I'm running every day, burning off all that pent up sexual energy. To be honest, with Gavin having a body like he does, I'm bit self-conscious. So it makes me want to run more. I'm getting toned in all sorts of places, which is awesome. I've taken up painting, which I've wanted to do for years. And I take a bikram yoga class too."

"Yeah, and?" Em asks. "Why do you still sound… I don't know… Bored? Unfulfilled?"

I fiddle with the straw in my empty water glass. "As it turns out, I can't paint."

Max scoffs. "Oh, that's an understatement. I keep waiting for them to offer her money back to stop coming to class."

I reach my arm around his neck and give him a noogie. "That's why I love you. No sugarcoating here."

He pulls away and gives me one back. I'm sure it does wonders for my hair.

"Children, knock it off," Em says sternly.

Max and I pull apart, looking like scolded school children.

"Now, continue," she commands me.

"As far as the yoga goes, I know I should love it, feel more connected and Zen. All I feel is hot and bored. It's just not doing it for me."

"Oh, honey," she says in a voice that's dripping with pity. "There's no mystery there. You just need to get laid."

I take a sip of my martini and sigh. "I know."

"Well, don't give up. I'll figure out how to get a little more pep in your step. You're coming to Boston soon. Then you move, and I'll come down to help decorate," Em says. "We'll have fun."

"Max, is the furniture in your room yours or Mer's?" I ask. "Just trying to figure out if I need to buy for that room or not."

"I told you, I'm moving in with my girlfriend!" he whines.

Em and I both crack up. Even she can see that it's a lost cause.

"Speaking of Meredith," Em says. "Explain to me how an FBI agent can afford that condo. I looked it up. It costs a pretty penny."

"It's Mer's parents' place," Max explains. "Her dad was some hotshot lawyer, and this was their DC apartment. They retired and moved to Arizona, but they've been keeping the place here for her. Now that she's been transferred, they're happy to get rid of it. The condo fees are a nightmare."

"Ahh," say Em and I in unison.

I slap the table. "Now that we've cleared that up, I'm going to run to the ladies'," I say as I get up. "Max, Em loves guns just about as much as you do. That should give you plenty to talk about while I'm gone."

I've had quite a bit to drink and have to concentrate on walking so I don't fall flat on my face, but I make it without incident.

As I come out of the restroom, I walk smack into one of the club's dancers, stepping on her foot. "Oh, I'm so sorry.

Clearly, I've had one too many. Are you ok?" *How embarrassing!*

She's stunningly exotic. Dark skin and almond-shaped eyes that are so dark they look black. Her waist-length black hair is so shiny she belongs in a shampoo commercial. "Not the first time or the last time tonight my foot will get stepped on. You get used to it," she says politely.

"Occupational hazard, I guess? Again, I'm really sorry." I smile and try to step around her without breaking any toes.

She grabs my elbow. "Lily, wait."

I stop in my tracks and stare at her. "How do you know my name?"

"You're Ash's wife, right?"

I pull my arm back. "I didn't expect he spoke of me when he came here. Yeah, I was his wife. You know he's dead, right?" I have no desire to sugarcoat it for her.

"I heard. I'm sorry. He was a decent guy."

I cross my arms over my chest. "No, he wasn't," I snap back at her.

"You're right. He wasn't. I was just trying to be nice," she replies, looking at the floor.

"Well, if you'll excuse me." I want out of this conversation. Now.

I try again to walk past her, but she continues to block my exit. "Are you here looking for Crystal?" she asks.

"Lady, I have no idea who Crystal is, and I don't want to know. I didn't come here looking for anything but a fun night out with my friends. I didn't even pick this place! My imagination has been working overtime from the second I walked in the door, picturing all the things and women Ash got into while he was here. I've been trying to block it out because that asshole isn't worth one more second of my time. Whoever Crystal is, I'm sure she and Ash had something real special, but I don't give a shit. He's not my problem anymore." I storm off, praying she doesn't come after me.

When I get back to the table, I try to act as calm as possible. I'm sure if Em heard about the exchange, she'd probably find this Crystal and gouge her eyes out with her stilettos.

Em looks at her watch, and informs us it's close to one in the morning. "Pumpkin time, everyone. I've got to talk to undergrads in a few hours." She claps her hands. "Up, up! Let's go."

We stumble our way to the exit, and Em asks the valet to hail two cabs. "You two're going home, and I'm taking my suite for myself." She turns my face in her direction. "And you! You go home, wake the Brit up, and have some nasty phone sex. It'll do you good."

As she hops in her cab, she calls out, "See you next week, Lil. Please bring better clothing options than the ones I saw today. Boston, it's been a real slice. Take care of my girl." She blows kisses out the window as the cab drives away.

He looks longingly after her cab. "I'm totally in love."

Max and I decide to walk home as it isn't too far away. After my encounter, I'm riled up, and the walk should do me good. Max keeps me laughing the whole way, and slowly the memory of that wretched woman fades away. By the time we get home, I'm calm and fairly sober. As we walk in the door, I kiss Max on the cheek.

"Thanks for being so awesome, Max. Sabrina doesn't know what she's missing."

He laughs. "You really don't think she's going to take me back?"

I lean against the wall as I unbuckle my sandals. "She can't unsee the video of you going down on another girl. I know you say you had to as part of your undercover stuff, but she saw it. I'm sure the image is burned into her brain. If it were me, every time you got close to me, that's all I would see."

He throws his hands up in the air and paces. "She shouldn't have been going through the case file! She knew nothing good would come of it."

"But she did it anyway, and there's no coming back from that. Unless you give up going undercover, and even then..."

He scrubs his hands along his five o'clock shadow. "It's part of my job. It's not fair that she ask me to give it up."

"There's your answer," I reply.

He collapses on the sofa.

I kiss him on the top of his head on my way to my room. "Good night."

Something occurs to me as I reach my door. I turn around and ask, "Why the hell would someone take a video of that anyway? I can't imagine a scenario where you giving oral sex would be a critical part of a case."

"That's confidential," he mutters.

"Sounds like bullshit to me. I'm guessing that's what Sabrina thinks too."

After closing the door, I strip down to my underwear and climb into bed. Using my fingers to count the time difference, I realize it's almost eight in the morning in London and I may be able to catch Gavin on his way in to the office.

239

"Isn't this a wonderful way to start my day?" he says when he answers.

I yawn. "I just got in and thought I'd give you a ring."

He chuckles. "Max sent me a picture of you in a rather revealing outfit. I figured you were up to no good. "

I pull the covers up around me. "Em's in town. We went to a burlesque bar and drank many, *many* drinks. Max came with us."

"Max got to meet Em, huh? I'm jealous," he says in a teasing voice, but I suspect he means it. It's not the first time he's pointed out that Max carries out all the day-to-day boyfriend duties in his absence. If the roles were reversed, I know I'd be green with jealousy. He hasn't said anything directly, but I'm guessing that's the reserved English gentleman in him.

"Yes," I respond. "They bonded over their mutual dislike of my outfit."

"Your legs look amazing, but as the man in your life, can I veto you wearing it in public? Can you even call that a skirt?"

"Shut it, Oxford. I've heard all I want to about my skirt." I hear some sort of machinery in the background. "Where are you?"

Clanging and clattering echo through the phone. "Sorry, luv. I'm in my studio. Let me turn that off."

"You have a studio?" How do I not know about this?

"I haven't been in here in a while, but since I've gotten home, I've been inspired."

I pull at a stray string on the sheets. "Oh." I guess being home inspires him.

"Stop right there, Lily. I can hear those wheels turning in your head. You're the inspiration, my dear."

"Oh," I say with much more enthusiasm. "You're lucky you have a creative side. My paintings look like my paints threw up on the canvas. Not in a cool Jackson Pollock way either. Bad motel art is better than what I make."

"You just need a good instructor. We'll paint together one day, and it will be glorious," he promises.

"Well, everything is more glorious with you." Just hearing those words come out of my mouth makes me want to gag they're so sappy. But I can't help it. That's what this man does to me.

There's more clanging on his end. It sounds as though he's putting things away. "Speaking of being with me, what are you doing next Wednesday?" he asks.

A surge of excitement rushes through me at the thought of getting to see him, until I realize I won't be in town. "I'll be in Boston working on an assignment. Are you going to be in DC? Maybe I can find a way to get back." I grab my laptop off of the desk and boot it up, ready to search for airfare.

"No, Boston's perfect. I'm flying to Connecticut for a meeting with the Coast Guard on Wednesday. Can we meet in Boston that night? Will that work with your schedule?"

"Oxford, this is the best news I've heard in ages." I squeal like a little girl. I hadn't even realized I could squeal until now. "The conference I'm covering ends on Wednesday. I was going to spend a few days with Em, but she'll understand."

"It's only for one night. I have to be back in London for a meeting on Friday. But I figured one night was better than nothing," he says.

"It's amazing and just what I need right now." *In so many ways.*

We keep chatting until I get very sleepy.

"Luv, you're starting to snore," he says, waking me up. "I'm going to ring off so you can get some sleep."

I wipe some drool from my chin. "I don't snore!"

"Sure you don't."

"Shut it, Oxford."

"Good night, luv. Sweet dreams."

After hanging up, I have a long night of very happy dreams.

****

When I wake up, I'm just too tired to run, so I skip going to the bookstore to work. Before long, Charlie has sent a bunch of panicked emails. He claims he's worried something happened to me on my run in and wants me to check in. Nothing cools a hot guy down faster than desperation. I think it's time to cut Charlie loose. The relationship, while good for my ego, isn't good for my relationship with Gavin. If Gavin had a Charlie, I'd be furious.

Around noon, I'm still in my pj's going through notes when Max comes home with Sully and Greene in tow. "Oh, the three stooges. Either you have stopped by to take me to lunch or you have good news for me," I say as they come in. They look so somber the "Imperial March" should be playing as they enter.

"You know I never bring you good news, smartass," Sully says. The man is such a charmer. It's shocking he's still single. Max walks to the kitchen and grabs a bottle of tequila and a shot glass from the cabinet.

"Oh, you grabbed the Patron," I remark. "You must have fabulous news. Okay, boys, spill before the anticipation kills me."

Max points to the dining room table. "Sit, then shoot." He pours one and slides it across the table toward me as I sit.

Greene pulls up the chair next to me. I know it must be very bad if they're having him break it to me. He's the only one with a shred of empathy.

"Lil," he says. "Two days ago, a man was taken into custody. In an attempt to bargain, he offered up information about other crimes he was involved in. One of the things he said was that he was hired to watch you."

I take my shot and motion for Max to pour me another. "By whom? How believable is this information?" I ask.

"We believe it's reliable. He knows far too many specifics for it to be bogus," Greene explains.

I take the next shot and roll the glass between my palms. "Who hired this guy? And what does he mean by 'watch' me?"

"From what we can gather, he was hired by a man with ties to the Moreila drug cartel. They keep themselves fairly insulated. It's next to impossible to pin anything on them, but that's what it looks like. We uncovered some evidence that Ashton was tied to them, but nothing conclusive. This guy's given us some information that's helping us connect some dots."

"What kind of dots?" I ask.

Sully drums his fingers on the table as though he's trying to decide how much he wants to tell me. "We think Ash owed the cartel a shitload of money. At least five mill.

243

Maybe more. This joker was supposed to sniff you out and see if you had the money, and if you did, get it back."

Five million dollars? What kind of moron would ever put Ash in charge of five million dollars? This situation has become so much worse than I could ever have imagined. "So, was he following me? I'm sure he could figure out from my lavish lifestyle that I don't have five mil hanging around."

"He was hired to follow you, but from what he says, they weren't happy with his intel. Apparently, you're boring and don't give anything away," Sully replies.

I point at him. "See, I've been following the rules. Even Pablo Escobar thinks so."

Max slams his hand on the table, making me jump. "Dammit, Lily! This's serious. They've hired someone else, and he said this guy will chop you into pieces to get the information. He claims he doesn't know who it is or how this new guy operates, but he knows the guy works freelance and is very good at his job."

I motion for another shot. "So, what do we do?"

"We'd like to catch this guy before he has a chance to act. We want to try to draw him out. If he's supposed to be following you, we'd like to set up some exercises where we send you out and follow you to see if anyone else follows you," Greene explains.

I take my shot, then wipe my mouth with the back of my hand. "You want me to be bait?"

"Yeah, basically," Max says.

"Okay," I reply.

Max looks at me like I'm crazy. "That's it? 'Okay'? Do you understand what we're asking?"

"Lily's tough," Sully says. "I knew she'd be down for it."

"Let her hear the details first," Max retorts. He points at Greene. "Go ahead."

"We thought we would start using the car. If someone's watching you, they're probably keeping an eye on it. You'll go and get the car, run some specific errands, and then put the car away," Greene explains.

"Okay, let's get started." I get up to grab my purse.

"Slow down, eager beaver," Sully says. "We'll start tomorrow. We've got to get all the moving pieces in place first."

They try to give me more details, but I ultimately decide it'll be easier the less I know. I shoo them all out. As soon as I close the door, my body shakes with fear. The phone practically jumps out of my hand as I try to call Gavin. No answer. I text and email too but get no response. I'm so desperate that I actually call his work number.

"Mr. Edward's office. Mrs. Smythe speaking." Mrs. Smythe sounds like a British version of my third-grade teacher, a miserably bitter woman who was so hardened, we used to joke her face would crack if she tried to smile.

I find my voice and shakily say, "May I please speak with Gavin?"

"Mr. Edwards is not in," she replies. "Who may I say has rung?"

"Could you please tell him that Lily called, eh, I mean rung."

"Oh, Ms. Clark," she replies as though it pains her to say my name. "I will inform him as soon as he is available, though that may not be for several hours. He is at a testing site, and there's no mobile reception. It will be some time before he returns to London. Good day."

Dammit. Why does my boyfriend have to live so damn far away?

Before I make it back to the tequila bottle for another shot, the door opens. "You didn't think I was going to leave you alone to freak out, did you," Max says, bags filled with Chinese takeout in hand.

I run to his open arms and bury my face in his chest. "Thank you for coming back."

"Come on, let's eat in Mer's gigantic bed and watch *Deadliest Catch*. I'm so behind."

I grab the take out bag from him and open it. He's ordered extra potstickers for me. I kiss him on the cheek. "Best roommate ever, except for when you bring me bad news. I'm thrilled you'll be moving with me." For once, he doesn't protest.

We bring the food to the bedroom and set up the containers on a tray to prevent them from spilling.

"Let me ask you something," I say as I break apart my chopsticks. "So the guys that Ash was on his way to meet when he died were mafia. And this other group is a Mexican cartel. It seems crazy to me that he could be so involved with two different organized crime groups. Could you be wrong?"

Max puts his container of almond chicken down on the tray. "I wish I were. Crime syndicates always need outside partners. Lawyers, accountants, bankers, shipping and transportation, and people who are willing to help them launder money. From what we can tell, Ashton was an experienced money launderer. But what made him even more attractive was that he had connections. We're not sure how he got in so deep, but he had contacts everywhere. It made him very attractive to various types of criminal elements."

I drag my spring roll through the duck sauce. "Sounds like Ash. He was always Mr. Popularity no matter where we went. People are drawn to him like magnets."

"We're still going through his records and computer, but he was in deep. The Italians, the Mexicans. He even had some deals going with the gangs in Baltimore. Most white guys would get shot setting foot in that territory. But somehow, your husband pulled it off. That just tells you he must have been able to deliver on his promises. Otherwise, he would have been dead a long time ago."

I smile sardonically. "I'm so proud. My husband, tearing down racial boundaries one criminal act at a time."

Max shoves a dumpling in my mouth. "Don't think about it. It won't get you anywhere."

After chewing enough to speak again, I say. "One last question, then I want to send all my Ash memories back to hell where they belong. What's the difference between a cartel and a mob? The Italians seemed to be okay letting me go. Why do we think the Mexicans won't just do the same thing?"

He wipes his mouth and takes a long pull from his beer bottle. "The mafia and cartels are two totally different animals. The mafia are organized, with rules and structure. Each mob has a slightly different way of working. Some are broken down by families, others by geography, but each one has a hierarchical organization that's run like a business. Yes, they're violent, but there's an order to it. Cartels used to be that way, but once all the leaders ended up dead or in jail, all hell broke loose, and it became every group for themselves. Picture *Lord of the Flies*."

An image of Ash, half-naked and covered in war paint, running around a fire on a beach, flashes through my head. I know that's not what Max means, but I can't help laughing to myself. Max's tone is intense, and I know he takes this stuff seriously. Not wanting to interrupt, I nod as I munch on my Kung Pao Shrimp.

He continues, "No rules, no order, no boundaries. Survival is dictated by power. If you want something—territory, product line, whatever—you have to take it. The more violent, the better. The threat of retaliation must be so intimidating that it's a deterrent. People have to be too frightened to fight back."

"So what do they do to people who steal five million dollars?"

"Make an example out of them," he replies.

I swallow, fighting the lump forming in my throat. "Enough drug talk. Let's just watch the show.

At some point during our marathon, I fall asleep. I don't wake up until the next morning. A lot of tequila mixed with the knowledge that a drug cartel has a bounty on my head leads to surprisingly deep sleep. I don't really feel rested when I wake, but at least I got through the night.

Today's bait day. Max has left a note that I need to be down to the meeting spot by ten to go over everything, so I get up and get showered. What does one wear when acting as contract-killer bait? I go with a simple white sundress.

On my way out the door, I check my phone. Max must have turned the ringer off last night because I have nearly two dozen missed calls from Gavin. I skip to the final voicemail.

"Lily dear, I've just spoken to Max. Please tell me you're not going along with this blasted plan. Using you as bait is crackers! I'm furious with Max for even suggesting it." He releases a long sigh. I can just picture him raking his fingers through his hair while he thinks of what to say next. "If you're going through with it, please stay safe. I know it's tempting to try to catch this guy once and for all. I wish I could be there with you. I'm stuck in the lab for the next few days doing product testing. Mobile reception is limited. Ring me when you're done, and I'll get back to you as soon as I can. Please be safe, luv."

Since I can't talk to him, I send him a long email, outlining all the reasons I need to go through with this plan and all of the things I'm petrified might happen. Writing it all out is cathartic and actually alleviates my stress. With a newfound feeling that almost resembles confidence, I lock up the condo and head out. I know an agent's watching me leave, trying to spot anyone who might be following me from my building.

As planned, I head down the street toward the metro. When I get to the top of the stations stairs, I find myself fact-to-face with Charlie.

"Hey there, stranger! Where've you been?"

Christ, Charlie. Not now. I say the first thing I can think of that will make any man run. "Hey yourself. I wasn't feeling so hot yesterday. You know, girl problems. I'm on my way to the OB/GYN right now. It's pretty ugly."

After that comment, he should be running in the other direction, but he continues walking with me and instead looks determined to keep by my side. So I decide to turn it up a notch.

"The cramps are just out of control. And the blood!" I shudder. "There's just way more blood than normal. I feel like I should be dead with all the blood loss."

"Man, that sounds horrible! I hope you feel better!"

He's *still* there and not showing any sign of leaving. Until now, I've never met a man who doesn't bolt at the first mention of female issues. Who is this guy?

Since he's not deterred, I guess it's time for the big guns. "I think I may have a yeast infection to top it off. There's that smell-"

He suddenly looks down at his watch, finally showing a hint of squeamishness. "I've got to run. I'll catch you later. I hope you get... all that sorted out." He turns on his heel and heads back up the stairs.

Hanging on all the way to the yeast infection? Charlie's officially moved from sweet to creepy in my book.

When I get to the meet location, an apartment in a non-descript building in Columbia Heights, there are already about thirty agents there—way more than I was expecting, which is highly intimidating. They break down the plan. Today, I'm meant to take the car out and drive a prearranged route, make a bunch of designated stops, and then return to the garage.

Then "the fun starts" or so Max says. We'll come back to the apartment to debrief, which is when we'll go through all of the photos and video they film to see if anyone looks familiar. We could be there all night.

An hour before go time, the agents scatter to hide in mailboxes and behind bushes or whatever it is they've got to do before I hit the road. Meanwhile, I'm left to sit and stress. My phone chimes, alerting me to an email.

Sorry we couldn't connect before you start your "mission". Good luck, luv. I'm sure it's scary, but you are the strongest, bravest person I know. If anyone can do it, it's you. You'll be an excellent spy. Just pretend you're British, and you'll do just fine.

Love,

Gavin

He knows just what to say to make me smile.

Before long, Max tells me it's time for me to get going. So, I go collect Franklin's car and dutifully follow my map, trying to look as casual as possible. I'm nervous, but after I get moving I begin to relax. There are thirty agents watching me, after all. If anyone tries anything, one of the many someones watching my back will jump out of the shadows and get him. It's also completely possible that there's no one following me. So, I go about following my list of errands, trying to appear as normal as possible. Throughout the mission, I never see anyone, agent or bad guy.

When the day is over and I have to return the car, the garage attendant practically has to pry the keys out of my hand. Not only is the car fun to drive, but when I'm behind the wheel, I can almost remember what it was like before my life got turned upside down. Life with Ash may have been all thorns and no roses, but at least there wasn't someone lurking in the shadows waiting to take me out. As much as I don't want to turn in the car, I know that the sooner I put this all to rest, the sooner I get to keep the car full time. It's excellent motivation to put my all into catching this stalker.

After I say good-bye to the car, I take the Metro back to the meet location. While I wait for the elevator, I send a quick text to Gavin, letting him know my covert activities are done for the evening and I rocked them. No need for the British inspiration with the *Mission Impossible* theme song playing through my head the whole day. An *American* classic.

When I reach the apartment, the boys are getting things set up, so I take a seat out of the way. I play with my phone and notice several Google chat messages from Charlie, all from before the yeast infection conversation. Bet I won't be getting any more of those. Yeast infections are such reliable boy repellant.

The debriefing takes hours. The agents managed to take a million photos, and I have to look through each and every one of them to see if anyone looks familiar. By the end, I'm certain I've now seen a picture of every jogger, dog-walker, and nose-picker in the whole damn city. And after six hours, all the faces look the same.

With today being a bust, the plan is to have the agents follow me every day for five days, varying the errand locations, and see if we notice recurring people. It's going to be a long five days. On the other hand, it'll give me time to catch up on errands, and I'm going to get a cut and foil on the FBI's tab.

When I get home, there's a package for me at the front desk. It's wrapped in British flag wrapping paper. My heart soars, and I hope that it means that Gavin's here. The card reads:

Lily,

Before you get too excited, no, I'm not here. A friend of mine was going to Washington today, and I asked her to bring this to your apartment. Far faster than FedEx.

Since I can't be there to hold you tonight, I send this as my proxy. It's by far my favourite article of clothing I own. I hope it brings you comfort.

Wishing I were there,

Gavin

I open the box at the front desk, unable to wait, and get a whoosh of Gavin, as though he's somehow found a way to package his scent. Underneath the tissue paper is an Oxford sweatshirt that looks as though it has been through hell and back. I'm amazed the thing is still in one piece, considering all the holes and tears. Despite its decrepit state, it's soft as cashmere from the apparent years of wear. I absolutely love it. In fact, once I get it on, I may never take it off. I'm certainly never giving it back.

In addition to the sweatshirt is a stuffed Paddington Bear, sporting a tag that says, "Made with love in England."

I run upstairs, shower, and put on my new sweatshirt. It's heaven. I send him a text that says:

Love the present. Who knew you were such a Paddington Bear fan? BTW, threw away that dreadful sweatshirt that got mixed in with the bear.

I was hoping to get a witty reply from him, but I don't hear anything the whole evening. When I'm ready for bed, I take a selfie and send it to him and say:

Just kidding. Best. Present. Ever. Hope you don't expect to get it back, because it's now my absolute favorite thing that I own.

Over the next four days, the agents follow me as I go about my typical routine. They tail me on my run and then watch me work all day before following me home. I really feel for these guys. They have to watch me stare at my computer all day. What a shitty assignment! They send a female agent with me when I go to yoga, which is disappointing. I'd really wanted to see Greene or Sully trying to do the bird of paradise pose.

I spend my workdays staring at the blinking cursor. I have so much work to do, but I can't focus. Instead of writing, I keep looking over my shoulder to see if anyone's watching me. The one saving grace is that Charlie doesn't show up once at Politics and Prose the whole four days. The last thing I need right now is to have to deal with him. He pings me a few times on Google chat. Seems he has a bug or something. I haven't responded. Hopefully he'll get the message.

Over the course of the mission, I spend more time with Max, Sully, and Greene than I ever imagined I would. It's a good thing I love these boys because otherwise, I'd kill them before we've found whoever's tailing me. By the end of the week, we've managed to find three different guys that show up three or four times throughout the surveillance footage. Now, my part's done, and the boys get to track them down.

Before I know it, the conference I'm covering in Boston starts tomorrow. Max says he doesn't see a problem with me going, as long as I don't go off schedule and I stay in crowded areas. I suspect he's sending an agent to tail me in case I go rogue, but it's not necessary. I'm frightened enough to toe the line. I'm scheduled to spend my days at Harvard and then go home to Em's. Em has promised that we'll order takeout and spend our nights in. I have no idea what the plan may be for when I see Gavin, as I haven't been able to connect with him since before my joyride in the car, but Max says he'll take care of it.

Before I catch my flight the next morning, the real estate agent comes by the condo with the closing documents for my new place. After a million signatures, I'm officially a homeowner. Well, a condo owner. I've already packed up my few things in Meredith's apartment. Max has said he'll move them for me this week. I must have reminded him a dozen times to remember my peace lily. I can't forget the proof of the only time Gavin has ever backed down. As I lock up Mer's apartment one last time, I say a quiet good-bye. I've had a lot of memories in this place. Time to go and make some new ones.

TWENTY-ONE

Boston in the fall is beautiful. When I land at Logan, I find Bruce, Em's driver, waiting for me at the curb. He drives me over to the Harvard campus with just enough time to spare for me to wander around a bit and get my bearings. The next three days are dreadfully boring. Nerdy doctors talking about... well, it's hard to tell what they're talking about because they don't speak English—they only speak doctor. I wish my client had picked someone with a science background for this. I'm in over my head.

By Wednesday, the clock is ticking, and I'm desperate for an angle for my article. But for that I need a translator. During the lunch break between lectures, I scour the conference room for the perfect guy: nerdy, but not so introverted he'll be afraid of me or won't give me the time of day. I need a Leonard, not a Sheldon.

I spot the perfect target, and I go in for the kill. After popping an extra button at the top of my blouse, I prepare to pull out a tool from my toolbox of feminine wiles that I'd always sworn I'd never use. A hair twirl and a few high pitched giggles later, I'm just a dumb blonde who just can't understand all this complicated science "stuff." Dr. Ian Crammer is more than happy to explain things to me. He sits and talks with me until I understand the material well enough to write about it. Not only that, but he takes me around and introduces me to the most influential people at the conference. I guess he probably wanted someone to see that a girl was chatting him up. If that's the case, I suppose we both win.

By the end of lunch, I have everything I need, so I head out to get a mani-pedi and a wax before Gavin arrives. I'm not sure exactly what time he's supposed to get in. Poor guy is going to be exhausted after flying all night and then sitting in meetings all day. I know he made it harder on himself so that he could squeeze in a visit with me. But I'm thrilled he has.

I'm not sure where we're staying, and I haven't been able get a hold of him yet today. So I futz around Copley Place. Buy some very sexy lingerie, an amazing deep red backless cocktail dress to wear to dinner, and some fabulous stilettos on killer sale to go with it.

At five, I finally receive a text from Gavin. He wants me to meet him at the Four Seasons—penthouse. I should've known. Excited beyond measure, I practically run to the hotel. My heels echo on the black-and-gold marble floor as I walk with determination, searching for the elevator. I've pushed the button a dozen times, as if that will make the car arrive quicker, when my feet suddenly leave the floor. My left shoe falls off my foot as I'm spun around. "I couldn't wait another second," Gavin says in between kisses.

After we've been kissing for what seems like forever, he puts me down. I open my eyes and see the whole lobby staring at us. Guess we've made a scene again. His chest puffs up, telling me he's as proud as can be, but I'm mortified. I snatch my shoe off the ground and scurry onto the elevator. Thankfully, he collects my forgotten bags, which I had dropped during our public kiss-fest.

The elevator fills quickly, pushing us to the back of the car. Gavin's hand presses possessively across my stomach, and I lean my head against his chest, his heart pounding in my ear. Closing my eyes, I float in the heavenly smell of his cologne. He pulls me tight against him. My contours hug his shape, as if I were drawn to fit around him. Being encased in the sensory experience that is Gavin is blissfully orgasmic, even fully dressed. In the weeks since he left DC, I've felt out of sorts, but being next to him for this three-minute elevator ride, I feel myself coming back together.

He threads his fingers between mine just before the elevator car opens, then kisses the back of my hand before leading me to our hotel room. Few words have been spoken between us, but the anticipation is palpable. He winks as he slides the key card in, unlocking the door. The green light clicks on, and in one smooth movement, he pulls me in the room, kicks the door closed, and has me pinned against the wall.

Gavin brushes a stray lock of hair out of my eyes. "I didn't think it was possible, but you're even more beautiful than I remember."

Unable to hold back another moment, I kiss him. We become a tangle of tongues and limbs, crashing together, eager for more contact. My fingertips trace the toned muscles of his back as his arms envelope me, pulling me so close that I can no longer ignore the already impressive bulge in his pants. A deep groan escapes his lips when I wrap my legs around him, desperate for friction. He pushes me harder against the wall. I'm sure there'll be a bruise tomorrow, but the slight pain will be such a delicious reminder of this moment.

Gavin's movements are raw, almost violent with desperation. He cups my ass, digging his fingers into the backs of my thighs, making me gasp with delight. The unbridled passion between us is intoxicating, making me want more. Harder. Faster. We've always been passionate, but never this carnal with desire.

"You're wearing far too much clothing for my liking," he growls. He puts his hands on the hem of my blouse, preparing to pull it over my head, when his phone rings. From the look of disappointment on his face, I realize he can't let the call go to voicemail, so I unwrap myself from around him.

He releases his hold on me, as he leans forward, resting his forehead against the wall. "Bloody hell," he rumbles. He roughly pulls his phone from his pocket. "Edwards," he barks at the caller. He bickers with the person on the other end, and then throws his phone against the nearby sofa.

He runs his fingers through is hair. "Bollocks," he mutters under his breath.

"Problem?" I ask.

"My secretary has committed me to having drinks with one of the senators from Massachusetts. It seems she's also in Boston." If the way he disdainfully spits the words hadn't already told me how livid he is, the icy glint in his eyes would be a clear indicator.

I straighten my disheveled clothes as I make my way to the sofa. "Do you have to go?"

"She's on the Senate's committee on Armed Forces, and I'm in the middle of negotiations with the Army." He hastily grabs his phone from the couch. "I'm canceling. I told Mrs. Smythe that I was unavailable this evening, and I know that the Senator has no –"

I hold my hand up. "Gavin, go," I insist. "You flew here for work. I'm just an added bonus. You need to go. Do you think we can still meet for a late dinner? Maybe you can use it as an excuse to keep the meeting short."

"Eight thirty at the Top of the Hub," he replies.

"Wow, a proper date," I tease. "I'll see you at the bar there." I stand behind him and gently push him toward the door. "Now go."

He turns to face me and gives me a kiss that reminds me just what I'll be missing while he's gone. "I'll see you soon," he says, handing me a spare keycard before walking out the door.

The evening isn't going exactly as planned, but we'll still have dinner. We can pick up where we left off after that. For once, I've actually had some prep time before our dates. Every time I've been with Gavin, I've been completely haggard, dressed in someone else's clothes, with finger-combed hair and no makeup. It's nice to have a chance to look my best.

I use every minute of my free time re-primping: carefully blow-drying, curling, and finding that perfect amount of product to keep my hair in place without my hair becoming crunchy. I even put on eye makeup, which has always been an adventure to me. It only takes me four tries to get that smoky look that the YouTube video makes look so easy. Before leaving the room, I stop in front of the mirror and give myself one last onceover. I have to say I look amazing. Judging by the stares I get as I walk through the lobby, either the back of my dress is tucked into my underwear or other people agree.

Outside, the valet hails a cab, and I take the quick ride to the Prudential Center. After quickly scanning the lobby, I take the elevator to the fifty-second floor. According to the hostess, Gavin hasn't checked in yet, so I walk to the bar and order a glass of cabernet. Rather than sit, I stand so I can take in the panoramic view. Between the cloudless sky and the floor-to-ceiling windows, I'm free to take in the spectacular pink, orange, and lavender hues of the fading sunset.

"The view is stunning, but it has nothing on you."

I suddenly feel a strong hand at the small of my back and the brush of familiar lips on my neck. "You look positively lethal. I'm now regretting suggesting dinner. Shall we return to the hotel and see how long it takes me to get you out of that dress? If I were to wager, I'd say less than three seconds."

I turn to face him and waggle my finger. "Now, now. All good things come to those who wait. I'm looking forward to our date."

He guides me to the hostess stand. "Let's order quickly," he demands. "I only have another twelve hours with you, and the list of things I want to do to you is growing by the second."

The hostess seats us at a table by the window overlooking the bay. The sommelier brings us a bottle of Opus One, a wine I've always wanted to try but would never dream of spending the money on. When the server arrives, Gavin's more than ready to order. I know I'm going to order the halibut, but I play coy and say I need more time, just to drive Gavin crazy. He shows me up by ordering for both of us. Surprisingly enough, he managed to pick exactly what I was going to order.

I hand my menu to the server. "Touché. I guess that point goes to you."

"You should know better than to play games with me, Lily. I always win."

While we sit and talk, I catch him up on my days of playing bait. While I do this, I slip a foot out one of my dangerously high heels and gently run my foot along the inner part of Gavin's thigh, smiling benignly across the table at him. Not blatantly enough that he knows I'm doing it on purpose—at first. As he shifts in his seat, I become more pointed with my actions.

Gavin looks back at me cool as a cucumber. My foot exploration has discovered that he most certainly is excited, but you would never know it by looking at him.

"What are you doing, Lily?"

I shrug. "Nothing, Gavin. Nothing at all."

"If you keep this up, I'll throw you over my shoulder and drag you out of here before the meals arrive. Hell, we might not make it out of the lift at this rate."

I bat my eyes with a look of angelic innocence as I continue to massage him with my foot.

Suddenly, he stands and slides his chair around the table next to mine so my foot can no longer reach him.

I take a sip of my wine, looking at him sideways over the lip of the glass. "You're no fun."

"Oh, I'm plenty of fun," he relies. "Just remember you were warned." His arm nearest me disappears under the table, and I suddenly feel his fingers on my knee. He slowly glides his fingertips up my thigh until they reach my thong. He toys with the lacy edge, teasing me. His fingers follow the lace from my hip bone down, all the way back to my ass. Each time he passes the center, he gently grazes me, sending a jolt of sensation through me. Each second that this goes on, I become more and more sensitive. My body craves his touch.

All the while, he rambles on about God only knows what. I don't hear a thing. All I can do is feel what he's doing to me. All my other senses are blocked. I try to look as calm as he does, but I'm not sure how convincing I am. Just when I think I've gotten myself under control, he slides his fingers under the fabric and glides them through my wetness.

I let out a little moan of delight and shock.

He clucks his tongue. "Now Lily, you can't do that, or the game has to stop. You don't want me to stop, do you?" His thumb massages my clit, and I feel an orgasm building. I don't want him to stop but I can't imagine how I'm going to do this without alerting the entire restaurant. "You're going to have to try harder than that. You wouldn't want to make a scene now would you?"

I muster all the self-control I have trying not to throw my head back and scream in ecstasy. I subtly rock my pelvis to the rhythm of his thumb. My body craves release. Getting caught up in the sweet torture of anticipation, my breathing becomes erratic as my body starts to ride the building wave.

Suddenly, he pulls his hand away. I feel my orgasm slipping, my body reeling at the loss of contact.

"I told you. You're going to have to try harder than that," he scolds me. "Do you want me to continue?"

I nod my head, knowing the words won't come out.

He points a finger at me, the finger I know was just inside me moments ago. "One last chance," he says. "If you look like you're about to explode again, I'll have to stop, and you'll have to wait until we get back to the hotel. Understand?"

I nod again. I'd have agreed to anything he said at that point, as long as he returned to the matter at hand—his hand, to be precise.

His fingers, still wet, slowly return to me. They toy with my thong, rebuilding the anticipation. At last, he pushes the fabric aside and runs his fingers between my lips. Up and down, up and down, several times. My clit is desperate for his touch, but he masterfully avoids it every time. I'm barely holding it together. I want to tear my clothes off and fuck him right there.

After seven long laps around my sex, feeling every part of me but the one part I desperately want him to, he finally starts to circle it with his finger. Slow circles with such a gentle touch that I have to bite my lip so I don't scream out, "Faster, dammit!" I try to keep my patience by rotating my hips to match his circles. He picks up the pace of his rotations, going just a little faster.

I feel the orgasm mounting from deep within. I force my eyes open and try to look as though I'm listening to whatever he's babbling on about. He circles faster and faster. My thighs clench around his hand, allowing me to push my clit into his finger, enhancing the sensation.

He softly says my name, looking deeply into my eyes. He must sense I'm close. I don't take my eyes off him as I grind myself against his finger. With a few more short rocks of my hips, I come hard. I muffle my scream by biting down on my lip so hard it bleeds, but I never lose eye contact.

He pulls his finger away and brings his hand back above the table. He continues to stare at me intensely as he sucks his finger clean.

"I told you I'd win," he says arrogantly.

I take a long sip of water and say, "I'm not sure I lost, Gavin."

"Trust me, however good it felt, watching you was a million times more satisfying. I definitely won."

Perfectly timed, our meals arrive, but I can't eat a thing. My earth-shattering orgasm hasn't scratched my itch. It's only opened the flood gates of desire. I push the fish around my plate with my fork and drink my wine, but I'm somewhere else. I'm back in our room, peeling his clothes away and taking him over and over until I'm finally satiated. Gavin's always the one in control, but with my burning need for him growing with each passing second, there's no room left for his control.

I've never felt urges this brazen. Just thinking about the way the evening could play out causes a blush to creep across my face. I may be blushing, but I'm not embarrassed. Not one part of me is ashamed of the borderline indecent way in which I want him. I feel alive, and it's delicious.

"Lily, you have not heard a word I've said, have you?"

I set down my fork and knife to the side of my plate. "Nope. You've no one to blame for that but you."

He chuckles as he cuts his steak. "Oh, my dear. You started it. I just finished it."

I take a sip of my wine. "Well, I'm not finished. I want more, and I want it now."

He swallows hard, probably not expecting my boldly direct response.

I put my glass down and look him square in the eye. "I need your cock deep inside me, and I don't think I can wait another moment. So, what're you going to do about that?"

He stands up, pulls out his wallet, and throws a wad of hundreds on the table before pulling my chair out. "Your wish is my command, milady."

Using my best model walk, I head to the elevator, hoping that I look sexy rather than like a complete idiot. He stands behind me as we wait, kisses my neck, and whispers, "Have I mentioned how amazing your legs look?"

I had been wondering if he'd noticed.

"Now, should I fuck you in the lift? Hmmm?" His hand snakes around and reaches up my skirt, going straight to my sex, "Still wet." He pulls his hand away and licks his finger.

The elevator doors open with a ding. I've never had sex in an elevator. What if someone else comes in? When the doors close, he pushes me against the wall and kisses me hard, pushing his body against mine. His hand goes back up my dress and tears my panties off. I'm prepared for him to take me here and now when he backs away and says, "A lift ride is far too short for what I've planned for you." He turns around and straightens his tie as though everything is perfectly normal.

I lean against the wall, desperately trying to catch my breath, completely frazzled by what has just happened.

He pushes my torn panties into his pocket as I hear a ding, and the doors open to a crowd of people. He grabs my hand and guides me through the mob.

He calls a cab, and we sit in tension-filled silence all the way back to the hotel. I can't even find words to make idle chitchat. I attempt to pull myself together and try desperately to look as poised and calm as Gavin does. It feels as though I have "just been naughty" written on my forehead.

He strolls through the hotel so confidently and with such a refined grace that I actually get distracted watching him. He wears a charcoal grey suit that must be tailor-made because it fits him perfectly. The lines of the suit highlight his toned physique. His commanding strides and that sparkling smile make him seem inhumanly perfect. He's practically a walking Ken doll. Except, of course, he has all his well-endowed male parts. I still can't quite believe I'm the one who's here with him.

He looks over his shoulder and catches me staring. Gavin grabs my hand and pulls me to him. He kisses me with so much fire it feels like a last kiss. When the elevator dings, he doesn't break away, but rather picks me up and carries me onto the car. I hear a round of applause break out behind us in the lobby. I erupt into laughter, and he looks down at me, quirking an eyebrow as though I've gone crazy.

"How long 'til that's on TMZ? They won't recognize it's me. Every other shot they have of me I'm a disaster, unshowered, and wearing something from the FBI closet."

"I told you. I give fuck all about the tabloids. I have one thing in mind, and the rest of the world can implode for all I care."

We kiss all the way back to our room. Somehow, he manages to unlock the door and open it without breaking our kiss. Once the door closes, he becomes primal, as though he's been holding it all back while in public and now it's time to unleash the beast. His jacket, shirt and tie seem to fly off. He tugs at my dress, and I fear he's going to tear it off me when he stops.

"I like this one, and don't want to rip it to shreds. I'd like to see it again." He slowly slides it off me. Once it's put safely on a chair, he returns to me while unbuckling his belt. In one swift motion, his pants are down, and the next thing I know, he's thrusting into me.

For having gone a few weeks without sex, Gavin has amazing endurance. He picks me up, and I wrap my legs around his waist. He pounds into me against the wall until we think we hear it crack behind me. He then lays me down on the table, pushing deeply into me as he licks my nipples. As he expertly maneuvers us into position after position, each creates more pleasure than the last.

I'm spread-eagle on the table as Gavin kisses his way down my stomach. His tongue finds my clit, and I scream his name. The time for slow and seductive has passed. Raw, carnal desire overtakes me. I greedily fuck his mouth 'til I come hard. He flips me around and comes at me from behind, burying himself deep inside me. His cock hits that magic spot as he thrusts, and I come again. I scream his name so loudly I think all of Boston must be able to hear me.

Finally, he carries me to the bed and places me softly on it. Gavin sweetly kisses all over my body until his mouth finds me again. I can't imagine it's possible to come again.

My body is already so sensitive, but he kisses me softly, using his finger to gently play with my clit.

At first, I'm too sensitive. One touch and an intense jolt shoots through me, more pain than pleasure. I squeeze my legs closed, but he gently pushes them back open. "Trust me," he says before kissing me. My body is on overload, every muscle is tense. He gently traces a lazy pattern along my thigh, "Relax," he whispers.

After a few moments, my muscles soften and my legs fall open. He runs a fingertip down my leg, from my ankle to my core. He grazes my clit. I'm still sensitive, but I don't push him away. The sensitivity turns to desire, and I want nothing more than to come. I gyrate my hips in rhythm with his fingers. I'm moments from falling apart when Gavin turns me to lie on my side. He lies behind me and pushes himself deep inside me. His hand reaches around and touches me, resuming my nearing orgasm. He feels so good inside me that I don't want it to end, but yet I'm desperate to come. One last hard thrust pushes us both over the edge.

My body is spent. Every muscle pushed beyond the brink of exhaustion. Every nerve feels blissfully numb. My brain is in a euphoric haze. Fucking Gavin gets me higher than any drug, and is far more addictive.

When I catch my breath, I look over at him and say, "So, you like the dress?" We both laugh, spent, and slowly surrender to sleep.

When I wake up at three o'clock in the morning, I'm starving. Thinking back, I realize I never got to eat dinner. So, I sneak out of the bedroom to the living room to order room service. While I'm ordering, Gavin stumbles out, arching his back in a big yawn.

I hang up the phone. "I'm sorry. I tried to be quiet."

He wipes the sleep from his eyes. "Lily, stealth is not in your skill set. Plus, it's nine in the morning London time, so I'm a bit jumbled anyhow. Did you—?"

"Order ice cream? Yes. And yes, there's enough to share. I kind of went on an ordering spree. We have a munchie smorgasbord coming. "

"That's why you're aces." He scoops me up in his arms. "Back to bed with you, luv."

We spend the next few hours talking and catching up on all the things we haven't had time to share on the phone. These casual moments with him, when we're both relaxed and enjoying being with each other, are even better than sex—I know it's a bold statement considering how good the sex is, but it's true. These quiet moments spent together have reminded me why the pain of the long distance is worth it.

Before we know it, the sun starts to come up, and we know the countdown to takeoff has begun. We're both tired but don't go back to sleep. As we lie there, it occurs to me I haven't told him the biggest news.

"Hey, guess what! I'm now the proud owner of a two-bedroom-plus-a-den condo in DuPont Circle." Gavin doesn't respond, which I find strange. His silence makes me feel uncomfortable, so I ramble on, trying to fill the quiet. "Max says he isn't moving in, but he totally is. It has twenty-four hour security and a pool in the building. Not as nice as Mer's or The Four Seasons, but nice enough. Greene and Sully give it their approval."

He looks at me through narrowed eyes, seeming confused and maybe slightly irritated. "You've done *what*?"

"I… bought a condo," I stammer. "I had to do something. Mer's moving out in two days. It didn't make sense to rent. Rentals are so expensive in the city it's like throwing money away. I finally got the money from the sale of the land, so I bought something."

He seems deeply unsettled by this, but I can't understand why.

"I'm sorry I didn't bring it up sooner," I say, trying to smooth things over. "We haven't spoken very often in the last few weeks, and it all happened so fast. I just signed the papers before I came up here."

His face turns red, and he bites his lip—not in a sexy way.

"Hey, Oxford. You want to tell me what is cooking in that pretty head of yours? You don't look like you're thinking about what to get me for a housewarming gift."

He throws the covers back and stands. "Nothing's wrong. I've got to shower." He walks away, leaving me dumbfounded.

Should I follow him and push the subject? Should I let it go? I choose to get dressed, as there's nothing quite as humiliating as being naked with someone who's pissed at you.

He returns from the bathroom dressed in his suit, looking painfully handsome. He busies himself but doesn't look as though he is really accomplishing anything. Just a lot of crashing and banging.

"Gavin," I say as sweetly as possible, hoping to hide my annoyance at his childish behavior. "Clearly something's bothering you. You're pouting like a teenage girl. Can we talk about whatever's bothering you? Please. I don't know when the next time I'll be able to see you is. Please don't leave like this."

He slams a few more things around and then finally says, "You'll never come to London, will you?"

Whoa, holy outta left field Batman! I stare at him, hoping an explanation might scroll across his forehead like the ticker at the bottom of the screen on the news channels. "What are you talking about?"

He puts his hands on his hips, looking down at me. Damn, he's intimidating when he's angry. Those glacial blue eyes bore into me as though trying to capture my heart, holding it in a vice until he decides what to do with me. "Have you thought about it? Have you considered coming to London?"

I should have expected this reaction, but I didn't. It never even crossed my mind. Disappointed in myself for not anticipating how the news would affect him, I avoid his gaze. "I told you. I need time to—"

His terrifying glare is unrelenting. His arms flail as he speaks, driving home just how angry he is. "Not now. I mean ever. Is that ever something you think you'll do? Although, with everything going on, now does seem like the rational choice. But let's put that aside because why would we ever want to do anything rational? Is coming to London something you will consider doing?"

"I know that's where you need to be. I know that if I want to be with you, that's where I will need to be. Beyond that, I don't know. I don't have a date in mind or anything. I'm just living one moment at a time."

"Lily, I don't think you have any intention of moving to London. I'm beginning to doubt if you'll even come for holiday."

Tired of feeling bullied, I stand, ready to go toe-to-toe. I will not let him think he can bully me. "Why the sudden need for an answer now? What happened to not pressuring me?"

"I don't want to pressure you. But I can't be blind and deaf either. I don't think you'll ever move, and I can't leave. This relationship is a train wreck of heartache waiting to happen." He turns his back on me and walks toward the window.

My stomach churns as I feel him pulling away. "I can barely think about tomorrow, let alone the future. I still have people after me. I-"

Gavin spins, the exasperation is written all over his face. He shouts at me, "You wouldn't if you came to London! *I* can keep you safe. For Christ's sake, I own a goddamned defense company. My house's a bloody fortress. Fuck, Lil. I'll pay the damn debt myself if it puts an end to this."

I shout back louder than I should. "I'd spend the rest of my life looking over my shoulder. That's not a life! I won't do it. I need to see this through 'til the end."

"Define 'the end'," he demands. "When they kill you? That's what you're hanging around for? And you expect me to just sit here and watch it happen? If you think I'm going to stand by and watch that happen, you don't know me very well."

I throw my hands in the air. "If you think I'll be bullied into abandoning something that's important to me, you don't know *me* very well!" I bark back.

He lowers his voice dramatically. "What about us, Lil? Are we important to you? Will you see us to the end?"

"I don't want us to end," I say just above a whisper.

He folds his arms across his chest. "Then we have to be allowed to start. That can't happen with an ocean between us."

We stare at each other from across the room, the tension palpable. The room phone rings, and our connection breaks when he turns to answer it.

"My car's here. I must catch my flight," he says, replacing the receiver. "I'm sorry we spent our last few moments having a row, but you really need to think about this. I'm sorry the entire burden is on you, but I cannot leave London. I have tens of thousands of people who count on me. You need to give some thought to what being together will actually mean. I'm too emotionally invested in this to keep going if there's no hope." He gives me a hard, angry kiss and then leaves, slamming the door behind him.

What the fuck just happened?

TWENTY-TWO

I have the room until late checkout at four, but I'm so hurt and angry with Gavin that I may just take up residence and have the hotel send him the bill. I call down to room service and order up a bottle of Dom and some orange juice. It's a shame to waste good champagne on a mimosa, but that's just the sort of spiteful mood I'm in. It'll go perfectly with the eggs Benedict with the added caviar I ordered. To cap off the spending spree, I order a pay-per-view movie I have no intention of actually watching and crash on the bed. He's always wanting to pay for things. *Well, here you go, Gavin! I hope you get the bill and choke on it.*

Replaying the morning in my head, I can't figure out where we went off track. The night and the early morning had been exceptional. The perfect balance of sex and sweetness. Then out of nowhere, it all went to hell.

If I'd thought about it, I should've seen it coming. I know that any future between us will have to be in London. I'm not against that at all. I'm actually excited about it. The thought of starting over, somewhere fresh, is exciting, but I'm just not ready.

This isn't the first time I've had to start over. When my parents died, when I went to college, when I moved to DC—each time, I was dependent on others for my survival. I had to be what they expected me to be. This is the first time the thing I have to be is me. Now, I just have to remember who that is. If I jump into moving to London, I'll morph into who I think Gavin wants me to be. It won't be a conscious choice; it'll just happen. I hope to hell I don't lose him, but if I don't take this time for myself, I know I'll lose me. I won't go through that again. Not for him, not for anyone.

Perhaps I should plan a trip across the pond, though. Maybe that's all he's been waiting for. I've shot the idea down every time he's offered without even considering it. It might salvage our relationship if I just pick a day and tell him I'm coming—if he still wants me to, that is. Right now, I have no idea where things stand.

The early morning mimosa and emotional brain scramble give me a headache, heartache, and heartburn. The bathtub calls out to me. After filling the mini-pool up with bubbles, I just sit and soak. An hour later, I wake up to a pounding on the door. I listen for a moment. The banging continues, and I think I hear the doorknob rattle. The oxygen is instantly sucked out of my lungs when I realize I haven't set the security latch.

What if Max was wrong? Maybe the men from the cartel have been sitting here waiting for Gavin to leave so they can pounce...

Shrugging into my robe, I tiptoe to the door with my back to the wall. The pounding finally stops, and I breathe a sigh of relief, until I hear what sounds like someone trying to use a key. Maybe it's some jackass trying to get into the wrong room. Or maybe it's a psycho killer here for my head. I know I should hide, but I can't. I have to know who's there. I look through the peephole just as the door flies open, smacking me right in the nose. Blood squirts everywhere, and I see stars.

"Bloody hell! What have I done?" says a voice that sounds very much like that of the man who's supposed to be on a plane right now.

I pull up the bottom of my robe and hold it to my nose as I stumble toward the sofa and sit down. "Gavin? What the fuck?"

"I'm so sorry, luv. Just stay right there." I hear him scurrying around. When he returns, he pulls my robe back, and blood gushes down my face. He presses a cold towel packed with ice to my nose. "I couldn't get on the plane," he says, cleaning the blood off my face. "I couldn't leave like that."

I wince when he touches a tender spot. "Well, isn't that peachy? Now you get to take me to the ER! Lucky me!"

He continues to clean, even when I pull away. "This isn't quite how I thought this would go," he replies.

"You broke my heart. You didn't think breaking my nose would be the icing on the cake?"

"I deserve that," he replies with a sigh. "I was being a prat. I couldn't leave without saying I'm sorry. My plan was to give you a good rogering until you forgot all about my temper tantrum. I hear multiple orgasms can cause memory loss."

I fold my arms across my chest and try to look as angry as is possible with an ice pack on my face. "Well, clearly that isn't on the agenda any longer."

"Can I take a look at it?" he pleads. "Please. I actually know quite a bit about broken bones."

"Really, where'd you learn that? Did they give bone structure training on the set of a Calvin Klein shoot?"

"Cheeky monkey," he says under his breath. "You know I was a medic in the military and completed three years of my physician's training, smartass. Are you going to let me look or aren't you?"

I slowly pull the towel away to let him look. "That's right. I forgot."

"Look, I'm sorry for the way I reacted. I'd like to blame it on how little sleep I've gotten this week and how thinly stretched I am, but there really isn't an appropriate excuse. I overreacted. I should never have behaved that way." He sits down beside me to get a better look.

The tension in my shoulders begins to melt. "I'm listening."

As he gently feels around my nose, he continues. "Whilst I was in queue for the plane, I thought about how we left things. I just simply couldn't leave us so... fractured. I canceled my meetings for tomorrow and thought I'd come back here and make it up to you. I thought maybe we could hire a car and go to Washington. You could show me your new flat."

He forces my eyelids open and looks into my eyes. "As it turns out, I need to go to the chemist and buy gauze to pack your nose." He looks at me critically. "I don't think it's broken. But, I suspect it'll be swollen and you'll have a couple black eyes. I don't think you need surgery, but check with a plastic surgeon in a week, when the swelling has gone down."

His head falls into my lap. "I'm so sorry, luv. What a mess I've made." After a few minutes, he sits up. His face is flushed, and his eyes are red. I have no idea what to say to him. He taps my leg. "All right, then. I'll be back in a few minutes. If you have any paracetamol, you should take some. If not, I'll pick some up at the chemist."

"Some what?" I ask.

"Anti-inflammatory," he explains. "Tylenol or aspirin. Do you need anything else whilst I'm there?"

"No, thanks."

He nods and quietly leaves the hotel room.

Twenty minutes later or so, he returns and stuffs me up with cotton. He's actually quite gentle. I can tell he's done this before. "It's already looking better. I think we might be able to get rid of the packing in a day or two."

When he's finished, I go to the bathroom and check out his handy work. "I'm rockin' the broken-nose look," I say with excessive sarcasm. "I hear gauze is the new black."

"I said I was sorry," he mutters from the other room.

The room is still filled with tension. I'm pissed off and not ready to give him an inch.

"Are you mad because I almost broke your nose or because I acted like a spoilt child?"

"Both," I snap.

"Are you going to be mad at me forever? Don't I get any credit for abandoning my flight to come back and apologize? That was romantic, wasn't it? Worthy of a John Cusack movie, if I do say so myself."

I shrug as I look through my makeup bag for something stronger than aspirin. "Yeah, I guess it was romantic. Not that it cancels anything out. You were out of line."

"I know. I told you I would be patient, and I wasn't. Just because you lost your place to stay doesn't mean you're ready to pick up and move. And just because you buy something here doesn't mean you can't move later. It's really good business actually. I should have commended you for being so savvy."

"Damn straight." Not that I had been thinking that far ahead or anything, but I'm willing to take credit for it.

"So, can we please go to Washington so you can show me your new flat?" He points at my nose. "It may hurt to fly, but we can take the train or hire a car."

"Fine. But don't think this changes anything. I still hate you."

He heads out to pick up a car while I get ready, avoiding looking in the mirror as best I can. Somehow he manages to rent a Mercedes 600 SL. There must be a rich guy's car rental place I don't know about because I don't recall ever seeing anything so swanky at Enterprise.

"Remember to drive on the right. I already have a broken nose. I don't need a head-on collision to make it worse," I say as I get in the car. As soon as the words come out of my mouth, I realize the twisted irony of them. If there hadn't been a head-on collision in the first place, Gavin and I would have never met.

Fate's a wicked bitch. I don't say another word during the first leg of the trip.

Somehow, before picking me up, Gavin had time to put together a playlist of sad, weepy love songs to bludgeon me with on our road trip. I listen to two straight hours of gut-wrenchingly gloomy songs. As soon as *Ain't no Sunshine When She's Gone* starts to play, I give in.

"All right!" I shout. "I can't take any more. I'll talk to you. Just promise you'll stop with the lite rock sad music assault."

He cracks a devious smile. Sneaky bastard.

We talk the rest of the way to DC, and the ice between us slowly melts. When we arrive at the new building, I realize I haven't been in since before I signed the papers. Gavin grills the security guy, whom I look at apologetically. Poor guy has already been put in the hot seat by all the FBI guys, and now the boyfriend. By the time he's done talking to the guard, Gavin has committed to buying a new security system for the building. It seems doghouse Gavin likes to throw money around to compensate for being a jackass.

While we're in the elevator, a lightbulb goes off in my head. "Call Marcus at the Four Seasons. We can't stay here. I have no furniture. I can't believe I hadn't thought about that," I groan.

"We could go mattress shopping. I'd wager we can find a shop with same-day delivery." He winks. "All we really need is a bed."

"Gavin. I have a broken nose. The last thing I want to do is go shopping. I want to lay in bed, drink wine, and eat chocolate. I still have to decide if I want you to stay or not."

He sighs "I'll call. Will you show me around first, at least?" He flashes those damn baby blues at me, and I'm putty, but I try not to show it.

The elevator doors open, and I motion for him to follow me. After unlocking the door, I give him a brief tour. My limited budget has forced me to compromise on amenities, but I'm happy. The kitchen could use an upgrade, but it has gas for cooking. The closets are small, but the bathtub is huge.

Based on his reaction to the news of my condo, I'd expected him to nitpick the place to death. Surprisingly, he actually likes it. Or at least he acts as though he likes it. After the twenty-five cent tour, I notice how empty the space really is. All I have are my two lowly suitcases and three tiny boxes. My whole life is packaged up in those few boxes that wouldn't even fill my miniature closet.

Poor cell reception inside forces Gavin to step onto the balcony to call the hotel. When he returns, he finds me sitting on my boxes with tears streaming down my face. He sits down on the floor next to me. "Want to talk about it?" he asks.

I get up and walk to the bathroom. I'm lucky enough to find some toilet paper left by the previous owner. After blowing my nose, I say, "You know, I'm not against moving to London at all. I'm actually looking forward to it. I just want to get myself sorted first. Ever since my parents died, I've been shuffled about. I've been all right because I'm good at adjusting to my surroundings. I'm good at putting the version of myself forward that's most appropriate for each situation. But I've been doing that for so long I'm not sure who I am anymore."

He motions for me to sit on his lap. I comply, and he wraps his arms around me in such a way that I feel as though I'm in a protective nest.

"If I run to London now, I'll just end up molding myself into who I think I need to be. I don't want that. You don't want that. I want to have something to bring to our relationship. I won't just latch on to your life. But right now, my life consists of three tiny boxes and two small suitcases. Half the stuff in the boxes I got from you!"

"Life isn't about things. You know that," he says. "You're working toward getting yourself together. Don't sell yourself short. You're working. You're writing. You're reconnecting with old friends, making new friends. Focus on your accomplishments because they're plentiful."

I sniffle and nod.

"Are you happy?" he asks.

I consider his question for a minute. "Yes, I think I am. I was really excited about buying this place. I've never had any place that was mine. Actually mine. This is a big deal for me."

He wipes away an errant tear. "Then I pissed all over it. I can't begin to tell you how sorry I am. Even if one day you move to London, you must keep the flat. That way you can come back whenever you want. I'm back here often enough that the place will be in constant use. To be honest, I'm surprised I haven't thought of buying a place of my own."

"Will The Four Seasons be able to stay in business?" I tease.

"That's their problem. You're the only one I care about," he says as he kisses my forehead, being careful not to bump my nose. "How about we go to the hotel and order take-away?"

I nod and reluctantly lock up.

TWENTY-THREE

After a quick drive across town, we get settled into Gavin's suite once more. He tucks me into bed and orders dinner for us from downstairs. Chewing hurts, so he only orders me a bottle of cabernet and a pint of ice cream. Dinner of champions.

While he's in the shower, I hop onto the IKEA website and start thinking about how to outfit my new condo. While it would be fun to shop at the hundreds of swanky design shops in the DC area, I'm definitely on an IKEA budget.

Gavin comes out of the bathroom only wearing a towel, looking irresistibly and infuriatingly hot. I focus on the screen, determined to mask my arousal. I want him to think he's still on my shit list. Plus, I have two black eyes and cotton coming out of my nostrils. I couldn't look more repulsive if I tried.

"What're you up to?" he asks, slipping into fresh boxers.

"Your favorite hobby: online browsing."

He flops down onto the bed next to me. "Ohh, can I help? I do love to point and click!" When he sees the site I'm looking at, he says, "IKEA? Really?"

"What's wrong with IKEA?" I ask.

He shrugs. "There isn't exactly anything *wrong* with it. I just happen to have great disdain for mass-market particleboard. I know lots of people love IKEA, and I'm sure it's very nice mass-market particleboard. But it's just not for me. I'm a bit of a furniture snob. I support fine craftsmanship."

What an arrogant prick! How can he be so out of touch? "Those that can afford a suite at The Four Seasons can afford to be furniture snobs. The rest of us real folks can't be so picky. I'd tread lightly here if I were you, Gavin."

"I didn't mean it like that. Please don't take it that way. Just like some people have a thing for wine, I have a thing for furniture."

I stare at him in disbelief. "Like you go antiquing?" I try to picture Gavin in a musty old shop, arguing with someone's grandmother about the price of an end table. I just can't see it.

He laughs. "No, not like antiquing at all. That sounds dreadful. All those nannies quibbling about doilies supposedly owned by some duke four centuries ago." He shudders. "I've mentioned my studio. In addition to painting, I do some woodwork. I like to build my own furniture. I have an appreciation for the artistry. I swear I'm not trying to be a toff."

The defensive edge to his tone is surprising. This seems like an innocuous enough conversation topic, but it feels as though it's getting under his skin for some reason. "Thou dost protest too much, methinks. Have I struck a nerve?"

Room service arrives, and Gavin leaves the bedroom to retrieve the food. He returns with my ice cream. Slightly melted, just as I ordered. They really cater to every request at this place. I put my laptop away as he sets up a picnic on the bed. When he takes the lid off his meal, I scoff. "Mac and cheese with truffles and lobster pot pie? Even your dinner is pretentious."

A hurt look crosses his face as he pushes the meal away. "I ordered this because it was the only thing on the menu I thought you might be able to eat without it causing you pain. I was hoping to share."

I'm an ass. "That was nice of you," I remark. I look down and push my ice cream around the bowl. "I'm sorry for calling you pretentious. Seems like it's a hot button for you."

He refolds his napkin. "It's an uncomfortable subject for me, yes. I grew up with money, and I've seen all of the ugly things privilege and excess can do to people. Despite where I come from, I've always tried very hard to stay down-to-earth."

I slurp up some ice cream. "I wouldn't have guessed it was a big issue for you. You seem to have no problem telling me you can solve my problems with money," I reply, unable to resist getting a jab in.

He lets out a frustrated sigh, as though he's trying not to say something he might regret. "That's not fair. I've only ever offered my money to protect you. This is an extraordinary circumstance. I don't generally go around flaunting my financial status. No matter how low-key I play it, it always changes things. People fixate on the money, and suddenly, it's the only thing they can talk about. It's revolting."

Showing my abundance of class, I wipe an ice cream dribble of my chin with the back of my hand. "Well, as you would say, I care fuck all about your money."

"Yes," he laughs. "You've made that quite clear."

Stuffed to the gills, I push my tray to the side. "To be honest, I haven't really given your money much thought. I went to a boarding school where everyone had more money than I could ever dream of. At first, I felt like it kept them on this higher plane that I could never reach. Their money never impressed me, but it kept us separated. In time, I learned to overlook it. It doesn't matter to me how much money someone has, because it will always be more than I do, so I decided not to care."

"No matter how little I've cared about money, it's always ended up controlling me. The only time I was truly free was when I walked away from it all, but I was too young and rebellious to appreciate the freedom for what it was."

It's interesting that the thing that had always made me feel stuck on the outside looking in as a girl is the same thing that has imprisoned him. I try to picture him growing up, poor rich boy that can't trust if anyone really likes him for him or his moneybags. Then it occurs to me. "Oh god, are you a lord? I'm not calling you Lord Gavin. No way in hell."

Finally a smile. "I'm technically a lord, and yes, I think Lord Gavin will do just nicely."

I laugh, and it hurts like hell, so I punch him in the gut. "No more making me laugh!"

He grabs his stomach and rolls to the side. "Yes, Lady Lily," he groans. He collects our trays and takes them to the kitchen, returning soon with his laptop in tow.

I lay back and close my eyes, losing track of times as he sits on the bed beside me and works. Rethinking everything he's just said, I begin to wonder. "Have you ever worried that I'm only after your money?" I look over at him.

He glances up from his laptop. "Of anyone I've ever met, you've been the least interested in my wealth. You might be the only woman I've been with that didn't look at me with pound signs in her eyes."

"I can't remember, is that better or worse than dollar signs? The whole conversion thing throws me off," I say jokingly.

He rolls his eyes and goes back to work. The subject isn't entirely settled for me though. "Not because it matters, but I'm curious," I say. "Exactly how high up in the economic stratosphere are you?"

He stops typing. "High. So please stop fretting about me paying for things."

I pull the blanket further up around me. "My concern isn't really about the money. It's about me taking care of myself."

He continues to type as he speaks. "It's ironic. My whole life people have only wanted me for money. The first person I actually want to share my money with wants nothing to do with it."

"Don't know what to tell you, Oxford. You can't always get what you want, but sometimes you get what you need."

He kisses the tip of my nose. "Thank you, Mick Jagger. But I think you're both."

"You'd best remember that." I close my eyes to rest when I get a brilliant idea. I sit up and look for my clothes. "Have Marcus pull the car around Gavin. We're going on a field trip."

He closes his laptop. "Where to?"

"I'm going to show you the wonder that is IKEA."

"Lead the way," he says with a smile.

I still look as though I've been on the losing end of a boxing match, so I grab a pair of Jackie O sunglasses and a ridiculously large hat from the lobby store.

It's a quick drive up 495 to College Park. Even a half hour before closing, the store is still crowded. It was worth trekking out here with a busted nose just to watch Gavin take in IKEA for the first time. While he never warms up to the "wood" furniture, he loves everything else. How can he not? Everyone loves IKEA. We fill two carts before we remember that we've driven in a convertible with limited trunk space. We leave with a few things, and I promise that the next time he's in town, we'll rent an SUV and come back.

We return to the hotel and spend the rest of the night pointing and clicking my way to towels, plates, and glasses. Gavin passes out, but I shop on for hours, loving every second of it. This is what I'd missed out on years ago when I hadn't been allowed to register for my wedding. Ashton demanded we abstain from registering so that people would only give us cash. Then, when we shopped for ourselves, he'd throw a temper tantrum if we didn't get exactly what he wanted. Tonight, I've actually picked out what I want for a change. I'd never thought picking out stemware could be so liberating.

In the morning, the blinding morning sun wakes me up in a cold bed. I pull a pillow over my head and try to go back to sleep, but Gavin's cranky voice echoes from the next room. From what I glean from one side of the conversation, someone must be furious he's still in the States. It had never occurred to me that he'd suffer backlash for staying. He's the CEO. Who does he answer to?

A few moments later, he stalks into the room. "Up for a walk? I really need some fresh air."

I sit up and stretch. "Sure. Just let me get my disguise on." It takes great effort, but I manage to get dressed and brush my teeth without looking in the mirror. I'm not ready to see how bad I look. Once my hat is donned and glasses are on, we walk to the canal.

The walkways by the canal are packed with joggers, stroller-pushers, and dog walkers. Gavin masterfully navigates us through the human gridlock. His fingers are threaded through mine, and he occasionally brings my hand to his lips for a sweet kiss.

Once we break free of the crowd, I say, "So, you want to tell me what's going on? I only overheard bits and pieces, but it sounded like a miserable conversation."

"Work," he grumbles. "Never-ending work."

"You're the boss. Can't you just make someone else do it?" I don't really have any business sense, but it seems like he should be able to delegate.

He laughs. "It doesn't work that way. I wish it did, but it doesn't. Next week, I have to fly to Oslo, Cairo, and then Tel Aviv. It's going to be hell." He explains how his company is rolling out a new product. It's top secret, so he can't go into details. But if it's successful, it could save thousands of lives on the battlefield. Apparently, he's the only one in his company that can sell it the way he wants, so the buck stops with him. I can hear in his voice how much the business matters to him and his worry that he's dropping the ball.

I lightly hip-check him "It's tough being the boss, huh?"

"Yes, but I wouldn't change it for anything. As much as I hated my family's company growing up, I know what we do makes a difference."

"And you get to see the world. One boardroom at a time," I joke.

"I've seen the world. It's not as glamorous as it sounds."

"I've never left the US," I reply. "Well, with the exception of some trips across the border when I was living in Arizona. But that hardly counts. Nogales and Tijuana are not really jet-setting destinations. "

"Really, you've never gone abroad?" he asks.

I shake my head. "Nope. Never had the money. We were supposed to go to Tahiti on my honeymoon, but it didn't work out. Not long after that, I stopped sleeping with him, so he never saw the point of taking me anywhere."

He puts his arms around me. "When you're ready, I'll take you around the world. Show you everything."

"Oh, think of the frequent flyer miles," I say deflecting. While I would love to be taken around the world, I'm not holding my breath. I'd learned a while ago that men love to promise the sun, moon, and stars but delivery is a whole different story.

His arm drops from my shoulder. "You doubt me?"

"It's not you I doubt. It's life," I reply. "Life's an endless assault of curveballs. I mean, look at us, the only reason we're together is because your crazy crashed into my crazy. If one of them had been five minutes later, neither of us would even know the other existed. In a world that random, it's hard to trust that anything's going to work out. So, don't expect me to hold my breath for an around-the-world cruise."

The muscles in his body tense as his gait speeds up. "Wow, I had no idea you were such an optimist," he said sarcastically.

The conversation has suddenly taken an ugly turn, something I seem to have a knack for causing. It isn't my intention to cast a dark cloud over us, but I refuse to go along to get along ever again. I'm going to be honest with myself and with him every step of the way. "I'm optimistic. Cautiously optimistic. It's not like I don't have hope. I do. I'm just careful with it."

His face falls. "You don't trust me?"

I pull a leaf off a tree as we pass and pull it apart as we walk. "I do trust you. I just don't get my hopes up. Trust me, Gavin. It's not you, it's me. I'm a 'believe it when I see it' kind of girl."

"Well, I guess I'll just have to show you then."

"I hope that you do," I say, all smiles, trying to reverse the dark mood I've brought down on us. I search his face, waiting for a reply. I normally love Gavin's ocean blue eyes, but when he's upset, they're like liquid blue pain. It hurts to look at him. The silence goes on long past comfort. "Are you pouting because I'm not always sunshine and rainbows?" I ask.

"I'm not pouting," he argues.

"Okay, fine. You're sullen and brooding. Is that better? You haven't said a word in over a mile."

"You've given me a lot to think about," he says flatly.

I'm not exactly sure what that means, but I let it go. I'm fairly certain I don't want to end up wherever that conversation would lead.

The rest of the walk back to the hotel is silent. I can tell he's really upset when he won't even hold my hand. I try to catch his gaze, but he won't look at me either. I'm not exactly sure what I've done, but it seems to be undoing all that lies between us.

Back upstairs, Gavin opens the door to the suite but blocks me as I try to go in. He lifts my chin with a finger so I have to look him in the eye. Not saying a word, he studies me with a fierceness I can't identify. I don't know if it's anger, resentment, sadness... Maybe all of the above.

"You going to talk to me about it or are you going to burn holes in my soul with your eyes?" I ask, breaking the silence.

"You don't want to come to London because you don't trust that this will work."

"Was that a statement or a question?"

"Take it however you'd like." He sounds as though he's giving up.

"Gavin, I'd be fundamentally insane if I were to move four thousand miles away and not at least have doubts. Not doubts in you. Not doubts in our connection or the relationship that we're building. Just doubts in the way the universe works. Life is crazy and unpredictable. The same sort of crazy twist of fate that brought us together could just as quickly tear us apart. I still believe happily ever after exists. I just won't be broken if it doesn't happen for me."

"One day, I hope to break down your guard and see you build some trust. In me. In the world."

Beating down the emotions his statement stirs, I flash him a big smile. "One day, I hope you take me around the world and then you can say your favorite line."

"What's that?"

"Well, then you could tell me how you were right and I was wrong," I say jokingly, hoping to ease some of the tension.

He smirks, giving me a small sign he might be okay. "I do like to be right."

"Will there be beaches on this trip? 'Cause I could seriously use some beach time. Just you, me, frozen fruity drinks, and crashing waves."

"I'll see what I can do." He leans down and kisses me. I can still feel his brooding just beneath the surface, but hopefully he won't let it linger too long.

His poor mood slowly dissipates over the rest of weekend. By the time he leaves on Sunday evening, we're both back to smiles and laughter. The poor guy's flight lands at six in the morning, and he has to go straight to the office for a full day of meetings. The ironman lifestyle he leads is insane, and I worry he's going to burn out. Despite the exhaustion, he says it's been worth it so he could see me. After seeing him off at the airport, the cab brings me and my IKEA purchases to my new condo.

Coming home to your own place is a powerful feeling. I lean against the doorframe and take in my condo. *It's all mine!* While looking on in reverie, I notice an envelope lying on the island. I tentatively open it. The note inside reads:

Dear Lily,

Don't be mad.

I simply cannot have you sleeping on the floor. Or with Max! This is the same mattress I have at home. I know you'll love it. If you hate it, donate it. But I know you won't hate it. I have impeccable taste. Just look at my girlfriend.

Wish I were there to break it in with you.

Gavin

I rush to the bedroom to find a giant mattress already lying in the middle of the floor. I immediately flop onto it.

It turns out Gavin's right—it's an amazing mattress, like sleeping on a cloud. I spend all of Monday sleeping, only waking to call him to thank him profusely for his gift. He sounds pleasantly surprised, seeing as I'm not the best at accepting gifts. He says he was sure I'd hate it on principle. When he puts it that way, I sound like a real charmer.

Things still feel strained between us, but I hope they'll get better. As awkward as things have been, I know I want to keep working things out. When we're off, I feel like a part of me is broken, which is ridiculous considering the short time we've known each other. Ridiculous but undeniably true.

By Tuesday, the swelling in my face has gone down. I have an assignment due as well, so it's back to the grindstone. My laptop hums as it boots up for the first time in days. I find no less than *ten* emails from Charlie! I ignore them for the moment and move on to more pressing matters.

As I get settled in, the home office looks like a better and better option. Well, a room that one day will be a home office. Until then, my kickass bed makes a good workstation.

The next few weeks go by like a blur. Max finally moves in. It's nice to have my partner in crime back. He and the boys have been busy conspiring with Gavin to beef up the security in the building. They think they're doing it on the sly, but Max accidentally leaves schematics and notes all over the place. Part of me wants to stomp my feet and tell them to stop meddling. But that's just my pride talking. Since the threat level is still uncertain, increased security is a welcome bonus.

Moving a few blocks further away from the studios has given me an excuse to give up yoga and painting. Despite attempting to throw all of my canvases away, Max keeps digging them out of the trash pile and hanging them up to torment me. He says that one day I'll look back on them and be happy I have something from my "cartel period."

With fall in full swing, it's getting too cold to run. Desperate to keep the runner's legs I'm so proud of, I think about joining a gym, but Max has a better idea. Since the condo is still basically devoid of furniture, we decide to turn the living room into a sparring gym with mats he's "borrowed" from the FBI training center. Our workouts start out as basic self-defense instruction, but as I get into it, Max begins teaching me a blend of martial arts. There's nothing like kicking the crap out of something to burn off frustration.

My blog reaches fifty-thousand followers. I just can't believe how far it's come in just a couple of months. A few A-listers tweet about it and boom—more followers than I can fathom! One afternoon, out of the blue, a publisher contacts me about a possible book deal. I make plans to head to New York in November to meet with them. After I tell him, Gavin sends over champagne, Baccarat flutes, and so many flowers that we run out of places to put them.

Knowing that people are actually reading, I put even more work into the blog—especially the marketing, which turns out to be a full time job in and of itself. My freelancing slows down a bit as a result, but I know I'll be okay moneywise for a few months.

Gavin calls to tell me he has to go on a crazy three-week long business trip soon, some sort of marketing/networking extravaganza. It sounds pretty swanky, and he says that most people bring a spouse or partner. His hints are as subtle as a freight train, and I'm petrified he'll come straight out and ask me to go. Being introduced as his girlfriend? The thought alone sends my insecurity meter through the roof. There's bound to be a lot of pressure that comes with being Gavin Edward's arm candy. People are used to seeing him with Brooke Livingston. Before that, it had been an endless string of supermodels. I can't fill Brooke's shoes. My ego couldn't take all the disapproving glances.

I hurry off the phone before he can ask me to go on the trip and spend the next two days dodging his calls. I call back during times I know he can't answer. He eventually emails begging me to join him, to which I claim I can't because of the publisher meeting coming up, saying I want to stay focused on that. It's bullshit, but it's the best I've got.

Not wanting him to leave without us talking at least once, I bite the bullet and Skype him.

"Hey," I say, flashing him an over the top smile, trying to set a positive tone.

I can tell I've caught him in the middle of something. He has a bunch of files in one hand and a legal pad in the other, with a pen tucked behind his ear. Working Gavin is so sexy. His tie is a little loose around his neck, and his hair is ruffled. Clearly, he's buried in work. But he looks smoking hot doing it.

"Hey yourself. How are you, luv?" People flit in and out of his office in the background, handing him files, taking files.

"Busy," I lie. "Been writing up a storm trying to prepare for this meeting in New York."

He stops what he's doing and looks into the screen. "I can't tell you how proud of you I am. It's so exciting."

"Thank you. That means a lot. It's just an introductory meeting, so I'm trying not to get my hopes up. It could be something, or it could be nothing."

Someone appears beside him and hands him a piece of paper, which he scans and then looks up. "Cautiously optimistic, right?"

"Exactly," I reply. "You ready for your trip?"

He looks around his office. "As you can probably see, its bedlam here. There's so much to complete before we depart. I literally haven't left the office in three days."

Looking closer at him, I can see the stress wearing on him. He's so sexy that it's easy to miss the bags under his eyes. "You work too hard."

His cell phone dings. He picks it up and scrolls down the screen with a scowl on his face. "Par for the course when your name's on the building," he says, looking terribly serious.

I desperately want to see that million-dollar smile. "How many bags are you taking? My guess is seven."

I'd expected at least a chuckle or snicker, but he simply stops what he's doing and stares at me. I guess I should have done this good-bye over the phone. The elephant in our virtual room wouldn't have been nearly so imposing. I wouldn't have had to see the hurt and disappointment in his eyes.

After what feels like an eternity, he says, "Over the next few weeks, I'm going to have limited opportunities to talk to you, so I don't want our last conversation before that to be like this, but I'm also not going to sit here and lie to you, pretending I'm not sorely disappointed you're not joining me on this trip. Even if just for a few days."

"Gavin, we've been over this. It isn't good timing for me. You can't expect me to drop everything just because you have a cool trip. I have a life."

"I don't expect you to drop everything. Your meeting isn't for ten days. You could easily come before. Or you could come after your meeting, and we could celebrate."

"*If* there's something to celebrate," I mutter.

"Fine, we could wallow in disappointment. At least we could do it together and in a beautifully luxurious resort."

"Gavin—"

"Is it really so awful that I want you to be a part of my life? Truly? That's all this is, Lily—me trying to bring you into my life. When I met you, I had twenty-four hours a day with you for a week. Then I left, and now I only get these short bits of time. It isn't enough. I want more. I want more than for you to be a voice on the phone that I sometimes get to see every few weeks. I want to share my life with you, not just have you be one more thing that I schedule into my day." He's clearly hurt. His voice, his face, his eyes are all filled with frustration and disappointment.

"Gavin, I'm just not ready for this."

"Ready for what exactly?"

I throw my hands up. "For this. Going with you on this trip would be a big deal."

"Aren't you the one that's always saying you want more than to be shuffled into clandestine hotel rooms? This would be a proper trip. It isn't a big deal. It's just you and me. How is it different than meeting me in Boston?"

299

"It just is. It wouldn't be just you and me. It's you and me and people from your company. There'd be so many expectations."

He sighs and looks sympathetic. Maybe he's calming down? "I understand where you're coming from. But luv, we'll deal with it together. I'll support you in every possible way. Whatever it takes to make you feel comfortable. I just want some time with you. It'll really be an amazing trip. You can skip the business part, and we can just sneak away."

"You're still missing the point, Gavin. They're used to seeing you with a—" I stop myself. I don't want to go there. "You know what? This isn't going anywhere."

"Finish what you were going to say, Lily. They're used to seeing me with what?"

"Gavin, just let this go. Please. I can't go with you. I'm sorry. I just can't right now." I don't know why I can't talk to him about this, but I can't. I know I need to. If we're ever going to be able to move forward, I'm going to have to get past Brooke's ghost. But I'm not there yet today.

"Stop shutting me out. Talk to me."

"Gavin, please. Let's just drop it."

Chaos erupts behind him in his office—phones ring, people rush in demanding his attention, his secretary buzzes by. He sighs and runs his fingers through his hair. "Lily, I don't know how you expect things to get better if you don't talk to me. I don't know about anything anymore. I think I should go. We can talk more about this later, I suppose. Goodbye, Lily."

The screen goes black, and he's gone.

Pangs of regret hit me like a kick to the gut. I've just screwed up big time. I can feel it.

I know I should have agreed to go with him. How many girls are offered amazing trips to spectacular resorts to spend time with their gorgeous boyfriends? While my feelings are valid, I know I'm overreacting. But knowing it and doing something about it are two different things. I'm being a coward, and it disgusts me.

I know I can't make it up to him right now, but I decide surprising him by going to London for Christmas might be a good idea. I hop online to book my tickets. Afterward, I send him a package with a copy of Frank Sinatra's "I'll Be Home for Christmas" and my travel itinerary.

Hopefully, my homecoming present to him will smooth over my absence on this trip. I make sure to write the date very clearly on the FedEx form. I want him to know I sent the package before he left. I know it doesn't make up for my stubbornness completely, maybe not at all. But it's a step, and it's all I can manage right now.

I try to work the rest of the day and get nowhere. I can't think about anything but Gavin and the mess I've made. At lunchtime, I trudge to the kitchen to scavenge for food, and I find a box wrapped in brown paper on the kitchen island. There's an envelope labeled "Lily" taped to the top of the box. Hoping it's from Gavin, I tear into the envelope.

Lily,

Your adversaries are growing impatient, and thus you are in imminent danger. Bring this file to the FBI immediately. While they've already boggled the tip I spoon fed them, hopefully this information will help them keep you safe.

Keep up with the martial arts training. You'll need all the protection you can get.

301

You've surrounded yourself with good men. Your choice in roommates has kept you safer than you realize.

Trust no one. Even if they have a badge.

Keep your head down and stay safe. And for the love of Christ, stay out of the papers. Cost me a pretty penny to call the dogs off you last time.

LG

Well, fuck me.

TWENTY-FOUR

I stare at the box for over an hour, too scared to open it. What the hell's actually in there? Money? Drugs? My mind flashes to a movie scene—a young Brad Pitt staring at an open box with his wife's head inside. Lorenzo wouldn't send me a head. Would he?

I try calling Gavin but an automated voice answers, saying, "The party you are trying to reach is out of the service area." Seriously? An international man of mystery like him isn't on a global plan? I send an email, but it bounces back as undeliverable . I know he said that he'd be out of reach a lot, but it seems like he's simply checked out.

My mind races. How am I going to explain to Max how I got this box? Everything I come up with I'm sure Gavin's new security system will be able to disprove. Then again, Lorenzo did manage to slip the box in here undetected. I don't have much time to mull over my story before Max comes home from work. I opt to go with a version of the truth.

When he walks in, he drops his keys in the dish by the door, then walks to the fridge to get a beer. He looks at the box. "What's this, Lil?"

I shrug. "Not sure. It was by the front door when I went to get the mail."

A look of horror crosses his face. "And you picked it up? What if it was an explosive? Fuck, Lily. I've got to call this in."

An army of FBI techs shows up to determine if there's a risk of a bomb or any kind of biological agent. Even though I know there isn't, I play the part of the clueless recipient as best I can. When they declare the coast clear, all but two techs depart.

As soon as they walk in the door, Greene and Sully are yelling at me for picking up a strange, unmarked package.

"Yeah, yeah. I'm the worst, and I'm lucky to be alive. I've got it, Dads. Can we please just open the damn thing?"

The box contains several file folders. The first folder contains a series of photos and a note written in block lettering: "HE SAW YOU, BUT YOU DIDN'T SEE HIM." The photos have captured a man in a hat with a camera clearly taking pictures of me. Based on what I'm wearing in the photos, I'm certain it's from the days during our surveillance mission. The guy with the camera is right there, in the middle of everything, but we never saw him. There are dozens more from the past few months. He was there when I went to painting class, yoga, Meredith's. There are even photos of me in Boston, at the conference and when I went to meet Gavin at the Top of the Hub. This guy has been following me for a long time.

The guy could be anyone. He does a masterful job of just blending in. Instead of *Where's Waldo?*, it's *Can You Spot the Sociopath Sent to Kill Me?*. I stare at his ever-present figure, trying to place him, but the shots are too grainy for any such luck.

The second envelope holds more information on places Ash may have stashed his money. There's an address for an apartment we hadn't known about, a storage locker, and two banks where he may have had safety deposit boxes.

The third envelope has more details on the cartel and how Ash became connected with it. There are pictures of Ash with a group of men that Lorenzo has identified as members of the cartel. Pictures of Ash with stacks of cash. Transcripts of conversations between Ash and the cartel members talking about him cleaning their money. How the hell these men— who are supposed to be cynical, hardened criminals that don't trust anyone—couldn't see through his bullshit is beyond me. I can't even read Ash's lines with a straight face he's so clearly full of it.

"Well, Lil. Looks like your fairy godmother delivers again. Something you want to tell me?" Greene asks.

"No. I'm as shocked about this as you are," I respond, hoping I sound convincing. I'm genuinely and visibly shaken up by the new information.

He cuts me some slack and backs off, not asking again.

Needing to catch my breath, I step onto the balcony.

Max appears beside me moments later. "It's going to be— "

"Stop right there, Max. Don't you dare say that it's going to be okay. You don't know that. This guy has been five feet away from me for months. Right under your noses. I'm not

305

safe. Not by a longshot. At any given moment, he could jump out of the shadows. What did your guy say? They'd torture me until I give up Ash's money. Well, that's a great fate for me because I know *jack shit* about the money!" I yell into the night. "Hear that asshole? I've got no fucking clue where the money is!" As if he could hear me or would believe me. Angry sobs overtake me.

Max pulls me to his chest and strokes my hair, whispering reassuring words in my ear.

"I hate him so much it hurts, Max. If I could kill him all over again, I would and wouldn't think twice." Tired of wasting tears on Ash, I pull away and wipe my eyes. "Let's go to the gym. I want to hit something."

We head down to the gym in the FBI building. It's much nicer than my living room. Max and I spar, and he gallantly allows me to kick the crap out of him. He doesn't get on me about technique. Today is all about anger management. I fight till I can barely stand, and at that point, he forces me to call it a night.

"Let's go get drunk," he says. "Home or bar?"

"Home. With my luck, my sociopath stalker would buy me a drink, and I wouldn't even know it. I think I'll to try to catch Gavin quick first though."

When I get home, I try Gavin's cell again and get the same automated response as before. Right now, I want nothing more in the world than to talk to him. He always seems to say just the right thing to calm me down. Maybe it's just the accent, but either way, I'm missing him deeply, which makes me feel even worse for not going with him. He did everything short of begging me to go, and I'd shot him down because I'm a coward. Now I need him, and I can't reach him. This situation completely sucks, and it's entirely my fault.

Max tries him on his cell as well and gets the same result. We even ask Greene and Sully to try calling, but no one gets through. Max promises to do some digging, but it won't help me just now. Feeling defeated, I pull on Oxford's sweatshirt and get into bed. At around ten, Max bounds into my room.

"Get your ass up."

"No. My whole life is totally fucked up. I've pushed away the one good thing in it. I just want to lie here and wallow."

"That's all well and good, but I live here too. I've listened to you crying for two hours now, and I've had all I can take. I'm doing my job as a good roommate, and I'm going to get you stinking drunk. Let's go."

He drags me to his room and puts *Mad Men* on his mammoth TV—my favorite show on television and the best show to play drinking games to. Whenever someone drinks on the show, you drink. Whenever Don makes a girl swoon, you drink. Whenever someone does something morally questionable, you drink, etc. By the end of two episodes, we're both three sheets to the wind, and I'm finally numb enough to drift off to sleep.

******

The sun wakes me up earlier than I would have liked, but I can't go back to sleep. I try Gavin again, but his phone tells me yet again that he's still out of his service area. Desperate to speak to him, I call his office.

"Mr. Edwards' office," Snooty Smythe answers.

"Good morning, Mrs. Smythe. I know Gavin isn't in, but I've been trying to reach him, and his cell phone is out of service. Do you have another way of reaching him?"

"I'm sorry, Ms. Clark. I cannot give out that information." She doesn't even try to mask her arrogant condescension.

Seriously? "O-kay... Can you please let him know that I'm trying to reach him? It's kind of an emergency."

"I will pass your message along to his staff abroad, and they will prioritize your message appropriately. Good day." With that, the line goes dead.

What the hell does that mean? Did he instruct her to give me the brush off, or is she just naturally that much of a bitch? Are we over?

Needing to get a handle on what has just happened, I go for a run to sweat out all the tequila. Each time my foot strikes the pavement, my anger grows. By the time I make it back to the condo, I'm fit to be tied.

"*Max!*" I scream as I lock the door behind me. "Get your ass up. I'm done being a sitting duck. If they want his money, I'm damn well going to try to find it. I can't spend another day hoping this is just going to go away. And I *will* not sit here in fear."

He stumbles out of his room looking disheveled. He's in boxers that hang indecently low, and his curly hair looks like a 'fro. "Okay, Slugger," he answers. "Let's go to my office and look through the files." He kisses the top of my head before ambling back to his room. "Just stop yelling. I still have tequila brain."

We get dressed and meet Sully and Greene at the office. They've already been at work on Grimaldi's file and tracked down the apartment Ash had been paying for. The name on the lease is a Crystal Steiner.

Huh. So Crystal finally makes an appearance. "We need to check this out," I tell Max.

"When we were at that club with Em, a dancer came up to me asking about Ash. She wanted to know if I was looking for Crystal."

He puts down the file he'd been looking at. "Why didn't you tell me before?"

I shrug. "I didn't want to get into it. Em would have tracked her down and strangled her with her stockings."

He gets a dreamy look on his face. "Have I mentioned that I'm in love with that woman?"

"Yeah, yeah." No matter how much I try to deter him from his little infatuation with Em, he's still stuck on her. "Have you told Sabrina you've found your soulmate?

He throws a wadded up post-it at me. "Very funny. Speaking of that, I think S and I are done for good this time."

"I'm sorry. You and I can be single and miserable together."

"Hell, no. I'm a playa, baby. I'll never be miserable." Freckled white guys with crater-sized dimples should never use the word "playa". They just can't pull it off.

I groan and roll my eyes as he collects the files on his desk and shoves them into his messenger bag. "Come on. Let's go track this chick down."

I slide my jacket on just as Greene runs up to us. "We've found her," Greene says. "She died about a month ago. Cause of death was an OD, but someone beat the hell out of her first. Raped her every which way. She was a longtime user and had been known to turn tricks now and again. Her file says she went clean after she had her kid. DC homicide didn't think it passed the sniff test and have been holding on to it. Now that we have this connection, it's pretty obvious what really happened to her."

I feel like I've been slapped in the face. Grimaldi told me that living with Max had kept me safer than I knew. I haven't really understood just how much until right now. The cartel's only being careful with me because I'm under the watchful eye of the FBI. Crystal didn't have that luxury.

She was only twenty and probably had no idea what she was getting into. I'm sure Ash must have come around with his big wad of cash and made her all sorts of promises. It worked on me when I was twenty. Why wouldn't it work on her? Whoever she was, she didn't deserve this. More importantly, her kid didn't deserve this, didn't ask for this bomb to be dropped on his life. The poor kid's life is permanently screwed up because Ash couldn't figure out that stealing from Mexican drug lords was a bad career move.

Max pulls out his keys. "They're going to keep working at the Crystal angle here. Let's you and me start with the banks," he says, turning to me.

I nod and follow him to the parking garage. We drive out to Eagle Bank in Old Towne Alexandria. We arrive armed with a key ring full of random keys the FBI collected during their seizure of Ash's things. One of them has to be the right key.

When the banker pulls out the box, I know the money isn't in there. You can't fit five million dollars into something barely bigger than a lunchbox. The banker leaves Max and I alone to look at the contents. The box is stuffed full of file folders filled with photos of influential men in compromising situations.

"Looks like Ash was in the blackmail business as well," Max says. As he flips through the folders, his eyes grow wide. "Holy shit, he has the director of the DEA in here. A couple of Congressmen, some federal judges. This is some powerful material."

"I can't say I'm surprised. I knew that Franklin couldn't have gotten all of his government contracts simply because he was good at what he did."

"That's Washington for you. You can only stay in the game if you're paying them off or keeping their secrets."

Glancing at the files, I say, "I wouldn't be surprised if there aren't more files somewhere."

"Maybe," he replies. "Maybe Ash set these aside for some reason. His death must have made some people very happy. They may not be too happy if they find out their secrets have been uncovered by someone else," Max offers.

"Oh, fabulous. Just what I need—more people out to get me. This just gets better and better."

He puts his arm around me and kisses me on the temple.

"I'll be okay. I promise. Let's bounce and head to the other bank."

We put the box back and head to Nations Capital Bank on Pennsylvania Ave. This one is a ten-by-ten box, but it's empty. If he'd had money here, it's long gone.

"I watched *Breaking Bad*," I say. "I know how big a stash of five million should be. The storage locker makes the most sense. We should've started there." I pull out the key ring and rifle through the keys. "The file said the unit's on H Street, right? And look! I'm guessing this little key here that says 'H Street Storage' is probably the right one."

Max opens the door for me as we exit the bank. "You're such a smartass. Fine, we'll go. But then, I'm taking you home. It's been fun playing detective, and you've saved me all sorts of warrant paper work. But, I don't want you getting sucked too far into this," he states.

"The Mexicans are looking for money I don't have, and if Crystal is a cautionary tale, they'll use me as a heavy bag until I either die or give them what they want. Sticking my head in the sand is no longer an option."

He unlocks the car with his remote. Unlike Gavin, he doesn't open my door for me. "I hear you, Nancy Drew. But you need some space from it so it doesn't eat you alive. This is heavy shit. Spend too much time in it, and it'll turn you black."

His words stick with me the whole ride, and my stomach is in knots by the time we reach the storage locker. I pray the answer to my problems lies behind the unit's door. But as always with things concerning Ash, I'm abundantly disappointed. The unit is full to overflowing with knock-offs: purses, shoes, jeans, wallets, luggage. No money.

I pick up a cute clutch. "Do you think they'll take some fake Prada in lieu of their five mil?" I ask.

"Don't let this get you down. You'd be amazed where people hide money. It could be stuffed inside the linings of that Louis Vuitton crap over there. I'll get the crime scene guys down here."

I scoff. "You're giving Ash way too much credit. Hiding money in the lining of a suitcase is beyond his creativity level."

Deflated, I walk back to the car while Max locks up. Halfway there, Greene calls to say that they're still waiting on the warrant for Crystal's place.

"Do we need a warrant?" I ask as Max reappears beside me. "Ash's name was on it, right? So then, technically, it's my place, right? I'm sure the key is on this ring."

Max shrugs as we hop into the car. "It's a bit of a grey area, but if you were to go and open it up and I just happened to be there, I think we'd be in the less-illegal section of the grey area."

"I need to find this money, Max. I couldn't care less if you can use whatever we find in court. I just need to get in there."

"Let's roll, then."

It's a short drive to the address in Falls Church, but far enough for panic to set in. I need to find a mountain of cash in this apartment. If not, I'm out of options. Game over. Do not pass go, do not collect two hundred dollars.

We pull up to a lovely little complex tucked away on a tree-lined street. I have to hand it to him—Ash found a cute place for his mistress. A nice place for a kid.

I try six different keys before I get to the right one. When we enter the three-bedroom apartment, it's evident we aren't the first ones to check here. The place is trashed. The couch has been torn to shreds, all of the tables and chairs are overturned, the walls have huge holes in them, and a bunch of floorboards have been pulled up. The bedrooms look as though a tornado has gone through. Every mattress has been gutted, and there's stuffing everywhere. Someone was definitely looking for a hiding spot.

There's no money here. Short of a miracle, I'm walking dead. Noticing a sledgehammer leaning against the wall, I see an outlet for the rage boiling inside and grab the heavy instrument. With each swing that smashes into the dry wall, I release a primal scream along with a rush of long-suppressed emotion. Fury that he left me holding a five-million-dollar bag that's conveniently missing the money. Utter sadness from the hopelessness of my position. I don't even hate the cartel as much as I hate Ash. In a warped way, they're just carrying out their jobs according to their own rules. Ash knew what he was signing up for. The part that breaks my heart is that my life clearly had no value to him. I knew our relationship had diminished, but for him to act with no regard for me or my safety whatsoever just shows he didn't care about me at all. I was nothing to him.

My assault on the wall doesn't last long. Sledgehammers are heavier than they look. Cathartic, but heavy. Panting, sweat dripping down the side of my face, I drop the hammer. "Take me home, Max."

As I walk back through the entryway, I notice the remnants of what I assume was a bookshelf. Broken glass from picture frames litters the ground. From a splintered shelf, I pick up a picture of a little boy. He's the spitting image of Ash. I set the picture back down, feeling as though I've seen a ghost.

Max allows me to stew silently on the ride home. There's so much to take in, and the weight of it is suffocating.

As we pull up to the condo, Sully calls. Max has to go back to the office, which is good. He's in agent mode, and I don't need an agent right now. My emotions are out of control, and he wouldn't know what the hell to do with me.

Needing to vent to someone that will understand, I call Em.

"What's happenin', hot stuff?" she answers.

I pace my kitchen while I talk. "Shit's hit the fan, and I'm feeling like I'm losing it." I catch her up to speed with the Cliff's Notes version.

She clucks her tongue. "Cocksucker motherfucker."

"I know, right? I'm so mad at Ash right now I'm going to explode. How could he be so stupid? So selfish? And a kid? Fuck. He looks just like him."

"Another Ashton Preston? That's just what the world needs. That boy should have been sterilized."

I fight back a sob. "I'm trying to deal with it all, but I'm maxed out."

"That's because you're trying to do what you always do, and it's not going to work this time. This is some serious shit and you aren't going to be able to gloss over it and make it pretty. Ash fucked you over and left you with a volcano of shit that's about to erupt. That's not okay. You have every right to be fucking pissed."

"I'm pissed. Beyond words! My anger is so out of control it's taken over. I want to crawl out of my skin because all I feel is rage and there's nothing I can do about it. Ash is gone! I can't punch him. I can't yell at him. I can't make him fix it. I don't even know if this is fixable. Five fucking million dollars! To a fucking drug cartel. How am I going to get out of this? It's too big. It's too much!" I collapse to the floor and let the tears come.

"You know I'll give you the money," she says. "Gavin'll give you the money. I'm not sure money alone's going to solve it, though."

"I'm so sick of cleaning up his messes," I sob. "I just want him out of my life. I want to be free of him." My angry ranting turns to open weeping. "I'm being punished for marrying him. I knew I didn't love him. I thought marrying him would give me a stable life. I wouldn't have to worry about money. I was going to get the job of my dreams. We had great sex. I didn't need more. But damn, I'm paying the price for it now."

"You married him because you never had to care about him. You never had to love him. You keep everyone at arm's length and you like it that way. Hey, I get it. I do the same damn thing. I'm not judging. If you keep them away, it won't hurt when they leave."

I wipe the tears from my eyes. "Yeah, unless your parting gift is a mountain of debt and a bounty on your head."

"Babe, I hate to tell you, but you married the devil."

"I wish I'd never met him."

"May he rot in hell."

I clutch my chest, as though it will help soothe the pain. "How do I make it stop? How am I going to get out of this? I need Ash to be purged from my life!"

"You're a survivor, Lily. You're the toughest person I know. You'll find a way to get through this. But you have to stop pretending it's all okay. You have to face it and fight it. Take it head on. Stop being a victim. You'll either end it or it'll kill you. But either way, you'll be out. I've got to go, Lil. I'm doing a report on CNN. Call me later."

Cocksucker motherfucker. I'm in deep shit.

TWENTY-FIVE

Perhaps it's the decreasing daylight as Thanksgiving approaches. Maybe it's that I haven't been able to connect with Gavin in almost seven days. Or maybe it's that a Mexican drug cartel has hired some serial killer to jump out of the shadows and murder me. Well, torture me first... but what's the difference, really? For whichever reason, I'm feeling blue. Maybe blue is an understatement.

I've been in bed since Max's impromptu Take Your Roommate to Work Day. I get up to use the restroom, and that's it. Eating seems uninteresting. Showering sounds exhausting. I've only changed to rotate through the three Gavin shirts I have. I've tried writing on my blog a few times, but after posting the new entries, Em had called immediately and ordered me to take them down before I ruined my brand. After the third bad one, she took over administrative controls.

To make matters worse, at the beginning of the week, my email was hacked. I'm still not exactly sure what was done or why, but my password was changed, and I was locked out.

After Google finally got me back into my account, my whole history had been deleted: contacts, received mail, sent mail, the whole shebang. It was totally wiped clean. I didn't even know that was possible. The FBI boys panicked about it and are having IT look into it. Max thinks that since I haven't been leaving the house, the cartel guys needed to go through my email to get a read on what I've been up to. As if they hadn't already fucked with my world enough.

Gavin's dropped off the face of the planet, and it feels like my heart has been ripped out of my chest. Every day that the cartel drama goes on, I feel the deep impact of his absence. I miss the way he calms me down and helps me see things rationally. Even though I hate how he wants to swoop in and save the day, I think knowing that he could and would if I let him gave me a sense of security. I didn't feel as though I was going through it alone, and now I do. I'm completely alone, and it's my fault. I pushed him away. The evil one, I marry. The good one, I push away. Damn, I'm a train wreck.

I've called his office and left messages—messages saying it's an emergency—and yet, he does nothing. Not even a postcard! If he cared for me as much as he's said he does, he would put aside our issues and call me. I may have pushed him away, but he's being a stubborn ass. If I didn't miss him so damn much, I'd tell him to go to hell and never speak to him again. But the truth is if he were standing in front of me, I'd run to him with open arms.

Max has even called and hasn't been able to break through Snooty Smythe's Chinese wall around Gavin. She'll only say, "I'll deliver the message to Mr. Edward's staff, and it will be prioritized appropriately." Aren't I a priority? She won't even give Max Gavin's itinerary, even when he pulls the FBI agent card. Although, Snooty *is* British, so maybe we need an MI-6 card.

On the eighth day of my self-imposed bed rest, I hear a knock on the door.

"If you're here to kill me, go away," I yell. I hear Max pad across the condo and then open the door. Hushed whispering from the entryway disrupts my quiet sulking. There's been a lot of that this week. Max has been worried, I know. I've got one foot down the rabbit hole.

"You have got to be kidding me!" Em shouts as she bursts through my bedroom door. "You're going to get your ass up and hop in that shower now. When Boston Max said you were in a bad way, I didn't believe him. I thought some chocolate and tequila and you'd be golden. This is beyond bad. I mean it, Lily. If you are not in that shower by the time I count to ten, I will bring the shower to you, and it will be unpleasant. Ten! Nine!"

I know she'll do it too. Em does not do idle threats. She's ruthless. In our sorority house, she had always been in charge of hazing and vengeance. Her tactics had kept the shrinks in Tucson busy with broken debutantes for four whole years.

By the time she reaches five, I'm out of bed and shuffling to the shower. As I close the bathroom door, I hear her attacking my room.

"I'm going to burn these sheets. I think there's something growing on them. Wait... You have gummy bears stuck to your sheets? This is disgusting." She storms into the bathroom once I'm in the shower.

"Just come on in," I sneer.

"Fuck, Lily. I said to go gangbusters. Not bury your head in the sand. Are you really going to let Cocksucker beat you?

Because that's what you are doing. You're drowning in his crap. You've just given up. That's fucking bullshit," she scolds. She's clearly pissed, and I know she won't pull any punches to save my feelings.

"You need to fight back. Get some goddamn control. I don't know how, but you sure as hell aren't going to figure it out holed up in your bedroom. I told you that you're a survivor because you are. You keep getting dealt shitty hand after shitty hand, but you always make it work. Until now. It's time to wake up and start surviving."

"There are clean clothes for you to change into while I fumigate that sweatshirt. When you get out of the shower, you'd better be ready to start getting your shit together. Because this weepy pity party ends right now," she orders, slamming the door behind her.

I hear more hushed whispering from down the hall as I step out of the bathroom. "You can stop talking about me. I'm right here."

"I've hired people to defunkify this place while you and I go to the spa. If Juan Valdez tries to take us out on the way to get a seaweed wrap, he'll have to face me, and I'm packing heat today."

"What?" Max and I say in unison.

She shrugs. "You think I'd come into this clusterfuck and leave my gun at home? No sir."

Em armed? God help us all.

"We have to leave for New York to meet with the publisher in three days, and you can't go looking like this." She motions to my disheveled self.

Looking in the mirror, my skin seems pale and a little broken out. I have enough extra baggage under my eyes to

320

take me around the world twice. My hair is stringy and tangled. I definitely need some work if anyone's going to believe that I'm some sort of an authority on starting over.

"Juan Valdez is the coffee guy," I correct her. "I can't imagine Ash was in debt to him for five mil, but you never know."

Em stays for the whole three days, even spending the nights at my condo, which tells me I must be in really bad shape. Every day, she takes me to a killer spin class taught by an instructor whom I affectionately call Hitler's Spawn. He kicks my ass every class to the point that I can barely walk when we're done. But that's okay because we go for massages right after. And facials. And mud baths. And any other service offered by a spa in the DC Metro area. I may feel hollow on the inside, but at least I look fantastic.

Em also takes me to a "holistic" doctor's office, where I get B12, botox, and God knows what else shot into me. Hours more are spent shopping, looking for just the right outfit for the meeting in New York.

At night, we hang out with Max. We play drinking games and watch movies. Em and I reminisce about college and, in equal parts, bore and entertain Max. He shares undercover stories that I'm confident are equal parts fact and fiction. Max tries to impress Em with his cooking skills by making over-the-top food each evening. I think I see something happening between the two, but I know better than to say a word, not wanting to jinx any chance of my two best friends getting together.

At the last minute, Max decides to join Em and me on the trip. He says it's for security, but I think it has more to do with Em. Either way, I'm thrilled to have him with us.

As I'm getting ready to go to NYC, I feel grateful to have such a pushy bitch as a best friend. She's snapped me out of my funk just in time. The only lingering sadness is that I still haven't heard from Gavin. He knows my meeting is tomorrow, and I keep hoping that he'll call to wish me luck. His continued silence probably tells me all I need to know, but I don't want to listen and check my cell incessantly.

By the time we board the train to leave, a fed-up Em confiscates my phone.

"This trip is about you making your life better. You can't get your head in the game by checking your call log and email every ten minutes. You don't need his luck, because you're going to rock it all on your own."

She's right. I don't need his luck. I've got this.

The meeting with the publisher goes better than I ever could have expected. The team I meet with has some spectacular ideas, and I think the discussion is going to lead to something tangible—maybe a book, maybe a column. Not wanting to rush into anything, I'm careful not to over-promise or bite off more than I can chew. Having said that, I leave the meeting feeling pretty damn excited.

Afterward, Em desperately wants to go out to celebrate, but Max puts his foot down. With the bounty on my head, he thinks that clubs are too much of a security risk. So she ends up spending most of the night pouting, or at least pretending to, which results in Max fawning over her. Eventually, he gives in somewhat and calls a few FBI friends to meet us for dinner at some hole-in-the-wall Italian restaurant that makes the best Bolognese sauce I have ever had.

Max's friends are quite handsome and a laugh a minute. None of these guys fit the uptight stereotype I'd attributed to

FBI agents. The evening out isn't exactly dancing 'til dawn at some famous club, but it's not a bad substitute. When you can't throw the party you want, throw a party with a bunch of hot men packing heat.

The whole group comes back to the Plaza with us, where we end up taking over the piano in the bar and singing badly into the wee hours of the morning. I don't think this sort of behavior is a common occurrence at the Plaza, but who's going to say no to a girl with an Amex Black card and six men with badges and guns? And who doesn't love hearing "Piano Man" and "Sweet Caroline" sung off-key over and over and over again?

I see many borderline sweet moments pass between Max and Em over the course of the night. Despite my complete frustration with love right now, I really hope that things go somewhere for them. They couldn't be more different, but oddly, I think they could work together. If Em heard Max had to have a physical relationship with someone while undercover, she would probably say, "Well, this way he won't be rusty when he finally gets home. Nothing's worse than getting back together and having bad sex."

Hung-over and possibly still a little drunk, Max and I take a morning train home while Em catches a cab to the airport. As always, I owe Em big time for knocking some sense into me.

After our train gets in to Union Station, poor Max has to go straight to work. He assures me that it's not the first time he's gone to work a tad under the influence, nor will it be the last. He says it helps him think like a criminal.

Once I get home, I climb straight into my heavenly bed. I may be pissed at Gavin for disappearing without a trace, but this mattress does dull the anger. A little. I sleep straight through the night and into the next morning, when I'm woken up by the phone.

"Ms. Clark. Lily Clark?" a voice asks when I pick up.

"That's me," I answer, groggy.

"We've a package here for you. According to the slip, it should have been delivered weeks ago, but it's been held up in customs. Will you be around this morning?"

"Yeah. I'm around." As soon as I hear the word "customs," I cringe. I can only think of one person who could be sending me something that has to go through customs.

"Great. We'll be at your building in twenty minutes."

Dragging myself out of bed, I throw some sweats on just in time to answer the knock at the door when they arrive. There's a bunch of guys standing outside the apartment with a box roughly the size of a Prius.

A rough-looking guy with a bushy beard and skull cap looks at his clipboard. "Lily Clark?"

"Yeah," I reply. "I'm not expecting anything. Are you sure it's for me?"

He looks at his board again. "You're Lily Clark, right? It says here: Lily Clark, this address, from a G. Edwards."

Just hearing his name makes me gasp. "Yes, that's me." *What the hell did Gavin send me?* I look at the shipping date, and it's marked a week and a half before he left on his trip. Before he went into radio silence. Before our fight.

The guy pushes past me and starts looking around my apartment. "Any idea where you want it?"

"I don't know what it is," I reply. "Can we get it in here, take it out of the box, and then figure it out?"

324

He shrugs, returning to the hallway, and barks orders to his crew.

They somehow manage to get the massive thing through the door. I'm still not sure how, despite watching the whole thing. It's like a magic trick. When they finally get all the wrapping off, I see the most extraordinary desk. Gavin hadn't been kidding when he said he had a thing for furniture. The desk is beautiful, unlike anything I've ever seen. The wood is adorned with carvings so detailed it must have taken someone weeks to handcraft... If I had all the desks in the entire world to choose from to write at, this would be the one I would pick. This is a desk I could write at for the rest of my life. Some girls may be wooed by jewelry. I've never been one of those girls. And Gavin has figured out how to woo me.

I can't even wrap my head around how much this must have cost. The shipping alone!

After they put my desk in my office,—which now actually looks like it could be an office—I go through all the drawers looking for anything else from Gavin, but I come up empty.

"Is there a note that came with it?"

He shoves the clipboard in my face and holds out a pen. "No ma'am, this is all we have. Sign here and here, please."

I sign, and they leave. I call Gavin again, trying all his numbers, but to no avail.

I've just sent another email that I'm sure will just bounce back when I get a call that some books I'd ordered at Politics and Prose have come in. I'd forgotten all about them, and would rather just ignore them for the moment, but I prepaid. Needing some time to think, I opt to run over.

It hadn't occurred to me to check the weather. It's freezing out, but the cold is good for me. When it feels as though your toes are about to break off, there really isn't any energy left to think about other unpleasant subjects. Like why my boyfriend sends me furniture and then disappears.

You don't send furniture to a girl you are about to break up with, right? That's not a break up gift. Way too personal and intimate. And freaking expensive! But he did send it before the fight. I replay our last few exchanges in my mind as I run, and I remember how hurt he'd been. How unfair I was. This excessive radio silence must mean one thing: It must be over.

I arrive at Politics and Prose with all my fingers and toes intact, but now feeling heartbroken as well as frozen, I decide I'll catch a cab home. I grab a cup of tea first and try to thaw a little. While warming up, I whip out my laptop and lazily scroll through Google news only to find a picture of Gavin under one of the headlines: *British Bad Boy on the Prowl Again.*

Please, no, not this.

I click the link and am faced with pictures of Gavin in the company of half a dozen different women, all supposedly taken in the last two weeks. One woman in particular appears with him a number of times at several different events. There's a picture of them lounging in their bathing suits looking very chummy. She's strikingly beautiful and looks just as good in a bathing suit as he does. I hate her.

I can't bear to look, but at the same time, I can't stop myself. Gavin once said that the people they show in the tabloids aren't real people, but characters in the fictionalized drama created by the media. I so badly want to believe that right now, but I look at the pictures and it's him I see. His gorgeous eyes. His amazing smile. His washboard abs being groped by some skank in a bikini. It isn't fiction. It's reality.

My initial pangs of heart-wrenching agony shift. I go from sad to livid in less than sixty seconds. So mad I can't see straight. I need to get out of here. I slam my laptop shut, almost hoping I've shattered it so I can send him back the pieces. I bolt to the door and smack into Charlie as I try to head out.

"Whoa, where's the fire? And where have you been? The place isn't quite the same without you!" He beams at me.

"Charlie, I've got to go. Something's happened, and I just need to get out of here," I say through gritted teeth. I'm angry, have no patience, and just want to be alone. It takes all I have to be civil.

He touches my shoulder, nudging me back toward a table. "Why don't we sit down and talk about it?"

I sidestep him and move out of his reach. "Charlie, don't take this the wrong way, but I need to be alone right now."

Screw the cab, I need out of here now! I rush past him out the door and take off down the street. I hear him calling after me, which only makes me run faster.

Despite the freezing cold, the need to clear my head is more pressing, so I end up running all over the city. I'm careful to stay in high traffic places, especially down by the Mall and the monuments. I desperately try to organize my thoughts, but I'm a jumble of anger and heartache. Have I really read him so wrong? Is Gavin just another lying, cheating jackass? If he is, I need to swear off men because I never saw this coming.

But I had seen it coming. I was just dumb enough to ignore it. How could he possibly be committed to me? We went through something tragic together, and guilt and loneliness got mistaken for love. In the back of my mind, I'd known it was just a passing thing, until he'd convinced me it was real. The second things become complicated, he fucks everything that crosses his path? Bastard.

I can't feel my fingers or toes, but I keep running. Every time I slow down, I want to curl up in a ball and never get up again. But that's not an option, so I keep pushing.

Freezing, tired, and heartbroken, I return to the condo. My legs are so tired that I barely make it home. When I open the door, I'm hit by the overwhelming smell of flowers. I walk in to see Max eating at the center island surrounded by vase after vase of arrangements of purple flowers. Hydrangeas, lilacs, tulips, roses, orchids, lisianthus, and a bunch I don't know the names of—all in my favorite color. I notice a lot of hyacinths sprinkled throughout, the apology flower. Every inch of kitchen counter is covered, and six more vases sit on the floor.

"You're lucky I was here. I stopped in to change before my meeting and a florist exploded in the hallway. I'm guessing all this means Gavin has been in touch?" He waves his finger around, pointing at the flowers.

I walk from vase to vase, smelling the flowers. "Not a word," I reply. "Are you sure they're from Gavin? Was there a card?"

"They're from G," he responds. He counts off his talking points on his fingers. "A. Who else has this much cash to spend on flowers? This all costs some serious cheese. B. Who else is going to send you flowers? And C. Some guy named Marcus was here with the florist deliveryman. Apparently, Gavin recruited him to orchestrate this craziness. There was supposed to be a note, but it didn't come through on the fax or something."

"Did he say anything else? Like where Gavin may be?" I ask.

"Nope, he had to run. Maybe he had to flower-bomb someone else. I'm guessing this is about what I saw in the scandal rags today."

The sweet smell of the flowers had momentarily made me forget the reason they're probably here.

"You saw it too?" I growl. "I'm so mad and so freaking confused. I don't hear from him for two weeks. This morning, I wake up and get a call that I have a package that's been stuck in customs. They deliver it, and it's a desk. From him. No note or anything. Did you see it?"

He takes a bite of his sandwich and nods.

"It's perfect, and I love it. Then, an hour later, I open Google news, and my heart's shattered. Then I come home to this. What the hell's going on?"

"There is no way any of the crap in the tabloids is true. You have to remember, I spend every day of my life reading people, and I'm never wrong. Gavin's a good person. He'd never step out on you, even when you're whatever it is that you two are. Plus, at least three of those pictures are of him just standing next to a woman. They aren't posing or anything. He could be standing next to her in line at a bar for Christ's sake," he points out.

He takes a long sip of his beer. "Gavin's a media target, and I'm sure it's hard for you. You'll have to decide if you can hang with it because it's part of his package. If you can't, that tells you something." I'm about to respond when he laughs so hard he spits out his beer mid-sip. "You two make quite the pair. He is being chased by paparazzi, and you're being chased by the Mexicans. Match made in heaven."

I throw a dish towel at him. "That was not beer-spitting funny." I pull out my laptop to show him the pictures. "Look, I hear what you're saying, but what about the black-haired chick in the gorgeous gown with the crazy toned arms? His arms are around her in that one."

He points at another picture of Gavin with *her*. "Do you see the 'picture smile'? They're posing. Gavin doesn't pose for paparazzi." He pulls me by the elbow to the bathroom and positions us in front of the mirror. "How would we stand if we were taking a picture?" He pulls me close, mimicking exactly how we'd stand if someone said, "Say cheese."

Not wanting to acknowledge his logic, I leave the bathroom, and he trails after me. "Posing or not, it doesn't mean he's not screwing around. I mean, what do we really know about Gavin? He could have a girlfriend in London, and we wouldn't have a clue. He could've been sleeping with half of Europe for all I know."

Max glares at me. "Not all men cheat, Lily."

I put my hands on my hips. "Maybe this one does." I shout at him.

"I'd bet my badge on it. Gavin isn't the type. I know, firsthand, how much he cares about you. Do you know how many times he and I have talked about you?"

I sit down on the mats of our makeshift gym. "No. I didn't know you talked about me at all."

"He's always calling me to check in on you. To find out about the case. If you're safe. Men that are sleeping around don't do that. I can hear it in his voice, Lil. I know this crap isn't true."

"Have you heard from him in the last two weeks?"

He stares at me blankly.

"I didn't think so. We have no idea what's going on with him."

He walks to the office and leans through the door, presumably checking out my new desk. "You know he made that, right?" he says, walking back into the living room.

I rub my still-frozen feet. "What?"

"Yeah, it's his hobby. He makes furniture. It's perfect for you because he made it for you."

I'm having a hard time wrapping my head around the contradictions around me. So he makes this for me and then goes radio silent? I'm so confused I feel as though my head will explode. I can't take it!

Max sits next to me and takes over my foot rub. "Snooty Smythe finally told me today that, 'Mr. Edwards is experiencing technical difficulties,'" Max says in a perfect Smythe impression. "So maybe he *can't* communicate versus doesn't want to. When is he due home?"

"Sometime this week. I'm not exactly sure."

"Let's hold off on panicking until then. Deal? Okay, let's hug it out."

He tackles me and pins me to the mat. "Careful, Lil, if someone took a picture of that, they could say all sorts of things. Maybe we're having an affair. If we are, you'd better start putting out."

"In your dreams, Max." I laugh.

He cups my face. "Ah, there's my girl's smile. It only took threatening you with sex. I'll try not to be offended."

I hug him and kiss him on his cheek. "I won't put out, but I'm sleeping with you tonight. I don't want to go anywhere near that bed. You raise some good points though. Maybe this is all explainable, but I'm not there yet."

He whispers seductively in my ear. "I snore. And sweat. And kick. It'll be the night of your life."

Ugh. Maybe I will rethink my "Everything Gavin" embargo.

After ordering me to think positive and stay off the internet, Max leaves for his meeting. With all this conflicting information, I need something more concrete to help me understand. Looking at all of the flowers, I'm reminded that Marcus had a hand in this massive display of affection. He may be the only one who has actually spoken to Gavin. I call him just to see.

"Marcus, this is Lily Clark. Thank you so much for your deliveries today. I've never seen more beautiful arrangements."

"It's my pleasure, Ms. Clark," he replies. "The very least I can do. I'm sorry that Mr. Edwards' note didn't come through. He wrote something for you, but I think he may have faxed it the wrong side down. Only blank pages came through."

"Orchestrating the deliveries was above and beyond the call of duty. I can't thank you enough. Do you by chance know where Gavin is? I can't get ahold of him, and I would like to thank him personally."

"Yes, I do. Sounds like he is having quite the hard time. Something about his mobile not working. He sounded very displeased when I spoke to him. He reached out to me because he couldn't get a hold of you himself. You can find him at the Ritz Carlton in Dubai."

"Marcus, one day I will explain this all to you, but until then, know that I'm more grateful than words can express." I say as I Google the hotel number. Overcome with excitement, I dial immediately after hanging up with Marcus. Once the line starts ringing though, I hang up. *What am I going to say? Do I really want to hear what he has to say? Am I ready to hear that it's over? What if he tries to string me along?*

Deciding I would rather know than not, I take a shot of tequila and call back.

I'm surprised that the front desk clerk speaks English and connects me. After about the twelfth ring, a breathless, Marilyn Monroe-sounding female voice answers. "Mr. Edwards' room. Ms. Philips speaking."

Trying very hard to keep my cool, I ask, "Is Gavin available?"

"Whom, may I ask, is speaking?"

I want to reach through the phone and scratch this snobby British chick's eyes out. Something about her rubs me the wrong way. "Could you please tell him it's Lily."

Her prim and proper tone changes to annoyed and intolerant. "Oh, it's just you."

What the hell does that mean?

I hear muffled sounds and incoherent shouting in the background.

"Lily, Mr. Edwards is very busy. I know you want his attention, but he needs to focus on work. He doesn't need to be distracted by his latest hero project. That's all you are—a project. You understand this, I hope. You American girls just fall part, and then he needs to run to save you. You're something to keep him occupied until something better comes along. Stop ringing his office. Stop leaving your pathetic messages. It's time you accept that this long-distance storybook romance is over. Do we have an understanding? Yes? Good. Okay, then. Ta-ta." There's a click, and the line goes dead.

I put the phone down, feeling as though I've just been sucked into a cyclone and spit back out. After taking a second to process what's just happened, my blood boils. "Oh, hell no! I am done playing games," I say to my empty condo.

Too angry to think about how much these calls are costing, I dial Dubai again.

"Hi, I just called a few minutes ago and asked for Mr. Edwards' room. I got his assistant instead. Is there a direct room line for him?"

"I'm sorry," the desk clerk says. "I've been directed to filter all calls through Ms. Philips' room."

"Did Ms. Philips give you that request?"

"I'm not at liberty to say, ma'am"

"Of course. Let me guess, she's stunning, black hair, looks great in a bikini?"

"Um—"

"Never mind," I say. "First, could you please take down my name and number and give it to Mr. Edwards personally? Please tell him it's urgent." I give him my info and then add, "Could you please connect me with Ms. Philips again? Thank you."

"Mr. Edwards' room."

"Listen, you British skank. I have no idea what your deal is. Maybe you have a thing for him, or maybe you're just a secretary with serious control issues. Maybe you're screwing him. Don't know. Don't care. Your pitiful attempt to intimidate me reeks of desperation. If Gavin were done with me, as you say, he'd tell me his own damn self. He wouldn't delegate it to staff. Gavin's not one for games, but you seem to be. I'd think long and hard about how this is going to end for you, Ms. Philips. Sounds like career suicide to me."

She tries to speak, but I cut her off. "Oh, and for the record, I don't need him to save me. I don't want him to save me. I can do that all on my own. There is only one of us that's pathetic on this phone line, and it isn't me. Good day."

Infuriated, I spend an hour or so pummeling the heavy bag that Max installed recently despite my misgivings. Now, I'm very glad he did. I don't want to believe the tabloids. What Max says makes sense, and I pray it's true. Plus, I can smell that stink of trouble radiating from that assistant of his even from the other side of the globe. I'm not sure what the story is, but I know there is a story. I punch and punch until I don't have any fight left, and then I sit out on the balcony to cool down. It's below freezing out tonight, but the sting of the cold air feels good.

I'm so damn tired. Not only from the hell I've just put my body through, but from the hell I call my life. Even if Gavin is completely innocent of the tabloids' claims, he's still brought all of this crap into my life. Well, not all of it... Ash is to blame for his share. But to live with the paparazzi and the distance. It's too much. I'm not sure how much more I can take. Why can't I find someone that's normal? Boring even? Someone that works nine to five as an accountant or a pharmacist. I'm over the drama.

Growls from my stomach snap me back to reality. Between all the exercise and the emotional hysterics, I must have burned a million calories today. A cheesesteak and onion rings with a chocolate shake and carrot cake for dessert sounds like the perfect meal. I call in an order at Bub and Pop's for delivery. The second I hang up, I remember Bub's doesn't take credit, and I have no cash. No choice but to run to the ATM down the block. Just what I need—more exercise.

On my way home, I see Charlie sitting on the steps to my building. *What the hell is he doing here?* I've been very careful not to tell him where I live. In fact, I haven't seen him since before I moved, except for when I ran into him earlier today. *Did he follow me home?*

He catches sight of me before I can think what to do. "Hey there," he shouts as he jogs my way. "I was worried about you. I thought I'd see if I could catch you." His hands are red and raw, as though he's been sitting in this blustery cold wind for quite some time.

I'm not comfortable with this situation at all. Maybe I'm being paranoid. After all, Charlie's been nothing but kind. Annoying and kind of creepy, but kind. But that still doesn't explain how he knew where to find me.

"I'm okay," I reply with a fake smile. "Just having a bad day. It was… thoughtful of you to want to check on me."

He looks over my shoulder at my building. "It's sure chilly out here," he says. I'm trying not to be paranoid, but I'm not going to do something stupid to prove it. There's no way in hell I'm inviting him in.

"Sure is…" I say looking around, hoping he'll decide to be on his way. I look down at my watch. "I should really get back in. Have a few things going on."

"Why don't we go for a walk? You look like you are a bit flustered. Some air might do you good," he suggests.

Clearly, he isn't taking the hint. "Okay, a short one, just around the block. I'm exhausted, and I have delivery coming any minute now."

We walk in silence for a bit. Eventually, he speaks, more like yammers, trying to fill the void. I don't hear him. All I can think about is getting home and shutting out the world. Especially men.

"Are you even listening to me, Lil?" he asks in a curt tone.

"Sorry. I'm terrible company right now. My brain's checked out for the day. I should really head back."

"What I was saying is that you really shouldn't waste your time with someone that doesn't appreciate you. I saw the tabloids. Why do you waste your time on that jackass boyfriend of yours? You're smart, gorgeous, sexy, and funny. The list goes on and on. You're what every guy dreams of. You're so much sexier than any of those girls he's been caught with."

I don't remember telling him about Gavin. I suppose I might have mentioned it, or maybe Charlie remembers me from the tabloids. The whole exchange feels off somehow. "Thanks, that's really sweet of you to say," I offer, hoping to nip the subject in the bud.

"You need to take care of yourself. Try to get your life back on track, it sounds like."

"That's good advice," I reply. "Speaking of which, I should really get back."

"Why don't you come home with me?" he suggests. "Let me make you dinner. Sounds like you need some pampering. You certainly deserve it."

"Thanks anyway, but I think I just need to go home and get some rest. So let's head back, okay? The delivery guy is probably there waiting for me." This is beyond awkward. Why, oh, why did I go on this stupid walk?

I try to turn back toward the building, but Charlie blocks my way. He grabs my hand and leads me further down the street, a bit more forcefully than I would care for. "Come on. I won't take no for answer."

I try to pull my hand away, but he's holding on too tightly. "Charlie, I really need to get home. You've been really kind, and I'm grateful, but I really do need to get going."

He has me by the wrist and isn't letting go. Yanking on my arm now, he's practically dragging me toward a row of parked cars. The more I resist, the harder he pulls.

"Charlie, I'm going to say this one last time. Let. Me. Go. NOW!"

I look around to see if there's anyone who can help, but there's no one on this tiny side street he's led me to. I try again to pull away, but I'm yanked back toward him, causing me to lose my footing. I fall to the ground, and my head smacks against the pavement. Hard. I'm dizzy and disoriented. The pain is throbbing, and I want to close my eyes and rest, but I know I need to push past it. Struggling to stay conscious, I try to remember my training. I pull myself to my feet and try to regain my balance.

Charlie still has my arm and is dragging me with him. I resist with all of my might, but in my traction-less flip-flops,

I slide across the pavement. I suppose this is what I get for wearing flip-flops out in November.

His long finger nails dig into my skin as I pull against his grasp. The more I squirm, the deeper they slice into my wrist. I make to scream, but before I can get a sound out, his free hand connects with my wind pipe. Pain explodes in my throat as I gasp for air.

I steady myself enough to launch a solid kick to his balls. He doubles over but doesn't let go of my arm. Then I give him three swift knees to the kidneys and a hard kick to the face. He howls, but still does not let go of my arm. Instead, he grips harder. I feel as though my arm is going to be ripped out of the socket.

He tries to kick my legs out from under me but misses. I give him a knee to the groin, then another one to the gut. While he's bent over, I throw the entire weight of my body onto the shoulder of the arm holding my wrist in one barreling move. I feel his shoulder dislocate, and he finally releases my arm. While he's hunched over, kneeling, I kick the back of his head, and his forehead smacks into the pavement.

Once I hear his head crack on the ground, I turn my back on him and run as fast as I can to my building. The doorman is missing. So much for the security upgrades. Afraid Charlie'll see me waiting for the elevator, I book it up the stairs. Twelve very long flights later, I finally make it to my apartment. My weary body makes it through the door and to the phone to call Max. The call goes straight to voicemail. I don't get out more than, "Get home, Max," before I black out.

TWENTY-SIX

I come around to Max calling my name. I'm on the floor of my apartment and feel as though I've been run over by a dump truck, but can't quite remember why. Max is talking to me, but I'm not processing anything he's saying. It's as though my brain's been scrambled. When I try to sit up, searing pain shoots up the back of my skull. That jolt makes it all come back. Charlie.

When the world comes into focus, Max is right in my face. He looks me in the eye and says, "Well, there you are. Nice of you to join the party. Want to tell me what the hell happened here?"

"Charlie," I whisper. I'm surprised how much it hurts to talk. I motion for Max to get me some water.

After I have a long drink, I try again. "He was waiting for me outside the building, said he wanted to talk. I told him we could go for a short walk, but he attacked me," I rasp. "He dragged me down the sidewalk. I'm guessing he was trying to get me to his car."

I pause for a minute to collect myself, still trying to put it all together. "I never told him where I live, Max. I don't

340

know how he found me. Or why he found me. I thought he had a bit of a crush, but this was nuts. He was talking about Gavin and how he doesn't deserve me. Said he wants to pamper me."

He puts his arms around me. "Holy shit, Lil. Why have you never told me about this guy? Fuck. We need to get you to the ER now. Greene," he says, turning to face the other agent. "Did you call for the ambulance yet?" He looks back at me. "You're covered in blood, but I don't see anywhere you're cut too bad. Can you tell me where it hurts?"

I want to tell him it's not all my blood, but Greene interrupts. "I did the second we saw her. I called tech too. They need to process the scene." Greene comes closer and kneels, running his thumb over my forehead. "I don't know how you get into these situations, kid. Look, I know you're tired and you want to rest, but I need you to tell me where this happened. I need to send my guys over there."

"On Newport, between 21st and 22nd."

"What the hell were you thinking?" Sully bellows from the other side of the room. "Some guy you don't know shows up at your building that you never told him about and you go for a walk with him? Damn it, Lily!"

"Nice to see you too," I croak. "I thought he was harmless."

"Doesn't look too harmless to me!" he continues, yelling still.

"Sullivan!" Greene barks at him. "Back off."

Sully storms out of the condo.

"He's just worried about you. We all are." Greene says, trying to soothe me.

Seconds later, the EMTs come rushing in. They check my vitals and then put me on the gurney. After a quick elevator ride, they load me up in the ambulance with Max in tow.

"How'd you get away, Lil?" he asks. "I see your wrists are all sliced up. I'm guessing he was holding on pretty good."

"You're perceptive, Max."

He holds my hand as the EMT beside me continues to check me over. "This is my job, babe. I'm an FBI agent, remember? A damn good one. So, he had you by the wrists, and then..." He motions for me to continue.

"I kicked him in the junk and was able to break away. I beat the crap out of him and ran. I'm pretty sure I dislocated his shoulder, and he's going to need stitches for sure."

"That's my girl!" He kisses me on the cheek and gives me as big of a hug as he can while I'm on a gurney and hooked up to an IV. "I'm so proud of you!"

I regale Max with the blow-by-blow for the rest of the ride to the hospital.

Being brought to the hospital by the FBI has its perks. I'm seen right away and have the nicest nurses. The doctor gives me twelve stitches to the back of my head and informs me I have a mild concussion. The cuts and bruises are annoying, but he promises they're nothing to worry about. There's a chance I have some damage to a tendon in my shoulder, but it's too soon to tell. I know that I walked away from the encounter in much better shape than Charlie, and I'm more than a little surprised when Greene shows up to tell me he hadn't still been lying on the sidewalk when they got to the scene.

I feel great about fighting him off but so stupid for letting him into my life.

After the doctor leaves, Sully comes in. "Hey kid," he says. "Sorry about earlier. I shouldn't have gone off on you like that. You just really had me worried."

"It's okay, Sully. I understand. You were right. It was stupid. I was so worried about being forced to invite him in that I just wanted to keep him away from my building."

He brushes my hair back from my face. "Shh… You did great. How'd you find this guy, anyway?"

"I have a knack for bringing bad boys into my life." My dark humor makes him laugh.

"I saw the video taken by a security camera across the way. Got a good look at you walloping the guy. I'm proud. You were pretty badass."

"Thank you." A big smile spreads across my face, remembering how empowering it had felt to successfully defend myself. "You should have seen it, Sul. I kicked the ever-loving crap out of him. Thank God Max has been teaching me how to fight."

"Yeah, Max has finally proved himself to be useful," he jokes. "Okay, Lil. You've got to tell me everything about this guy. We need something to go off of because he's in the wind."

I tell Sully everything I remember about Charlie. What he looks like, how we met, the random things he told me about himself. Sarah, a tech, comes in and checks for skin under my nails, takes samples to test for DNA, and then takes thirty minutes' worth of humiliating pictures of every bruise, scrape, and cut on me. Thankfully, she does her best to get through it quickly. Sully tells me bad jokes and crazy stories to try to distract me in the meantime. It doesn't really work, but I love him for his effort.

After Sarah leaves, Sully sits on the edge of my bed and holds my hand—a surprisingly intimate move for him. He looks me in the eye and says, "Kid, I'm going to find him and I'll make sure he's punished. You'll be safe again, I swear it. We've got everyone on it. I actually have to get out of here now to meet up with the DC guys and get some updates. I'll check on you later." He gives my hand a squeeze and leaves. It's crazy how these guys have become my family. I can't imagine he gets this close to all his cases. I may not be lucky in love, but I've been very lucky in the friend department.

When the warmth of Sully's hand in mine has cooled, my hospital room feels empty. People have been popping in and out, wishing me well, but I know that soon I'll be discharged and I'll go home alone. There won't be anyone there to wipe away the tears that'll inevitably fall. There won't be anyone to calm me when I wake from the nightmares I'm sure I'll have. I miss Gavin more than I'd ever thought possible. Even so, I've proved tonight that what I've been telling Gavin all along was right: I can save myself. I don't need him to swoop in and be my hero. But, I never thought about how painful the aftermath would be to face these monsters all by myself.

I was a badass tonight, and I'm damn proud of myself. But does being strong and independent mean you have to be in isolation? I'm not sure I've ever felt so alone.

After being in the hospital for hours, I'm ready to get out of here. It's almost ten in the morning, I haven't eaten since before my ordeal, and I'm exhausted. I don't have my phone on me, so I can't call Max. The nurses won't say when I'll be released. I'm moments away from walking out of the hospital on my own when Max finally comes back.

"Hey, Slugger. How're you holding up?"

"Sore, but okay. I'm ready to get out of here. Can we go home?"

He frowns and shakes his head. "Not just yet. Still waiting on the tech guys to come down. They want to try something that may be able to lift fingerprints off your skin."

"Max, that only works on TV. It never actually works in real life."

"When did you become a forensics expert?" He cups his ear. "Hmm, what's that? You're not? That's what I thought. How about we leave it to the experts, okay? If I've learned anything, it's that you never piss off your woman or your tech. Either can royally fuck your shit up. So I do everything I can to stay on their good side. If the man says he needs to try something, then we try something."

"Pearls of wisdom from Max McCarthy. I'll have to remember that."

He sits down on the edge of my bed and puts on his agent face. Bad news is coming. "So, Lil, we have to talk about something. There's no Charlie Murphy anywhere in the country that comes up matching this guy's description. All the stuff he told you was bogus. He didn't grow up in Iowa, didn't go to Northeastern. It's all a lie. We're now thinking he was the man hired by the cartel."

I'm such an idiot. How did I not see that before? They send a man to investigate me, and I invite him to lunch. *Brilliant, Lily.*

We're interrupted by a knock on the door. A man wearing an FBI windbreaker comes in pushing a wheelchair.

"Steve! I was just talking about you," Max says. "Lily, meet Steve, the most important man at the FBI."

His shameless ass-kissing cracks me up. "Steve, great to meet you. I hear you're going to CSI me."

"Nice to meet you too, Lily. The hospital's given me a lab downstairs to play in. We need more space and sterilization than your room allows." He rolls the wheelchair over to my bed. "Your chariot, milady."

Max gathers his bag, preparing to leave. "Alrighty then. Steve, take good care of my girl here. I'm going to go get back to work so I can catch this guy." He shakes Steve's hand. "Can you take her home after, or should I come back and get her?"

"Max, my man, not to worry. I've got it all taken care of," Steve answers with a smile.

Max heads out, while Steve helps me into the chair and wheels me down the hall.

I try to strike up conversation, but I can't quite keep his attention. He seems distracted. I notice he keeps looking around, in a kind of twitchy way.

"Steve, you okay back there?"

"Yeah, I'm good. I know you've got some interesting people after you, so I'm trying to keep my eyes peeled."

I suppose the tech guys are more lab rats than field agents, so I understand his anxiety. He maneuvers us through the hospital labyrinth, bringing us to a small room with several long tables that reminds me of my high school chemistry lab.

"So, Steve, what's the plan? When I've seen them do this on TV, it's always on a dead person, and they have to put them in a tent or something." I turn to look at him and find a gun in my face. "Um, Steve."

"Shut up, Lily," he snaps. "Just. Shut. Up." Steve paces, pulling out his cell phone. Based on the notification sounds, the texts are back and forth rather quickly. He exhales audibly and shoves his phone back into his pocket. From the other pocket, he pulls out a small vial and sprinkles a bit of white powder from it onto his thumb.

Shit. Shit. Shit. Lorenzo had warned me not to trust anyone. I'd never imagined it would be an FBI agent to seal my fate. He has to be connected to the cartel. Game over. They've finally got me. Instinctively, I do what I always do when I'm backed into a corner: I talk. "Got a bit of a coke problem, do you, Steve?"

"I told you to shut up." He snorts the powder and then points the gun back at me. "They'll be here for you any minute, and then I'm out."

"Oh, is that what they said? 'Do this and you're out?' That's a laugh. In case you can't tell, these guys don't like to leave open lines of credit. How much do you owe them, Steve? How much?"

He wipes some stray powder from his nose and rubs it on his gums. "Forty grand."

Dear God, who taught these guys how to run a business? They let this guy on a government salary run up a forty-thousand-dollar tab. As if he's magically going to run into forty large one day? They gave Ash five million. Did they really think they'd ever see that money again?

Steve continues to pace and snort. I don't waste any more of my breath on him. He's a dead man walking, and I think deep down he knows it. By selling me to the devil, he may have killed us both.

About ten minutes later, the door to the room finally opens. "Hello, Lily," Charlie says in a poorly mimicked Jack Nicholson voice. He struts over to me with a swagger I've

347

never seen from him. He's no longer the sweet farm boy I'd come to know. Nope, this is the psycho killer who's been haunting my dreams. I take great pleasure in seeing the bruises on his face and his arm in a sling. He approaches my wheelchair and gives me a smug smirk before smacking me with the back of his hand, right across my face.

I spit out the blood pooling in my mouth. "Wow, Charlie, that was a serious bitch slap," I say. "If you were a chick, I'd be impressed. But you're not, and this isn't some 1980's soap opera where a slap is impressive. So, I must say, kinda lame."

I should really keep my bravado in check. Charlie punches me right in the temple, and everything goes dark.

TWENTY-SEVEN

Why can't I have déjà vu of the best moments of my life? My tenth birthday when Billy Baxter held my hand before we played pin the tail on the donkey. The day I found out I was a National Merit Scholar and earned a free ride to school. Any of the time I've spent with Gavin. Why can't I relive those moments? I guess because that's just not how things work for me.

I'm waking up yet again with the world out of focus. There's a searing pain in my head, and I have no idea where I am. If this were a movie, I'd tell the writer to get a new trope.

Wherever I am is bitter cold and pitch black. I don't see anything, not even stars. From the smell and the way my eyes are itching and swelling, I'm guessing I'm on a farm, possibly inside a barn. Hay and I do not get along.

I'm tied to a chair, the ropes over the cuts and bruises on my wrist. Warm blood trickles down my hand, as every time I move, the ropes reopen the still-fresh cuts.

"Oh, good. You're up!" Charlie's disembodied voice says with enthusiasm. He's not shy about showing how much he's enjoying having caught me.

"Seriously, Charlie. You had to take me to the one place I'm deathly allergic to? Killing me with hives is taking the pussy way out, don't you think?"

"The name's not Charlie, babe. And I don't give a shit about your allergies. I'm done playing with you. I've got a job to do, and we're going to finish it. Together." He turns on a small lantern.

Even though the light is minimal, it still takes my eyes a moment to adjust to the sudden brightness. My suspicions had been correct. We're in a barn. But other than that, I can't make out anything in the weak lantern's glow.

"My employer wants to know where your husband hid his money," he says with a smile. "You're going to tell me. Nod if you understand."

"Listen, Not Charlie. I get that they want their money. I'd love to give them their money. I don't know where it is. I know you've checked all of the places I've checked. I don't know anywhere else to look. Tell Pablo Escobar I'll be happy to do a payment plan to pay back whatever Ash stole. I've got good credit. Maybe we can work out a good interest rate?"

Something crackles, a sound like someone dropping a whole box of pop rocks. Before I can figure out what it is, a searing jolt of pain hits me. It's like the exact opposite of an orgasm. While my whole body is lost in its wake, instead of feeling ecstasy, there's only sheer, blinding agony. When the wave of pain dissipates, I ask, "What the fuck was that?"

He waves a long pole in front of me that I guess must be a cattle prod. "Playtime's over. We tried this the nice way, where I pretended to be the doting admirer. You were supposed to tell me the information without a fuss. That didn't work. So now, I ask, and you answer. If you don't, then I use the cattle prod again."

"Thank God you only need one arm to work that thing since I dislocated your other one. Did you get that looked at, by the way? I do worry about you, Not Charlie."

He zaps me again. The surge of pain is worse than before. He must have cranked up the juice. I see stars, and there's a ringing in my ears. Eventually, the raw pain settles into an ache, but my body still tingles as though the electricity is still coursing through my veins. I've really got to learn to stop poking the bear.

"Okay, Not Charlie. I get it. But I still don't have anything to tell you. Ash was a lying, cheating, corrupt asshole. Had they done their due diligence beforehand, they would have figured that out. Seriously, do they not do any sort of background checks on the people they get into bed with? They blindly trusted him with five million dollars, and that's on them. Let's call it a bad investment. How this has become my problem is still a bit hazy to me."

Not Charlie paces behind me. With the way his voice carries in the barn, it's hard to pinpoint exactly where he is, which is disorienting. Obviously his intent. "You think you're so clever. But your smart mouth isn't going to talk you out of this one. They don't care about you. They won't be impressed by you. They won't care if you flirt with them and bat your pretty eyes. They get their money, or they kill you. There's a beauty in the simplicity of it. I'm going to let you sit here for a while and think about it. Maybe you'll have an epiphany about the money's location by the time I get back. It's below freezing tonight, so think fast."

He storms out of the barn, taking the lantern with him. I'm now freezing, alone, and in the pitch black again. I cannot think of a single way to get out of this. I'm tied too tightly to wriggle free. No matter how hard I struggle against the ropes, they don't budge.

There's nothing for me to tell him. No leverage, no bargaining chip. This is foreign territory for me. I've never been in a situation I can't talk my way out of.

Goddamn you, Ashton.

Not Charlie may have left the barn, but I hear his voice faintly in the distance. He's yelling at someone, but I can't make out a word he's saying. After what feels like forever, he storms back in.

He sets the lantern down on a small bench. "Apparently, someone doesn't want the pretty girl's corpse to be too bloody, so it's time for plan B."

"Oh? I thought they didn't care about my pretty eyes," I sneer.

"Don't push me. If I send you back to them in pieces, they'll get over it."

A big smile spreads across my face. I may not be able to fight him off, but I won't give him the pleasure of knowing how scared I really am. "Well, if I'm going to die anyway, I might as well go out pissing you off."

He picks up a knife and a whetstone. He sharpens the knife as he walks toward me. "You really don't quit, do you? You know, I've been doing this sort of work for a while. Never, in all these years, has a client been so off about a mark before. They said, 'She's a mousy doormat whose husband ran around on her.' Clearly, you're not the same girl."

"Oh, I'm the same girl. I was just in hibernation. You're a sociopath. I'm sure you can relate. You know all about adapting to your surroundings, don't you, Not Charlie? You seem to have gotten over your fear of blood!" I have no idea what or who has saved me from more physical torture, but I'm thankful.

He chuckles. Behind me now, I hear him opening cases and shuffling things around. I focus all my energy on trying to picture what he's doing, but it could be anything. He must be wearing heavy boots because every step he takes reminds me of a pouting toddler. Stomp. Stomp. Stomp. Those stomps are now headed my way.

I feel his presence behind me. My whole body tenses, waiting for a blow or a zap. Instead, he pushes my hair off my neck and blows gently on the exposed skin. I would rather he punched me. Physical abuse would be so much better than being touched by this sicko. He softly kisses my neck and moves his way down to my collar bone, each kiss a bit more intense than the last. His hand glides across my body to massage my breast. He pulls the neck of my sweater aside and then runs his tongue from my shoulder to my ear in one long, disgusting lick. "We're going to have a good time tonight, Lily. I'm going to put that sassy mouth of yours to work."

I bite down on my lip to muffle my scream so hard that I draw blood.

Suddenly, I feel a pinch and a painful burning in my neck.

"I can make your last few moments in this world as excruciatingly painful as possible, or I can be merciful. Don't forget that. I'm in control here, and you will obey me."

Shivers overtake me when I think about what he could do to me if he really wanted. I have no idea what he has just given me, but I could soon be in for a world of hurt.

He walks away and says rather cheerfully, "Now, onto Plan B. Since I can't beat the truth out of you, I'm left with a less elegant method. A confession elixir—my own personal blend of cocaine, MDMA, and some other secret ingredients. When you work for drug dealers, you score brownie points for using their products in fun new ways. I think this combination has great potential. I'm working on a name. I like Verity. Good, right? Nice little play on words there."

"Branding a big factor in your line of work, is it?" I ask. "Sociopaths won't buy just any truth serum. It has to have a catchy name like 'Can't Shut Up Cocktail.' Do you trademark something like that? Do you start a website? How does all that work anyway? Do hit men have a Facebook group? Marketing's a bitch, you know. You should think about that before you launch this poison on the market."

He groans. "I sure hope I don't have to listen to hours of your crap. I've already had to suffer through so much of it playing your secret admirer. You're not as charming as you think you are." He pulls the knife out of his back pocket and grabs my chin. "What I wouldn't give to cut out your tongue."

Despite being so scared that I'm worried I might pee my pants, I already feel the drugs starting to take effect. While ninety-nine point nine percent of the time, I'd avoided drugs, I'm not a drug virgin by any stretch. After spending four years at a school that sends more kids to rehab than grad school, I've gotten glimpses of what I might be in for. But I think I can try to fight the high. Your high is as bad as you let it become. If I stay focused, I can buy myself some time. My goal is to distract him as much as possible until I can figure out a plan.

He forces my eyes wide open. "Ah, your eyes are giving you away. You're starting to feel it already, eh?"

"'Eh?' What are you, Canadian?"

He claps and looks up to the roof in frustration. "And the bitch is still here! Is there anything that makes you less infuriating?"

"Tequila," I retort. "But that wasn't in your special blend."

He slaps me hard across the face. "One more love tap for good measure won't hurt anyone." He wipes the blood away from my lip and kisses me gently. It takes all I have not to vomit on him.

Standing tall, he shifts the bulge in his pants, causing me to gag. "Tell me about Ash's money."

I take my time and think about my words carefully. "He never had money of his own. Ash always mooched off everyone else. His father, his friends, his mistresses. Mexican drug lords. He was an equal opportunity scumbag."

"Where did it all go?" he asks.

"Up his nose. Paid for hookers and strippers. Where do you think it went? If your damn bosses had only asked me for a reference, I would have told them Ash should be nowhere near the drug trade. I've watched *The Wire*. I've listened to Biggie. What's the first rule? 'Don't get high on your own supply.' Ash never had the self-control to follow that."

He taps his chin and circles behind me again.

While he's rummaging around, I say, "Tell me something. How'd the total get up to five mil? After he didn't give back the first four they thought it was a good idea to give him more?"

He laughs, but doesn't answer my question. I'm about to say something else, but the returning crackle of cattle prod stops me. "Keep talking Lily. Where did your husband put the money?"

"*Late* husband, thank you very much," I deflect.

He stands in front of me again with the prod in his hand. "Whatever. Where's the money?"

"If you were any good at your job, you'd know that we've had nothing to do with each other for the last five years. I'm the last person who would know. You should have one of his girlfriends tied up here."

"I did that already. She didn't know anything." He caresses my cheek. "She was a wild ride, but I think you're going to be so much sweeter." His hand travels down the length of my body. "Oh, I love my job."

I want to scream. To spit in his face. But I don't have the luxury of getting emotional. I have to stay calm and keep stalling. "I'm so pleased you have such job satisfaction, Not Charlie. Most people don't get up in the morning excited to go to work. Clearly, you do. You've found that the secret to a happy life is bringing others to their deaths. Your mom must be proud."

I may sound tough, but it's all an act. I remember Crystal's story. She OD'ed on this asshole's private reserve. I saw pictures of her body. I know what he's capable of.

"Where did your husband hide the money, Lily," he says calmly.

"*Late husband!* Dammit, Not Charlie. If you're going to kill me anyway, can you at least stop calling him my husband? I hate him very much right now, and thinking that I'm still tied to him makes me very angry! If you really think this is going to go anywhere, you'd best knock it off."

"Or else what?" he laughs.

I look at him through narrowed eyes. "You think you're in control here, Not Charlie. But you're not. The drug is. Well, I am, really. I can talk about what you want me to talk about or I can ramble on about anything. You let go of control once you shot me up. Sure, it's probably going to make me OD soon, just like Crystal. I can spend time talking about Ash or about how I'm still mad that little Erik Miller didn't do the hokey pokey with me in the third grade. Your choice."

He pulls a syringe from his back pocket. "Maybe you just need more?"

"Maybe your product just sucks."

He punches me in the gut for that one.

I cough and try to catch my breath. Damn, that hurt. Once I've regained my composure, I go right back at him. "You know, Not Charlie, I saw you coming a mile away. You know what gave you away? No man, and I mean *no* man, stays for female problem chats. For future reference, real human boys, not monsters like yourself, run for the hills when a girl's period is mentioned. You stayed through the flow and cramps convo all the way to the yeast infection! No man does that. I knew you were fucking nuts right then and there."

He looks at the syringe in the light and adjusts the dosage. He's going to give me more. I better think faster. "Thanks for the notes. I'll work on that with my acting coach for my next gig," he says, voice dripping with sarcasm. "Tell me about Ashton."

I'm struggling to keep some control of my thoughts and where they go. I use whatever focus I have to think of random things about Ash. "He used to get the clap so often the girls at the doctor's office would call him The Clapper! I'd long since stayed away from him and his penis at that point. Yuck! I got texts from them almost twice a month. 'The Clapper is back!'"

"Tell me about his money," he growls.

I've got to slow down again. If I don't try to keep it together, this is where I could screw it up. "He used to only snort coke with hundreds, because he thought they were handled less and thus cleaner. *Hello!* You're putting a toxic chemical straight into your brain, and you're worried about catching the flu? I never understood that."

He grabs my chin and forces me to look at him. "Stop trying my patience."

I look up and away, defying him. "You're going to kill me. These are my last moments on earth, and I'm going to talk about what I want to. Sorry, my friend. You've lost all control here, so spare me your *Dexter* act. What're you going to do? Hit me again? Ohhh, scary! Now, where was I? Oh, money. Right. He used to leave money everywhere. He put money in his sock drawer, in his glove compartment, in the toilet, under the sink, in the hot tub filter. But all those places burned to the ground. Maybe your money did too. Did anyone think of that?"

Not Charlie has lost his cool, picking up and throwing whatever's within reach around the barn. I'm getting to him. My plan is working, so I keep pushing harder.

"Let me guess. You use this drug mostly with men, right? Women are a very different kind of chatty than men. Men may ramble about sports, sex, or whatever. But a woman can go on and on about all sorts of subjects. Especially when you get me all touchy feeling from the MDMA-coke combo. That's really your flaw there. You want me to talk about my ex, and all I want to do is tell you how I feel when you furrow your brows like that. You should really stop that by the way. You'll get wrinkles."

He rushes back over to me and yanks down hard on my hair. "Where. Is. The. Fucking. Money."

"I. Don't. Fucking. Know." I say, purposefully spitting when I talk.

In a rage, he hits me with all he's got, punching me with his full strength. He picks up the chair I'm in and throws me. I think he expects the toss to hurt me, but all it does is break the chair—and give me my window of opportunity.

With the chair in pieces, the ropes have loosened, and I'm able to wiggle out of them before he notices. I stay lying down, feigning injury.

After trashing the barn a bit more, he walks over to me. "I can toss you around this barn like a sack of potatoes. Who's in control now, bitch?"

I punch him square in the balls. While he's doubled over in pain, I untie my legs. Once I'm standing, I wail on him in a way I've only seen in the movies. By the time I'm too exhausted to throw another punch, I'm pretty sure he doesn't have any teeth left, most of his ribs are broken, and he has heavy internal bleeding. Not Charlie won't be hurting anyone else anytime soon. Even if he does wake up, I think I've destroyed his chances for procreation.

Just as I'm about to make a run for it, the barn door opens. My heart stops. A man in black points a gun in my direction. Looks like I've gained a two-second reprieve only to be back in the crosshairs.

TWENTY-EIGHT

I hold up my hands and slowly back away from Not Charlie. The shotgun follows my movements, but in the dark, it's impossible to read the man holding it. Without dropping my head, I glance around the barn floor at my weapon options. Nothing that would allow me to get to him before his shotgun got to me. The crunching of hay draws my attention to the space behind the gunman. We have another guest.

"This was not the scene I was expecting to come upon." I recognize Lorenzo's voice instantly. He stands in the doorway. Even through the shadows, this man, whom I'd thought unflappable, looks flapped.

I put my arms down as the man with the gun lowers his weapon. I let out a breath I didn't know I'd been holding. "If it isn't my knight in polyester pants. I couldn't be happier to see you."

He looks around the barn as he walks toward me. "Do I want to know what has happened here?"

"Probably not."

He looks me up and down. When he reaches out to touch me, I flinch. "Are you okay? Did he hurt you?"

I shrug. "He zapped me a few times, and he's loaded me up with a drug that's supposed to make me give up my dirty secrets."

"Did you?" he asks with a raised eyebrow.

"Look at him and look at me. How would you rate his job performance? Now, can you get me out of here? I know where the money is."

Lorenzo stops in his tracks. "What? How? We've looked everywhere for that money."

I kick Not Charlie in the gut one more time as I walk past. "He was right. Once you get talking, the truth eventually comes out. It came to me as I was babbling about something else."

We leave the barn and walk to his town car. Before we get in, I stop to give him a hug. "Thank you, Lorenzo."

"You're welcome, but it doesn't seem like you needed me."

"I was ten seconds away from trouble when I got lucky. It could have easily gone the other way. If you hadn't come, I don't know what I would have done."

"I was always coming," he replies. "It just took longer than expected to get things settled. I couldn't just barge into a cartel operation without calling first. There's etiquette to all of this."

"Underworld etiquette? Does one take a class in that?"

He laughs. "No such luck. This is how we weed people out. Those that learn quickly and play by the rules make it. If you don't, you don't last for very long." He gives me squeeze and says, "Now get in, before we freeze."

I don't need to be told twice.

"Lily, meet Albert," Lorenzo says once we've settled into the back seat, pointing to the very large man driving. Albert must weigh three hundred pounds—earned, I suppose, by eating too many cannoli. Through his reflection in the rearview mirror, I see he has deep pockmarks on his face that I guess are from a rough adolescence burdened by acne.

"Everyone calls me Big Al."

"You smell familiar, Big Al. Is it fair for me to guess you were a part of my previous kidnapping?"

He winces.

"It's all good. Consider your karma scrubbed clean by coming to save me."

"So where to, boss?" Big Al asks.

Lorenzo looks to me. "Lily?"

"Potomac. Frankie's house. You haven't razed it yet, have you?"

Lorenzo looks at me with curiosity. I can tell the man is not used to being surprised. "No. It has remained untouched since the first fire."

"Then we're golden." I lean my head back and close my eyes. My body feels strange. Floaty and euphoric. I feel my heart pounding, but it seems distant, as if it's outside my body.

"I know the way," Al says.

They allow me to rest for a bulk of the drive. In my head, I'm formulating a plan. In order to pull it off, I'll need my wits about me.

When I notice we're close to Potomac, I say, "Thank you again for coming to my rescue. For the future, can you please give me some way to contact you??

He shakes his head. "I contact you, Lily. That's how this works."

"I get the whole cloak-and-dagger thing. But perhaps this all could have been avoided if we had been able to stay in touch. Can we get a bat signal or something for you?"

"Bat signal?"

"You know, something for me to flash up into the sky when trouble is lurking."

"My dear, with the way trouble finds you, that signal would be up non-stop," he replies. "Speaking of trouble, you may have escaped your captor there, but you still have very real problems with some gentlemen from Mexico."

"I think I know where the money is. If I'm right, I'd like for you to arrange a meeting. I'll deliver their money, and they can promise to forget I was ever born. I won't spend my life looking over my shoulder. I want them to look me in the eye and swear that I'm clear."

He taps his fingers on his legs. "These men look people in the eye and lie all day. Their assurances mean very little."

"That's where you come in. You'll keep them honest. I know you will. I've played this out in my head a million times already. There's only one way I walk away from this alive, and that's if they feel good about letting me go. I can't be a threat of any kind. If I can't make them okay with that, then I might as well just off myself now. You promised me protection, and I'm begging you to deliver."

"What makes you think I can provide that level of protection?"

"You'll work it out. And if you don't, they'll kill me. Anyway, it won't matter if the money isn't there. If it's there, can you arrange a meeting?"

"Yes," he says with a nod.

"You know how to contact them? Was their info on the bottom of the ad for the bounty on my head?"

He laughs. "You certainly do make things colorful. I was speaking to them before I came to collect you. They're expecting me to find some sort of resolution here as well."

"So we're all on the same page then? I feel stupid for stressing myself coming up with a plan that was so obvious to everyone else."

"Don't feel that way. You're new at this. Consider this your internship in... what did you call it, underworld etiquette?"

We pull into the driveway and park next to the garage, or what's left of it anyway. Just a short time ago, this lot was where it all began. Forced into a stinky police car on a hot summer's day.

There's very little still here. Just the sad ruins of my former home. As I get out and walk around, my mind flashes back to times with Ash. Looking at them as still shots, I can see how someone might have thought we were happy. Maybe at certain moments we were. But those times were few and far between. Most of the time, we were mutually indifferent. No wonder he had no problem serving me up to the cartel.

When I was asked where Ash had hidden his money, I'd thought of all the random hiding places I used to find his crap—drugs, phones, condoms, money, porn. He had hiding places everywhere. Usually, he got caught because he screwed it up. Like the time he put pot in the hot tub filter without sealing the bag. Clogged up the filter and caused the whole system to burn up.

I'd completely forgotten about the pool filter. The *underground* pool filter. Franklin hadn't liked all the machines being out in the open. He thought it looked tacky. So when they carved up the land to put in the pool, they left room to build a filter room next to it. One of the pieces of pool deck was designed to lift up to a set of stairs leading down to a little room containing the pool filter, heater, and pumps. I had only been down there once, years ago, when the pot had burned up the filter when the pool guy was on vacation. After that, I'd never thought about it again.

I walk across the yard to the pool deck. After pausing to say a prayer, I lift the trap door and climb down the stairs. By the time I reach the bottom of the short stairwell, I can already see that I'm right. Clear plastic bins sit stacked along the far wall. Bins stuffed with cash, even more than five million by the look of it.

I run up the stairs to see Lorenzo and Al waiting for the results of my treasure hunt. "Call your Mexican friends. I have a debt to settle."

TWENTY-NINE

I'd be the first one to admit that I put on a great show of confidence. Some swagger and a whole lot of bravado will convince a lot of people of a lot of things. I sure hope it works this time because I'm scared shitless. Why did I want to meet with this guy again? Why can't Lorenzo just handle it? What the hell was I thinking?

There's no backing out now. This meeting will either lead to my clemency or my execution. Either way, I pray that, after this, it'll all be over and over quickly.

I smooth down my hair, as though it could make a difference to the outcome. They just want their money. I'm sure they couldn't care less that I look like I've rolled around in a barn. "So tell me who they are again?"

"You don't need to know their names. Nor do you want to," Lorenzo explains. "But these are the men of authority for their organization in this area."

I play with the cross around my neck. "So, I'm not meeting the head guy, right?"

"Lily, no one ever meets the head guy. How do you think I've lasted as long as I have? No one knows who I am. Even so, the man you're meeting will be able to provide you with the assurances you're looking for."

I will my hands to stop shaking, but I fail miserably.

He reaches over to clasp my hands and pulls them to his chest. "If you go in there like a scared little girl, you'll be treated as such, and I don't expect you'll like the results."

I look him square in the eye. "Lorenzo, I've got this. I just have to get my jitters out now."

The car comes to a stop. I hadn't been paying attention during the drive—not a wise move from a survival standpoint. I have no idea where we are. Too late to worry about that now, I suppose.

We're in a park of sorts. There's a lake with a small pier, and the beginnings of trails lead off into the woods. A sign that states that camping is prohibited. As it's the middle of the night, I suspect we're completely alone out here. No one to hear me scream.

Lorenzo motions for me to get out of the car. He makes no move to follow, though, so I guess I'm on my own. There I see a man sitting on a bench looking out at the lake. Like Lorenzo, he's rather unassuming. He's probably about fifty-five, and everything about him is run-of-the-mill—average height, average weight. He'd blend into any crowd in America, right down to the Members Only jacket. I'm assuming he's my date.

I slowly walk toward him, trying to gather any confidence I can muster. Or at least fake it 'til I make it. I sit down next to him but have no idea what to say, so I wait for him to speak. I can tell from his breathing pattern that he's calm. I try to mimic his rhythm in hopes of finding that same level of ease.

It's freezing out with a slight breeze, and I'm shivering. Focusing on keeping my teeth from chattering helps deter any thoughts of my impending doom.

The man turns to me and raises an eyebrow. Looking me over with curiosity, he touches my chin and tilts my face to the right and left to examine both sides. "Looks like you've experienced Mr. Snyder."

"Ah, is that his real name? Well then, yes, I have experienced some of his fine hospitality. He signed me up for his deluxe spa package, a lovely combination of deep tissue beating and electroshock therapy. I'll be sure to write him a stellar review on Yelp."

The man doesn't respond at first, and his silence makes my stomach jump to my throat. I'm going to get myself killed because I can't keep my sarcasm under control.

Finally, he looks me in the eye and says, "You're funny. A little humor is good." He doesn't laugh, but I can tell he's amused. "You wanted this meeting, Ms. Clark. Tell me what I can do for you."

The wind picks up and chills shake my frame. "I'd like to give you your money and then have your assurance that my debt will be cleared."

"Our mutual friend has told me that you did, in fact, find the money."

I dig my nails into the wooden slats of the bench. "Yes, I found it this evening."

He scoffs. "I find that surprising. We've had a lot of people looking for that money for quite some time now. People who are very good at what they do."

369

"Charlie—I mean Mr. Snyder—said something that sparked a memory. I swear I had no idea until a few hours ago."

He looks at me critically through narrowed eyes. With each passing second, I convince myself more and more that he's not buying my story. I hold my breath, anticipating a strike. "I believe you," he says. "Based on the way you look, Mr. Snyder did his best to make you very uncomfortable. If you knew where it was, I'm sure you would have told him. But then, if that were the case, you'd be dead."

Gulp.

"But then again," he says with a shrug. "I hear that he was the one to lose all his teeth in your relationship. You certainly know how to turn the tides, Ms. Clark."

Could I have possibly earned this guy's respect? My muscles relax a bit, and I loosen my grip on the bench. "I just want this to be over. I want to give you the money and go on with my life. I don't want to have to look over my shoulder for the rest of my days."

"I can understand that. Uncertainty is an unforeseen consequence of our lifestyle. From what I understand, this was not a path you chose. Rather, it was chosen for you."

I snort. "Only if you don't think I made that choice when I married a spineless ass-hat." I actually get a smile out of him at that one.

"I was never fond of your husband."

"Late husband," I correct. "And neither was I. See, we have so many things in common."

"While I can see that this wasn't your choice, I'm sure you can understand that you pose a risk. Uninsured risks must be eliminated for my organization to survive."

370

"On the surface, I can see how you may think that, but in reality, I know absolutely nothing. I know Ash was in debt, that his debt was placed on my head, and that I met some guy in a park to talk about spa packages. Hell, I don't even use any of your... products. I wouldn't make a good witness for anything. But more importantly, why would I say anything? What would I have to gain?"

"People do funny things, Ms. Clark. Especially ones who live with FBI agents."

I think about my response to that for a moment, choosing my words carefully. "I've lived with an FBI agent for months and never once have I told him about our friend over there." I nod in the direction of the parking lot. "Also, I just spent the day being tortured for information—beaten, shocked. He even gave me a truth serum, and I still didn't give him anything... but grief. I think I've demonstrated that I can handle the pressure without cracking.

"And, since I'm laying it all out here for you, I'm so over all this drama. I would never, ever do anything to put myself back in your crosshairs. All I want is to get the hell out of here and rebuild my life. I'll keep writing, maybe get a dog—you know, normal people stuff. The only drugs I want to hear about ever again are in Grateful Dead songs."

He cracks another smile. "You certainly are entertaining. I'll give you that. You have an innocence that I don't get to see very often."

"Nature of your business, I suppose. Not too many vestal virgins coming your way."

He tips his head back and laughs. "Oh, you're no vestal virgin, Ms. Clark. I've seen the photos. Remember, we've been watching you very closely. I'm not sure I can ever go to Top of the Hub again without thinking of you fondly."

Well, if he doesn't kill me now, I may just die of embarrassment. I feel myself turning beet red as I try to come up with a response and fail.

There's a twinkle in his eye, and I know he's enjoying my humiliation. Once his laughter dies down, he sits there staring at the lake once more. I have no idea what I should say, or if, for once, I should just keep my mouth shut. He has a pensive look on his face, and I assume he's weighing his options.

He starts humming the Grateful Dead's "Casey Jones," and my mind races through the lyrics, trying to determine if this is a good sign or a bad one. Not so good, if I recall. Something about two trains about to collide and being better off dead. Hopefully, he just happens to like the song.

"What will you tell the FBI?" he says, snapping me out of my thoughts.

I hold my hands up in defense. "I told you, I won't say anything. I swear."

"If I grant your request and allow our relationship to dissolve amicably, what will you tell them? How did you escape? They have an investment in you at this point. They'll need to hold someone accountable."

I know he's right. This isn't a movie where the picture fades to black after the lost girl comes home. Tons of money and man-hours have gone into this investigation. They'll need something to show for it, or people will lose their jobs. People like Max, Sully, and Greene.

"How comfortable are you with letting our dear friend Not Charlie take the blame? Perhaps Not Charlie was just an overeager suitor who couldn't deal with rejection. I'm sure if they find his place, they'll find all of the photos of him stalking me. I wouldn't even have to lie. I can't imagine he would be dumb enough to have records that he was working for you."

He rubs his chin. "Continue."

The wind picks up and blows my hair around, forcing me to tuck it behind my ear. "I'll say he snatched me from the hospital and smacked me around until I got away. I won't bring Lorenzo into this either, so I'll just pretend that I've been wandering through the battlefields in Manassas all this time."

"That's a plausible story," he agrees. "But I know they have aspirations of catching a bigger fish."

"Don't we all? As it turns out, someone will realize they had an overactive imagination and made some grandiose connections that weren't really there. It'll turn out Charlie wasn't hired to kill me at all. He just had an unhealthy crush. It may not be as sexy as taking down a cartel, but it will make one hell of a Lifetime movie."

He taps the bench with his fingers. The way he sets his jaw makes me think he's mulling the story over, trying to pinpoint the flaws. "I would be burning a good employee. That isn't good for morale."

Wanting to squash his doubts, my bravado kicks into gear. "He got his ass handed to him by a girl. You may want to reconsider his value. And really, isn't this the risk you take when you go into this line of work?"

"You'll have to sell the story. To the FBI. To the press. You must never deviate. Do you really think you can keep it up for the rest of your life?"

"That's the easy part."

"What is the hard part?"

I smile. "This conversation."

He snickers and then stares off into the lake again.

"Fine, Ms. Clark. I will consider our business relationship terminated on good terms. You'll be watched. If I catch wind that you are sharing any information about our encounter, the situation will be rectified. Permanently."

"Understood."

"You may not use any of this in your work."

"My work?" I ask.

"Your writing. I don't want to see this on your blog."

"You follow me?" He rolls his eyes and gives me a look that tells me not to be flattered.

"Well, if you do, you'd know I haven't mentioned a thing yet. I have no motivation to change that. Rose Evans leads a typical normal life. She would never sit in a park with a stranger in the middle of the night freezing her ass off," I say with a wink. "Look, I'm going to do everything I can to pretend that none of this ever happened. I want this whole ordeal to feel like a really screwed up dream."

"You know I have people everywhere. If you change your mind, I'll know. And then it won't be only you that pays that debt. Anyone I think you may have confided in will be eliminated."

I cringe thinking about all the people I'm putting in jeopardy by sitting here.

He points to the parking lot. "Now go. The sooner you get back, the sooner the heat dies down. I expect nothing short of an Oscar-winning performance. Remember, your life depends on it."

"I suggest you get some popcorn and a box of tissues. I'm going to put on a hell of a show."

He chuckles again. "Goodbye, Ms. Clark. Don't make me regret this."

"I won't. Please don't be offended if I say I hope to never see you again." I walk away before he can respond, but I hear him laughing as I go.

THIRTY

Walking back to the car, I feel a million pounds lighter. It could be the fact that I can't feel my body from the waist down.

Al opens the door for me when I reach the car. After I get in, I see him palm something to Lorenzo.

"What was that?" I ask.

Lorenzo smiles. "He bet me that you wouldn't make it back."

I put my seatbelt on. "That's really disturbing. Al, you are officially off my Christmas card list."

Lorenzo takes off his fur-lined coat and covers my legs with it. "I knew you would. You are far too charming for Carlos not to bend. Plus, you're very much like his daughter. That girl has him wrapped around her finger."

"Well, let's hope I can charm everyone else while I try to pull off this final part."

"Which is?" he asks with a raised eyebrow.

I slide my arms into the coat on my lap, hoping the soft fur will stop the frostbite from setting in. "I have to convince everyone that my kidnapping had no connection to the cartel."

"If you do this, then you're no longer in his debt?"

"Yes. Well, I'll sort of be on probation. I'm in the clear as long as I don't step out of line. If I break the rules, then all bets are off."

He pats my leg. "I have faith you'll be able to fulfill your part of the agreement. Where shall we take you?"

"Somewhere near the barn. Not too near because they're looking everywhere. How far could I have walked in this amount of time?"

Big Al turns down the heat so I can hear him chime in. "I know just the place. Just say that you escaped and ran through the battlefields until you found civilization." Manassas is filled with Civil War battlegrounds, miles and miles of them—an easy place for a wounded girl to get lost. "I'll drop you off, and then you'll have to walk a mile or so until you hit a gas station. They'll call for help for you there."

"Sounds dramatic. Can you turn the heat back up please?"

Al laughs and cranks the heat back up. We sit in pleasant silence for a few minutes, enjoying the calm before the storm. We take the back way to Virginia, through the mansions of Potomac—so many people there, sleeping comfortably in their gigantic beds without the fear of execution hovering over them if they say the wrong thing. Not so long ago, I was one of them.

Before the opportunity passes me by, I know I have to take advantage of being in close quarters with a mob boss. "Okay, gentlemen, I have to ask: What'd you think of the ending of *The Sopranos*?"

Lorenzo rolls his eyes at me, but surprisingly, Big Al has some very impassioned feelings on the subject. Lorenzo and I both laugh at his rambling from the backseat until he wears himself out.

"If I haven't said it before, thank you, Lorenzo, for all that you have done for me. I'm truly grateful," I say.

"It was my pleasure. You did most of it on your own though. I was just the getaway car."

I nudge him with my shoulder. "I'd have probably been killed a long time ago without your watchful eyes."

He nods. "That's true."

I had been joking, but clearly, he isn't. I know I'm playing in the big leagues, but I still haven't gotten used to the rules they play by. I know they won't hesitate to kill me if they aren't happy. I must never forget that.

"Presuming there is a positive outcome to your performance, I suggest you make yourself scarce for a bit afterward. I'll have time to make sure everyone stays true to their word while you get safely out of the line of fire."

"I was thinking of leaving the country for a little while."

"To be honest, I haven't been able to figure out why you haven't done that yet. Seems like that would have been the most sensible move. But, I try not to judge."

"That's clear from your judgey tone," I retort, getting another laugh out of him.

Looking out the window, I can see we're getting closer to Manassas, and I know my short reprieve is just about over. While the hardest part may be behind me, the next act isn't going to be a picnic.

Lorenzo turns to me and says, "You can do this. You will do this. And you will do this well."

I shift in my seat to better look at him. "Will I see you again? I wasn't kidding about needing a bat signal. I can't stand that I have no way to reach out to you, even just to see how you're doing. This isn't just a one-way street, you know. I care about you. So come on, a signal? We can call it the Lorenzo Lantern."

"I don't think shining a light into the sky would be good for my anonymity. I'd rather not throw away a lifetime of caution as I enter the home stretch. If you stay with Mr. Edwards, I have full faith that you'll be safe and taken care of. If you're left to your own devices, however, I feel confident you'll see me again soon, when you're up to your eyeballs in trouble again. Your taste in men leaves much to be desired. You're lucky fate has intervened on your behalf."

Gavin.

We pull down a dark dirt road.

"We're here," Al says.

"Yay," I say under my breath. I look at Lorenzo. "I guess this is it."

"I'll always be here. You just won't know it."

"Carlos said just about the same thing. You guys should carpool. Reduce your carbon footprint and all that."

He shakes his head. "I've never had such a sassy charge."

I shrug. "You call is sass. I call it moxie."

I lean over and hug him. "Thank you, for everything. I imagine you don't get too many hugs in your line of work."

He laughs as he hugs me back. Then he pulls back to look me square in the eyes. "Stay out of trouble. And know a good thing when you see one."

He kisses me on the cheek as Big Al opens my door.

"All right, Al. I need your help," I say, getting out and circling the car. "I don't look enough like I've just been beaten and traipsed through fields for hours. I know I don't look good, but you need to freshen me up. Give me your best shot."

He steps back, shaking his head. "I'm not hitting a woman. You should go roll around in the field a bit. It'll scrape you up."

I step forward and tug on his arm. "Nope, I need a big open wound. Something that says that a big, bad man was mean to me. I know you can do it."

He squares his stance, trying to look intimidating. "I'm not doing it."

"Al, I need this. If I don't play the part, they won't buy it. So come on. Suck it up and slap me."

BAM! He lets one rip.

Son of a bitch, that hurt. I spit out blood and rub my jaw. "That was good, Al. Real good." I lean my head in though the open backseat window. "Pay up 'Zo."

"What do you mean, 'pay up'?" Al asks.

Lorenzo hands me a twenty, laughing as hard as I've ever seen him laugh.

"I bet 'Zo that I could get you to hit me. Hope you've learned to never bet against me now, Al. Catch you on the flip side," I say, smiling as I walk away from my fairy godfather. Hopefully, for the last time. I hear the car drive off behind me.

I'm freezing again, but right now, the cold feels amazing. I know I'm alive. I take Al's advice and roll around on the ground for a bit. I use the tall grass to scrape up my legs and the rocky soil gives me some bruises. I had already been pretty freaking dirty, so that part's well covered now.

Only knowing Manassas a little bit, I have a general idea of where I am but not a specific one. The longer I wander around though, the more credibility it will give my story, so I'm glad to be a little lost.

After a while, the adrenaline wears off, and I finally feel every cut, bump, and bruise I've collected. I haven't slept in over thirty-six hours. I can't remember the last time I ate or drank. I'm getting lightheaded and dizzy. Playing the role of the victim won't be hard.

I'm not one for crying in public. I tend to internalize. But I can't do that now. I need to sob like a little girl and sell my story about the man who wouldn't take no for an answer.

In the distance, I see the gas station Al mentioned and a McDonalds. The gas station would afford a bit of privacy for my scene. The jam-packed McDonald's screams instant YouTube fame. I debate my two choices as I hobble toward them. I must do exactly what someone would do if they had been wandering the wilderness all night in the freezing cold.

I'm suddenly overcome by the smell of coffee, hash browns and pancakes. The fast food joint is packed with some sort of high school sports team, families with toddlers, and a group from a local assisted-living facility. *Get ready, America. It's showtime!*

"HELP! Please, someone help me!" It's supposed to be pretend, but I'm having a hard time finding my breath all of a sudden. I think I may have overdone it by running. My chest feels as though it's being crushed.

As I enter the restaurant, all heads turn my way. I hold myself, shivering from cold as well as fear. I see some people piecing it together.

"Is that the missing woman from the news?" I hear someone ask.

"Please, help me!" This isn't make-believe anymore. Something's actually wrong with me. Sharp pains shoot through my chest. That's what I get for thinking of pulling off a stunt like this. Instead of feigning a problem, I now have a real one on my hands. I should have known better than to fuck with karma.

My knees buckle and give out, and I fall like a sack of potatoes. The back of my head hits the ground hard, re-opening the wound there. A stream of warm blood pours down my neck. I hear people scurrying around me. Someone calls 911, but also News Channel Four. You can always trust the average Joe to have his priorities straight. No one tends my wounds, but I hear the constant click of cell phone cameras. For once, the tabloid-crazed media is working in my favor. And it might just kill me.

Fighting for consciousness, I run through my story in my head. My life depends on how well I play this off, so my story has to be spot on. But my body, mind, and soul are so spent, completely drained of any energy. It hurts to breathe, and the room feels as though it's spinning. I just want off this tilt-a-whirl.

So I give in to the darkness…

THIRTY-ONE
Gavin

I'm in hell. For the past week in Dubai, we've endured a record-setting heat wave. It's been 45°C, with over sixty percent humidity—almost 25°C higher than their record temperature in November. I've suffered through a week's worth of golf outings and tennis matches that I've had to go to with a plastered on smile, when all I've wanted to do is stay in my room and drown in scotch.

The company's fiscal year is made or destroyed on these trips, and as CEO, it's my responsibility to make the magic happen. This year, I'm going through the motions, but my heart isn't in it. I haven't spoken to Lily since I left on this trip, and I'm gutted. She's all I think about. I can't concentrate on work. Everyone expects me to be my typically charming self, and I just don't have it in me.

Only two more days until I can go home and sort things out. The trip has been grueling. Golf at dawn, meetings past sunset, black-tie dinners that go on deep into the night. While it may sound glamorous, it's exhausting. Especially since I can't seem to keep my mind on business.

I spent the whole of this morning on the golf course, and now I have thirty minutes to shower, get dressed, and get downtown for the afternoon's meetings, where I'm expected to give a speech. I wish I had time to stop and call Lily. My picture was splattered over the tabloids yesterday, and I can only imagine how upset she must be. The stories are all completely preposterous, and I hope that she trusts me enough to know that. But I honestly don't know what she's thinking.

The last time we spoke, we'd had a row. A few days after, I'd gotten an email from her insisting that she needed space and asking me not to contact her. A bloody email! It has practically killed me to respect her wishes. If my mobile hadn't been pinched at the airport at the beginning of the trip, I probably wouldn't have had the self-control not to call her. The only time I'm near a telephone with any sort of privacy is when I'm back in my room. And with the time difference, it's never a good time to make that call.

After I'd seen the pictures in the tabloids, I knew I had to do something. I didn't care what she'd said in that email! I'd sent her flowers and a letter that was probably far too emotionally charged. I had Marcus attend to it personally to make sure everything was done perfectly.

I do my best to get ready quickly, but I'm still running late as I head out. As I'm walking through the lobby to the valet, the concierge, Nav, stops me.

"Mr. Edwards, I have a few messages that I was asked to deliver to you personally. The American gentleman caller who left the last one said he has been leaving you voicemails at your room number and, as you have not returned his calls, he insisted I give this to you and urge you to call him back immediately. I apologize for the profanity in the message, sir. He demanded I write it word for word."

"Thank you, Nav," I say, puzzled. This is the first I've heard about any voicemails. I hand him a tip and take the messages from him. The first is from Lily, asking me to call her, which surprises me. It's marked urgent, and I'm instantly unsettled.

The next is from Marcus.

The FBI has just been here to question me about Ms. Clark. I think you should contact them as soon as possible.

The final message is from Max.

You limey bastard. You'd better drop what you're doing and call me right fucking now. (202) 555-8785.

"Nav!" I shout across the lobby. "I need a private phone straight away."

He takes me into his office and closes the door. I can't dial Lily's number fast enough.

"Hello," a strange, male voice answers her phone.

"I'm looking for Lily. Is she there? Put her on, please."

"Sir, I'm going to have to ask your name."

Who does this bloke think he is? "Gavin Edwards. Who the bloody hell are you?"

"Mr. Edwards, I've been told, if you called, to have you call Special Agent in Charge Max McCarthy. Do you have his number?"

"Yes, can you please tell me what the hell is going on?"

"Please speak with SAC McCarthy."

I hang up immediately and call Max.

"McCarthy," Max answers.

"Max. I just tr—"

"Where the fuck have you been? Do you have any idea what's been going on here, you selfish prick?"

"Max, mate, pl—"

"Don't 'mate' me," he shouts. "I can't fucking believe you. You son of a bitch... After all the shit you've put her through, you call now? What the hell are you thinking? You know what? I don't have time for this. At least one of us should be focused on Lily right now. If you give two shits about her, get your ass on a plane right now. If not, go to hell and don't come back."

"Max, what is going on?" I scream into the phone. "*Max!*" He's already gone. This doesn't make any sense! I try calling him back, but it goes straight to voicemail. Desperate, I call Greene and get voicemail again. Finally, I try Sully.

"Sullivan."

"Sully! Please tell me what's going on. I can't get a hold of Lily. Max just screamed at me and hung up. I'm freaking out here, Sul. What's going on?"

"Jesus, Gavin. Where the hell have you been?"

"I've been on a trip for weeks. Everyone knew that. Why's this shocking everyone?"

"G, I don't have time to get into this. Lily's been kidnapped. We're pretty sure it's the cartel. I need to get back to work. You need to get on a plane and get here. Call me when you land."

I stare at the phone long after he's hung up. This can't be happening. It's just not possible.

"Mr. Edwards? Can I be of service?" I hear someone talking, but the words don't register. I never even heard the door open.

"Mr. Edwards, are you alright?"

I snap out of my daze and see Nav in front of me.

"Nav…" I say, still disoriented by the news. "I need to get to Washington, DC straight away. Can you get me a flight? Charter a plane if you have to. I need to leave now."

"Yes, sir. I will look into it right away."

Lily. Missing. I try to wrap my brain around what's happening, and my mind is flooded with horrific thoughts of what those bastards could be doing to her. I should've kept her safe. Now I'm on the other side of the fucking planet, and I can't do a goddamn thing. I bolt from the office, ready to head back to my room, when I run into my team waiting in the lobby. *That's right. We're supposed to be on our way to a meeting.* I'd completely forgotten. I pull George, my second-in-command, aside.

"Gavin, you look ill. You're white as a ghost!"

"George, there is an emergency in DC. I have to leave right this moment. You need to handle the rest of the trip. There's only today and tomorrow morning left. I'm sure you can manage it. Make apologies for me. Just tell everyone I had a family emergency."

I let go of him and stagger toward the elevator, when he grabs my arm. "What's going on? I know I don't have to tell you how important these last meetings are. Can't it wait until tomorrow?"

"No, mate. It can't. I just spoke to the FBI. My girlfriend has been kidnapped." I hear myself say the words, but they don't feel real.

"That's horrible. Yes, man, you need to go. How can I help? "

"Just take care of things here. I can't think of anything else at the moment. I just received the news a few moments ago. I'm still in a bit of shock, I think."

"O," George calls over his shoulder. "Get over here!"

Olivia Phillips, or O as we call her, is a junior executive. I've known her my whole life. Our mothers were best friends, and we grew up together. She's the closest thing I have to a sibling. When Lily had said she couldn't join me on the trip, I invited O to join the group. She's still working her way up in the company, so coming on this trip was a great opportunity for her to expand her horizons. O's background is more on the tech side of things, but I know she's wanted to learn the business side as well. She's been filling the role of my assistant on this trip, but we've ended up fighting the whole time. I've been such a wreck that I've been fighting with everyone.

She storms over, looking at her watch. "Why haven't we left yet? We should have been at the meeting site ten minutes ago. What's the hold up? You're giving the presentation, Gavin. We shouldn't be late."

"George is going to do it for me. I have to go. There's an emergency in the US. I must get there."

Nav walks over and hands me a print out. "The next commercial flight doesn't leave until one in the morning, sir. But there's a chartered jet that is leaving in an hour and a half."

"Wonderful. I'll be on that one then. Thank you, Nav." I pull a pen from my suit pocket and scribble down a phone number. "Can you call this number and ask for Special Agent in Charge Sullivan? Please give him the flight information and tell him to have someone pick me up at the airport." I turn to George and say, "I'm going to pack. Go to the meeting. You have all my notes for the speech." As I head to the elevators, I hear someone in heels running up behind me.

"Gavin, what are you doing? You can't leave," O insists.

"Yes, O, I can and I will. Now go to the meeting and make my apologies for me." I step into the elevator, hoping she'll leave it at that.

Surprisingly, she steps in as well and keeps at me. "You can't be serious, Gavin. Really? You have a speech to give and the last round of meetings tomorrow. Surely your needy little plaything can wait two days to see you. That stupid American cow cannot be worth throwing hundreds of millions of pounds' worth of business down the pan! You have employees to think about."

I point my finger in her face. "Don't you dare question my loyalty to my employees or my company. And do not *ever* speak of Lily in that way again. O, I love you, but you are skating on thin ice. Now, piss off."

The elevator doors open, and O exits right alongside me. "Gavin, you need to stop and think about this for a moment. When Brooke disappeared, you dropped everything and ran after her while your staff held the company together. Last month, you flaked on a major meeting so you could stay in the US with your latest pet project. And now you are going to leave again? I'm questioning your loyalty. And your blasted sanity. I get that you need to be the hero. You need to ride in on your white horse and save the damsel in distress. Can't she stay in peril for forty-eight hours longer so you can fulfill your goddamn responsibilities?"

I slide the keycard into the lock and push the door open. I block the doorway, wanting her to leave me the hell alone.

"She's been kidnapped, O. By some very dangerous people. I need to be there."

She brushes past me. "Wire them the ransom and be done with it," she spits. "The FBI can fly her here after they sort it out. You don't need to be there."

I pull my luggage from the closet and toss it onto the bed. I throw my clothes haphazardly into the open cases. "You're a coldhearted bitch, you know that? How do you live with yourself?"

"You're damn right I am, and I'm bloody proud of it. Now stop packing and go to the meeting."

I stop what I'm doing and stare at her. "Have you not heard a word that I've said? I'm leaving. Go do your job, get to the damn meeting, and get the hell out of my way."

She throws her hands up into the air and storms out, slamming the door behind her. *Good riddance.* I need to get to the airport as fast as possible, and I don't need her slowing me down. I throw the rest of my things into my suitcases and take a car to the airport.

The flight from Dubai to DC is sixteen long hours. I wish I could fall asleep, but my brain won't stop thinking of all of the horrible things Lily could be going through. Not knowing what's happening to her is agony.

I'm seated next to a woman I've actually met a few times. She's an actress or a model or something. I can't really recall. She won't stop talking though, and it's driving me mad. I just want to sit and get a handle on the situation. I give fuck all about her or her job or whatever the hell she's babbling about now. She's flirting and giving me those Mile High Club eyes, and I want nothing to do with them.

I order a scotch and tell the flight attendant to keep them coming. I don't want to land in DC sozzeled, but if I don't calm my nerves, I'll never make it through the flight. Maybe after one or two, I'll actually be able to nod off.

Five scotches later, I finally pass out. Sleeping proves to be worse than staying awake though. My dreams are plagued with images of Lily in various scenes of danger. Each one is worse than the last. With each horrific scenario, I feel more and more horrible for not being there already, even though I know that when I get there, I'll only feel helpless because there'll be nothing for me to do but wait. Awake or asleep, it makes no difference. I torture myself for the duration of the flight.

THIRTY-TWO
Gavin

As soon as I'm off the plane, I'm sprinting through the airport to baggage claim. When I get there, I find Meredith already waiting for me.

"Hey there, Hot Stuff. What is it with you and girls that can't stay out of trouble?"

I give her a huge hug, in part because I'm thrilled to see her and in part because I really need it. "It's so good to see you. I thought you were on assignment."

"I came back when I heard Lily was missing. I head out later today."

"Thank you for coming to get me. Mer, please tell me something. All I know is that she's been kidnapped. No one would tell me anything else. I'm losing my mind. Please tell me what the hell is going on."

"You do know how hot you are when you beg, right?"

"Mer…" I glare at her. How can she be so flippant? I know she's a good agent, but shouldn't she be taking this seriously? Bloody hell!

"Sorry, just trying to insert a little humor. Come on. Let's get your luggage. I'm sure you've got enough to clothe a small island country."

"Please just tell me something. Anything!"

"Not here, Gavin. Let's get your things, and we can discuss it in the car."

I want to tell her I'll leave my luggage behind, but I know she's testing me. If I'm calm, she'll open up. If she thinks I'll fall apart, she'll be reserved and only tell me the bare minimum. I want to know everything, so I need to at least appear to keep it together. I collect my luggage, and we head to her car in silence.

Once we're on the motorway, she finally speaks. "She was found this morning in Manassas. She wandered into a McDonalds and collapsed. I'm not sure of the extent, but she'd suffered significant trauma. When I left the hospital to get you, they were still running tests and working on her. You'll know more when we get to the hospital. As far as I know, she hasn't regained consciousness yet."

"How bad, Meredith?"

"Bad, Gavin. It's bad. They tortured her."

I can't respond. There are no words to express the darkness that has overtaken me. Each time I'd let my imagination delve into the horrors she may have been enduring, I'd stopped myself, thinking it couldn't be as awful as I feared. Hearing all this is my worst nightmare realized. I feel as though my soul has been ripped out.

Mer touches my arm. "We're looking for the bastards that did this, Gavin. We'll find them. This's what we do." Meredith continues to talk, but I don't hear another word.

393

When we arrive at the hospital, Meredith stops me before we enter. "Look, Gavin, there is going to be a lot going on in there. Lily'll be protected by guards at all times until we know more. I can't say when you'll be able to see her or for how long. But I can tell you that fighting the guards will only make things worse for you. So stay calm, do what you're told, and don't make this harder than it already is. She's the number one priority right now. Not you or how you feel about her. Got it? Let everyone do their jobs, and this will go smoothly."

I nod and follow her through the maze of people. She's required to show her badge at several stops along the way. The whole hospital is locked down like a fortress. I'm relieved that there's so much security, but it also makes me aware that the danger they feel she is in is still lurking. The FBI wouldn't allocate this amount of resources unless there were a serious threat.

We make it through the labyrinth, and I spot Greene and Sully at the end of the hall, talking to a doctor. More than anything, I want to storm over and demand information, but I know that will only end up getting me pushed out of the inner circle. I wait as patiently as I can.

I wish I could read lips. Greene looks over and makes eye contact. I give him a look, pleading for him to have mercy on me. He turns his back to me to speak to Sullivan. A moment later, Sully comes over. Not a good sign. Greene's the soft one. He's either sent Sully over to intimidate me or to put me in my place.

He shakes my hand. "G, glad you made it. Wish it were under different circumstances. At least she's alive though."

"Sul, please. I've been sitting on a plane for sixteen hours, imagining the most ghastly things. Tell me what you know."

"Hearing the details isn't going to scrub those images from your mind. I can promise you that. No matter how much you hear, you weren't there. You'll never really know. You'll always wonder. It isn't going to be easy either way," he warns.

He shares the same information I'd received from Meredith earlier. The doctors are still running tests. They have no idea who took her. No leads. No ideas.

"What are you doing to figure it out, Sully?" I ask him. "It seems like half the damn FBI is here just hanging around the hospital. Aren't you supposed to look in every warehouse, farmhouse, doghouse and whatever other house you find? Are you or are you not the bloody FBI?"

He looks around and nods. "We do need to get half of these dick wads out of here. Gavin, I know you are upset. Here's the deal: you can be emotional or you can be a part of the team. You can't be both. Well all care about her, so don't think you're the only one torn up inside about this. If you're going to get pissed off and start yelling, then I have to treat you like a boyfriend and escort you to a babysitter. If you want to help and be part of the conversation, then calm down and focus."

I know he's right. The situation isn't his fault, and I know he's good at what he does, but it's hard to remember that at the moment.

He whistles loudly to get everyone's attention. "If you've been standing here with your dick in your hand for the last two hours, I suggest you get out of this hospital, get out on the street, and do some goddamn investigating. We need to get this guy, and we need to get him now. The longer we wait, the colder this case gets. If you can't remember all the details of the case, watch the damn news, because the press is working harder on this case than you are. Get out there, and don't come back until this guy is in cuffs. *Now move!*"

As the agents scurry around, organizing their plans, I notice Max walking toward me. "You're brave to show your face around here," he says with open hostility.

"Max, I'm here because I love Lily. This shouldn't come as a surprise to you. Why don't you explain why you're so pissed off?"

He keeps walking toward me, and I can't tell if he's about to punch me or emotionally collapse. He looks terrible, as if he hasn't slept in days. He's pale, and his eyes are swollen and red.

He tightens his fists, and I firm my stance in case he takes a swing. "You went MIA, man," Max yells at me. "You swooped in here and got her all caught up in your fairytale Prince Charming bullshit, and then you went poof. Gone. If she hadn't been crying her eyes out about the damn tabloids, she wouldn't be in here. This, my friend, is your fault."

"Max, I didn't go anywhere. She sent me an email telling me she wanted a break and to give her space. I went out of my mind for three weeks trying to respect her decision," I explain, straining to stay calm. My fists are clenched so tight that my fingernails dig into my skin, and it's taking all I have to not lose it.

"What the fuck are you talking about? Her email was hacked weeks ago. She hasn't had access to it in ages."

I pull my iPad out of my bag and show him the email. "This is what the fuck I'm talking about Max," I say through gritted teeth.

Gavin,

This is all becoming too much for me. Let's use the time you're gone as a clean break.

Please don't call or email. I need space and time to think. Contacting me will only push me away. Please respect my space.

I'll call you when I'm ready.

Lily

He reads the email and pushes the iPad back at me. "I don't know what is going on, but that email is bullshit. There is no way she wrote that."

"Then who did? Do you honestly think the cartel hacked her email to break up with me? That's mad! It has to be from her. I pushed her for more of a commitment and she couldn't take it."

Sullivan storms over to us. "Hey, assholes! Did you forget this is a goddamn hospital? That girl is fighting for her life, and you two are screaming about a damn email? What the hell is wrong with you? Sit down and shut the hell up, or you're both out of here. We don't have the time or energy to referee the two of you. Now kiss and make up, or get the hell out."

We both obediently sit down, but the tension remains.

"Now, if you ladies would like to know what we found out about the email, I'd be happy to tell you," Sullivan continues.

Max stands back up, yelling again. "Enough with the power trip, Sully. Stop being a prick and clue me in about what's going on." He shoves Sullivan.

Sully walks away in a huff.

"Max, you're out of line," I shout at him. "Control your bloody temper!" I chase after Sullivan. "I'm trying to wrap my head around all of this, mate. Nothing makes sense. Please, tell me what you know," I plead.

Sullivan sighs. "The IP address that her computer was hacked from is in London. We traced it back to your company's server." He pauses and gives me an appraising look. "But it's not your personal IP address, so it clearly wasn't you. At least, not you on your computer," he growls.

"You can't really think it was me?"

He glares at me for at least a minute, as if he is trying to decide. "I should, but I don't. You'd better think long and hard about who in your company would want to fuck with your girlfriend."

I'm flummoxed. I can't imagine how anyone at my company could be connected to Lily. Or why they would do something so stupid. What reason could someone from my company have to break Lily and me up? It doesn't make any sense. Other than a select few, my employees don't know anything about my personal life. There are a few diehard *Covent Gardens* fans who took Brooke's death hard, but to do something like this? It's barmy!

I want to ask Sullivan more questions, but he's called away by another agent. Still stunned, I sit down in the first chair I can find. A woman walks over and sits next to me.

"You must be the Brit," she says.

I raise my eyebrows, a bit surprised by her abruptness.

She holds out her hand. "Emily Harrington."

"Ah," I remark. "The infamous Em. A pleasure to meet you. Although it feels improper using a word like pleasure right now."

"I hear you. Look, you've got to cut Max some slack. He's taking this hard, and he's coming off the rails. Whether we like it or not, we're her only family, and we have to stick together to get her through this. All of us."

"I understand he's gutted. I am too. I don't fault him for it. I know he blames me. Hell, I blame me. I should've protected her. I should have been here or dragged her stubborn ass to England and kept her under lock and key until this mess got sorted. But I didn't, and now she's here. I get that he's cross. But he knows more than he's telling me, and that pisses me off. All I've wanted since I spoke to him yesterday is for someone to tell me what really happened. I'm in the dark, and it's excruciating."

"He doesn't blame you," she explains. "He blames himself. He's calm now. You should go talk to him. I'd tell you, but it isn't my story to tell."

I walk over to Max, holding my hands up in truce.

"She went out to the ATM, to get some cash for take-out," Max says abruptly. He shakes his head. "That girl never has cash. She was all boohoo because of the damn tabloids and wanted some junk food from the neighborhood deli, but they don't take credit, so she went to get some cash. This guy she knows was waiting for her and attacked her."

All of the air leaves my body and my heart feels as though it's seizing. I have a million questions but can't seem to get any words out. "Was she… I mean, did he…" I stammer.

"No, he didn't rape her, if that's what you are trying to ask."

I nod.

"Our Lily, man," he swallows hard and then continues. "She kicked the crap out of him. Just beat him to a pulp. When we watched the security video, it looked like she broke a couple of his ribs, dislocated his shoulder, and probably broke his nose. She's a tough chick."

"Wait, she got away?" I'm more confused than ever.

"Yeah, she made it home. We took her to the hospital where one of *my* fucking tech guys handed her over to that creep. He was supposed to be taking evidence, but instead he gave her to the guy that attacked her. The perp shot Steve, the tech, and took off with Lily. This guy's good, too. He changed cars somewhere, and we lost him on the cameras. She was just gone, and we had no fucking clue where they went. We had all our people on it, and no one could pick up a trail." His words hang in the air like a smoke cloud. She could have been gone forever, and we might never have found her.

He taps his forehead against the wall. "It's my fault, dude. It's my goddamn fault. I handed her over to the tech. She didn't want to go with him, but I told her to go. I told her she would be safe." I can see he's fighting back tears, but it's a losing battle.

"Max, you didn't do this to her. This isn't your fault."

"That's bullshit, and we both know it."

I don't try to say anything more, because I know it won't help. The painful tension is broken when a doctor approaches.

"I'm Dr. Walker. Are you here for Ms. Clark?"

"Yes," we say in unison.

"Ms. Clark has suffered multiple forms of trauma, but she's stable now," Dr. Walker says. "She was electrocuted and sustained severe blunt force trauma. She also had high levels of a range of narcotics in her system when she was brought in and is lucky she didn't overdose. She was dangerously dehydrated as well and had a significant electrolyte imbalance. All of these factors contributed to Ms. Clark's ultimate cardiac arrest and the onset of multiple seizures, which we feel we now have under control. As I said, she's stable, but still unconscious. We now have to monitor her carefully. Her body has been through a lot, but she's young and healthy. There's a good chance she'll wake up and come out of this okay."

I should have a million questions, but the only words I can find are, "Can I see her, please?"

"Yes," Dr. Walker answers. "You may both come with me now and visit for a few minutes. But after that, let's limit it to one in at a time. I know there are many people who care for her, and the FBI is still working an active case. Her recovery is my only priority. All drama is to be kept outside of her room, or I will revoke visitation. Have I made myself clear?"

Such a smug sod. I do my best to keep my annoyance at bay and completely disregard his little tangent. He walks Max and me to her room and is courteous enough to give us some privacy.

With all the horrors that have been playing out in my mind, I'd thought I would be prepared when I saw her. Nothing could have prepared me for this. My heart seizes when I set eyes on her. My lungs stop working. It's as though my brain can no longer function. My dear Lily is black and blue everywhere. I couldn't possibly count all of the cuts and scrapes covering her. She looks so small and fragile. Oh, the pain she must have endured!

Max takes one look at Lily and walks back out. Em, who had been lingering in the doorway, runs after him. I hope she can help him because I don't have it in me. Seeing Lily like this has shattered me.

I sit down beside her and reach out to hold her hand, but I stop myself. Deep cuts run all along her hands and wrists. I'm afraid to touch her. I don't want to cause her any more pain.

"Hold her hand. Trust me, it will do more good than harm," a voice behind me insists. "Hi, I'm Susan. I'm your nurse for the night. Believe me, she needs you to talk to her and be there for her. That's what'll bring her out of this. She's a fighter. She's been through hell and back and is still here. Don't worry, you won't break her so easily." Susan checks Lily's vital signs and then slips out of the room.

I pick up her hand and swear to never let go again. It takes all my restraint not to climb into the bed and hold her. I stay by Lily's side all night and well into the next day. Em is kind enough to bring me something to nosh on in the morning, but I'm not hungry.

I must nod off at some point because the next thing I know, I'm startled awake by the sound of Max screaming in the hallway.

"Max, you have got to calm down," Greene shouts back.

"I'll calm down when you start doing your job," Max bellows. "How the hell has it been days and you still don't know anything? How's that even possible? The guys that did this to her are probably long gone by now. This case has gone cold because you guys dropped the ball. She's my roommate. I should be out there!"

"Max, you son of a bitch! Sit your ass down before I knock you down," Sullivan growls. "I'm sure as hell not going to find him when I have to keep coming back here to deal with your sorry ass. You're too damn close to this, and you know it. You can't be out there, because you're only seeing red. You can't be an agent right now. You're no good to her out there. She needs you here. "

Dr. Walker storms into view and threatens to kick everyone out of the wing permanently. Em pulls Max away, and Sully and Greene join me in Lily's room.

"Sorry about that, G," Sully says. "Max isn't used to being on the sidelines and doesn't know what to do with himself. He's a good agent, one of the best, but right now, he's not thinking clearly. He's no use to us out there."

"I don't think any of us know what to do with ourselves," I reply. "So have you found anything?"

Sullivan lets out a long sigh before answering. "I'll give it to you straight. We've got nothing. The guy that took her is a ghost. I'm just as pissed off as Max is. The difference is I can't go mouthing off about it."

Greene gets a call on his mobile and motions for Sully to be quiet as he answers. "They've found something," he says after he hangs up. "An abandoned farm out in Manassas, about ten miles from where Lily was found. There's an abandoned barn with a lot of blood in it. And a cattle prod. We've got to—"

Alarms start blaring, and the room suddenly fills with doctors and nurses. Susan pushes the three of us out of the room and into the hallway, where I'm left to watch helplessly as they try to save her.

THIRTY-THREE
Gavin

Three harrowing days and no sign of improvement from Lily. The doctors were able to stabilize her after she went into cardiac arrest again, thankfully. But she hasn't shown any signs of waking up, and the doctors are now using "if" instead of "when". I refuse to imagine a world that doesn't have her in it. I know she'll wake up. I don't know when, but I know with every fiber of my being that she will. Until that moment, I'll keep praying.

The search continues for Lily's abductor. The FBI and DEA feel confident he's linked to the cartel. Sully and Greene have tried to bring me into the loop, but I can't do it this time. When I'd been helping them with Brooke, I wanted to be on the inside. I was able to be a part of the team without becoming too emotional. I'm not capable of that now. I can't stomach thinking about what's happened to her. When I do, I'm consumed by rage and frustration. I'm no good to Lily like that.

Max comes and goes. The FBI is letting him help a bit with the investigation, but I think they're mostly allowing it to help him keep his sanity. He still stops by twice a day and often spends the night at the hospital. Being on the job again gives him a sense of purpose and an outlet for his guilt and anger. He's still a bear to be around, but at least he's stopped picking fights with everyone.

I spend the days just talking to Lily. She told me once that she loves Jane Austin, as if there were a woman alive who didn't. I've bought the whole collection on my kindle and read from them to her daily.

Em kicks me out for an hour or so a day so that she can attend to Lily. Facials and other such things that she insists her friend needs. "When she wakes up I want her in perfect condition," Em insists. "If the roles were reversed and she let me wake up with oily skin and bushy eyebrows, I'd never forgive her. Plus, you need to get out and shower. Lily is fighting for her life. When she wakes up, she deserves to see sexy Gavin, not frumpy Gavin who hasn't showered or brushed his teeth in a week." She shoves me out the door.

I've tried to stand my ground, contending that I need to stay in case Lily wakes up. But Em's informed me that if I don't do as she says, she'll tell Dr. Walker that I'm disrupting Lily's rest and need to be removed. I can tell Em is a girl who's used to getting what she wants and isn't afraid to play dirty. I don't for one second think she's bluffing.

I hate leaving the ward because it's bloody hard to get back in once you've left. There's still security at every turn. It seems as though the guards standing post manage to change every time I'm out, and the new guard always refuses to let me pass. It's a nightmare.

On my fourth day at the hospital, I'm paged while taking a shower in the physician's locker room. I throw my clothes on and sprint back to Lily's room, praying that she's awake. Greene, Sully, Max, and Em are all there, drinking champagne. *She must be awake!* I run past them and rush straight to Lily's bed. Her eyes are closed.

"Gavin, I'm sorry. I didn't think when I had you paged," Em says. "She's not awake. They found the guy though. He's dead. The search is over."

I'm relieved that at least that much is over and that the bastard is gone, but it's hard to be happy when I'm recovering from the disappointment that Lily still isn't awake. Refusing to give up hope, I sit back down at her bedside and pick up where I left off in *Pride and Prejudice.*

Once the others leave, things are quiet—that is until Max drops back in and asks to go for a walk. I agree.

As soon as we get out into the hallway, he says "I've been looking into that email you got. Your IT department has been very helpful. Top notch guys you have there."

"Thank you," I say, waiting for him to get to the point.

"The IP address traces back to an Olivia Phillips. Anything you want to tell me?" he asks.

"O? That's crazy! I mean, I believe you. I just can't fathom why she would pull something like this." I'm completely gobsmacked.

"Gavin, it's not that hard. She's got a thing for you. Do you two have a history?" he asks in an accusing tone.

"What? God, no! She's like a sister to me. Our parents were friends, and I've known her since we were children. She's got an on-and-off thing with my best friend, James. Plus, she's an employee. I'd never cross that line."

"Seems like you have some shit to work out."

"It seems I do. Can I borrow your mobile?"

He pulls his phone out of his trouser pocket. "Sure. You ever going to get yours back?"

"To be honest, I haven't thought about it once since I've been here."

My first call is to my IT department. Not that I don't trust Max, but I want to hear from them firsthand. They confirm that "Lily's" email was sent from O's computer. To make matters worse, they've looked into the integrity of my email account, and it's been tampered with as well. They aren't sure of the extent yet, but they're working on it. On top of all that, the replacement mobile that O had told me was on backorder arrived the day after mine was stolen. O had signed for the package herself.

Next, I call my secretary. If there's been something improper going on, she'll get to the bottom of it. Mrs. Smythe has the interrogation skills of a seasoned SIS officer. She informs me that Lily and Max had been calling for weeks. O had insisted that all messages be funneled through her. I thank Mrs. Smythe and ask her to connect me with O's office straight away.

"Hello, Gavin," O says cheerfully.

"Olivia."

"Oh, dear. I must be in trouble. You only call me by my proper name when you're cross with me."

"Olivia, you've one chance to come clean."

"Gavin, I haven't a clue what you're talking about."

"Last warning," I growl.

"Gavin, really. I'm completely at a loss," she says innocently.

My blood is boiling. Such betrayal from a lifelong friend! "Fine. Play it that way. You're fired. Clean out your desk and get the hell out of my building."

I hand Max back his phone, determined to deal with her properly when I return to London. She isn't worth another moment of my time at present.

"Damn, you don't mess around," he says.

"She's lucky she's four thousand miles away and I'm too much a gentleman to make a scene," I retort.

"Come on, heartbreaker. You've got to fill Greene in. He's still trying to figure out if the cartel is behind any of Lily's troubles. He'll be relieved to know that this part is only the doing of a scorned woman."

I explain the story to Greene. Recounting the details, I become incensed. All of that pain and hurt caused so unnecessarily. All the times Lily reached out for help and felt that I had ignored her. When I'm finished with the story, I decided to go for a walk to cool down. I don't want to go back to Lily's room carrying all this anger. But once my temper has cooled, I head back.

Bloody hell, another guard change!

THIRTY-FOUR
Lily

Oh, great. A screaming match. Clearly no one has taught these people how to use inside voices.

"You cannot go in that room," someone shouts.

"I've been in there for days. I understand that this is your first shift, but I assure you I'm permitted in there," a more familiar voice shouts back.

"Sir, this patient is in protective custody. No one's allowed in there but medical staff and FBI agents. Those are my orders."

"Call the bloody agent in charge. I was just talking to him."

Is that Gavin? It can't be.

"Sir, I'm going to need you to calm down and wait downstairs. If you really have access to this patient, we'll work it out down there."

"I *need* you to let me in there. If you won't call Greene, I will!"

"Gavin," I say in a voice far weaker than I'd expected. Realizing that no one must have heard me, I know I need to sit up to get this party started.

I open my eyes and struggle to sit up. "Gavin," I try to say again, but no sound comes out. My throat is parched, and my mouth feels as if it's been coated with glue.

I suddenly feel as though the world has completely stopped and everyone is staring at me. I think even that damn beeping has stopped. In this place, where you can't pay for a moment of quiet, I think you could hear a pin drop.

The glorious quiet lasts for a millisecond before the room is flooded with doctors and nurses. I see the police officer pushing Gavin away. He puts up a fight, until Em drags him away. I'm just as surprised to see Em. How long have I been sleeping?

The doctors practically scream questions at me, and my brain goes on sensory overload.

"Can everyone stop yelling at me? One at a goddamn time, okay?" I try to shout with my raspy voice. Thankfully, they stop after that. I look around at the shocked faces and pick the one cute guy out of the bunch. "You, McDreamy, go."

They all laugh, and I think I've made McDreamy's day. Not too original, I know. But at least I've gotten them to all calm down. I think that once they've seen I have my wits about me, they turn the panic level down a few notches.

They ask all sorts of questions about how I'm feeling and tell me to push this, pull that, follow the pen light. After about ten minutes of that, I cut them off.

"Enough. My turn," I squeak at them. "Can someone please tell me how long I've been out for and what the hell is going on? I know why I'm here. I remember everything up until the McDonalds. Then what?"

McDreamy answers, "Well, the FBI will be in to talk to you about that. What I can tell you is that you've been asleep for close to five days."

"Five days! How is that possible?" As soon as I let out the yell, I regret it. My throat hurts so much.

"When you came in, you were dangerously dehydrated," McDreamy explains. "In addition, there was evidence that you had suffered numerous electric shocks. That in combination with the dehydration put great stress on your heart, and you had a heart attack. In addition to the heart attack, you had an electrolyte imbalance that set your whole body into a tailspin. You had a series of seizures and then fell into a coma. Since then, we've been hydrating you, monitoring you, and waiting for you to wake up. You've had quite a few close calls. Your heart's doing better, but it's still weak."

Ashton literally broke my heart. That bastard.

They talk at me for a little while longer, but I don't hear a word they say. The nurses check me over and take blood for more tests.

"Okay, Ms. Clark," McDreamy, whose name is really Drew, says. "We're going to get out of here and let you rest. I know this has been a lot to take in. The FBI is eager to get in here and pester you, but I'm keeping everyone out of here for a few more hours to make sure you have some time to relax and feel settled. I've put your room on lockdown. They may have the badges, but I'm the gatekeeper, and I'm on your side. Got it?"

"Thanks, Drew," I whisper.

"I'm not opposed to McDreamy, you know," he says with a wink.

"Good to know. Hey, there was a British guy here a little while ago. Can someone get him back?"

"Gavin? Yeah, we all know Gavin," he says with a hint of disdain. "None of the nurses have gotten any work done since you've been here. They're all too busy swooning over him like high school girls. I'll send him up after you've had some rest."

"Why does that not surprise me? I'll see what I can do to get your ladies back to you," I say, returning his wink.

McDreamy stays true to his word. No one but him and my nurse, Natalie, comes into my room for over eight hours. It gives me time to get my head together. My throat had felt like sandpaper, but after a few ice pops, I feel better. I can't believe I've been out for so long. I don't feel great, but I don't feel that bad. I'm wondering how much of my unconsciousness was due to a coma versus my body demanding some much needed rest.

I'm busy fiddling with the bed settings, trying to make it more comfortable, when I'm smothered by a big body that smells like Polo Sport.

"Don't ever fucking do that to me again!"

"I love you too. How'd you get in here? I thought I was safe from the FBI for a while?"

Max releases me from his hug and scoots onto the bed next to me. "I'm not the FBI. I'm your ever-loving roommate that's been out of his mind thinking you were dead. I'm not included in the authority embargo."

"Then how did you get in here?"

"I bribed your guard. Got him the phone number of a nurse he likes."

"Of course you did." I roll my eyes. "So, Gavin's here?"

"Yeah. I'll let him tell you about it. All I'll say is that there were some big misunderstandings. Don't be too hard on him. He'd be in here now if I hadn't told him they were running tests and that no one could see you until tomorrow. Then I said there was cricket on TV, and now he's clicking his way through the channels trying to find it."

"There is no cricket, is there?" I ask.

"Nope. I wanted you all to myself. Once he comes up, I'll never have the chance again," he says after kissing my temple. "This's all my fault, Slugger. This whole thing."

Oh, boy. Time to get my head in the game if we're going to talk about my adventures. "Max, none of this is your fault."

"I told you to go with Steve. You kicked that guy's ass to get away, and then I just handed you right over."

"He would have gotten me anyway, Max. He was obsessed with me. Like *Fatal Attraction*, going to boil my bunny obsessed. You can't take that blame. Speaking of crazy Charlie, what has he been saying?"

"He's dead."

"Oh, shit. I killed him?" I didn't think I'd killed him. I'd hated the guy, but I really don't want his blood on my hands. The heart monitor starts beeping like something out of a video game.

"No. Lil. You didn't do it. We found him in his apartment two days ago. He'd hanged himself. Left a note. If he couldn't have you, he didn't want to live. Total psycho."

"Oh?" Clearly someone has been working behind the scenes because I know there's no way anyone would ever have found his house, and if they had there wouldn't have been anything there. Charlie, or whatever his name was, was too good for that. Looks like either Lorenzo or Carlos took my advice after all. I doubt I'll ever know if he really hanged himself or if he had help. I'm not sure I want to know.

"Someone had beaten the crap out of him though. Really worked him over. Busted out most of his teeth!"

I blush. "That was me. That's how I got away."

"Damn, Lily. I'm seriously in awe. I think you may be the strongest chick I've ever met."

I shrug. "I had a good teacher."

"Yeah, you did. Anyway, this guy clearly had it bad for you. He had thousands of photos of you. He had your underwear, and lots of it too. Which means he was in and out of our apartment as well. There were pictures of you that he'd clearly... um... made deposits onto."

"Ew, Max. That's enough. Gross." I don't even want to know how they got my underwear or managed to manufacture that lovely detail.

"The craziest part was what I call the Gavin Wall of Death."

"What?"

"He had this wall of pictures of Gavin and all the ways he was going to kill him. Like he had a noose drawn on him or had him decapitated with his head on the counter and what we think was supposed to be his heart in a blender. Really crazy shit. The guy was totally loco."

Wow, I've got to hand it to them. They went all out with the psycho angle. It's made my job way easier.

Suddenly, Sully and Greene burst through the door.

"Max, you bastard! You know you aren't supposed to be in here. You're not on this case." Sully points to the door. "Out now."

Max kisses me on the forehead, and then withdraws, holding his hands up to show he won't fight them on leaving. Sully gives him a smack upside the head as he exits.

"You're worse than Gavin!"

Sully then takes out his wallet and gives Greene a five dollar bill.

I raise my eyebrows.

"The docs were supposed to keep everyone out until we talked to you. Standard protocol. My money was on Gavin being in here," he says. Seriously, when did I become the popular game to bet on?

He comes over to the bed and gives me a warm embrace. The man's as tough as nails and has the exterior of a cactus, but when he lets down that wall, he's pure sweetness. After the hug, I can almost feel his prickly wall go back up.

"My turn," Greene says. He sits next to me on the bed and leans in for a hug. I can tell he doesn't want to let me go. But after a few minutes he does. He looks me in the eye, and I can see the worry that has been consuming him. "Let's get business out of the way so that we can let Gavin in here," he finally says, breaking the awkward tension. "He's been out of his mind. I don't think he's left the hospital since he got to town. He's a complete wreck. We've all been."

I feel awful hearing that, but I'm not sure what I'm supposed to say.

Crap, show time. For the plan to work, I need to sell this story, which means it's time to come up with some creative fiction real fast. I sure hope I can remember everything that Carlos and I agreed I should tell them.

"All right, kid. Tell us what happened," Sully says as he pulls out and starts his recorder.

"I was with Steve, here at the hospital. Charlie was waiting for us. I don't remember what happened next, but the next thing I knew, I woke up in a barn, tied up to a chair. It was so damn cold, and it smelled awful. He left me alone in the dark for a while. I'm not sure how long, but long enough that I was freaked out of my mind.

"He came in and didn't say anything for a bit. He just circled me. I could tell each time he walked around that he was getting more and more frustrated. I couldn't really blame him. I had beaten the crap out of him. I'm sure he was really pissed.

"He slapped me around a bit. Not really saying anything. Eventually, he started babbling about what a bitch I was. I figured he was talking about the fight. But as he went on, I could tell it was about more than that. He was mad about everything. He said I'd broken his heart. The more he talked, the more I started to see the bigger picture. He was hired by the cartel to follow me. Just like your informant said.

"As it turns out, the whole mess with the cartel has been over for weeks now. You guys know about Crystal, right? He had her in that chair, all drugged up, and she'd told him where the money was. It was in the walls of her apartment. That's why they sledgehammered everything. After that, the cartel was happy, and his job was done. But he wasn't done with me.

"He'd been trying for a while to connect with me, but I kept brushing him off. That day, he just couldn't take it anymore. He saw me in the morning. He'd seen everything going on in the tabloids and thought it was his chance. He was sure Gavin and I would be through, and that if we weren't, we should have been. He went on and on about how Gavin was cheating on me and I deserved better.

"He couldn't understand why I would choose Gavin over him. Or at least that's how he saw what I was doing. Now that I had 'made my choice,' he was livid. It was unforgivable, and he wanted to make me pay.

"He injected me with something. I have no idea what it was. With the way it made me feel, I'd guess it was a date rape drug of sorts. He yelled at me over and over again about Gavin, and each time I didn't answer the way he liked, he would zap me with the cattle prod, which hurt like hell, by the way.

"It all got out of control after that. I was sobbing and telling him anything I thought he wanted to hear. He zapped me more for that. With every zap, he became more and more out of control. Eventually, he got so enraged that the zapping wasn't enough. He came up and shook me really hard. I felt like a crash test dummy. He lost control and I ended up crashing to the floor. When I hit the ground, the chair cracked a little, enough that I was able to wiggle out of the ropes.

"He didn't notice that the chair had broken. He was too busy kicking me in the gut. Once I got out of the ropes, I used part of the chair to hit him over the head. It didn't do much, but it caught him off guard. Enough for me to take him down. Well, I'm sure you saw how he was.

"I had no idea where I was, so when I got out of the barn, I just started wandering. It was so dark out there. It was a total crap shoot of where to go. I followed the sound of traffic in the distance. It took just about all night for me to get to that McDonalds.

"And that's it. The whole sordid tale. I still can't believe that this wasn't some big conspiracy like we thought. Just a crazy stalker."

We sit in awkward silence. Greene and Sully seem to be speaking to each other through telepathy. I can tell from their facial expressions that there's something going on between them.

"Come on, guys. I know you have questions."

Sully breaks the ice. "So you're telling me that this had nothing to do with the cartel?"

"From his ranting, I think it started out that way, but once they found the money, they moved on. He also said something about how they were frustrated by all the press about me. I was too hot of a target. They wanted him to leave me alone, but he didn't see it that way. He wasn't going to let go just because the job was over."

"Well, we aren't completely surprised," Greene said. He tells me all of the same information Max had told earlier, and I pretend to hear it for the first time.

They have me retell the story, and I'm fairly confident I match the first version well enough. They ask a lot of questions, but it's nowhere near the sort of interrogation I'd been expecting.

"So what happens now?" I ask when they seem to be done with their questions.

"Well, since he's dead, the case essentially is closed. We need to reevaluate if you're still at risk with the cartel. From what you've told us, I don't think you are. Between what you've said and what we found in his apartment, it really does sound like he was working for the cartel, but more like he went rogue," Sully says.

"It's a bit early to say so, but this whole mess might really be over for you." Greene takes my hand. "Lil," he continues. "I… We're just so sorry you had to go through all of this. We hear stories like the one you've just told us all the time, but they never get any less horrific. Especially when they're from someone we've come to care about. I…" He trails off, looking lost, as though he wants to say more but can't find the words.

"It's okay. Really. I'm alive. I made it through. I'm sure there'll be nightmares. I'm sure I'm going to be jumpy and not want to be by myself for a while. I think my days of running alone, especially at night, are over for now. But I fought back. I saved myself. I got to kick out all of his teeth. There's a lot of closure in that. I'm not a victim. I'm going to be okay.

"It's over," I continue. "The hell Ash put me through is finally over. I feel like a curse has been lifted."

"You've always been good at finding the positive, kid," Sully says.

Just then, a doctor comes to the door and pokes his head in "Gentlemen, do you mind exiting for a moment? I need to check on Ms. Clark."

"Alright, kid. We'll go find G. If he hasn't spontaneously combusted yet."

"Thanks, guys."

They leave, and I let out a huge sigh of relief.

As the doctor comes closer, I see he looks very familiar. "Doctor, huh? Doctor of what exactly?"

"I actually do have a PhD in economics," Carlos says.

"You don't say? Hmmm. Wonders never cease."

"I'm only here for a moment, to let you know we have this room closely monitored. I just heard your little presentation. You sold it better than I expected. It may just work."

"You all set the foundation for it. You made it easy. Down to the tiniest, most disgusting details."

"Some of the more crass things were not our fabrication. Your story has more truth to it than fiction."

"Oh, that is just so gross. So, do I pass? Can we go back to me never seeing you again?"

"So eager to get rid of me? Well, I can't say I blame you. Although, I think under different circumstances, we would have gotten along very well."

"That may be the case. But while the balance of power still lies in you just having to give the word to have me killed, I think our friendship is best to stay as is."

He smiles. "Yes, you've passed, as you say. Just keep it up." He hands me a flash drive. "This is a recording of what you just told the FBI. Memorize it. Keep it consistent. Mistakes will draw suspicion. Suspicion will not be tolerated. Are we clear?"

"Yeah, and it'll also raise suspicion if you're caught in here. Now scram."

"Did you really just tell me to scram?"

"Are you still here?" I'm totally pushing my limits, but I know deep down he finds it hilarious. I hope.

He wags a finger at me and says, "You, you're funny." With that, Carlos turns and walks out of my life, hopefully forever.

THIRTY-FIVE
Gavin

Sully and Greene find me outside. I can't stand to be in the building for one second longer knowing that Lily is awake and I can't see her. It's like telling myself not to breathe or my heart to stop beating. I wanted so desperately to be there when she woke so she wouldn't feel alone.

"G," Sully says. "You okay?"

"Losing my bloody mind, Sul. How are you?" I snap. "When can I go see her?"

"Now, man. What are you waiting here for?"

I don't respond. I just sprint. I'm fairly certain that I knock over a few people on my way to her room. I don't see anyone though. My mind's eye can only see her. When I make it to her floor, there's no one blocking the way for once.

When I reach the door, I freeze, paralyzed with anxiety. What will I say? It's been so long. She's been through so much... so much that I wasn't here for, so much that I didn't protect her from.

"Gavin, are you going to look at the door or open it?" Max asks. I hadn't noticed him until he spoke. "Don't be a pussy. Get the hell in there. She's asked for you."

"You saw her?"

"Please, dude. Like there was really cricket on TV. We're not in London, mate. Now stop thinking about how you want to punch me and get in there."

She lies on the bed, eyes closed. She looks positively angelic. The color's returned to her cheeks. She looks so peaceful that I don't want to disturb her, but I can't not touch her. I sit down beside her. So many times over these past few days, I've battled my fears, my fledgling hope—my guilt over my fledgling hope. It's been such a dark time, and I pray she won't be able to see just how dark when she looks at me. I sit down, unable to bring myself to wake her. I lean my head against the mattress and try to figure out what I'm going to say when she opens her eyes.

I must have been so exhausted that I fall asleep, because I suddenly wake to someone running her fingers through my hair. A smile spreads across my face as I look up and see Lily's beautiful eyes looking back at me.

"Hi," she says.

"Hi."

"Nice of you to wake up."

"I could say the same to you." I smirk.

"Well, I needed my beauty sleep. I went a bit haggard wondering if I was ever going to hear from a certain British gentleman again."

"Lil, I…" I try to think of a clever response, but I just can't make light of the pain she's experienced. Some of which was directly inflicted by me.

423

"Gavin, really, let's not do this now. I don't have it in me, okay? Just keep flirting with me and make me smile. We can get into all the ugly parts later. They're not going anywhere. Please, for now, just pretend that we're not in a hospital but some hotel room you've smuggled me into."

I can tell she's fighting being swallowed up by all the torment in her life. It's heartbreaking. I can't take the pain from her, but at least I can save her from drowning in it.

"Well, you don't have any luggage, so we have that part right. Sadly, we can't roll around naked in the sheets for days on end just now. We have too much of an audience for that. Unless you're into that sort of thing," I jest.

"Oh, I've had quite enough of people watching me roll around in these sheets to last a lifetime. I haven't even been conscious that long, and I'm already over it."

"I'm afraid you're stuck with it for a little while longer. Until I can break you out of here, anyway."

"I look forward to that."

We banter back and forth for hours. It's not as natural as it once was, but it isn't forced either. I'm uncertain what this feeling of reserve means for us. The connection we have is still unquestionably strong, but we both have walls up. Even with the walls, I have no doubt that I care for her as deeply as I ever have. Quite possibly more.

We chat casually about nothing in particular until she falls back asleep. We've mastered the art of avoiding the elephant in the room—something we have been doing since we met. I watch her, in complete awe of her strength and her resolve. She seems larger than life. I pray I haven't lost her.

She wakes up again around three in the morning. "Why're you still awake?"

"I can't stop staring at you."

"Well, I *am* sporting this season's hot trend, the bruised and battered look. Cuts and contusions are very hot right now. Or maybe it's just the fact that I haven't showered in like a month."

"You're always stunning. It's impossible for you not to look gorgeous," I tell her.

"Says the Calvin Klein model who still manages to look like he just walked off a runway while in the hospital. How do you do that? This lighting makes everyone look bad. Except you, apparently!"

"Em made me leave the room for an hour every day to get some fresh air and shower and change. While I was gone, she filed your nails, exfoliated you, and did all sorts of other girly things."

She runs her fingers along her lower leg. "My skin is ridiculously smooth. I was wondering about that."

"I'm anxious to get you out of here so I can find out for myself!" I expect a witty comment back, but Lily just looks at me somberly.

"So, what happens next, Gavin?"

"Lil, do you really want to talk about this now? I mean, I will. I just thought you'd want to wait."

"I do want to wait. But I think we need to."

I take a deep breath, "Okay, do you want to start or should I?"

"Did you sleep with all of those women?"

I shake my head. "I didn't sleep with any of those women. There were so many events scheduled on this trip. Since I was traveling solo, I was constantly being asked to escort someone to that evening's event or this partner's dinner party. Seemed like there was an endless supply of executives' daughters and nieces who were just dying to meet me. It was insanity. I had women latching on to me at every opportunity. I couldn't get a moment's peace. I felt like I was on that show where there's the one chap and the parade of batty women."

"*The Bachelor?* Is this supposed to be making me feel better, because it's not."

I grab her hand and kiss the top of it. "I'm sorry, luv. What I'm trying to say is that, yes, there were lots of women on the trip that I had to be around for business. But that's all it was: business. I was miserable the whole time."

"Is that why you wanted me to come on the trip so badly? So you wouldn't be compelled to have dinner with all the lonely hearts?"

I thread my fingers through hers. "No, Lily. I wanted you on the trip because I wanted to experience it with you. For so many years, you've been isolated, alone. It's a travesty that you lost so many years, so much wasted time. You deserve better than that. I never want you to have to live like that again. I want to give you the world, one blessed memory at a time."

Tears well up in her eyes.

"Don't cry, luv. My intentions weren't all sweet. I'm also a selfish bastard, and I just want you with me all the time."

"If that's true, why didn't I hear from you? I called and left messages. And what the hell was up with your phone?"

I tell her all about O's meddling, and she's fuming by the end.

"Lil, I can't stop thinking that if I had gotten those messages, I could have been there for you. I never would've left you alone if I had known how dangerous things had become. I could have prevented all of this."

"I spoke to her. Did she tell you?" Lily asks.

"No, I had no idea." I know I shouldn't be surprised by anything O has done at this point, but I still am. "I had no idea you had called my office. I never spoke to Mrs. Smythe. O handled everything."

"After you sent the flowers, I spoke to Marcus to find out where you were. I called and spoke to her. She's a raving bitch! Let me guess, she's the one that was in most of those pictures with you."

"Yes. She was a part of my team, so we were together the whole time. Along with a group of twelve other people."

"I could tell when I spoke to her she was up to something." Lily's face is flushed, and she has fire in her eyes.

"Luv, you're getting all worked up. You have to calm down, okay. Please. I've fired her. Security dragged her out of the building. I never have to see her again."

She lays back and closes her eyes. "You're right. I think we've rehashed enough for tonight."

"Are you okay?" I ask. *Are we okay?*

She smiles. "I'm better than okay. My psycho stalker is gone. You aren't sleeping with half of Europe. For the first time in weeks, I can actually relax. Life is good."

She pulls my hand up next to her face. Moments later, she's fast asleep.

427

THIRTY-SIX
Lily

I finally get to check out of here. If I thought I had to stay one more day in this fishbowl, I might slaughter the next person that asks me "how we're doing today." There ain't nothing "we" about this crap. I've never been so excited to put clothes on in my life! My skin has started rebelling against the scratchy hospital gown. But Em has been kind enough to bring me yoga pants and my Oxford sweatshirt. Heaven!

Five days of observation after my return to consciousness, McDreamy feels it's safe for me to blow this pop stand. He's ready to have his hospital back as well. Between Gavin, my FBI boys, all the protective custody people, and all of the extra "staff members" that are really plants from Lorenzo or Carlos hanging around, I think the hospital will be at max capacity as long as I hang around.

I'm more than ready to get Gavin out of here too. I can tell he's carrying around a mound of guilt, and it's clearly sucking the life out of him. Sometimes, he seems fine, but if he has too much time to think or if anything at all reminds him of the past month, he goes to a dark place. I hope that once we get out of the hospital, a constant reminder of what happened in itself, he'll let it go.

"Ms. Clark, make sure you follow up with your cardiologist in two weeks and then once every three months after that. You need to do everything in your power to keep your heart rate low. Get plenty of rest, drink tons of water, no caffeine. Alcohol is okay in small doses. Limit your activity. And that means all kinds of activity," McDreamy says, looking over at Gavin, who's waiting for me by the nurses station. "You may be better, but it won't take much to put you back here."

I hold a hand to my chest, feigning shock. "What? You don't want me to come back?"

"I never want my patients to be repeat customers, Ms. Clark. But you especially."

I tap my finger on my chin. "I'm not sure if that was an insult or a compliment."

"Don't overthink it. Just take care of yourself. Now, get the hell out of here," he says with a laugh.

"The British invasion has finally come to an end. You get your flock of ladies back." I hug him and give him a kiss on the cheek. "Later, McDreamy."

I find Gavin sitting in a chair by the nurses' station. Sometimes I forget how stunning he is. His blond hair is messy and yet perfect at the same time. He manages not to have even the slightest hint of a dark circle under his eyes, despite the lack of sleep. And that smile. Oh, that smile could melt the polar ice caps. He may single handedly be responsible for global warming. He finally catches sight of me, and I get to see those sapphire pools that make me melt.

Three nurses at the desk are falling over themselves trying to get his attention, but they don't manage more than a polite smile out of him. He only has eyes for me. I love getting the opportunity to break up "flirt with Gavin" time. I walk up to him and sit right in his lap. "Mr. Edwards, would you please do me the honor of getting me the hell out of here?"

He smirks at me and scoops me up, giving me the kiss to end all kisses. I'm sure I can hear the whole floor stop to stare at the spectacle he's making. He does like to make a scene. I'm not sure if the show is meant to piss of McDreamy or if he just wants to leave all his admirers something to remember him by. Or maybe he's just really missed me. Either way, I know I'm not the only one that could use a change of panties after that kiss.

"Sorry, luv. I've been waiting to do that for a long time."

"You are such a show off."

"No, luv. That was entirely for my benefit. In fact, I think I'll do it again." I was wrong. This is the kiss to top all other kisses.

I hear McDreamy yell, "I said all activity, Ms. Clark!"

"Will you two get a room? My God!" Em shouts at us. "You're lucky I love you, Lily, because for over two weeks, I've had to put up with him and his wrecked state. And now all this kissy face? I wouldn't tolerate this for just anyone, you know."

She won't admit it, but I know Em's been the glue that has held everyone together. She made sure the boys ate and occasionally showered. She claims it was all for her benefit, that she didn't want to smell them any more than she had to, but there's a nurturer underneath that hard façade she puts up. I'm so glad she's here.

"Time to jet. I can't deal with these fluorescent lights for another second," she states. She blows a kiss to McDreamy. "Later, Doc." She says there's something going on between them, but I think it's just to piss Max off. It works, and Max storms off, mumbling something about getting the car.

When we're finally ready to leave, several agents escort us to a back entrance to the hospital. It sounds like the press has been an ongoing parasite the whole time I've been here. I had blissfully forgotten all about the press during my stay, but that daydream has come to an end. Reality is such a cruel bitch.

Max picks us up in a souped-up FBI Suburban with pitch-black tinted windows and flashy rims. I feel like I need to have released a hip hop album to be worthy of such a ride, but I'll take it. The ride home is weird and toxic with tension. No one knows what to say or how to act now, and it's beyond frustrating. Em tries desperately to spark a casual conversation and fails miserably, which only draws attention to how strange everything feels.

We arrive at the condo to find the press camped out at the building as well. Max says they haven't left in weeks. We park in the underground garage, but a few reporters still manage to chase us down there. Between the press and the awkward tension, I finally snap once we're in the elevator.

"Enough, boys. I'm not dead. I'm not broken. What I am is pissed off that you are both acting so weird. Get over your guilt and do it quick."

"Thank you, Lily," Em says with an exaggerated sigh as we enter the condo. "I've been dealing with your broody butts long enough. Granted, you both look sexy as hell while you're doing it, but real life is not a cologne ad. Broody gets old real fast. Lily's alive! She has gone through hell and back and come out in one piece. She's free of Cocksucker forever! Can we please start to celebrate that? I think this calls for tequila!"

"You think everything calls for tequila," Max and I both say at the same time.

"Really, boys, I need you to snap out of it. You both have jobs to do," I inform them.

"Jobs?" Max asks.

"Yes. Max, you're going to run out and buy me french fries, onion rings, two milkshakes, and a big-ass burger. All that is for me and only me. If you want something, order your own, because I'm not sharing. Gavin, you're going to help me pack."

"Pack?" they ask in unison.

"I used to know two highly articulate men. Now I have parrots. Yes, pack. Do either of you think I'm going to stay here one more day with all this madness? Hell no! I'm getting on a plane to London tomorrow morning."

Max smiles and goes to order my take out. Gavin just looks at me, confused.

"All right. Hop to it. I'm going to take the longest shower of my life and try to scrub this hospital stink off me!"

When I get out of the shower, Gavin's waiting in my room.

"Why are you going to London?" he asks.

"Because I hear it's lovely this time of year," I say sarcastically. "Why the hell do you think I would go to

London? I clearly can't stay here. Being in the US has proven to be detrimental to my life expectancy."

"Thank God you're finally getting with the program, Lil," Em says, appearing in the doorway. "And G, don't even think about helping her pack. This's my department. You just sit there and look pretty." She heads back out to the kitchen to criticize Max's choice of food—to give us some space, I suppose.

"It's time for a change of scenery," I explain. "You Brits are supposed to be more genteel, right? I'm hoping that means fewer people will try to kill me on a regular basis there."

"When did you decide this?"

"After the last time we spoke. I mean, the last time before all this stuff happened. The whole kidnapping and coma thing has really sealed the deal though. You don't seem excited about this at all. Have you rescinded your invitation? Given away my side of the bed?"

He runs his fingers through his hair and sighs in what I guess is frustration, confusion, or tension. Maybe a combination of the three. "No, of course not. It's all just quite a surprise. This is about the last thing I expected to hear from you. After everything you went through and how you thought I'd just disappeared. You needed me and I wasn't there for you. Just another example of my drama causing you harm. I thought you would need time."

He raises good points, but I'm not deterred. Before all of this went down, I'd been crushed by his actions. Or what I'd thought were his actions. But even before he explained to me what had really happened, I'd gotten over it. He was here by my side every day. Each time I wake up and see him beside me, I know where I need to be. But is it was he wants?

"Gavin, do you want me to take time? Are you trying to talk me out of this?"

"No! Not at all. You know there's nothing I want more than to get you on British soil."

"It always comes back to England with you!" I roll my eyes at him.

I still haven't had a chance to fill Gavin in on the actual events that took place. It was far too risky at the hospital. Soon I will tell him, and I hope it'll snap him out of this funk he's been in. When he gave me the abridged version of his story, I knew he was struggling. These past few weeks haven't been easy on him.

I catch him staring off into space. "Penny for your thoughts."

"I keep thinking about my flight here. I had no idea if I would ever see you again. I'd never been so petrified in all my life."

"It's over, Oxford. We've got to let go of it." I kiss him deeply. He still feels as though he's far away, but my kiss seems to be drawing him back in.

When he pulls away, he says, "I'm trying, luv. I swear I am. Your bruises may be healing, but they're still there. Every time I look at you, my mind flashes back to all of the horrible things you have been through... how I could have stopped it."

"Gavin, listen. I'm only going to say this once more: this is not your fault. You could not have stopped it. You have to start being happy that I survived instead of being brokenhearted that it happened."

The rest of the night is a very quiet one at my condo. The boys stare at the TV while Em helps me pack. I have no idea how long I'll stay in London, but I'm looking forward to it. It seems as though I'm the only one though. Between the two boys, five words at most may have been said all night, all of them monosyllabic. I can't imagine how awful it would be if Em weren't here.

While the boys are lost in a football game, Em hands me a present. She's made a scrapbook of pictures of Gavin from tabloids from over the last two weeks. There are actually some pictures of him in which he doesn't look perfect. I can tell they're from at the hospital. He looks distraught. Broken.

These 'imperfect' shots are few and far between. In most of them, he still looks like a supermodel.

"Hey, Oxford! You're pretty sexy when you're brooding," I tease. Em nailed it. He does look like he's in a cologne ad!

"Oh, Em," he yells. "Did you really give her those rubbish papers you've been saving?"

"Sure did! She loves them," Em says proudly.

I hug her and kiss her cheek. "Em, this is perfect. Just what I needed to make me smile. Thank you for taking care of my boys."

"Anything for you. I really love Gavin, and well, you know how I feel about Max."

"No, I actually don't know how you feel about Max. Do tell..."

She stammers a bit. "Well, if you don't know, then I'm not telling you."

I snicker and allow her to change the subject.

I'd been looking forward to quiet time with Gavin after we all went to bed, but I pass out as soon as my head hits the pillow. He's been treating me like glass since I woke up, and I'm desperate for him to return to normal. I miss him.

His strange behavior continues into the next morning as we pack up to leave. I'd thought he would be happy to be going, but he doesn't seem like it. He's so distant.

Em says good-bye to me at the condo. She isn't one for big emotional airport scenes. I also think she's had about all she can take from the broody bunch. She's always looking for an opportunity to go to London though, so I expect I'll see her again soon.

Max drives us to Dulles giving me the cold shoulder the entire way.

"Max, you going to tell me why you're upset, or are we going to keep playing this game?"

"I'm just sad you're leaving so soon. This was really hard on me, on all of us. I just got you back, and you are leaving again."

"Max, you knew this was my plan."

"That was before you got snatched."

"Because I got snatched is why I need to go now more than ever. I need you to get that."

He's quiet the rest of the drive. He walks us into the airport looking as though someone has stolen his puppy. When we get to security, I ask him, "You going to flash your badge so you can sulk all the way to the gate, or are we going to part as friends here?"

He scoops me up into a hug so big I can't breathe and whispers in my ear, "I love you like we're blood. I'm going to crazy miss you. You're taking my roommate and one of my best friends, and I hate it. At a time when I have so much to make up to you."

436

I whisper back "I'm okay. We're okay. You have nothing to fix. Just be happy for me. Please. I'm sure I'll be home soon. We both know I'm going to hate it there. Like the Brits know how to make a decent burger and shake. I'm not going to make it," I say it loudly enough for Gavin to hear, trying to get a rise out of him.

He doesn't even respond. It's as though a zombie has taken over his body. He'd never let a burn like that slide normally.

"We're good, Max. You have to forgive yourself." I kiss his cheek and step aside.

Max and Gavin have a boy good-bye: a bro hug followed by a "see ya," topped off with the guy head-nod. They've been through so much together in the last two weeks that I would have expected something more personal. But they're boys. They can communicate anything via grunts and nods.

Max grabs me for one last hug and plants a very wet kiss on my cheek. He pulls away with a big smile on his face, looking very proud of himself for leaving me covered in slobber.

He looks at Gavin and says, "You'd better take care of her, G. Or I will personally come across the pond and kick your ass. If I hear about any more tears, I will end you. You feel me?"

Gavin would typically jump all over him, but he just looks solemn and says, "You have my word, Max. If any harm comes to her, you can come and wallop me."

I watch Max walk away, and then we head over to security.

Gavin's funk is wearing on my patience. When I hear our flight announced over the loudspeaker, I storm off to get in line. At the last minute, I change my mind and drag him off to the British Airways lounge.

"Lily, we should get to the plane."

"Sit."

"We don't have time."

"Sit," I command.

He obeys. "Okay. I'm sitting."

"Is this how it's going to be?"

"What are you talking about?"

"This? Us?" I point back and forth between us. "Is this how we are now? Because this is killing me. I can't go to London with you like this. I get that you have to deal with your own feelings about what happened. Can you do that without shutting me out? I know you wish you could have done something to stop what happened to me. But you have to realize everything that happened probably still would have happened even if you had been here. You have to let that go. You can't change what happened. But I'm hurting now. I need you now."

"I know you do, and I'm sorry. I can't begin to tell you how sorry. I know I'm fucking it all up."

"You need to jump out of this rabbit hole and get back to me. Like now. I can't do this by myself, Gavin. I'm running away to London to run toward us. If there isn't an us waiting there, then I don't know why I'm going."

"You're right. I—"

"Of course I'm right, Oxford. I'm always right. Nice of you to start figuring that out."

Finally, a smile.

"Hey, there's that smile I fell in love with." Oops. We haven't used that word yet, and that may be the lamest way possible to tell someone you love them for the first time.

His smile spreads ear to ear and then turns into a mischievous grin. I've let the cat out of the bag, and he's going to torture me with it. Thank God Gavin is back.

"I'm sorry, but what did you say?"

"Okay. Good talk. Let's get on the plane." I turn to head toward the gate.

He grabs my hand and pulls me back to him. "Oh no. You're not getting off that easy."

"Gavin, it's been weeks since I've gotten off." I hope sexy talk will distract him.

"Well, we will certainly have to remedy that, once you are given the go-ahead by the doctor. But that's not the point, and you know it."

"Gavin, we have to go. They aren't going to hold the plane for us."

"Lily, fuck the plane. What did you say?"

"Why?"

"Because, if I've learned one thing through this whole sordid mess, it's that I love you more than I ever thought possible. I need you like I need oxygen. When I'm not with you, I feel like a shell of myself, utterly incomplete. I love you, and I thought I heard you say that you love me too."

Well, hot damn.

"You would show me up by saying it better than I did."

"Lily, I'm British. Of course I was going to say it better. We're far more eloquent."

"No, your accent is just prettier so it sounds better. That doesn't mean that you are!"

439

"Lily."

"Gavin."

"Say it."

I roll my eyes. "Fine, Oxford. I love you too. Are you happy now?" I'm trying to act put-off, but I have a huge smile and feel as though a weight has been lifted.

"I've never been happier."

"So does that mean sulking, broody Gavin has left us?"

"Yes, I think so."

I jump up and wrap my legs around him, giving him a whole body squeeze while planting a million kisses on his face. "Thank you! Thank you! Thank you! You had me worried there. Now, let's go catch this plane."

We make it just as they're about to close the doors. As we get settled into our first class seats, he says, "I can't wait to show you everything. I think you're really going to love London."

"I hope so. I'm really looking forward to it."

"Once you're there, you will finally get it."

"Get what?" I ask.

"That everything's better in England."

"Oh, it's on, Oxford. It is so on."

LILY AND GAVIN'S STORY
CONTINUES IN
When Fate Isn't Enough

Coming February 25, 2015

Turn the page for a sneak peak!

I used to think dating the hottest man in the room would be amazing—that I would revel in being the envy of other women. All the mean girls in my life would finally suck it.

During my eight-hour flight to London, I learn that dating the sexiest man on the plane is nothing but trouble. Every time I run to the restroom, I come back to a flight attendant or female passenger batting her overly mascaraed eyes at him or pushing her cleavage in his face. By the third hour, I'm *so* over it. Gavin and I started our relationship under unusual circumstances, so I'm used to it just being the two of us held captive somewhere. That's shielded me from the piranhas in push-up bras. I can't say I blame them. Gavin Edwards may be one of the sexiest men to walk the earth. He has dark blond hair and chiseled features. He's kept his body in pristine condition from his days as a model. In fact, his body may actually be better now. But his most striking feature is his eyes. He should have to register those baby blues as a weapon. Once I'm caught in those azure pools, I turn to mush and would do anything he asks. Such and unfair advantage.

"Oxford, tell me that it is not always going to be like this," I say when I sink into my seat after another trip to the bathroom.

"Like what?"

His hypnotizing blue eyes make me think for a second he might not actually know the impact he has on women. But then he flashes me that "you will be putty in my hands" smile, and I remember that he knows exactly what he's doing.

"Like this," I gesture toward the flight attendant. "Women throwing themselves at you all the time. This trip is supposed to be an escape from stress. If I have to be on hussy-watch every time we go to the grocery store or take the dog to the vet, I may lose my mind."

"I don't have a dog," he retorts.

"But maybe we'll get one, and if we do, clearly we need to get a male vet because if we get a woman vet, she may want to play doctor with you."

"You are positively adorable when you're jealous."

I snatch the bag of peanuts off of his tray. Oh, honey roasted. I adore first class. "It isn't really jealousy as much as pity. They're so pathetic, and I just don't think I can stand to watch it day in and day out. Like take Double D over there. Does she really think that if she unbuttons one more button, you're going to leave the woman in your lap to go join the Mile High club?" Gavin laughs and starts to say something, but I interrupt him. "If you're already a member of the Mile High club, I don't want to know."

That only makes him laugh harder. I love to watch him smile.

He twists a lock of my long blonde hair, seductively flashing those eyes at me. "Has it really been that terrible?" he asks.

"Yes. We've lost so much time together. After all I've been through, I think I deserve your undivided attention."

He unbuckles his seatbelt and stands. "Stand up," he orders.

"Why?"

He gently tugs on my elbow. "Stand *up!*. Stop being difficult."

I stand and roll my eyes at him. "I'm standing, now what?"

He leans in and gives me the kiss to top all other kisses. The kind of kiss that leaves you dizzy, breathless and desperate for more. I can almost hear jaws dropping and drool forming puddles on the floor.

When he finally breaks away he winks at me. "That should solve that problem, luv." He sits and resumes working on his laptop, as though he didn't just kiss me stupid. "Oh," he continues. "In case there was ever a doubt, you've always had my undivided attention."

I can feel my face flush as I sink into my chair. "I feel like *I* should be asking you to join the Mile High club."

Gavin returns to his seat and refastens his seat belt. "If it weren't for that pesky heart problem you have, we would have."

I was recently kidnapped by a sociopath trying to find money that my late husband—may he rot in hell—stole from a Mexican drug cartel. In the end, I kicked the ever-loving crap out of my kidnapper and got away, but my heart did not escape unscathed. I now have to keep things sedate until I get the doctor's go ahead.

"So are you going to kiss me like this everywhere we go to ward off the gaggles of women trying to get in your pants?" I ask.

He brings my hand to his lips, then kisses the top. "If I have to. If it were up to me, I would retire, buy an island, and do nothing but naughty things to you all day long."

"Why can't we go with that plan? It sounds mighty good to me."

He cocks his head to the side, giving me a knowing glare. "You wanted find yourself again, re-establish your identity, and be independent. You don't want me taking care of you because you're perfectly capable of taking care of yourself. Does any of this sound familiar?"

He has me there. There's nothing worse than your own words coming back to bite you in the ass.

I met Gavin about four months ago when my husband and Gavin's wife were in a fatal head-on collision. Due to my late husband's connection to the drug cartel, and Gavin and I were placed in FBI protective custody for a while. I believe we have the worst possible answer to "How did you two meet?"

Gavin wanted to run off into the sunset, but I insisted that I needed time to get my life together and shake off all of the rust that had formed while I wasted away married to Ashton. Gavin had wanted to spoil me rotten and buy me everything my heart desired, and I insisted that I needed to do things on my own. My life was a train wreck, but I sorted it out myself. I literally kicked ass and took names. I can walk with a bit more swagger now, and I know that there isn't much I can't overcome.

"Well, can we do the whole island thing sometime? I mean, maybe you don't retire and buy the island, but can you rent it for a while?" I ask sheepishly. Normally I would have found some way to twist his words against him and give him a zinger, but all I can think about is him giving me a zinger! One kiss has me completely frazzled.

"Why, Lily Clark, you're positively randy, aren't you," he says a bit too loud. "You're blushing. You are just breathtaking when you blush." He kisses me again, but this time he isn't trying to show off. His kiss is soft and tender. "Have I told you how much I've missed you?"

"No, but you can."

He whispers sweet nothings into my ear until I fall asleep.

I'm woken by a hostile drink cart. The attendant's gotten the hint and doesn't hit on my boyfriend when she delivers his scotch, but she's a bit cranky now. I feel a bit cranky when I hear some persistent giggling coming from a few rows over. I look over at two women pouring through tabloid magazines and looking over at Gavin. He has been on the covers of the gossip rags for weeks now. My kidnapping and rescue became big news, and the media loved putting Gavin's beautiful face in the center of it.

He shares this week's cover with Olivia Philips, Gavin's longtime friend who has been hoping for more. Depending on the cover, she's heartbroken, or they're secretly carrying on while I'm in a coma, or she's pregnant with his child. Where do they come up with this crap?

"Maybe you should go sign an autograph?" I say, nodding toward his fans. "I'd do anything to stop their girly squealing."

Not wanting to encourage them by looking, he continues to work on his laptop. "Just ignore it. I'm not that interesting. It will settle down," he says flatly.

"While we're on the subject, what are we going to do about Olivia? And by 'we,' I mean you."

He stops typing, and faces me. "I fired her. I've cut off all contact. I'm not sure what else needs to be done," he says. "I'm still not sure why she pulled all those stunts, but I don't care to find out. I've cut her out of my life. Problem solved."

I look down at my nails, which for once are actually manicured thanks to my hospital bed beauty treatments courtesy of my best friend Emily. "According to *US Weekly*, she's having your child."

"Yes, and John Lennon is alive and well—he was just captured by aliens. They're looking for a story, and they're going to print all sorts of things. You just have to learn to ignore it."

"Hmm, so you say."

He closes his laptop and returns it to his bag. "Is this a roundabout way to ask me if I slept with her?" he asks pointedly.

"No!" The truth is I'm dying to know more about his relationship with a woman he swears is "like a sister."

"If you want to know, just ask," he says as he lays his head back and closes his eyes.

I don't want to give him the satisfaction of catching me in my passive-aggressive fact-finding scheme, but my curiosity outweighs my stubborn pride. "Okay, you've got me. It's killing me not to know. So spill it." He chuckles, and I shoot him a dirty look. "I'm thrilled you find my insecurity so amusing."

He takes the sleeping mask from my lap. "Insecurity is natural. The fact that you can't just own up to it is what I find adorable."

I wait for him to continue, but he goes back to trying to sleep. After a minute or so, I hit him in the arm. "Out with it!"

He takes the mask off and looks at me. "No, I have never slept with O. Just the thought disturbs me. I've known her all of her life, and I've never seen her that way. She's dated several of my friends, including one of my best friends, and that's a line I won't cross. Moreover, she's a spoiled brat. I overlook it because she's like family, but I could never overlook it enough to be in a relationship with her. I know everyone thinks she pulled this crap because she's interested in me, but I don't buy it. I think there's more going on here."

"Like what?" I ask. "Her actions are pretty textbook for a mean girl who's after a guy."

"I'm not sure, but I don't think that's it. But I have no desire to find out. Like I said, she's out of my life." Clearly he has no understanding of crazy women. Cutting her off is only going to add fuel to the fire.

"So you say, but I don't think this is that last we'll hear from Ms. Philips. What about all of the other women you were spotted with while you were gallivanting around the world? Any of them I have to worry about?"

He scratches the sexy scruff that's filled in the last few days and groans. "Luv, we've been over this. I was on a business trip, not a dirty weekend. As I went to those events unaccompanied, I was often asked to escort the daughter or sister or niece of a client. Most of them were dreadful."

I tap my fingers on the arm rest between us. "You didn't sleep with *any* of them?"

"Bloody hell, woman," he growls. "How many times are we going to go over this?"

I see fury in his eyes, and if we weren't on a plane, I'm guessing he'd be shouting at me. Always the refined British gentleman, he doesn't want to make a scene.

"No," he says through gritted teeth. "I didn't sleep with anyone.". "I was forced into spending time with them for business, and that is all it was. *I* did not seek out those women, and *I* did not engage them. You have nothing to worry about, no matter how bad it looked in the papers."

I hold my hands up and shrink back in my seat, showing him I'm backing down. "Settle down. Don't get your knickers in a twist," I say. "I trust you. I know you never would have stuck around through all the hospital drama if you didn't truly care for me. But I feel like we need to clear the air so that there're no secrets. I didn't think you would sleep with someone else, but if I don't ask…"

He doesn't veil his hurt. "That's *not* trust. I've been nothing but direct and honest since the moment I met you. Does that count for anything? I won't lie to you, either straightforwardly or by omission. I'm not sure what else I can do to prove that to you."

I wince because he's right. Gavin is the most sincere, forthright person I've ever met. He always says what he means without games. So many of the important people in his life lied to him without hesitation. His parents. Brooke.

Before I can respond, he says, "It's a whole industry created on embellishing facts and fabricating stories. Thousands of people make their living spinning fiction and calling it news, and it provides entertainment for the masses. It's hard to do, but you have to learn to see it as just that. Fiction." I lift up the arm rest so I can snuggle close to him.

"I'll try. I'm going to warn you, I will mess up. I'm not as strong as you. But I promise to try."

"Hopefully our lives will slip into blissful domestic tedium, and they'll move on to some other poor soul Someone that does something more exciting than taking the rubbish bags to the skip" he says while gently stoking my hair.

I can't help but purr from how comfortable and safe he makes me feel. "You have no idea how many women would drool over a picture of you taking out the trash. A man that does housework is like finding a leprechaun. Match that with how sexy you must look doing it," I say with a smirk. "I'd even buy that magazine and I have the real thing right here. Face it,.even when you're boring, you're gorgeous. Our press pals aren't going anywhere."

He sighs. "You're right," he says with disdain. "I promise they'll let up eventually. But, it's going to be a rough go of it until they do. After the last feeding frenzy, once they see me with one woman on a regular basis, you'll be like blood in the water to them."

"I guess we will just have to hide inside," I say with a sigh. I run my hand along his thigh. "I wonder what on earth we'll do to occupy ourselves. Can you think of anything?"

He removes my hand and places it on my lap. "Until the consultant checks you out, I think we'll be watching movies and I'll be kicking your ass at poker."

"Consultant? You won't sleep with me until you have my business plan analyzed? That's not fair." I've read enough English novels to know what he's talking about, but I can't pass up an opportunity to razz him.

"Don't be cheeky." He touches my chin and turns my face toward him. "Someone broke your heart, Lily. It's my job to put it back together. We're following all the rules until we know for certain your heart has healed. It's not up for debate."

I pout and stick my tongue out at him. "You always have to be *so* responsible, don't you?"

He kisses me with a tenderness that reminds me why I'm on this plane. He loves me, and I'd be crazy to pass up another second with him. The next few hours go by quickly. I read and doze while Gavin goes back to work. I'm woken from a nap by a *ding*.

"We are making our final descent into London, Heathrow Airport," the captain reports.

My heart races. This is a huge risk I'm taking. I hope I'm making the right call.

Gavin grabs my hand and whispers, "Stop worrying. This is going to be smashing. I told you—everything is better in London."

ACKNOWLEDGMENTS

Writing this has been quite a trip. Lily and Gavin's story started with the crazy notion of two people getting together after their spouses died in a car crash. From there it took on a life of its' own. It never would have gotten past the first chapter without the help of some amazing people.

My sister in law, best friend and writing partner Karin, you introduced me to these smutty books and got me hooked! Lily and Gavin would still be a crazy story in my head if it wasn't for your inspiration to start writing. You have been my cheerleader, my name creator and the best sounding board. For everything you have done to support me during this adventure and in every aspect of my life, thank you, thank you, thank you.

Paige Randall, I'm so lucky to have you in my life and in my books! You push me in ways I'll never be able to explain, and never let me settle. So much love to you!

Kimberly, this book would never have rereleased if you didn't kick me in the ass and keep me on target! The best thing Facebook ever did was bring you into my life, and I'm grateful for your friendship and writing partnership every day.

Devon, my rock star editor! Together we managed to pull it off! I adored working with you. In order for someone to be able to edit Lily, she had to be just as snarky! You fit the bill to a T! You truly understood the characters and their wild adventure. I'm so proud of the work we did together! Drinks are on me!

Jesey, you were the first blogger to give me a chance and I'm so lucky, grateful and proud to call you my friend. Thank you for your endless support, through good times and bad.

Kari Nappi, the lady with all the answers and the kindest heart of anyone I've ever met. Thank you for your boundless support, encouragement and enthusiasm.

A special shout out to the Schmexy Girls!!! For a group of women that I have never met in person, you have all become so near and dear to my heart. I can't tell you how heartwarming it was to come back into the mix and have a home to come back to! Best group of women I've ever met! We've laughed and cried over so many books, I can only hope you love Gavin as much as I do!

I owe infinite thanks to so many authors that have provided guidance, council, and support for me through every stage of the writing/publishing process. Indie authors are some of the finest people I've ever met, and the author community is strong and supportive. Heather Hildenbrand, Amy Bartol, Georgia Cates, Corinne Michaels, CP Smith. I can only hope to pay forward the kindness you have extended to me!

Thank you to all the bloggers that have supported the release of this book. I may be new at this but I know that without you, the only people that would be reading my book is people I'm related to.

A special thanks to Angela Pratt, a woman I can always turn to!

A big thank you to my most wonderful dearest friends that cheered me on while I took on this insane idea of writing a book. I know while I'm writing, I have a one track mind. All conversations lead back to my book, and I appreciate your patience, brainstorming, and tolerance.

One final thank you to my family. Thank you for putting up with the mountains of laundry, thrown together meals, and crazy deadlines.

Thanks for joining me on this adventure. Who knows where this may lead. It's been one hell of a ride so far!

Made in the USA
Charleston, SC
26 February 2015